SOLAMNIA THE EMPIRE

A loyal vassal betrayed seeks
revenge through any means.

A woman trapped takes the chance of
freedom, only to become a weapon.

A leader who achieved everything only to become
bitter and cruel faces a threat he never expected.

For a moment it seems that Solamnia has found
peace, but that peace is shattered quickly by the
revolts caused by the emperor's harsh treatment
of his lands and people. The return of old enemies
with new allies and new treachery means that the
emperor must make a stand to save the nation he
created. Solamnia will fall if the emperor does,
but the emperor cannot hold without his allies.

THE RISE OF SOLAMNIA

Lord of the Rose

The Crown and the Sword

The Measure and the Truth

THE MEASURE AND THE TRUTH

THE RISE OF SOLAMNIA
VOLUME THREE

DOUGLAS NILES

The Rise of Solamnia, Volume Three

MEASURE AND THE TRUTH

©2007 Wizards of the Coast, Inc.

Published by Wizards of the Coast, Inc. DRAGONLANCE, WIZARDS OF THE COAST, and their respective logos are trademarks of Wizards of the Coast, Inc., in the U.S.A. and other countries.

Printed in the U.S.A.

Cover art by J. P. Targete
First Printing: January 2007

9 8 7 6 5 4 3 2 1

ISBN: 978-0-7869-4247-3
620-95913740-001-EN

U.S., CANADA,
ASIA, PACIFIC, & LATIN AMERICA
Wizards of the Coast, Inc.
P.O. Box 707
Renton, WA 98057-0707
+1-800-324-6496

EUROPEAN HEADQUARTERS
Hasbro UK Ltd
Caswell Way
Newport, Gwent NP9 0YH
GREAT BRITAIN
Save this address for your records.

Visit our web site at www.wizards.com

To the Mountain Men:
Johnny Mac, Fred Baxter,
Pat Seghers, and Mike Wesling

THE RISE OF SOLAMNIA

The very name bespeaks history, legend, and ancient glory: *Solamnia.*

It hearkens back to the Age of Dreams and a time that ushered in the Age of Light. It is a place named for a man of legend who was a general, a rebel, an emperor who became greater than any king.

Vinas Solamnus was that rarest of heroes, a master leader of men who recognized the wrongness of his own cause, and who changed from an agent of imperial power to a champion of right and virtue. In the changing, he formed his own nation, at first a branch of the mighty Empire of Ergoth, but eventually an empire in its own right.

Solamnus founded the order of knights who still bear his name and who served the creed he laid down for them, prescribed in the Oath and the Measure. *Est Sularus oth Mithas*—my honor is my life. Such was the founder, and such is the nature of any man who swears fealty to the Knights of Solamnia.

As the Age of Light became the Age of Might, the Knights

of Solamnia became the best hope of the world, and waged a great struggle. Their triumph assured the survival of freedom, goodness, and mortal choice on the face of Krynn. A magnificent hero, Huma, proved the eternal truth and power bound up in the Oath and the Measure.

But in the wake of that war, beginning more than a dozen centuries before the start of our own story, that empire and that credo began to fracture. Facing forces of modernity and opposition on every side, the Solamnic Knighthood was driven into the shadows, blamed—wrongly!—for much of the wickedness in the world. The knights became outlaws, their cities and nations reduced to minor fiefdoms, the domains of warlords and petty dukes and merchants.

Through the Cataclysm and the long centuries of the subsequent Age of Darkness, the nation remained torn, its knighthood in disgrace and disarray. Again falsely accused, the Knights of Solamnia were driven into hiding, even hunted and killed. It was not until the return of the dragons, and the War of the Lance, that Solamnia's long night began to brighten into day. Another hero for the ages, this time the knight Sturm Brightblade, led the order toward the birth of a new era.

But it was a violent and grisly birthing. The crown jewel of Solamnia, the city of Palanthas, was subjected to special scourging, as the Dragon Highlord Kitiara led a brutal attack resulting in terrible damage. Magical storms wracked the city, and a convulsive spell caused the Tower of High Sorcery—a landmark of Palanthas from before the city even existed—to vanish from the known world.

When the Dragon Overlord Khellendros laid claim to northern Ansalon, an area that included Palanthas, the city's doom might have seemed all but assured. Yet somehow the citizens not only survived, but managed to prosper, through the trade that had always been Solamnia's lifeblood. Khellendros was eventually slain, and the Dark Knights ruled the land for a time, but soon after the War of Souls ended, the Knights of Solamnia struck in concert, reclaiming the heartland of their ancient regime by 40 SC.

Even then the lands of the historic nation lacked a soul, a binding force. Under the ostensible mastery of Lord Regent Bakkard du Chagne, appointed by the High Council as the Solamnic master of Palanthas, the old cities were divided among noble knights deemed worthy of holding power. Caergoth, Solanthus, Thelgaard, Vingaard, and Garnet were all ruled as independent city-states. They were in no sense a united nation.

Du Chagne was a merchant prince, who displayed the fabulous wealth of his treasury in pure yellow ingots enchanted to glow magically from the windowed room at the top of a tower he called the Golden Spire. Content to amass wealth in Palanthas, he let alone the cities on the plains, and the ruling dukes did as they pleased. . . .

Until a new threat to the peace on those plains appeared in the form of a half-giant barbarian named Ankhar, who called himself The Truth. Ankhar was the tool of an evil god, Hiddukel, the Prince of Lies, but he did not see that he was not his own master. Born in the Garnet Mountains, Ankhar gathered a horde of goblins, ogres, draconians, and the like, and in 42 SC he emerged from his lofty heights to lay waste to the plains in a war that raged for nearly three years. Garnet and Thelgaard were sacked, and Solanthus was subjected to a siege of more than a year's duration.

Then at last a leader who would reforge the ancient realm emerged. Jaymes Markham was not a man of noble ancestry; he bore no claim to the blood of kings or dukes. Yet he was a true leader of men and a general of surpassing skill. He was aided by the discovery of an explosive compound, a black powder he used with considerable effectiveness on the battlefields of Solamnia. He was aided, too, by a young mistress of magic, a prodigy of a wizard who embraced the cause of Solamnia and fought steadfastly at his side. Coryn the White was her name.

They became lovers, and they might have even been in love, once. But the man who would rule a nation discovered a higher calling. Jaymes Markham married Selinda du Chagne, the Princess of Palanthas and daughter of the Lord Mayor. Through her, he claimed rule—and gained access to her father's nearly unlimited funds. There seemed to be none to challenge him.

As the lord marshal of all the Solamnic armies, Jaymes Markham waged war against the invader, and proved that The Truth was, in fact, a hollow lie. Slowly, at great cost in blood and treasure, the humans and their allies drove Ankhar's barbarians back to the hinterlands. The three orders of the knights—the Rose, the Crown, and the Sword—served one master at last and finally defeated the invading horde in the Battle of the Foothills, a memorable day-long clash on the northeastern fringe of the Garnet Range.

With this costly victory, the last vestiges of ducal power were broken. The knights on the battlefield acclaimed their Lord Marshal as greater than any noble in their time. He became the master of all the elder nations of Solamnia—those that still flourished after the cataclysms—and he wove those lands into an empire, with himself firmly seated upon the emperor's throne.

CHAPTER ONE

THE EMPEROR RIDES

I t was important to be seen.

Jaymes understood this principle of command from his days as a sergeant of the line. To lead, one had to be observed in action, accepting the same risks as the men under his leadership. Once, he had practiced this principle as a captain of the Rose Knights, back when serving as Lord Lorimar's aide de camp. As Lord Marshal, he had made certain all the men in his four armies knew his face.

As the emperor, he would see to it that the people of his empire knew him as well.

So it was that, even as his army gathered outside the gates of Palanthas, planning and preparing for a new campaign, he took the time to ride through the streets of the great city. He had a personal guard of one hundred men, the Freemen, who would all have been honored to accompany him, but he did not require such a display just then. Instead, he would present the face of courage . . . and calm. With but a single man-at-arms, the loyal and capable Sergeant Ian, riding at his side, the emperor, astride his white stallion, slowly promenaded through the streets of Palanthas. It was not a horse he would ride on campaign, but it was splendid for show. He made his way from his palace, a new structure that loomed over the city's great central plaza, through the bustling mercantile districts, past the villas of nobles and merchants.

He rode through the New City, the teeming buildings outside the great wall—though he pointedly disdained the neighborhood dominated by the lord regent's palace and its great tower, the Golden Spire. Passing through the gates, back into the realm of taverns and guildhouses along the waterfront, the emperor accepted cheers from veteran soldiers, spoke kindly to women and children, complimented laborers and nobles alike on their work, their accomplishments, even their manners and dress.

At the intersections of the city's great avenues, he found crowds of people gathered, for the heralds had gone out before him and were busy making it known to all that the emperor had issued a decree. Jaymes did not stop and listen to the heralds—he knew what they were saying—but instead he watched the people, studying their reaction to his words.

"The emperor and his Legion of Palanthas march to bring the insurrection at Vingaard Keep to an end!" the heralds proclaimed, reading from scripted scrolls at twelve different locations in the city. They repeated the message every hour of the day, so every citizen who was interested had a chance to be informed.

"Those who challenge the lawful authority of the New Council and the Solamnic Senate are nothing more than outlaws, and they shall be dealt with as such! Lord Kerrigan of Vingaard has refused to obey the lawful orders of his liege. The New Army of Solamnia, under the command of Emperor Markham, goes to administer the lesson in a manner that shall make His Excellency's determination apparent to all!"

Some citizens muttered at the words, while others cheered, but all took note. And if the people who heard the news looked at him askance, Jaymes did not care. What was important was that they looked at him, saw him, knew him—and recognized his authority.

Perhaps he felt an occasional longing for the simpler life of a warrior. He spotted a dwarf at a waterfront inn who reminded him of his old trail mate Dram Feldspar, and the emperor had to suppress a desire to dismount, enter the tavern, and have a drink with the fellow. But that, he could not—*would* not—do. He was *of* the people no longer; they must come to see he was above them.

The first years of leadership had taken their toll on him in ways that could be detected even by a casual observer. Though he was not yet forty, his once-black hair was flecked with gray along the sideburns. His neatly trimmed beard was shot through with light hairs, giving the impression that it was crusted with salt. Crinkles of age ran from the corners of his eyes—the proof of too little sleep, of a host of problems that could never be completely solved.

Still, he rode straight and proud in his saddle, his strong features inspiring confidence in the men, his rugged handsomeness bringing flutters to the hearts of the women. His chest encased in black armor, with the mighty sword Giantsmiter hanging at his side, he cut a dramatic figure. Sergeant Ian carried his unique banner, the white field with the combined golden images of Crown and Sword and Rose, and the people understood that he was the Lord of No Sign and of All.

Reaching the waterfront at last, he and Sergeant Ian dismounted. The stevedores and sailors stood back in awe as he made his way to a massive trading vessel, the *Star of Mithas,* which had arrived in port just the previous day. Her owner and master was a minotaur of that eastern land, a towering bull named Horth Bearslayer. A new policy of the emperor's had allowed minotaurs access to the Palanthian docks—subject to high tariffs and tight regulation—and the ship's captain knew a benefactor when he saw one. He made a great show of welcoming the master of Solamnia to his own seafaring domain.

Horth Bearslayer covered his gangplank with red velvet and greeted the emperor with a formal bow—an honorific no minotaur offers casually.

"I am grateful for the chance to trade in these waters, Excellency," the minotaur said solemnly. "The wisdom of the emperor is shown in the freedom he grants his merchants."

"The success of the merchant is the pride of an empire," Jaymes replied. He spent a short time touring the vessel, which was huge and tall, with a hull made from logs as big around as an ogre's waist, and pronounced himself pleased. When he departed, the minotaur captain was beaming, and the people watching from the docks whispered that even greater prosperity lay in the near future.

On the way back to his palace, the emperor made one more stop: he climbed the steps of the great library on foot and was met at the door by one of the elder Aesthetics, a man named Pastorian.

"How can we serve the master of all Solamnia?" the Aesthetic asked with a low bow.

"I want to know more about the minotaurs," said Jaymes. "What are their numbers and locations? I desire a complete order of battle of all of their troop formations on Ansalon and estimates as to reserves on their homelands. I want to know who their rulers are, how old they are, who will succeed them."

"I understand, Excellency," Pastorian replied with another

bow. "I shall set my researchers on the task at once. Naturally, the information will take some time to collect."

"That's fine. You have the rest of the summer and the autumn to make your report. I would like to read your findings by the time of Yule—something to while away the winter nights."

"Of course, Excellency."

If the Aesthetic blanched a bit at the task and accompanying deadline, he could be forgiven. Given the widespread activities of the minotaurs since the conclusion of the War of Souls, the assignment was indeed daunting. They were known to be at war on the mainland, and they ruled the eastern seas with their mighty ships. The greatest efforts of the Aesthetics staffing the library would of necessity be devoted to the imperial commission. The true calling of the order, which was the recording of the day-by-day history of Krynn, would have to be diverted and delayed.

But Pastorian, too, had seen the emperor in action, and in that, as in all, the emperor would be obeyed.

Jaymes knocked on the entrance to his wife's suite of rooms, high up in one of the great towers of his palace. She opened the door quickly, saw him, and turned and walked back into the room. He entered, closed the door behind himself, and approached her. When he put a hand on her shoulder, she turned and looked at him.

Her face was expressionless, but he noted suspicion—or was it fear—in her eyes. For a brief moment, he longed for the warmth, the unquestioned love, he had once glimpsed there. That was gone most of the time, and he knew it was folly to try to get it back.

Selinda was gazing out the window. She gestured at the great army column, already outside the city gates, lined up on the road, waiting for its commander.

"So you're really going?" she asked. "Marching on Vingaard Keep?"

"I have to," he replied. "Lord Kerrigan leaves me no choice."

She spun around, glaring at him. "I thought your plan was to *unite* Solamnia? Forge one nation? Yet now you're breaking it apart!"

"You don't understand," he said calmly, while wishing devoutly that she did. "Unity requires sacrifice, so the parts will make the whole stronger. Kerrigan will not accept that essential truth. His realm was spared the scourge of Ankhar's war. Now Vingaard needs to make up the difference, give us men for my army, steel for the nation's treasury. He absolutely has refused to do either."

"And you are the new ruler of the nation. You've been emperor for less than a year, and you can't let this refusal go unchallenged."

Her sarcastic tone was lost on him. Instead he nodded, feeling a swelling of relief. Perhaps she *did* understand! She turned her back and walked to the high windows, the beautiful clear panes of glass that allowed her to look out over her city like a goddess viewing the world from atop a cloud. She had everything she needed in there; he had worked hard to make the rooms suitable for her.

He walked up behind her, leaning forward to inhale the sweet smell of her hair. Long and as bright as spun gold, her hair was a vital part of her beauty. His right hand caressed the curve of her hip, and he felt a swelling of affection and of proprietary pride. "You are still the most beautiful woman in all Solamnia," he said, "and so precious to me."

She didn't turn, didn't respond with the tender sigh that, a year earlier, would have been followed by a swoon into his arms. When she spoke, her words were controlled and aimed like darts at the window.

"I am a person, like any other. I wonder sometimes that I should be here simply because you find me beautiful."

"Why should that make you wonder?" His left hand found her other hip; he moved close behind her.

"I wonder if it was ever my beauty that attracted you. Or was it the fact my father is lord regent, that he controlled the treasury of Palanthas—and of all Solamnia?"

He shrugged, giving no indication of offense. "It was a useful circumstance, true. But did you not come willingly into my arms? We chose each other, don't you remember?"

Finally she turned to stare at him with pain in her eyes. "Then why are things so different now? Why do I *feel* so different?"

Jaymes grunted, dropping his hands. "I don't know," he replied. "And I have to be going." He started toward the door, then stopped and turned back to her. "One more thing. I want you to stay in your chambers until I return," he said. "There are too many threats abroad for you to venture out safely. You will be safe here and well cared for. Marie has a bed in your anteroom, and I've ordered a full platoon of guards to stand by, to make sure that you want for nothing."

"Want for nothing? I want to walk around the palace—the city!" she retorted angrily, crossing to him. "What kind of threats are out there that can't be stopped by an escort of your personal guards?"

He placed his hands on her shoulders and looked into her eyes, his expression maddeningly serene. "I don't want any chance of exposing you to violence—or the gods know

11

what else. Illness, pestilence—they're all about the city these summer months." With a meaningful look downward, he placed a hand on her stomach. His touch made her flinch, but he didn't seem to notice her reaction.

"Remember, it's not just your own health at stake," he cautioned.

With that, he gave her a perfunctory kiss, turned, and marched out the door. The sergeant of the guard did not even glance at her as he closed the door behind Jaymes Markham, Emperor of the Solamnic Nation.

❦❦❦❦❦❦❦❦❦

Soon after, Jaymes left the great city with the bulk of the Palanthian Legion: a force of five thousand men, some four hundred of them mounted knights. In the wake of the column rumbled heavy wagons hauling three bombards, the last surviving cannons from the six that had been employed in the Battle of the Foothills more than two years earlier. At that time Jaymes Markham had commanded the four armies that broke the half-giant Ankhar's invading army and dispersed the fleeing remnants into the wilds of Lemish. The outcome of that war had solidified Markham's control over all the realms of Solamnia. He had ushered in a new era of peace and prosperity for Solamnia.

The army passed through the city's Crown Gate, with the rugged Vingaard Mountains and the narrow cleft of the High Clerist's Pass beckoning on the horizon. It had been more than two years since the soldiers had waged battle, and that was enough time for the wounds to heal and the grim memories to fade. They were men of Palanthas, loyal to their captains, generals, and emperor. They would serve with dedication and courage.

To be sure, the time since the end of the war had not been spent in mere recuperation. Once the Lord Marshal had assumed control of all Solamnic Knighthood forces in the lands of the Old Empire and claimed the mantle of emperor, he had announced his goal was nothing less than the restoration of the ancient regime. While he had maintained the overall structure of his military—the forces were still organized into three armies, augmented by a legion of troops in Palanthas devoted to the emperor's personal service—he had tinkered with longstanding traditions in armor, weaponry, unit organization, and tactics.

The campaign they embarked on would put his improvements to the test. Most significantly, the regiment which had been the standard infantry formation for more than a millennium was broken into four, or sometimes five, companies of about two hundred men each. The companies allowed the army commander to maneuver his troops with greater precision than ever before. The ratio of light cavalry in each formation had been increased, often at the expense of the heavily armored knights that had traditionally been the backbone of the Solamnic Knighthood. Flexible, light, and fast, they would outmaneuver, rather than overpower, any foe.

The emperor had also encouraged the employment of the Clerist Knights, priests who were trained in magic at the ancient Solamnic centers on Sancrist and would cast their spells in the service of the cause. Under the overall command of Lord Templar, clerists were assigned to each regimental headquarters, and at least one apprentice accompanied every company on the field. By dint of their magic, the holy knights facilitated communications between the army commander and his individual units.

Another fundamental change in the way the knighthood

waged war was evidenced in the personal command style of the army leader. No longer was he seen, resplendent in a bright uniform, gilded epaulets gleaming as he rode a strutting, prancing charger. The modern emperor wore a woolen riding cape that was drab compared to the scarlet tunics worn by his footmen. He rode behind the advance companies of light cavalry and was surrounded by a staff of couriers, together with his chief clerist—Lord Templar—and a half dozen of the Freemen.

Such was the force of the Emperor's determination, and his authority, that the changes had been implemented with very little resistance from the officers and the ranks. For more than a year, his army had trained and studied and experimented. Finally, for the first time, the new style and tactics would be tested on the battlefield.

That was, if the rebellious inhabitants of Vingaard Keep did not immediately recognize the error of their ways.

The people of the city stared as the army marched off to war. Their mood was somber, with a few offering cheers for the troops and many shouting best wishes to individual soldiers—husbands, brothers, and sons—in the ranks. The emperor himself the citizens regarded warily, not so certain of the impending conflict as they had been of his necessary campaigns against the barbaric Ankhar. The troops looked straight ahead and marched in perfect cadence.

The emperor rode a nondescript roan mare with the casual ease of a natural horseman. His personal guard of Freemen, a hundred strong, rode white horses and looked alertly around as they rode close by their leader. Even as the party passed beneath the arch of the city gate, Jaymes could be seen talking and listening to his aides, confirming the order of march in the column, receiving detailed lists from the quartermaster regarding the provisions in the baggage train, and having a word with Lord Templar about the most recent auguries regarding the Vingaard rebels.

As the column, and the command party, headed around the first curve of the encroaching mountains, there were those among the emperor's men who noted that their commander had not once raised his head to glance back at the city they were leaving behind.

CHAPTER TWO

PARLEY AND PRISON

Lady Selinda Markham looked out the clear, glass window of her lofty chamber, conscious that the glass alone had cost the equivalent of a half year's pay for one of her nation's ordinary citizens. Though she had grown up with such luxury, only recently had she taken to considering its relative value. She knew that glass was a precious commodity, rare, valuable, and beautiful.

Yet it was only with great effort that she resisted the impulse to drive her fist through the expensive glass, to shatter the pane into a spray of shards tumbling to the courtyard so far below.

How *dare* he!

Selinda, like all other Palanthians, knew Jaymes Markham would brook absolutely no challenges to his claim of absolute power. But this—his imprisonment of her! It far exceeded his authority, Selinda believed. Even her father would never have had the audacity to speak to her as her husband had, only hours before.

While she looked through the window, Selinda's hand

drifted to her belly, touching the imperceptible *thing* that had taken root there, though it was not yet beginning to affect her slender shape. Her tower room offered views in three directions, but she did not so much as glance at the roadway heading into the mountains, the route taken by her husband's army. Instead, as she stroked her belly, the princess of Palanthas gazed northward, past the city's teeming docks, to the masts of the crowded harbor, and the sparkling blue waters extending to the limits of her vision on the northern horizon.

She knew her husband and his soldiers too well even to try to persuade the guards at her door to consider relaxing their duties and letting her out for a short while. They would hem and haw and shuffle their feet, but in the end they would obey the emperor. She would not be allowed to leave her chambers.

What a pretty prison I've made for myself! she thought, remembering back. She had been long been intrigued by the man, even though he was an outlaw when they had first met. Fascinated, she had paid wary attention to Jaymes as he exonerated himself, then rose by acclamation to the command of all the Solamnic Armies. As lord marshal, he had been surprisingly gracious to her. Then, one time during a visit, he had come to her chambers and they had shared a decanter of wine and talked; that was when she had fallen helplessly in love with him. Almost overnight his words had become music to her ears, his casual wishes her deepest desires.

She had wanted—no, *needed*—him with a passion she had never imagined—and one that she could barely recall. What a naïf she had been when he had proposed to her, and her world broke into song. The wedding itself, hastily arranged but conducted with all the pomp that was owed to their status, had been a like a dream. Later, when he took her into the bridal chamber, her love for him had soared.

It was a curious memory. At times the old feeling would return, when Jaymes would smile at her, or touch her cheek; then her heart would suddenly melt, while her mind . . . well, her mind just seemed to shut itself off. Only recently he had wielded that charm to take her to bed, some two months ago; she smiled at the memory. Then she frowned. The result was the child she had only recently discovered she was carrying.

Most of the time, Jaymes was all business, immersed in his work, in the politics of rule or the dictates of army command, while she was trapped in that room in the tower, fifty feet above an enclosed, barricaded courtyard.

Waiting to bear the emperor's child.

"No!" she cried aloud, banging her fist against the pane. She was startled by her outburst, and upset as she saw a thin crack spread across the expensive piece of glass.

She drew herself up, tried to calm her emotions, forced herself to think. Banging on the windows—or walls or doors, for that matter—was fruitless. If she was going to do something, get out of there, she would have to try clever means.

She thought for a long time, pacing slowly, looking out the window without really seeing the sunlit view, the blue waters, the glittering, busy city. Finally, she made up her mind, turned her back to the window, and strode to the door.

"Sergeant!" Selinda called.

The door opened at once to reveal the familiar mustachioed knight in his scarlet tunic and gleaming black riding boots.

"Yes, my lady?"

"Take a message to Coryn the White. Ask if she will come to see me at her earliest opportunity."

"At once, my lady," replied the sergeant. He saluted formally and closed the door. She heard him issuing orders to a runner.

At the same time, she heard the lock snap shut outside her door.

<hr />

The soldier strode through the upper hall of Thelgaard Keep. As he turned the corner leading to the general's council chamber, he almost broke into an excited run, his left hand bracing the hilt of the long sword he wore at his belt so he didn't trip over the weapon.

"I need to see my father, at once!"

The young captain's manner was so urgent that the guard might have let him pass even if he weren't General Dayr's son. As it was, the halberdier at the door all but stumbled over himself in his haste to get out of the soldier's way.

"Of course, Captain Franz, go right in!"

His riding boots scuffed across the smooth boards of the floor as he burst into the council room, where he found his father and several of his officers standing around a map. A glance showed Franz that the parchment displayed the central Vingaard Plains.

"Is it true that we have been order to march? To join the emperor in a campaign against our own people?" Franz demanded.

"Watch your tone, my son," the general retorted sharply. His glare was fierce, until it wavered unevenly with a glance toward the other men at the table. Franz could see his own misgivings mirrored in the concerned expressions of Captain Blair, master of the Thelgaard Lancers, and the Knight Clerist Lauder. General Dayr was silent for a moment as he slowly drew a breath. Finally, he addressed his son directly.

"Yes. The order comes through the Clerist's scrying tool. Lord Markham is leaving Palanthas this morning, and we are to march north from Thelgaard. We are to seal off the approaches to Vingaard Keep from the south and east while he comes down from the mountains."

"But those are some of your own men in Vingaard!" protested Franz. "How can you march against them!"

"They are men who swore an oath to support the lawful government of Solamnia!" the general snapped. "Yet they have sent a message that can only be construed as a personal challenge to the lord marshal!"

"He's not the lord marshal any longer, Father. He has appointed himself emperor. Isn't that going too far?"

"He is not the first emperor in Solamnic history. Sometimes a realm needs an absolute ruler, one who can dictate to the masses, to his troops—to everyone. It is an honorable title, one that has been claimed by strong men throughout our history whenever the empire has been in a state of turmoil," Dayr explained, as if tutoring a schoolchild.

"The only turmoil is *his* doing!" retorted the son.

"That is enough!" snapped General Dayr, suddenly filling out his uniform with his annoyance. His gray mustaches curled downward in walrus-like disapproval, and his cheeks were flushed beyond their normal ruddiness. Franz was reminded that his father was a man who had fought many battles, had risked his own life and ordered hundreds of men to their deaths, all in the service of the lord marshal who had proclaimed himself emperor. "Jaymes Markham has united this nation, restored a proud legacy, and given us—and the order to which we have sworn all devotion—a real chance to regain its former glories! He deserves my loyalty, and he deserves yours!"

Captain Franz immediately stiffened to attention, replying only with a curt "Yes, sir."

The elder officer relaxed, slightly, and indicated the map

on the table. "But I'm glad you're here, Captain," he said in a softer tone. "As cavalry commander, you'll play a key role on the march. I'll want the White Riders to accompany the column, of course." He turned to Blair. "And the lancers will screen the advance, as well as the right flank of the march route. Our left will follow the course of the Vingaard River, for the most part."

"Yes, General. When do we depart?" Blair was a stolid veteran of the past years' campaigns. Courageous but unimaginative, he had seen Thelgaard fall to the barbarian horde and had nearly lost his life when the city was ultimately reclaimed. If he shared Franz's discomfort with the current mission, he did not say anything. But his look was solemn.

"I want two companies of lancers on the road well before dark tonight. The rest of the Crown Army marches north with the dawn. Can you see to that?"

"I have four companies in garrison right now; two of them can depart by noon. And the muster has already sounded, so the rest of the men should reach the stables before evening."

Dayr turned to his son. "And the White Riders? When will they be ready to move out?"

"Within the day, sir. But Father—that is, General—what is the objective? Are we going to make war?"

General Dayr sighed. "Right now, we're going to show the knights of Vingaard the emperor means business. They'll see an army coming out of the mountains and another ready to cross the river."

"And then?"

"And then, I hope, they'll have the wisdom to yield to the emperor's will," replied Dayr grimly.

⊱⟡⟡⟡⟡⟡⟡⟡⟡⟡⊰

The road connecting Palanthas to the rest of Solamnia—and all the continent beyond—had been dramatically improved during the past two years. It was wider, paved with smooth stones in the places where wear and erosion had worn it away, and graded out over some of the steeper climbs. Nothing could change the fact that the road had to climb high through the steep Vingaard Rrange—the High Clerist's Pass was nearly two miles above sea level—but the emperor's dwarf engineers had done a magnificent job of making the highway as efficient and passable as could be.

With the aid of the explosive devices they were still mastering, the road crew had chiseled away at overhangs and ledges, broadened the shoulders, even carved deep notches out of some of the rolling ridges. One result of the improvements had been a dramatic increase in overland trade. Although the great city of Palanthas was first and foremost a seaport, the amount of goods leaving and arriving along the mountain road had increased threefold in the past year.

As the legion marched southward from Palanthas, they came upon more than a dozen trade caravans during the four days it took to reach the summit of the pass. Those mercantile processions pulled off to the side to allow the soldiers to pass. Some enterprising traders hastily established roadside markets, and the soldiers quickly purchased food, drink, and trinkets. The emperor was a strict disciplinarian, but he instructed his officers to allow these transactions to continue—so long as the men quickly resumed the march and maintained a double-time pace for an hour to make up for the delay.

Finally, the crest of the pass was before them. Despite the best efforts of the dwarf road builders, the highway passed through a series of sharp switchbacks during the final ascent, so the soldiers in the front looked down onto the heads of the men in the middle and tail end of the column. Even with the steep climb, the pace of the march continued unabated, and the men sang marching songs as they at last reached the high point of the long climb.

The fortress called the High Clerist's Tower commanded the only gap through the rugged sawblade that was the crest of the Vingaard Range. Most of the army column simply marched past the place, the men staring up at the lofty towers silhouetted against the stark blue sky, then continuing on with the relief of travelers who have completed a long ascent. As there was precious little level ground in the vicinity of the mighty keep, most of the troops headed down toward bivouacs five or six miles below the crest, on the flatland known as the Wings of Habbakuk.

But some of the army did stop at the tower, including the command party. Jaymes Markham rode into the small, deep courtyard and examined the high stone buttresses. This place had been savagely mauled in several wars, but—by his order—the damage had been repaired, and in fact the stout defenses of the ancient bastion had been strengthened by the addition of a curtain wall across the southern approach. A quartet of exterior towers had also been erected, with one pair overlooking the approach to the fortress from the canyon to the north and another pair commanding the road as it fell between the narrow gorge approaching the south gate.

The commander of the tower's garrison, General Markus, waited in the courtyard for the emperor's party. The Rose Knight, who had been one of the first to serve Jaymes, saluted him crisply. Markus was hailed by Jaymes as he dismounted and whisked the dust of the mountain road off of his cape.

"You've arranged for the feeding of the army in bivouac?" Jaymes asked immediately.

"Yes, my lord. My kitchen staff has set up camp between the Wings, and the men will get a hot meal tonight, and tomorrow morning."

The emperor nodded. "Good. Hold the second courtyard for the bombards; I'll want to inspect them when they arrive, and they need to be secured behind the walls for the time being."

"Here they come now, my lord," reported Sergeant Ian of the Freemen, as the first of the big wagons rumbled beneath the portcullis and entered the courtyard.

A team of eight oxen hauled the mammoth conveyance, which was built more sturdily than a heavy freight wagon. The axles were steel, the rims of the huge wheels banded with the same hard metal, while no less than thirty stout spokes supported each wheel on its hub. The bombard rested in the wagon bed, the barrel—its gaping mouth more than a foot wide—slightly elevated and extending to the rear beyond the body of the wagon. Dark steel bands ringed the heavy beams that formed the long tube, while an iron screw supported the bombard midway down its length. The screw could be adjusted to raise the barrel. Shifting the weapon's aim to the left or the right could be accomplished only by turning the wagon itself.

Markus was busy issuing orders as the second bombard rumbled into the fortress and an adjacent portcullis rattled upward, opening passage to another, similarly small courtyard nearby.

"All three of them will fit in there," the general said. "And there's a stable just beyond, so that the oxen can be tended."

Jaymes nodded, his mind already moving on to other matters. He leaned back and stared up at the lofty tower that was the centerpiece of the keep. The parapets once damaged by Chaos Armies and dragon overlords were newly intact and gleaming. A banner flew from the highest pinnacle, snapping straight in the high mountain wind, proudly bearing proof that it was a citadel of the Solamnic Knighthood. Three symbols in black—the Crown, Rose, and Sword—were etched against a background of snowy white. Each side tower—and they were numerous—held another flagpole with images showing the company heraldry, clerical affiliation, or other symbolic indications of tradition and authority.

"I have the maps arranged as you requested," Markus explained as he accompanied the emperor into the lower hall of the multilevel keep. "I've taken the liberty of placing them in the dining hall so that we can have dinner as you make your plan."

"*Refine* my plan," corrected Jaymes. "But the hall should work nicely."

Markus lowered his voice as the two men passed through an anteroom, and the press of aides and guards discreetly fell in behind them. "I have received a letter just this morning, Excellency. From Lord Kerrigan, in Vingaard. He has enclosed a message for you with the request that I deliver it, when possible."

Jaymes nodded, and the general passed over a small scroll, a fine skin rolled into a tight tube no fatter than his little finger. The wax seal, bearing the imprint of an eagle, was unbroken.

The general waited for a moment, but the emperor made no move to open the parchment in his presence. Rather, Jaymes followed Markus into a vaulted dining room, where, as promised, a series of maps were laid across several tables. The chamber was deep within the interior of the fortress, but several chandeliers blazed brightly enough to simulate full daylight. Jaymes looked up at the crystal objects and observed that the light was magical in nature.

"Better, and cheaper, to have the Clerists do it than to invest in a hundred candles," Markus commented, as Jaymes nodded approvingly. He approached the maps and studied the terrain that he already knew by heart.

"Now, we will emerge from the mountains here and approach Vingaard from the west. Dayr and the Crown army are coming up from the south."

It wasn't until several hours later, when the emperor was alone in his room, that he took out the scroll from the rebel leader at Vingaard Keep. The time was late, since the planning session had run long into the night, but he needed only a few hours of sleep before rising with the dawn. He allowed himself a flicker of satisfaction; he was as hale as he had been as a young man; four hours of slumber always made him feel rested and invigorated.

Jaymes ignited a few extra candles; his eyes, alas, were not as keen as they had been even a few years before. He broke the wax seal on the scroll, unrolled it, and read the message.

My Dear Emperor, Uniter of Solamnia,

I beg you to hear my words, and to grant me the privilege of a parley. We in Vingaard are more than willing to give the nation, and yourself, the due fruits of our prosperity. The benefits we have already gained—simply with the increase of trade over the pass that you yourself traverse at this moment—have dramatically improved the quality of life in our humble river town.

I also beg Your Excellency's forgiveness for the fact that our misunderstanding has progressed to this distressing state. I assure you that it was never

my intention to challenge the authority of the State,
or of the Emperor.

I will present myself to you on the road before
my city. I will bear no weapon, nor bring more than
a small party of loyal attendants to meet with you. I
merely seek a means to resolve this issue that allows
me to salvage an element of pride.

In Greater Solamnia, there is certainly treasure
for all!

> *Your Devoted Servant,*
> *Kerrigan*

No expression marked the emperor's face as he finished the short, polite missive. But he frowned slightly before touching the corner of the scroll to the flame of one of the candles.

The dry material caught immediately, flared into bright light, and burned very quickly. Jaymes dropped it on the stone floor and went to bed. He was sound asleep before it had stopped smoldering.

CHAPTER THREE

TO THE SPIRES OF VINGAARD

The three great towers of Vingaard Keep rose above the plain like a triple-peaked summit standing alone on a small island. The great Vingaard River, nearly a mile wide there, curled and meandered to the east of the ancient fortress. A smaller tributary, Apple Creek, guarded the southern approach to the castle and surrounding town. Apple Creek was a raging torrent as it rose in the heights near the crest of the Vingaard Mountains, but where it meandered across the plain to join the mighty river, it was merely a wide, sluggish stream with a muddy bottom and swampy, reed-choked banks. The waterway was not deep, though the soft bed made it a major impediment to the maneuvering of an army.

The Palanthian Legion marched out of the mountains and approached the keep along a road that followed the south bank of the creek. Soon after they had started across the plains, a message from General Dayr arrived, reporting the reasonable progress of the Crown Army. A day later, and ten miles short of Vingaard, Jaymes called a halt, putting his army into a fortified camp.

There was a sturdy span called the Stonebridge over the Apple, well downstream from where the legion camped, but none of the emperor's officers questioned his decision. The bridge and its approaches were within catapult range of the fortress, and if in fact this looming confrontation came to be, that was not a location for any sensible soldier. Besides, there was a ford near their camp, where the banks were dry and the bottom of the creek was lined with a bed of boulders and gravel—the only such crossing until they reached the mouth of the stream and the ancient bridge.

General Weaver, the legion's tactical leader under Jaymes's overall command, joined the emperor on a low hill overlooking Apple Creek. In the distance they could see the elegant trio of spires of the keep. "Any word from General Dayr?" asked Weaver.

"The Crown Army is only a day's march south of the keep," Jaymes replied. "As I expected, they are making good time. He's crossed over to the west bank of the river. What have you learned about the situation in our immediate neighborhood?"

The emperor gestured to a nearby grove of apple trees, and beyond it the vast stretch of airy woodland that extended for miles along the other side of the creek.

"The scouts have returned. They report a full regiment of pikemen in that grove, ready to block any attempt at fording. They have archers and heavy infantry to back them."

"We'd certainly outnumber them," Jaymes noted.

"Oh, of course," Weaver replied. "But it would be a bloody crossing."

"Well, maybe we won't have to shed blood. Any word from Lord Kerrigan regarding the parley?"

"I dispatched the message to the keep as you requested, Excellency, but there hasn't been—oh, wait. Here comes my man, Baylor—the one I sent with the message."

The two commanders rested easily in their saddles as the lone rider urged his horse to a gallop and up the gentle slope to the hilltop. He saluted briskly; Weaver returned the formal gesture, while Jaymes nodded.

"Lord Kerrigan accepts your offer of parley, Excellency," Baylor said, addressing the emperor. "He questioned me strictly on the guarantee of safe passage to your headquarters, and naturally I pledged to him that you gave your word he and his party would be allowed to come and go in safety."

"Go on," Jaymes said.

"He will arrive an hour before sunset, and wishes to discuss the possibility of ending this dispute in an amicable fashion. He sends assurances that he does not wish to challenge your ultimate dominion of the empire, and merely wants to negotiate some of the fine points of governance."

"Very well," replied the new emperor of Solamnia. He looked at the sky, squinting at the western sun. "We'll see him in a few hours, then. And then we shall see what we shall see."

⤬⊶⊙⊶⊙⊶⊙⊶⊙❖⊙⊶⊙⊶⊙⊶⊙⊶⤬

Lord Kerrigan was a tall, hearty duke with an ursine aspect and, under most circumstances, a hearty, infectious laugh. His red hair fanned across his shoulders in a cascade of curls, and his cheeks and nose flushed, either from exposure to the air as he rode the few miles out to the army's camp or—more likely—from an excessive fondness of strong drink and rich food.

He was accompanied by a knight in a black tunic adorned with the red rose, an elderly priest of Kiri-Jolith, and a younger man in a silk shirt and elegant riding boots. A quick search, supervised by Sergeant Ian of the Freemen, ascertained that none of the three was armed, and the pickets stood aside to let their horses advance, at a walk, toward the table and chairs set up outside the emperor's headquarters tent.

"The young fellow—that's his son, Sir Blayne," Weaver said quietly, standing next to Jaymes as they awaited the truce party's approach. "A good knight—served five years in the legion. Smarter than his father, I'd say. Back then he was a bit hotheaded, though."

The four men rode nearly to the circle before reining in. Stewards took their bridles as they dismounted in unison. Kerrigan stepped forward, his eyes frank and inquiring as he advanced toward the emperor. He began to extend his hand until something in Jaymes's face caused him to halt. Instead, he straightened.

"Excellency. Thank you for hearing my parley." His voice was friendly, though his expression had grown watchful and guarded.

Jaymes nodded and indicated the chairs that had been arrayed for them. The four men of Vingaard sat, and the emperor took his seat. General Weaver occupied the chair at his right hand, Captain Powell to his left. Lord Templar, the clerist, was the fourth member of the emperor's party.

"It is impossible not to notice you have disregarded the government's lawful requests for tax payments, as well as refusing to send recruits for the empire's army," Jaymes began. His tone was dry, almost bored, but his eyes bore a different intensity and never wavered from Kerrigan's face. "My agents have addressed this lapse by letter and emissary for nearly twelve months, now. I regret that it became necessary for me to bring my army into the field. Now you find us before your gates, after a march of no little expense and inconvenience."

"You're not at our gates yet," muttered Sir Blayne, drawing a sharp look from his father. Kerrigan cleared his throat gruffly, and returned the emperor's even gaze.

"Wait," Jaymes said, holding up his hand before the duke could speak. He glanced at the young knight, an almost-smile creasing his lips. "The only reason we are not at your gates, young sir, is that I do not want to kill your men unless I have to. Your regiment of pikes—and the hidden archers and swordsmen—in the grove across the stream wouldn't stand for ten minutes under a concerted assault from my battle-hardened men. But we are here to talk because we hope such an attack won't be necessary."

The young knight flushed. His hand brushed the curl of his mustache, and his eyes attempted to bore holes in the emperor's face. But he held his tongue.

"And, I trust, no attack will be necessary," said Kerrigan smoothly. "Naturally, I anticipated that your scouting would be thorough; my men were there for you to discover them.

"But, Excellency," he continued, "as I tried to explain to your emissaries—the burden you place on Vingaard is too heavy. Our economy is on weak footing, and our population is too small. To pay half the tribute you demand would be a hardship—to contribute half the recruits you require would be a terrible burden. To fully comply with your numbers would be to destroy all I have worked to build here. So I beseech you, Excellency, lower the numbers. Let us begin to work together."

"It seems to me you have been rather fortunate, here in Vingaard." The emperor gestured to the keep. Even ten miles away, it dominated their view with its lofty towers, the spires so slender they almost seemed to sway in the sky, defying gravity. "In the past few years, Garnet and Thelgaard have been captured and sacked by barbarian forces. Solanthus endured a siege of two years' duration and a destructive battle of liberation. Caergoth has been transformed into an army and naval base of unprecedented proportion. Palanthas has filled the coffers of the empire with the steel of commerce, and at the same time it has contributed countless men to the ranks of the legion and the knighthood."

He continued speaking, his eyes daring anyone to interrupt the emperor. "This magnificent road—the highway that runs almost past your fortress gate, that has opened trade routes to Kalaman and places as faraway as Neraka—is a tangible benefit of the new Solamnia. There are inns and wayhouses every mile, smiths working hard for the benefit of travelers—and all of them paying taxes into your treasury. While you, here in Vingaard, have farmed your farms, fished your river, and harvested your apples."

Sir Blayne clenched his jaw with visible anger, while the flush spread upward from Kerrigan's cheeks to fully encompass his brows and forehead. Even General Weaver, beside Jaymes, looked at his leader, who had adopted a sharp tone, askance.

The duke took a long moment to draw a breath and calm himself before responding. "Surely you are aware, Excellency, of the contributions made by the men of Vingaard during the campaign against the barbarian Ankhar! Our knights rode with the regiments of Crown and Sword and Rose—a hundred of my men fell in the crossing of the Vingaard, the very river that is our namesake! We were there when the siege of Solanthus was broken—we, too, bravely faced the fire giant in the Battle of the Foothills!"

Jaymes shrugged. "I am not disputing the sacrifices made by your men—they are as worthy, and no more so, than any other knightly unit. *Est Sularus oth Mithas,* naturally. But that was the story of wartime; this is a time of peace. And these figures are based on property, not men, and it is here that your realm has emerged without the scars that have marked these other places."

"So you would destroy us with taxes and conscription?"

The emperor shook his head. "These contributions will not destroy you. They should make you stronger—they *will* make you stronger, for the larger nation needs your contribution of steel and men in order to restore its place as Krynn's mightiest empire."

"It is too much, I tell you!" declared Kerrigan, his voice rising almost to a shout.

"You refuse to pay? Still?"

"I cannot pay!"

Jaymes nodded. His eyes flicked to Sergeant Ian, commander of the Freemen, who stood with his small company off to the side of the council. "Then arrest these men now. I want all four of them clapped in irons."

"Yes, sir!" replied the young knight, waving his men forward.

"This is an outrage!" cried Kerrigan, leaping to his feet, instinctively grasping for the hilt of the sword he wasn't wearing. "You gave us your word that we would parley under a truce!"

Jaymes stood too, not cowed by the duke's display of temper. "I changed my mind," was all he said.

⚖⊶⊙⊷⊙⊶⊙⊷⊙⊷⊙⊶⊙⊷⊙⊶⊙⊷⊙⊷⊙⊷⊙⊶

"Thanks for coming to see me," Selinda said to Coryn as the guard closed the door behind the white-robed enchantress.

"Of course—I would have come at once, but I have been busy in Wayreth for the last ten days."

Coryn the White embraced her friend, concern reflected in her dark eyes. The wizard's black hair fell in a loose cascade over her shoulders and halfway down the back of her immaculate white robe. The silky material was embroidered with countless images in silver thread, and the magical sigils seemed to glimmer and gleam in the bright, sunlit room.

Selinda noticed, with surprise, that a few streaks of gray had begun to appear in those thick, dark tresses. But Coryn's face was smooth and unlined, her features still those of a very young woman.

That was, except for her eyes. The enchantress, the Master of the White Robes, had seen much of the harshness of the world in recent years, and those experiences, Selinda could see, were taking a toll. She remained a very beautiful woman, but there was a maturity and sadness about her that Selinda saw more clearly than ever before.

"What is the news in the city and the land—of Jaymes . . . and Vingaard?" Selinda asked as the two women settled themselves on a settee beside one of the tall windows—not the pane with the angular crack running across it. The summer morning was balmy, and a slight draft of fresh air wafted from the open doors to the nearby balcony. "No one will tell me any real news, up here."

"And are you stuck here? Are you not allowed to leave?" Coryn had heard the rumors but hadn't credited them. She looked at the princess with upraised eyebrows.

Selinda felt the flush creep across her features, a mixture of humiliation and anger. She met her friend's gaze and spoke quietly. "Jaymes—the *emperor,*" she amended bitterly, "says it's because he doesn't want anything to happen to his—our—baby."

The wizard blinked and, unless it was Selinda's imagination, she started, for a fraction of a second. Then a mask fell across Coryn's face, but it didn't cover her eyes—and those dark eyes, the princess realized, seemed terribly wounded.

Then the mask was dropped. Coryn's expression warmed, and she reached out to take Selinda's hand.

"Well, that's bigger news than anything *I* can tell you. Congratulations, my dear."

Selinda looked away, changing the subject. "But what is the word from over the mountains? As I said, they tell me nothing."

"Jaymes took his army all the way through the pass and down to Vingaard Keep. I understand that he intends to stand firm and that he doesn't expect Duke Kerrigan to agree to his terms."

"So—there will be civil war?" asked Selinda, despairing.

"I hope it won't come to that—I trust it won't!" Coryn replied without a great deal of conviction, to Selinda's ears. "I'm sure they will come to some kind of understanding. The duke has to recognize how important the riches of his realm are to the restoration of empire."

" 'Empire.' Such an old-fashioned word, it seems to me," Selinda replied. "I would have thought that, perhaps, the modern world has outgrown such concepts."

Coryn shook her head firmly. "There will always be a struggle between order and chaos, between light and dark. And a strong empire—an empire that upholds the Solamnic Code, the Oath and the Measure—is the greatest defense we humans have for the future. It is the only thing that can protect us from the scourges that have befallen the elves, from the menace of minotaur invasion that has swept over so much of Ansalon. Of that I am certain."

"And Jaymes Markham is the only man who could forge

such an empire, isn't he?" the princess asked.

"Frankly, I have invested all of my hopes in him," Coryn answered. She looked sincerely at the other woman. "He has brought our fractured land together, led our defense against unspeakable evil. He is a great leader—though he has his faults. Even so, I never imagined he would keep you virtually imprisoned here!"

Selinda looked out the window for a long time before squeezing Coryn's hand and looking again at the enchantress, staring deep into her dark eyes. "Coryn, I need your help."

"What is it? I'll do anything I can," pledged the wizard.

"This baby . . ." Selinda spoke softly, and her face was wrenched by an expression of raw emotion—grief, rage, and frustration all twisted together. "I am so afraid—I don't know if I can bear it! What kind of father could Jaymes be? What kind of mother will I be?"

Coryn sat back, shocked. "But—you—you're pregnant!" she finally stammered. "The die is cast. I mean, it's natural for you to be afraid—all young mothers are. But . . . how can *I* help you?"

"I will not let my life be carried away by this current beyond my control!" Selinda declared in utter sincerity. "Will you advise me, help me? Is it possible . . . to bring about some delay? To let me think, give me time to reach some decision?"

The wizard stood and moved to the window. Selinda could see that Coryn was trembling, her legs shaking. The White Robe wrung her hands together, stared outside for several interminable seconds, then turned back to the emperor's wife.

"I—I don't see what I could do to help," she said, and Selinda sensed that she spoke candidly. "There is nothing in the repertoire of a white robe wizard that would enable me to do anything even if—"

"Even if you wanted to help me?" the princess finished bitterly.

Coryn sat back down and took both of the other woman's hands in her own. "I do want to help you. I meant that, and I still mean it. But I spoke the truth: I have no skill, no ability to change or delay this reality."

Selinda's eyes welled even as she clenched her jaw. "Isn't there anyone?" she asked. "Anyone I can turn to?"

The wizard thought for a very long time. "I don't know, not for sure," she finally said, speaking very deliberately. "But perhaps you could speak to a priestess . . . someone you know . . . a wise woman who could counsel you, could help you to understand, to cope."

The princess of Palanthas nodded as she worked to keep her expression cool and mask her disappointment. Of course, Coryn was speaking the truth—it wasn't a matter for a wizard of the white robes.

"There is . . . there is something I can do that might alleviate your troubles," Coryn said softly. She removed a slender silver band from a finger on her right hand. "I give this to you—it will assist you in escaping from your prison here."

Selinda took the tiny circlet and looked at the enchantress curiously. "How?"

"It's a ring of teleportation. Put it on your third finger—there, like that. To use it, simply twist it three times around your finger, and say the name of the place where you wish to go. It must be some place known to you, and you need to picture it very clearly in your mind. The magic will transport you to that place."

The princess had a look of awe in her eyes as she examined the little ring, gleaming and silver, on her right hand.

"Thank you," she said. "Indeed this will help."

The burly Freemen moved quickly, grabbing Duke Kerrigan and leaping to restrain the two nobles sitting beside him. Chairs tumbled over as the fourth member of the party, Sir Blayne, dived to the ground and, for just a second, eluded the grasp of the guards. The young knight no sooner broke free from the clutching hands than he abruptly disappeared from sight.

"Where'd he go?" demanded one of the Freemen, looking around in confusion.

His partner reacted with more imagination, diving onto the ground where the knight had disappeared, grappling with an unseen presence there. Abruptly a sharp smack sounded, and the guard's head snapped back. Blood spurted from his nose as he lay, stunned, in the tangle of chairs and feet and milling confusion.

"He's made himself invisible somehow," Jaymes declared calmly, pointing as one of the chairs was knocked out of the way. An edge of exasperation crept into his voice. "Surround him! Stop him!"

Then the bearlike Lord Kerrigan suddenly broke free from the two men holding him. With a strangled cry of rage, he lunged toward the emperor, his hands outstretched. One of the Freemen, blade raised, lunged to intervene, and the duke ran headlong onto the blade, forcing the swordsman back a step. With a groan, Kerrigan staggered, dropping to his knees.

"Damn!" snapped Jaymes, grimacing. He looked down at the stricken duke, a crimson blossom spreading across his chest.

And chaos still reigned in the camp. The emperor barked at his men, who ran around like clucking hens trying to locate the invisible Sir Blayne. "Fools!" he demanded. "He's getting away!"

Another man stepped forward from the army's entourage. He didn't wear a knight's mailed shirt; instead, his tunic was emblazoned with the Kingfisher. He was Sir Garret, one of the mages who like the clerists, had become an integral part of the emperor's military machine. Garret spoke a word of magic, holding out his hand, fingers splayed.

Immediately young Blayne appeared as the dispelling incantation took effect. The knight could be seen, crouched between a pair of guards, looking around wildly; at first, he didn't seem to realize that he could be seen.

"There he is!" cried a dozen men at once. As Jaymes's men lunged for him, Sir Blayne vaulted away with a wild spring—bursting out of the council circle as if he had been shot out of one of the bombards. He streaked toward the waters of nearby Apple Creek with shouts trailing after him.

"Run! Get away from here, my lord!" cried Vingaard's priest of Kiri-Jolith, firmly in the grasp of several burly Freemen.

Lord Kerrigan writhed on the ground, bleeding from the wound in his chest, breathing bubbles of blood from his mouth and nose.

"More magic, this one a haste spell," Jaymes remarked, standing above the dying man. "He surprised me. He was prepared for anything, your son."

"He was prepared—for *you!*" challenged the duke, struggling bravely for breath, the words bubbling thickly from his bleeding mouth. "He had your measure . . . I was a fool to think there was a reason . . . to parley."

Jaymes shook his head in irritation. That was not in his plan. "Lord Templar!" he shouted. "We need you—at once!"

"Yes, Excellency!" the Clerist Knight reported, dashing up to the emperor and kneeling beside the dying man.

"See if you can help him," Jaymes ordered irritably.

The priest touched the deceptively small wound, murmuring a prayer to his just and lawful god. The emperor ignored the healing attempt, gazing off into the distance instead, watching as the young knight darted right, then left, evading the rush of a dozen men-at-arms. Horses reared as he darted past a picket line. The alarm was spreading; a score of men moved to block his path.

Still running like a madman, Blayne dropped to his hands and knees and scooted right under the belly of a startled charger. The horse reared, feathered hoofs flailing in the faces of the pursuing men, while the fleeing knight popped to his feet, dashed past another line of picketed horses, and rushed to the riverbank.

He shucked his tunic off, the silken material seeming to hang in the air briefly as the human was bared. Then, inches ahead of his pursuers, he made a clean dive, plunging into the cool, deep water with barely a splash. He disappeared beneath the waters as the knights shouted and pointed and waded in different directions. But Blayne was halfway across the creek before he surfaced, swimming with amazing speed downstream, toward Vingaard Keep. The magic propelled him. Arms churning, legs kicking, he seemed to swim even faster than a man could run.

"Archers! Ready a volley! He can't outrun an arrow!" shouted an enthusiastic sergeant of longbows. His men, some fifty of them, had been standing guard duty, so their bows were already strung. They put arrows to the strings and drew them back. The sergeant raised an eyebrow, looking at the emperor.

Jaymes frowned and shook his head, a very slight gesture but enough to cause the sergeant to hold his command.

"Let him hie back to the castle," the emperor said calmly. "We'll catch up with him later, when we conquer the place." He looked down at Lord Templar, who was gently closing Lord Kerrigan's eyes.

"I am sorry, Excellency," the clerist said. "His heart was pierced—there was naught that I could do."

The emperor nodded, turning to the other prisoners. The Vingaard priest, squirming in the arms of two brawny Freemen, looked at Jaymes with eyes spitting hatred.

"So you'll take Vingaard?" he challenged, looking helplessly at his slain duke. "You have killed our lord! You will destroy our keep! And then what? Thelgaard? Solanthus? Palanthas? How long are you going to make war on your own country?"

"As long as it takes to build the future," Jaymes replied.

"You have no sense of honor, no sense of tradition—you mock the greatness of this country. You're a blight on Solamnia."

"And you think it's honorable to withhold taxes and men, the lifeblood of the nation, from its lawful ruler? Is that right? Is that the kind of virtue you espouse?"

"Est Sularus oth Mithas!" declared the priest stiffly.

"Your honor is your life?" Jaymes repeated the oath contemptuously, his tone drawing looks of unease from several of the knights in his own entourage. He ignored their expressions.

"That's your luxury, then—worry about your honor, your life. As for me, I must look out for the greater good."

CHAPTER FOUR

DARKNESS AT DARGAARD

Everywhere loomed chiseled faces of granite, their color so dark a gray that it almost looked black. The mountains offered no sheltered groves of aspen, no rounded shoulders gently cloaked in a mantle of firs or pines. The open rock faces seemed to have been assembled without a pattern: one summit was a knife edge of two cliffs rising back to back; the adjacent peak was nearly flat at the top, a broad smooth shelf of rock dropping off on every side like some great towering cube. The gorges were deep, shrouded with shadows, sometimes slashed by raging torrents of icy water.

Snow still lingered in the shadowed couloirs and swales, but it was a dirty kind of gray slush, thick and wet and slowly melting away. There was water in the mountains, but it mirrored the colors of the rocks. Lakes and ponds were flat and the color of slate, lacking reeds at the shore or lilies in the sheltered bays. The streams connecting those pools were the only breaks in the monotonous landscape: they tumbled through cataracts, over falls, through rock-choked chasms, like ribbons of froth against a backdrop of ash.

There were no houses in the heights of the mountains, not a farm or village, not so much as a single herdsman. Anyone who tried to live off the land would find a world that was barren, cold, and to all appearances lifeless. Even the sky was gray, like a lid of cold iron pressing close above the mountain summits.

There was one lone structure, an eminence rising from the mountain's gray stone. The color of the structure closely matched its surroundings, yet the sheer walls, looming gate, and lofty tower marked that building as a thing that had been constructed.

The dark castle occupied a cleft in the dark range. A deep moat, with a bottom lost in shadow, surrounded the entire fortress. The moat was spanned in one place by a long, slender bridge that had been built upon a single arch, with the span anchored at each side of the deep barrier. Tall, sheer walls looked down on the moat and the bridge, and the small valley beyond. A single keep rose within those walls, and that building was dominated by a tall tower—which was just a slight shade darker in color than the rest of the castle and the surrounding landscape.

A man stood in the window at the top of that tower, gazing out on the castle and the valley, the mountains, perhaps the whole world. He too was as dark and gray as the mountains, his skin swarthy, his once-black hair growing thick at the brows and on top of his head streaked with enough white to render it gray. A gray cape hung near where he stood, on a peg in the wall.

He wore a black cloak, wrapped like a toga about him, as he stared wordlessly, for a very long time, from his lofty perch. Leaning forward, he let one hand rest on the stone sill of the window, allowed the cool air to brush his features, chilling him as it evaporated the sweat beaded onto his forehead. He looked at the slate sky, at all the gray facets of his world, and he frowned.

"Hoarst? Why don't you come back to bed?"

Hoarst turned slowly to look at the woman who had spoken. Her shock of hair, snowy white, spilled across the pillow as she stared at him, lazily lying on her side. Her skin, as white as her hair, looked as cold as ice—though he remembered its heat against his flesh. She was Sirene, and she pleased and served him in many ways, willingly giving him her body, even sharing drops of her blood when he needed them for various spells and potions.

At that moment, she simply repelled him.

"Leave me," he ordered. "I will have need of you, but not until later."

The albino woman's eyes widened slightly, but she quickly scooted away, out the far side of the bed, gathering up her clothes and, barely taking time to throw a robe over her slender shoulders, darting out the door. Even in her haste, she remembered to close it very gently.

Hoarst exhaled slowly, relishing the precise control over his breathing. Disdaining the use of magic for now, he took an inordinate amount of time to wash and dress himself, heating a metal bowl of water over a small brazier, cleansing his face and hands, shaving carefully. He smoothed the wrinkles from his gray tunic and leggings before donning them and even buffed, slightly, his worn and comfortable boots. He took pleasure in the mundane tasks, which he could easily have accomplished merely by casting a few simple cantrips. He was saving even the tiniest expenditure of his power for something, anything, more interesting than his ablutions.

He picked up a gray robe and draped it casually over his arm as he finally emerged from his chamber in the high tower.

He took the steps one at a time, counting them silently as he rounded the spire again and again in a descending spiral. At one hundred four steps, he reached the door at the bottom, drew a slow, contemplative breath, and emerged into the heart of his stronghold.

What had once been the keep's great hall, Hoarst the Thorn Knight had converted into a huge laboratory for the working of his magic. A great oven had been installed along one wall, with benches of burners, centrifuges, glass vials, and a myriad of components arrayed on both sides. A pipeline of water had been diverted to run along the length of his primary workbench, with several spigots operated by hand screws, so he could turn on a flow of water at any one of them simply by adjusting the valves.

The other side of the room was devoted to rows of tall cabinets, which stood like wardrobes, each stocked with the odds and ends of magical experimentation: bats and rats and bugs, sometimes dried and whole, sometimes divided into useful components such as eyes, livers, and tongues. There were more than a dozen live birds, some of them tropical creatures of colorful plumage, but including a scruffy crow, several hawks, and a leering vulture, all caged in one corner of the room.

Above the great fireplace, poised over a warm bed of glowing embers, a cauldron large enough to hold a man's body was suspended. Within that vat bubbled a brew of dark brown, with bits of organic matter—the tip of a tentacle, a bit of leathery wing, an eyeball, something that looked distressingly like a child's hand—occasionally roiling to the surface. A miasma of steamy vapor lingered above the cauldron but also seeped outward to infuse every corner of the great room.

All that was Hoarst's creation, and all of it he ignored,

stalking through the laboratory and on through the anteroom, where three wide halls converged at the keep's front door. He gave no thought to the locked door at his left, though behind that door was the long stairway leading deep into the rocky ground. Down there, behind a succession of locked doors—and guarded by other, more devious threats as well—was the trove of treasure and possessions that made Hoarst one of the wealthiest men in the world.

Not very long ago, a mere stroll down into that dungeon, with its permanent light spell cast broadly over the piles of gleaming coins, the chests full of precious gems, the bullion and statuary, paintings and vases and chandeliers, would have gladdened his heart, rescued him from the deepest depression. Much of the treasure he had plundered from Palanthas, when he had been the chief Gray Robe of the ruling Dark Knight Council. Oh, there had been lords who outranked him, generals with greater authority than the Thorn Knight Hoarst. But he had feared none of them—no, they had feared him, and he had prospered by their fear.

The rest of the trove had been fair payment given to Hoarst by the half-giant Ankhar the Truth. The Gray Robe had served in the army of the great barbarian as his chief wizard, and for his service, he had been well rewarded. Ankhar's own treasure wagons had bulged, following his sacking of Garnet and Thelgaard, and the cultureless barbarian had willingly allowed Hoarst to pick and choose from among the objects of art, the enchanted items, and classical statues that had all been tossed together in a jumble.

As a result, the Gray Robe possessed a collection unmatched anywhere on Krynn, save perhaps the palace of some eastern king. Now and then, Hoarst thought about bringing those priceless objects up from the dungeon and scattering them around the barren castle to enliven his mood. It depressed the wizard to realize that he kept putting that off; he really didn't care to exert the energy, to take the trouble of deciding where to display his treasure.

Of course, his women would have helped. There were nearly two dozen there at that moment. He thought of them as his harem, using them as concubines as well as servants. They were all young and beautiful, and he had collected them from the many corners of the world. They varied in complexion from the alabaster Sirene to women of brown and darkest black. Some were voluptuous, others slender; some short, some tall. There were elf maids and humans among them, for those two races he judged to possess the greatest physical beauty. All were cheerful and accommodating—their cooperation assured, when necessary, by the careful use of a charm spell.

Sirene, the albino, had become something of a favorite lately, spending night after night in his bed. He knew the others were jealous of her, and that pleased him for, in their jealousy, the rest became all that much more eager to do his bidding.

Yet even the pleasure of controlling all those women grew thin and tasteless, feeling like merely another way to bore himself.

He turned to the right, away from the steps leading to his treasure trove. The kitchen lay in that direction and there would be fresh bread—as there always was in the morning—and that kindled a gnaw of hunger in his belly. He was grateful for the sensation, any glimmer of sensation.

Then he felt a chill, as if an unseen filter had passed above the layer of gray cloud, leaving full daylight in the courtyard beyond his windows but somehow sapping even the minimal heat of the day from the air. A knock sounded on the great doors of the keep, a booming thunder that originated only a few steps away and echoed through the lofty, empty halls like some kind of dirge.

Hoarst stepped to the door and opened it, his curiosity piqued. He encountered a man who was wrapped in a black robe, the cloaking so complete as to mask even the fellow's face. There was a medallion around the masked man's neck, a disk of gold displaying the emerald eye of Hiddukel.

"Who are you?" asked the magic user.

"I am the Nightmaster, High Priest of the Prince of Lies," said the other man, bowing formally and entering the hall.

Hoarst nodded, not displeased. Perhaps something interesting would happen after all.

⋖∘⊷∘⊷∘⊷◉⊶∘⊶∘⊶∘⊶⋗

The hobgoblin pulled back the leather flap and leered into the dark, humid hut.

"Lord Ankhar?" he hissed, poised to flee if his intrusion aroused the half-giant's displeasure.

But Ankhar had been lying awake on his dirty straw pallet, had known that the sun was up and had been for hours already. Nothing had compelled him to rise, so he had just been lying there in the heat of the swamp, listening to the drone of mosquitoes and flies. The hob's arrival at least gave the *suggestion* of something happening.

"What is it, Half-Ear?" growled the half-giant. He rolled onto his side and, with great effort, pushed himself up to a sitting position. The great roll of his belly spilled across his thighs, so heavy that it threatened to choke the breath out of his lungs, until he rose first to one knee, and finally to an unsteady standing position.

"Two ogre-lords have come up from Brackwater. They seek your judgment on a matter of dispute."

49

"Ah. Tell them I'll be there soon," the half-giant declared, scratching his belly and snuffling loudly. Half-Ear bowed and withdrew while Ankhar rooted around on the flat beam propped across a pair of stumps that served as a table—the hut's only piece of furniture. He pushed aside a pile of cloaks, a moldy half loaf of bread, one of his spare boots, and finally found the gourd of water. He half drank, half rinsed himself and tossed the empty container out the door. Finally he stretched, feeling the knots and kinks in his shoulders and back, wondering when it had happened that he started feeling old.

Emerging into the filtered daylight of his forest stronghold, Ankhar scratched his head and peered around. The camp was small by the earlier standards of his marching army, barely the size of a human village. But it was surrounded by a stout wall of timbers, with a pair of well-guarded gates, and three score small huts were crowded within its enclosure. His favorite companions lived there, a mix of hobgoblins, goblins, and ogres. They served his every whim and did all of his labor, and his reputation and size insured that they remained secure from any threats.

When they had first settled there, following the retreat from Solamnia, some of the humans in his army had dwelt in the headquarters village as well. For some reason, they had departed to set up their own town, just over the nearby ridge. No matter; Ankhar was undisputed lord of the small place.

Ankhar immediately spotted the two ogres who had brought their disagreement to the half-giant lord. Both wore metal helmets, one plumed with a scraggly array of stork feathers, the other wrapped around with a sash of some tattered material that might, once, have been silk. Those badges of honor marked them possibly as chieftains, or at the very least as warriors of importance and influence.

The half-giant got an idea as to the source of their dispute when he spotted an ogress, as tall and broad as each of the warriors, hanging back from the pair. She was seductively clad in a bearskin that she held tightly around herself, while her little eyes cast nervous glances from one ogre to the other. Finally she raised her face to meet Ankhar's gaze, and he plainly perceived the plea for succor in her beseeching look.

He puffed out his chest and swaggered forward, having already made up his mind as to how the dispute would be resolved. She was not displeasing to the eye, that wench, with full breasts swelling under the bearskin robe, a long mane of thick, dark hair, and ample flesh displayed on the calf barely glimpsed beneath the hem of her robe.

"What is this?" he demanded, placing his hands on his hips, looming over the two ogres, leering with a tusk-baring smile at the ogress behind them. She gasped and lowered her eyelids demurely. The pair of plaintiffs immediately began to bark, each trying to snarl loudly over the other's blustering accusations.

"He stole my bride—" snarled Stork Feathers.

"He took my wench—" declared Silk Band.

"She was in my lodge—"

"I paid her father—"

"Enough!" roared the half-giant, finally lowering his gaze to look at the two dumbstruck ogres. Ankhar pointed a sausage-sized finger at the ogre wearing the feathered crest. "Who are you?"

"I am Vis Gorger," replied the bull proudly. "Chief of the Gorge clan, and lord of two valleys. This ogre wench was awarded to me by her sire—she is part of a pledge of truce between his people and mine. I claim her as a fair prize and would take her now as a chieftain's bride."

The half-giant scratched his chin, apparently considering his argument—but actually, admiring the increasing expanse of plump calf exposed beneath the hem of the ogress's robe as she, inadvertently or not, adjusted her garment. Very nice!

"And you?" Ankhar said, switching his attention to the ogre with the sash. "What is your claim?"

"I am Heart Eater, bull son of the Ripper clan." He thumped his chest with a resounding boom. "This wench is Pond-Lily, and I claimed her for myself many seasons ago. She said she would come with me, pledged her word last year. I am a chief in my own right—lord of one valley, for now—and my honor has been sullied."

"You're an ogre," Ankhar retorted. "You have no honor. Neither of you. And you have no claim on this wench."

"What?" bristled Vis Gorger.

"How dare you!" charged Heart Eater.

"You—Pond-Lily?" spoke the half-giant. "Did you promise to go with this ogre last year?"

"Um . . . no? That is, great lord, I really can't remember," she replied in a musical voice, her soft doe's eyes cast downward. Very nice, indeed!

"A promise unremembered is a promise never made," declared Ankhar. "And you, Vis Gorger, will honor your truce, and you do not need a wench to seal the peace. This is my judgment: The wench—er, Pond-Lily? You will stay with me. As to the pair of you, go while you can still get away with your lives."

With a certain amount of muttering, growling, and dire glares, the bull ogres did just that. Before they were even out of sight of the great tent-city, Ankhar had taken Pond-Lily back to his shelter and embarked on some hasty negotiations of his own.

"You have made a very comfortable place for yourself," the Nightmaster commented, his words as dry as the impeccable red wine he sipped through the black gauze that covered his face. The elf maid who had served it beamed happily, and scurried away at Hoarst's dismissive gesture. "This place has been a wreck for decades. I shudder to think of the expenses you must have incurred."

Hoarst took a drink from his own glass and, shrugging, studied the masked high priest curiously. "It is true that I hired some masons and carpenters. But my magic sufficed to accomplish a great deal of the . . . improvements I have made."

"No doubt," said the Nightmaster. He drew a long, luxurious breath in through his nostrils. "Even so, the air positively *sings* of gold and gemstones. I should say a virtually unprecedented cache, stored somewhere below our feet."

"And if that is what it is?" asked the Thorn Knight, growing more guarded. "How is my treasure of interest to you?"

"Oh, I assure you, my good wizard, it does *not* interest me—except in that it allows me some understanding of your motivations, your desires."

"Go on."

"I am wondering if you would be interested in adding more gold to your holdings—an amount of gold that is, I believe, the largest intact collection anywhere upon Krynn."

"I am always interested in valuable items and trinkets," Hoarst allowed. He released a dry laugh. "I let an ignorant barbarian think that he was my master, simply because be paid me very, very well. But why are you coming to me with this proposal? I should have thought such a prize would be as tempting to the Prince of Lies as it is to any wizard."

The Nightmaster chuckled, a sound like wind rustling dry leaves in a cold woodland. "The Prince counts his treasures in souls collected. Such trinkets as gold and gems are merely a means to the end."

"So Hiddukel means to acquire *my* soul?" asked the Thorn Knight, his tone bordering on contempt. "I would have given him credit for greater subtlety in the attempt."

"No, you misunderstand," the dark priest clarified. Another chuckle whispered through the mask. "No matter your power, you are but one soul. The Prince desires to ensnare thousands, tens of thousands, and for this you could serve as an important—and very well-paid—agent."

"Go on," replied Hoarst, intrigued. "Where does the Prince intend to seek his souls in a land ruled by the Solamnics?"

"He intends to subvert the rule of the Solamnics. He proposes to take all the souls in Palanthas, and you can have all the gold in that city—including the lord regent's legendary hoard."

"A tempting offer. I have seen the bright ingots glowing in the room atop the tower he calls the Golden Spire. But the knighthood is stronger now than it has been for centuries, millennia even. Perhaps your master's ambitions are too lofty for his means?"

"The knighthood may be strong, but there are fault lines in the empire. Besides, it is not necessary to destroy the whole nation at once. That one city, Palanthas, would be a good start."

"Palanthas is well protected in its own right. There is the pass, and the High Clerist's Tower."

"Ah, you are right, but you are missing the point. Palanthas is vulnerable precisely because of that tower, that pass."

"I don't see how," the Thorn Knight challenged.

"Would you feel the same if I told you where you could find and recruit a formidable army that would jump at the opportunity to take that tower and close that pass?"

Hoarst thought for a long time then looked at the empty bottle of red wine. He snapped his fingers, and the elf maid reappeared. "Bring us another bottle," he demanded, all the while staring at the Nightmaster. So it was going to be a productive day after all. "My guest and I have much to discuss," he added quietly as he gestured at the woman to hurry from the room.

CHAPTER FIVE

NEW COMPOUND

The opening of the mine gaped like a dark eye hung on the cliff wall overlooking the remote mountain vale. The place was high up in the Garnet Range, at an altitude where only a few scraggly cedar trees conspired to form a clump that was barely a grove, the foliage was so thin and sparse. In the center of the vale was a lake of spectacular beauty, a blue that reflected the purity of the skies on cloudless days. Trout arrowed through the depths, silvery spears darting after the flies that alighted briefly upon the placid surface.

Three sheer cliff walls enclosed the lake and the little grove. A stream flowed out of the valley in the fourth direction, and a crude track—it would be misleading to call it a road—scored a rocky, rutted route parallel to that pristine flowage. A stout wagon rested at the terminus of that track, and a quartet of burly dwarves emerged from the mine with pickaxes and shovels balanced on their shoulders. They waved to the dwarf maid resting on the driver's seat of the wagon, and started down the narrow trail toward the lakeshore and their waiting conveyance.

"Shouldn't you be coming down a little faster?" the female dwarf called worriedly from her seat on the wagon.

"Don't you worry about that, Sal," replied the leader of the small group of miners. Dram Feldspar swaggered along with every appearance of extreme confidence, sparing not so much as a glance over his shoulder at the dark entrance of the mine. "Freddie's getting pretty damn good at setting those fuses just—"

The sentence was never finished, as a spurt of smoke and flying rocks erupted from the mine entrance, spraying the little valley with a wave of debris. A second later, the sound of the explosion—a dull boom that shivered the very bedrock of the place and echoed from the cliffs like thunder—swept across the four dwarves, knocking them over and sending them tumbling in a tangle of boots, beards, and flying tools.

The four miners picked themselves up rather slowly and dusted each other off, checking for broken bones. Fortunately, none of the flying rocks had struck flesh.

"Er," Dram noted sheepishly, acknowledging the crimson flush sweeping across his wife's round face as they limped up to the wagon. "Maybe we do need to be a little more careful."

"Well, if all you hurt was your pride, then you can go ahead and set another charge—might knock some of the pride out of you!" Sally Feldspar huffed, hopping down from the wagon, using the tail of her shirt to blot—none too gently—at a scuff on Dram's nose, caused when that impressive proboscis had slammed into the ground.

"Ah, geez," the dwarf said, blushing. "It ain't nothing, Sal."

"Can we go back to New Compound now?" she asked, ignoring his protestations as she licked at the corner of her shirt and used the moist cloth to wipe the dust from her husband's forehead. She looked at him hopefully, though she suspected the answer.

"Of course not!" he objected. "We've got to get back in the hole, as soon as the dust settles, and see how well the blast worked!"

"I suppose so," she sighed. She gestured to the wagon. "Well, you fellows better have a tankard to wash out the dust. And I brought along a hunk of ham and a few loaves of bread."

"Thanks, Sally. I mean it," Dram said, resting his hand on her shoulder. He smiled, his white teeth gleaming through the dusty tangle of his beard. "And I bet you brought the ham from Josie's smokehouse too."

"I did—but how did you know?" she asked, pulling back the blanket, which she'd had covering the sumptuous feast.

"I could smell it from twenty paces away," he said with a chuckle.

<hr />

It was late in the afternoon before the four dwarves reemerged from the "hole." Coated with gritty dust, they evinced pleasure in shining eyes and beaming grins as they made their way down to the wagon. Sally, meanwhile, had caught an impressive stringer of trout, which she had packed in a chest and covered with snow that she had scooped from a nearby, shady swale. She hitched the mules into their traces as the miners reappeared and had the wagon turned and ready to roll by the time they reached her.

"Good news, I take it?" she said drolly, taking in their obvious delight.

"You wouldn't believe the crack we put in that seam of

ore!" Dram declared, hopping onto the bench beside his wife, ignoring her attempt at evading him as he planted a sooty kiss on her cheek. "Why, there's enough digging to keep a team of a dozen working around the clock for the rest of the season!"

"Well, I'm glad for that, but I do wish you'd be a little more careful," Sally said, getting the wagon rolling with a cluck of her tongue and a quick snap of the reins. The other dwarves settled themselves in the back as she expertly steered the two-mule team onto the rutted, descending track. She kept one hand on the brake and, with a lot of jostling and bouncing, slowly guided them beside the tumbling stream, until the steep little valley spilled into a wider, more pastoral area.

The wagon forded the little stream with a splash that doused them all—Sally declaring the rinse-off did the four miners a world of good—then rolled onto the smooth road that would take them the rest of the way to New Compound. The bumps vanished, replaced by tightly meshed paving stones, the slabs laid with dwarf precision.

Soon the road crossed the river, and there a span of three stone arches made a gentle rise, with the middle arch set high enough to allow the passage of a good-sized boat underneath. From the crest of the sturdy bridge, the dwarves got a nice view of their destination.

New Compound had changed dramatically from the muddy, wooden-timbered frontier town that had sprung up, practically overnight, when Dram relocated his manufacturing operation to the Garnet Range. Though most of the residents—including Dram's wife and father—were hill dwarves from the Vingaard Mountains, they had made the migration across the plains with relatively little grumbling.

Under the orders of Jaymes Markham, then lord marshal

of the Solamnic Army, the entire town and manufacturing operation dedicated to the production of the explosive black powder had been obliged to be moved there, to be closer to the war. And, in fact, the powder—and the tubelike bombards Dram had invented—had proved decisive in winning that war, driving the barbarian half-giant Ankhar from Solamnia with the remnants of his scourging horde.

The great factory complex occupied half of the town, which was situated on a flat plain along the water where the river pooled into a lake before spilling out of the valley and down onto the central Vingaard Plain. Five tall smokestacks dominated the flat area, and two of them belched black smoke into the mountain air as Dram and his fellows watched from the wagon; a stiff wind, cresting across the foothills, carried the smoke away in the direction of Solanthus, leaving the sky over New Compound generally clear. Steam swirled around the great, stone firehouse, where boilers remained hot and sent their warmed water throughout the manufacturing complex, as well as providing service to some of the larger houses near the shore of the lake.

The greatest of those, through no accident, was the domicile of Dram Feldspar and his wife and child. As the wagon trundled off the bridge and onto the streets of the town—which was not protected by a wall or any other defensive positions—the mountain dwarf felt a proud, glowing sensation in his belly. He thought of that house, of the dwarf woman and their precocious child, and he could not restrain a chuckle of deep, genuine pleasure.

"What is it?" Sally asked, shooting him an amused look.

"Ah, just . . . I guess I never imagined I would so much enjoy coming to a place like this, having a real home, a real family." He blushed and glanced back to make sure that none of the three miners in the rear of the wagon could hear him. No worries: they were happily toasting each other and the day's work, their sloshing mugs half full of the ale they continued to draw from the keg Sally had so thoughtfully brought along. Dram looked back at his wife, his expression serious, his voice low but sincere.

"I owe it all to you, Sal. And I want you to know I'm grateful."

She squeezed his knee, looking at him through shining eyes. "You don't give yourself enough credit." She giggled. "For starters, you stood up to my father when he wanted to rip your liver out and cook it on a spit!"

"Well, that was just man-business," Dram said, embarrassed. He touched the knob on his skull, a bump inflicted a week earlier during the course of some "man-business" with his estimable father-in-law, Swig Frostmead.

"I mean, you make me proud, the way you don't give in to him. You're the only dwarf I've ever known that could take his measure." She looked away, and he thought he heard her sigh slightly. "I wish . . . I wish . . . someday . . ."

"You wish I'd stand up to Jaymes, don't you?" Dram spoke seriously, knowing his wife's mind all too well.

She looked at him again, and he felt as though she were looking straight through him, straight through to his soul. "I don't mean it like that. I know what he means—what he meant—to you . . . for all those years you were living like outlaws. And I know that the work you've done for him has been in the name of a good cause. You've united Solamnia, and that was no easy task. And the barbarians have been driven out, for good . . . I hope."

"Aye, all true. But he's changed, hasn't he? I'd be blind not to see it," Dram declared softly.

"Yes, he has. And sometimes . . . I worry about the future."

"You and me both, wife," Dram replied gruffly. "You and me both."

The cool stone walls of the house were pleasing, and Mikey squealed with pleasure as Dram and Sally entered the front hall. The little boy toddled from the nursery to greet his parents, while his grandfather stood back, beaming with pride.

"Mums! Dada!" Mikey chortled as Sally kissed him, and Dram nuzzled his son with his bristling beard. As usual, the lad was consumed by giggles at these ministrations.

"Thanks for staying with him, Dad," Sally said, going over to Swig and kissing his furry cheek. "Any problems?"

"Not a one," the grizzled hill dwarf said, beaming. "That little fellow is a real prodigy—why, he was using my pocket knife like a pickaxe, digging in the backyard. And today I showed him how to make two fists!"

"Uh, thanks, Dad."

"Don't mention it. You can call on me any time." Swig glanced at his son-in-law and cleared his throat. "But you got a visitor waiting. Rogard Smashfinger came down from Kayolin to see you. He's set up at the inn."

"Well, we'll send a message and have him come for dinner," Sally said quickly before Dram could head for the door. Her husband had been known to take six or eight hours, sometimes, when he went to personally fetch someone from the inn.

Sheepishly, the dwarf nodded. "I'll send one of the men down with an invitation. Tell him to come over as soon as he can."

"Good. I'll see to the kitchen," said the dwarf maid, bustling through the dining room, Mikey rolling along behind.

"Did Rogard say what he wanted?" Dram asked as Swig drew a couple of mugs of ale from the keg that rested in an alcove in the front hall.

His father-in-law handed him one of the foaming vessels and shrugged. "Nah. He seemed kind of out of sorts, though. I suppose it's the usual—he wants us to buy more steel."

Swig's guess proved prescient when, not long after, the mountain dwarf arrived. Rogard Smashfinger wore the fur cape and bejeweled bracelets, rings, and necklaces that marked him as a noble merchant of no small station, and in fact they knew that he was a cousin of Kayolin's king. It was Rogard who had provided the incredibly strong bands of spring steel that had allowed the bombards to finally be rendered functional. Three years ago he had been the master forger of that dwarf under-mountain realm, but his activities and dealings with New Compound had allowed him to take off his leather apron and don the splendid merchant's togs.

Rogard's gray beard was split by a grin that was just a little too friendly, and the gleam in his eye looked as if it had been placed there more by design than by genuine emotion. Even so, it was a relaxed trio of dwarves who retired with their cold ales to the sitting room.

The mountain dwarf from Garnet leaned forward, resting his elbows on his knees, and fixed Dram with a determined look. "So, now. I have ten wagons of steel bands forged and finished, ready to roll down here. When do you want 'em?"

"I'm not sure that I *do* want 'em, to tell you the truth," Dram replied. "I haven't been doing much work on the bombards lately. The emper—Jaymes, that is—still has three of them, and I think they'll be sufficient for the time being."

"You can't be serious!" objected Rogard. "Will you be

content to be just another dwarf mining town, here in the Garnet Range?"

"There's veins of gold and silver in these hills," Dram allowed grudgingly. "Turns out I've got kind of a nose for the stuff."

"Well, listen. If that's your purpose, then the king will have to take a little bit more interest in your operation. Seems likely that you'll owe him some taxes, seeing as how you're digging in *his* mountains!"

Swig sputtered so hard that he blew the foam off of his mug and all across his trousers. He leaped to his feet then made an effort to hold his temper when Dram calmly held up a hand. "Now, Rogard, I am a loyal subject of the king, having been born in that great city under the mountain. But I know where Kayolin is, and I know where we are. There's a lotta miles between us, and the king doesn't have any claim to these valleys around here."

"Are you going to tell the king that? Knowing his majesty like I do, I expect that's more the kind of decision he'll want to be making himself. After all, you led him to believe that you'd be taking this steel off his hands. He's been busy forging up there, while you were poking around in the hills, digging up nuggets and ore. I can't say he's going to be happy about it."

"How dare he tell us what to do?" demanded Swig, stepping forward and balling his fists. "Why, if that mountain dwarf mole ever stuck his nose out from under his mountain, he'd know—"

"Now, now, Swig," Dram said, standing and placing a restraining hand on his father-in-law's shoulder. "Let's mind our manners."

"Manners?" Swig sputtered. "Why, you're just as—"

"Dad?" Sally chirped sweetly, sticking her head through the door to the kitchen. "Oh, hi, Rogard," she said, offering a dazzling smile.

"Hi, Sally," the mountain dwarf replied, beaming at her then warily glancing back at Swig.

"Can you give me a hand in here, Pop?" she asked. "I need someone with a little strength . . ."

The hill dwarf looked angrily at the master forger then turned an appealing expression to his daughter. "But—we're just—I was gonna—I have to—"

"Go ahead, Swig," Dram said cheerfully, using his hand to steer the muttering hill dwarf out of the room, flashing his wife a grateful wink. Only when the two had disappeared into the rear of the house did he turn back to his visitor. Before speaking, Dram took a moment to refill their mugs, carefully sculpting the foam into a perfect head on each glass. He handed the drink to an appreciative Rogard.

"That old hill dwarf has a temper," allowed the guest.

"He's set in his ways. But he's true to his soul, and he's as brave a dwarf as you could ever hope to find."

"Don't doubt it. But it makes me wonder who's in charge down here."

"You just *saw* who is in charge," Dram argued. He meant himself, of course, but he had a momentary thought that it might have actually looked as if he were talking about Sally. No bother, that. It was close enough to the truth, anyway.

"Now, there might be some more of those bombards coming. I really don't know. I'm going to be sending Swig back to the Vingaards to bring a load of sulfur over the next few months. When I get that in, I'll be able to take stock."

"You're not going yourself? Don't you want to see the emperor in Palanthas?"

"He knows where to find me," Dram said with a shrug. "So no, I like it here just fine. And one way or the other, I can find a use for some of that splendid steel around here. Just not sure it will be ten wagons."

Rogard glowered but nursed his ale for a while before replying. Finally, he set the empty glass down and rose to nod stiffly to his host. "I'll tell the king that you'll have an answer for him in two months, then. I *think* he'll be willing to wait until then."

"He'd better," Dram replied, lowering his voice to a growl. "We're not without allies, or weapons, here in New Compound."

"Now, now, Dram. I'm sure there's no need to be thinkin' along those lines. At least, not if you can keep Swig out of the room. Good day."

Dram was holding his own mug, barely touched, when Sally came in a few minutes later. She looked around the empty sitting room. "He's gone? What about dinner?"

"Turns out he didn't have much of an appetite," Dram said sourly. A moment later he brightened. "But I do," he concluded, following his wife into a room full of wonderful aromas.

CHAPTER SIX

APPLE FORD

Blayne Kerrigan slipped through the marshes on the north bank of Apple Creek, no longer churning the waters, instead gliding like a reptile through the shallows. The haste spell continued to propel him with unnatural speed, but it would wear off soon—and by then, he was determined to reach the shelter of the grove along the dry ground just beyond the stream.

Father! He thought of Jaymes Markham's treachery with anguish. With a backward glance as he raced toward the river, he had seen the bloody blade of the Freeman emerge from the lord's back. He wished he had imagined it, but the image was too clear, too real.

Lord Kerrigan was dead.

Soon the protective canopy loomed overhead, and the young knight slipped behind a gnarled trunk and rose to his feet. He peered through some branches and saw the men of the Palanthian Legion in their red tunics, probing along the riverbank. A few unarmored footmen pushed into the water, but the muddy bottom prevented them from making much progress, and they quickly floundered back to the far bank. By that time Blayne had already slipped deeper into the grove, wringing the water from his tunic as he padded along in his bare feet—having kicked off his boots when he first entered the water.

He trotted along, still fired with energy. Apple trees surrounded him. Within moments he came upon an archer dressed in a green leather tunic. The man nodded at him as he passed, then looked questioningly over the young knight's shoulder.

"Lord Kerrigan and the others were taken. The emperor broke the parley," Blayne said coldly. "I saw my father cut down by one of the emperor's guards. I think the duke is killed."

The sentry's face tightened. "Red Wallace is waiting for you at the Grandfather Oak," replied the man, his hands clenching his bow and arrow. "And if that is true, then we'll get revenge for Lord Kerrigan's betrayal, my young lord. I promise."

"Thanks, Paddy. I know we will," Blayne said, touching the sentry on the shoulder as he moved deeper into the grove. He passed other camouflaged men and, though he didn't speak to them, the expression on his face seemed to communicate the grim news to the whole company waiting in the grove. He made his way through the ancient, gnarled apple trees until he reached a small clearing.

The open area was dominated by a massive black oak, a giant tree that dwarfed all others in the grove. Enormous limbs, heavy with early summer leaves, reached out as if to envelop the place. Great beards of moss hung from the lower limbs, masking the shadowy depths closer to the gnarled trunk. The top of the tree—a scarred and blackened stretch of trunk and twisting limbs, proof of a lightning strike many decades ago—lofted over the clearing like a skeletal monument to age, strength, and tenacity.

A lone man emerged from the mossy enclosure, still half concealed by the shadows beneath the dense foliage. As he stole forward, the crimson shade of his robe became visible in the growing light. Tiny images of silver and gold winked from the soft material, which included a hood that covered his head and concealed his face in its deep cowl. As Blayne approached, however, the Red Robe pulled back his hood and looked at him with penetrating eyes.

"The emperor took your father at the parley," the man declared, without preamble.

"Worse. He killed him; I saw a guard run him through."

"The bastard! I wouldn't have believed that even he would stoop so low!"

"His treachery disgraces the knighthood!" Blayne spat. "He promised us safe passage and lured us into his trap."

"It is a good thing that you were prepared, then," Red Wallace noted.

"Thanks to you, old friend," replied the young knight. "Invisible, I escaped their cordon. The haste spell allowed me to swim fast and cross the creek. Else I would be in chains, or worse." He spat noisily. "They count the White Robes even as their allies! How can those wizards countenance such wickedness?"

Red Wallace shrugged. "Sometimes even the cause of good will follow the path of least resistance. I believe the White Robes—with the lady Coryn at their head—feel the emperor will bring about the kind of orderly and law-abiding nation that holds such appeal for them."

"Even if they must break the law in order to pretend such a thing?" sneered Blayne.

"Did you get a look at them—the machines, I mean?" asked the wizard, changing the subject.

"Yes. They were the ugliest contraptions I have ever seen: nothing but great hollow tubes, black ironwood banded with steel. They're carried about by these massive wagons—I'm sure they have to be hauled by oxen."

"Do you think it's true—what we've heard about their power?"

"I can't be certain. Yet there was something about those black mouths that reeked of destruction, of killing. If they are brought within range of Vingaard Keep, our home, our families, our lives—yes, I know it in my heart, all will be lost."

Red Wallace grimaced as if in physical pain. Immediately shaking off that display of weakness, he put his hand on the young lord's shoulder and looked Blayne steadily in the face.

"With your father fallen, it comes to you to ready a response," he said. "What do you plan to do?"

For just a moment, an expression of consternation, perhaps even fear, flickered across the young man's face. Then his features hardened to match Red Wallace's.

"My father's plan remains in effect. If they try to cross at the ford, we'll meet them here with a line of pikes. We have a good chance of holding the line at the creek."

"Aye," Red Wallace agreed. "But you know they will probably just follow the road on the other side of the stream down to the river. They can cross the Stonebridge and march right up to the keep."

Blayne nodded. "We have light cavalry in position to harass the emperor, so at least we can slow his progress toward the keep. And we can fight him tooth and nail at the bridge."

"It can only be a delaying action," said the wizard.

"Yes, delay and harass," Blayne replied. He stared through the trees, remembering the scene at the emperor's camp. In his mind he saw the ranks of soldiers, the herds of horses, the tents and baggage wagons. Above all he remembered the three great war machines, the tubes of the bombards mounted on huge wagons.

"If we merely delay him, he'll bring those weapons up eventually, and Vingaard Keep will be destroyed," Blayne said thoughtfully. "So we must take him by surprise, strike at his strength."

"What's your idea?"

"The horsemen will harass him," said the young knight decisively. "But when the wagons are halted, waiting for the road to clear, I will lead a group of determined men from ambush. We'll attack with torches and pitch, and we will destroy his great weapons—*before* he can bring them to bear against our home."

≻◦◉◦◉◦◉◦◉◦◉◉◦◦◉◦◉◦◉◦≺

From the comfort of his command center in the fortified camp, which resembled a temporary city, with a picket wall of trees and neat paths lined with tents and exercise fields, Jaymes ordered General Dayr to bring the Crown Army up from the Vingaard. The two forces were to merge at the camp, which occupied the ridge of hills overlooking the lone ford across Apple Creek.

The vanguard of the Crown Army, led by General Dayr himself, came up to meet the Palanthian Legion.

"The lancers under Captain Blair are busy patrolling along the river," the general informed the emperor. "But I left the Stonebridge unguarded, as you requested."

"Good. The more of their men they put in the field against us, the easier it will be to conquer the keep later on," Jaymes said.

"What's the next step, then?" asked Dayr.

"I've already given the order. We will attack across the ford," the emperor replied. "General Weaver's legion will lead the charge. I'll hold your men in reserve—I'd rather blood some of my newer troops."

"Of course, Excellency." Dayr rode off to see to the deployment of his men. General Weaver quickly and precisely deployed his Palanthian Legion, and in a matter of less than two hours, the units had been moved into position, the attack prepared.

"General, send the first wave across the ford," ordered the emperor.

"Aye, my lord," replied Weaver.

The emperor and his two generals sat astride their horses on a low hillock overlooking Apple Creek, very near to the ford crossing. Nearby, a knot of couriers and signalmen awaited commands. All watched eagerly as Weaver gestured to his flagmen, who raised the pennant signaling the advance.

Immediately, three companies of light infantry moved in columns toward the bank of the creek, where the rutted gravel road sloped into the water. The warriors wore leather tunics and carried short swords and small, round shields. The first wave of the attack would be borne by those free citizens of the New City of Palanthas, who had enlisted in the past year. Fresh to war, they advanced eagerly, ready to impress their general and their emperor.

"Forward! Double march!" barked the sergeants.

The first attackers splashed into the water at a trot, swords and shields held ready, and began to slosh across to the other side. Just beyond the opposite bank, the road curved to vanish among the trunks of the trees in the hushed apple grove. The leading men broke into a run as they found their footing on the far bank.

A dozen of the New City men fell at once, amid a flight of slashing arrows visible to the commanders on the hilltop. They heard screams and saw many of their soldiers writhing on the ground.

Still pressing forward, the troops stumbled over the fallen bodies of their companions, and more went down under the relentless fire. The archers remained unseen, hidden in the orchard, but they obviously had clear fields of fire. The volleys were heavy, lethal, and persistent. The big, steel-headed arrows punctured leather breastplates and wooden shields, even pierced metal helmets.

The surviving troops darted into shelter behind tree trunks and among the dense hedges that lined the road. Wounded men crawled toward safety, while more than a score lay motionless on the ground, apparently slain. More missiles continued to shower the lead ranks, and within minutes all three companies were pinned down.

No further command was given—the plan was already known to company officers—as the next wave, the heavy infantry, moved into the ford. Those soldiers wore mail shirts that descended almost to their knees, with steel caps to protect their heads, and they wielded much larger, heavier shields. Their swords were longer too. They were brawnier veterans, and they hoisted their shields to protect themselves from the arrows. The soldiers advanced slowly, passing through the ford, scrambling up the far bank and pressing toward the trees.

A number of those men, too, stumbled and went down, tripping over bodies or potholes, and several soldiers who lowered their shields momentarily took gruesome wounds from arrows that pierced cheeks, eyes, mouths, and throats. Inevitably, the column spread to the right and left of the narrow road as men fought to find advantageous positions. Spread out and inching along, covered by the layer of shields, the second unit resembled a moving pincushion.

That heavier rank finally penetrated the grove and drove against the picket line of Vingaard swordsmen who awaited them. Steel clashed against steel, and shouts of triumph competed with shrieks of pain and moans of the dying. More Crown infantry pressed across the river, ignoring the continuing arrow fire as they progressed toward the concealed enemy.

The defenders fought stubbornly, working in pairs. The men of Vingaard Keep didn't bother with shields, but instead stabbed and parried from behind the stout trunks of the apple trees.

A bold Crown Knight raised a hoarse cry, lunging forward, chopping with his mighty blade—only to catch the sword in the tough limb of a tree. Before he could wrench it free, one of the defenders thrust from below, driving his keen steel right through the mail shirt and into the knight's belly. With a low groan, the stricken veteran released his grip on his own blade and sank back into the arms of his comrades, who dragged him back.

In a skirmish such as the one being waged, numbers would inevitably prevail—that was understood by the commanders on the hill and by the swordsmen on both sides. Company after company of the Crown Army marched across the ford, some veering right, others left, expanding the frontage of the attack. Ultimately, the men of Vingaard had to fall back through the trees, though they gave ground only grudgingly—and even then, at a high cost in blood and misery. As the shadows swallowed them up, they retreated more quickly, and the attacking soldiers gave chase, a tide of steel and fury, bent on avenging their losses and carrying the day.

That tide broke, very abruptly, against a levee of pikemen who materialized, as if by magic, between the trees. They had not been disguised by any spell but merely had been camouflaged and lying low. The long polearms were unwieldy in the grove, but Kerrigan and his son had arranged the line shrewdly. Seemingly a thousand men stood shoulder to shoulder against the attack, forming a barrier that bristled with razor-sharp spear tips.

Most of the attackers hesitated in the face of the surprising obstacle, although a few courageous Crown soldiers charged forward and were pierced to death. The defenders met the onslaught with taunts and jeers, drawing still more to reckless charges. But the line never wavered, and the attack faltered.

One Crown sergeant managed to break a pike and bash another to the side, creating a temporary wedge. He charged ahead with a howl but was chopped at from all sides by multiple blades, losing an arm, and getting a fiendish cut in his thigh, which spurted blood.

Everywhere swordsmen waited among the pikes, and whenever the solid line showed signs of a rupture, the swordsmen stepped into the breach and took on the charging warriors. The entangling trees prevented easy flanking movement, and the defenders had piled great nests of brambles all around on the ground. Sharp thorns hooked into clothes and skin; even the most sure-footed of the emperor's men were tripped up by the tangle of branches.

For thirty bloody minutes, the ponderous, chaotic struggle raged. Each side killed and each side died, and whenever the attackers gained a few feet, the defenders struck hard and drove the Crown soldiers back. When a man's sword broke, he seized another from a fallen foe or comrade, and when he was wounded, he dropped back, allowing a fresh fighter to take his place in the line.

Vingaard archers scrambled into the trees and showered arrows over the heads of their comrades, into the faces and breasts of the attackers. A rank of Crown men armed with crossbows came up behind the first line of the charge and returned that fire with admirable accuracy, their steel-tipped bolts puncturing the green leather shirts of the targeted bowmen with ease. The missile duel increased in ferocity until the opposing bands were engaged in their own lethal fight for supremacy, a battle that took place literally over the heads of most of their comrades trapped in the melee.

On the hilltop south of the stream, the emperor strained to scrutinize the fight in the woods, his face showing ill-concealed displeasure. From there he could not claim to know the details, but the reality was plain. As more and more of his men crossed the stream, they were bunching up in the grove, and the advance had bogged down. Men were dying in growing numbers, and their sacrifice had ceased to have any meaning.

"Sound the withdrawal!" he snapped finally.

Dayr signaled to his trumpeters, and a trio of heralds raised their brass instruments and brayed out the command to retreat. Immediately the men at the edge of the grove turned and raced toward the ford. Others broke from the shelter of the trees, coming down the road, converging from the right and left on the narrow ford.

"Dammit! They're panicking, running like fools!" snapped the emperor. He put the heels to his horse and, with Dayr trailing behind, galloped down the hill.

There were a dozen companies clumped together on the

near side of the river, waiting to cross, and they scattered out of the way of their enraged commander. Jaymes drew up his horse at the edge of the river, even as a hundred men splashed into the shallow flow. Fleeing, stumbling, falling, and choking, they clawed their way toward the safety of the south bank.

Jaymes pulled back his reins, and the roan reared. He brandished Giantsmiter; the blue flames that crackled on his legendary blade were visible even in the bright sunlight. The panicked men hesitated at the sight of their lord on his rearing horse.

"Hold your formations!" he shouted. "Remember your training!"

Some of the men responded, while others continued to flail through the water. More arrows showered from the woods, felling more soldiers. Even though Jaymes used the flat of his blade to slap at the first of the wretches to crawl up the near bank, he couldn't stem the tide. The officers and commanders shouted themselves hoarse, trying to organize a proper withdrawal. The men of the New City, new to battle as well, did not listen.

The enemy captain—Jaymes fleetingly wondered if it was Lord Kerrigan's son—saw his opportunity, and hurled forward his line of pikemen. The pikemen poured out the apple grove, their long weapons prodding at the disorganized retreat. Vainly, the Palanthian officers shouted and cursed, trying to get the ranks to wheel and face the deadly threat to their rear.

It was Dayr who saw what had to be done. He barked out commands to a large troop of longbowmen, who had been holding their position on the near side of the stream. Immediately they commenced a shower of arrows, which arced over the heads of the retreating soldiers, falling among the advancing Vingaard pikes. Quickly the pikemen halted their pursuit, withdrawing into the safety of the trees, as the weary and bedraggled attackers slogged through the stream and collapsed on the south bank of Apple Creek.

Jaymes rode his horse back and forth before the shamed, defeated men. Scorn dripped from his voice as he addressed them in loud, angry terms. "You men fought like you'd never heard the horn of battle before! I won't fault you for failing to break a line—but to run like whipped curs at the first call of retreat? I would never have expected it, nor would I believe it if I hadn't witnessed it with my own eyes."

"Forgive us, my lord!" cried one commander, standing amid the seated, soggy ranks. "Let us try again. We'll carry the line of these traitors—or die trying!"

A few of the soldiers raised a cheer at his brave statement, but most kept their eyes on the ground, humiliated and shaken. Jaymes spoke sternly. "You'll have the chance to fight again. When you do, this shame will be scourged. Until then, you will all live with the memory of your failure—and you will not march with the rest of my army, but stay behind to lick your wounds and ponder your failure."

Some of the men wept, others shouted in protest, but he ignored them all as he spun his horse and rode back to General Dayr. "We're going to have to march down the road and take the bridge after all. I'll leave these men here so the enemy will have to worry about another crossing—but I want the rest of the army on the march within the hour."

"I've got them ready now, my lord. These hills along the stream should conceal us for the first few miles, so perhaps we can surprise them by our decisiveness and speed."

"All right," Jaymes replied. He looked again at the ranks

of defeated, soaking men near the ford, his eyes narrowing with displeasure. He stared for a moment then shook his head and put his knees to his horse, ready to join the march column on the road.

CHAPTER SEVEN

><◦◦◦◦◦◦◦◦◦◦◦◦◦◦◦◦◦◦◦◦◦◦◦◦◦◦◦<

LORD OF THE WILDERNESS

><◦◦◦◦◦◦◦◦◦◦◦◦◦◦◦◦◦◦◦◦◦◦◦◦◦◦◦<

At first, Ankhar was enchanted with the ogre wench he had claimed as his prize from the two arguing chieftains. Pond-Lily had many natural charms: the swelling cheeks that gave her face such a fetching roundness, the twin globes of her immense breasts, the sturdy, admirable muscles of her hamlike legs. She was a pretty little blossom, a change of pace from the emerald-green wilderness.

But after a month of sampling the delights of Pond-Lily's physical attributes, he was forced to realize her name was a pretty fair estimation of her intelligence and conversational abilities.

In fact, he thought as he glowered into the dying coals of his campfire, there might be swamp flowers out there that had more personality, and more intelligence, than his current hutmate. That was probably why he was still sitting and sulking, long after most of the village had gone to sleep, reluctant to seek the comfort of his own sleeping pallet.

With a sigh, the hulking half-giant got to his feet, pushing himself off of his log with both hands. He couldn't help but notice the bulge of his gut, and he flushed with embarrassment when he thought of the trim physique that had carried him through his great war campaigns.

"Once I was master of half of Solamnia," he declared aloud, as if amazed by the realization. "Now I am a master of the swamp and of a wench who is a pond-lily by any name."

"How would you like a return to the power you once held—or to reach even greater heights?"

The question was whispered so softly that the half-giant whirled around, growling, ready to smite whoever had dared to sneak up on him and mock him. But no one could be seen.

"Who speaks to me?" he growled, his tiny eyes glaring from their fat-enfolded sockets as he stared into the darkness. "Who is there?"

A man—or at least, he thought it was man, based on size and shape—emerged from the darkness at the edge of the trees. The stranger was cloaked from head to toe in black, including a gauzy mask that utterly concealed his face. Most surprisingly of all, he approached the looming half-giant without any obvious display of fear.

"How dare you!" spat Ankhar, starting to take a step toward the interloper, to smite him with, at the very least, a powerful blow from the back of his hand. Surprisingly, however, the half-giant's booted feet remained frozen in place, as if he had stepped into soft mire that had suddenly congealed around him. He stared in amazement as the man approached casually and took a seat on a log very near to the one where Ankhar had been sitting.

Abruptly, Ankhar's feet came unstuck, and he stumbled, realizing that a magic spell must have gripped him for a moment. The man who had cast the spell had obviously released him from its thrall—so the interloper had to be regarded with suspicion, but also with a wary respect. The dark-cloaked man settled himself down and waited for a few moments until Ankhar, almost unconsciously, came back to the fire and sat down nearby his strange visitor. The half-giant's anger had dissipated in the face of his visitor's cool self-confidence, and he found himself more curious than angry.

"Who are you?" he asked

"Ask your mother—she will know me at once," replied the man, his tone somehow courteous even though he had refused to answer the question. Somehow, his calm certainty only made Ankhar more uneasy.

"My mother sleeps—the hour is late. Tell me yourself," he insisted.

Instead, the mysterious visitor said, "This is a nice village," his masked face turning this way and that as he took in the crude huts, the wooden palisade, the muddy central square. Again, his tone was innocuous, even pleasant, but the half-giant felt himself bristling.

"It is nice enough for my needs," he declared guardedly.

"But is it secure enough to hold your treasure? The vast wealth your armies took from Garnet and Thelgaard and other places of Solamnia? Don't you worry that some army will come and batter down your palisade, make off with your cherished hoard?"

Ankhar growled, a deep, menacing sound by any measure, though the black-clad visitor seemed hardly to notice. And in truth, there was little vitriol behind the chieftain's noisy bluster. Again, his curiosity was stronger than his anger. The growl faded out as he shrugged.

"My treasures were many, but they were taken by the knights after the Battle of the Foothills," he said. "I do not miss them. They were useless trinkets, heavy to haul around, not good to eat."

"I see," came the soft reply.

"Besides, such baubles are more the concern of humans. What need have I of steel and jewels, of great castles and high stone walls? I am happy here, and I am the master of all this place!"

"No doubt you are."

"I am!" Again Ankhar found the remark vaguely offensive, though it was offered pleasantly. It occurred to him—and he was not a terribly introspective fellow—that it was as though he were arguing with himself. "Warfare is hard and thankless work. And plunder, unless it is good to eat or useful like slaves, tools, or land . . . well, plunder is too much trouble. There is food in these forests, and a small amount of work will provide for all of my needs."

"All your needs?" needled the masked visitor.

"Yes—all of them!" barked Ankhar. He thought of Pond-Lily, waiting for him in the crude hut, reposing on the muddy straw pallet flat on the ever-damp ground, and he felt his conviction waver. "Why are you taunting me with these words?" he demanded.

"I do not intend a taunt, my great friend. And you are my friend, whether you know it or not. You and I have done great work in the name of the same master, in the past."

"I have no master!" The half-giant's voice rose with his temper.

Only then did he notice the lone chip of color on the black-garbed man. An emerald winked from a pendant at his throat. It was a small piece of stone, too tiny to notice in the dark—except up close. For just a moment, Ankhar could have sworn the green stone flared with some kind of internal light.

And with that realization, he recalled another green stone, the mighty arrowhead of emerald that once tipped his great battle spear, the talisman he had carried to war. When he had held that spear high, the power of Hiddukel, the Prince of Lies, had illuminated it with an iridescent strength that could light up a whole valley, driving back the shadows of night.

Now that battle spear lay in the mud of his hut, somewhere near the back wall. The green spearhead had ceased to glow when the half-giant's horde had been broken at the Battle of the Foothills. He had carried the weapon with him to Lemish out of habit, but whenever he looked at it nowadays the stone seemed to have gone cold, dark, lifeless.

"My lord! Lord Ankhar! Oh, great master, come and see!"

He bolted to his feet, startled by the urgent words coming from his hut. Pond-Lily was calling him, summoning him in a voice filled not with desire, but with wonder. He spun around and gaped in the direction of the hut, startled to see green light spilling from around its door-flap, and penetrating through the many gaps between the logs of the imperfectly constructed walls.

He crossed to the place in a dozen strides and pulled back the flap to find the ogress sitting up on the pallet, gazing with a look of dumb disbelief at the source of the illumination.

His spearhead, almost buried beneath the miscellaneous rubbish at the far wall, was glowing with a brilliance that hurt his eyes. He saw Pond-Lily reach out a tentative hand, as if to grasp the stone, and he cuffed her away with a savage slap.

"Don't touch!" he roared. "It's mine!"

Pouncing like a cat, he wrapped his hands around the haft of the spear. The stout stick was as big around as a man's wrist and some eight feet long. He lifted it reverently, shaking the weapon to break it free of the wet leaves, old food scraps, and other debris. Then he carried it out of the hut and back to the fire, where the masked visitor still sat, watching him with that featureless face.

But it was neither the half-giant nor the strange visitor who next spoke. Instead, there came a cackling laugh from the darkness, and a wrinkled old hobgoblin wench hobbled forth toward the embers of the fire. Laka, Ankhar's stepmother, had apparently been awakened by the disturbance. The coals in the fire pit seemed to take on a new life as she approached, flaring into brightness, casting a red glow that reflected off of the hob-wench's few remaining teeth, proving that she could still beam broadly.

"My lord," she said, surprising Ankhar by kneeling before the masked visitor.

"You know this man?" demanded the half-giant.

"Yes," Laka replied, climbing to her feet, taking Ankhar by the hand, and leading him to sit on a log beside the masked visitor. "He is the Nightmaster. The Prince of Lies has sent me a dream, saying the Nightmaster would be coming to see you, to tell you important things, and to charge you with a great task."

"Which is?"

"Listen to him," the hob-wench said impatiently. "You need to shut up for now and hear the words of the Nightmaster."

The half-giant was not used to being talked to thusly, but as always he bit his tongue, sat still, and did what his mother told him to do.

⊰⊶⊰⊶⊰⊶❁⊰⊶⊰⊶⊰⊶⊱

Hoarst traveled through the ether of time and space, the wings of magic carrying him in a moment a distance that would have taken him three days to ride by horse. In that burst of teleportation, he passed over mountains, steep-walled valleys, across a vast plain and a mighty river, and deep into an unfamiliar range of mountains. Finally, the magic cast him down into the low swale the Nightmaster had described to him. The Thorn Knight arrived at the same time of day he had departed—that was, just before dusk—and since he had taken the precaution of making himself invisible before he teleported, he arrived unseen by any of the men around him as he materialized. Unnoticed, he took stock of his surroundings.

The priest of Hiddukel had spoken the truth, he realized at once: there was a great military host gathered there, arrayed in a camp with admirable discipline, all approaches guarded by alert sentries. The valley was hidden by lofty mountains, surrounded by a natural palisade. A trio of dark lakes were connected like a necklace of black pearls by a frothing stream that flowed through the valley. Groves of fruit trees thrived there, and a quick glance around showed him hundreds of hectares were under cultivation.

The mountains around the place were steep and forbidding, limiting access to a pair of passes, one to the north and the other to the south. When the wizard scrutinized those mountain-flanked saddles, he saw that access was guarded by cleverly camouflaged fortifications. The bastions looked very much like the natural mountainsides, but Hoarst picked out subtly concealed platforms for archers and numerous overlooks where rocks had been poised, needing only a trigger or a little leverage before they would tumble downward, crushing hapless interlopers in the passages below.

His initial inspection completed, Hoarst looked for his intended destination, and found it in a great house overlooking the largest of the three lakes. Still invisible, he made his way down a smooth path toward the place. He passed a broad practice field, where hundreds of men in black tunics were being drilled by hoarse-voiced sergeants. Some worked on tightly disciplined pike formations, while others fired volleys of arrows at straw targets, or bashed at each other with swords that, while dull, seemed to be made of steel or iron. The wizard heard more than one bone get cracked in the few moments it took him to traverse the field.

The great house was new, a gleaming stone structure with towers at the corners and battlements along the top of the walls. The windows were small and narrow, for defensive purposes. The defenses were well designed, Hoarst realized, taking in the fact that the roadway was the only feasible approach through the marshy ground. The treacherous ground surrounded the great structure on three of four sides.

The Thorn Knight was pleased by everything he saw.

The front gates to the place were closed, but through the iron bars he noted a courtyard, with the doors to the house only twenty paces away. No guard could be spotted, but he knew there would be one. A quick spell of flight, the enchantment cast with an inaudible whisper, lifted the invisible mage to the top of the wall, where he spotted a pair of men-at-arms, who wore black, scale-armor shirts and steel helmets. One was snoozing with his back against the wall, but the other watched the road with every indication of alertness.

Of course, no level of alertness permitted a man to see that which could not be seen. Nor could a guard hear silence, and Hoarst made sure to move slowly so that not even any slight breeze would cause his invisible robe to rustle. He glided over the wall and swooped into the courtyard. At the last minute, he veered away from the front door, climbing through the air, banking around the corner of the house. He came to rest on the largest balcony of the house, a broad expanse of marbled surface that offered a splendid view of the nearby lake and the surrounding mountain peaks.

That was where he would find the man he was seeking. Pleased to note that the doors to the balcony were open, he strode into a vaulted chamber, the centerpiece of a splendid suite of rooms.

A man sat alone at a vast table, scribbling notes on a great sheet of parchment—a map. Hoarst silently came up from behind.

"Captain Blackgaard," the Thorn Knight said softly, allowing his spell of invisibility to fall away like a cloak shrugged off. "I was hoping I would find you here."

The seated man sprang to his feet, knocking his chair over and pulling a stiletto from his belt as he spun to face the intruder. Even startled, Blackgaard had the presence of mind to pull a blank sheet of scrip over the map, the Thorn Knight was amused to see, trying to conceal it from view. For a full breath, the knight's knife hand trembled, the tip of the blade pushed up against the wizard's heart.

"Gray Hoarst?" the captain finally gasped, lowering the knife and clapping a hand to his chest in astonishment. "You might have gotten yourself killed—or killed me from the surprise!"

Even so, the accusation was more surprised than angry. Hoarst chuckled. "If a mere shock is enough to slay you, good captain, then perhaps you are not the man that I need to see."

"Figure of speech," Blackgaard said gruffly, sheathing his knife. With a quick glance at the concealed map, he shrugged and crossed to a cupboard and opened the door. "Can I offer you a drink, old friend?" He was already removing a crystal decanter containing a dark brown liquid, so Hoarst replied in the affirmative and took a chair at the large table, a respectful distance away from where Blackgaard had been working.

The captain handed the drink to his visitor and they clinked glasses.

"I'm happy to see you escaped the foothills alive," Hoarst allowed, taking a sip of what proved to be a splendid whiskey.

Blackgaard chuckled grimly. "No thanks to our mutual boss. Last I saw, he was heading for the southern horizon. I rode away with four hundred men, with the Solamnics too worn out to chase us."

"It seems you have collected considerably more than four hundred men, in the meantime."

The captain, a former Dark Knight who had progressed naturally into the role of mercenary, nodded. "I have five thousand here, and an equal number can be mustered in a few days."

"This is an interesting choice of location," the wizard noted. "The north Vingaard Range? You're situated rather close to the Solamnics, aren't you?"

"It's close, true, but perfectly safe," Blackgaard replied. "This valley was part of the landscape that Khellendros devastated back in the day. All the people were killed or driven out, and it's been pretty well written off since then. No travelers pass this way. As you saw, we've managed to make a tidy little fortress here for our purposes."

"Ah, yes. But I wonder, are you and your men feeling suited for life as farmers and herdsmen? Or do you miss the beat of the martial drum? Are you still warriors, in your hearts?"

"That always depends," the captain replied cautiously, "on choosing the right fight, the right war."

"The right war? Or the right prize?"

"Same difference."

"Then you might be willing to wage war again, for the biggest prize of all?" Hoarst watched the other man carefully, already sensing the answer. He knew because he had glimpsed the map that Blackgaard had been studying before the mercenary had time to cover it.

"You mean, do I think of reconquering Palanthas?" asked the military man. He looked toward the concealed map, winked, and nodded. "I think we have much to talk about," he added.

※─◎◎─◎◎─◎◎※◎◎─◎◎─◎◎※

"Est Sudanus oth Nikkas."

My power is my Truth. Ankhar savored the irony of his personal credo. He had allowed himself to idle and cower for too long, had nearly forgotten the lesson that his mother—and his mother's unforgiving god—had taught him so many years ago.

"Est Sudanus oth Nikkas," he repeated, well satisfied. It was a phrase that had been taught to him by one of his old lieutenants, a former Dark Knight-turned-mercenary named Captain Blackgaard.

"What do you mean by that phrase you keep muttering?" Pond-Lily asked cautiously. She had just served the half-giant his morning porridge and stood to the side as he slurped noisily from the great bowl. Ankhar had been acting strange for the past few days, and strange for him was really strange, the ogress thought.

"It means, 'My power is my Truth,' " came the reply.

"Oh."

"I am intended for great things," the half-giant expounded. "I was once a great lord—"

"You still *are* a great lord!" she blurted with wide-eyed sincerity.

He patted her cheek so gently that, though he knocked her down, he didn't really hurt her very much. "Don't interrupt." As she picked herself up and sat meekly beside him again, he gathered his racing thoughts.

"I am a chosen one of the gods," he said, trying to recall the eloquent words that Laka had beaten into his head with her skull-capped totem staff over the past few days. "And it is a waste for me to live here, in the Lemish Forest. I am to be master of a great city!"

"A city! What city?"

He scratched his head, for the details were a little sketchy, in spite of his mother's yammering. "A city of the knights," he remembered. He growled, unconsciously. "I hate the knights," he added.

So it was that, just a few days after the auspicious visit of the Nightmaster, Ankhar, the chosen one, marched out of his safe village. He was accompanied by some henchmen from his previous campaigns—Bloodgutter the ogre, and Rib Chewer the goblin, among them. His goal was to assemble another horde and launch another war and conquer a certain city of the knights.

He bore his emerald-tipped spear in his right hand and wore a gem-encrusted gold crown, one of the few treasures he had brought from Solamnia after his defeat. With his henchmen dressed in great bearskins, each captain crowned with a feathered headdress, he led his entourage through the woods to the nearest ogre settlement.

It was the stronghold of Vis Gorger, a hill town, in a valley peppered with cave mouths. Inside of each was a house, an inn, or a shop. There he met with the ogre lord Vis Gorger, who was still resentful over the Pond-Lily affair, and refused to join the expedition or acknowledge that Ankhar was the Truth.

So the half-giant broke the ogre's neck, quickly and without warning or hesitation. The town's vice chieftain, a strapping male named Bullhorn, didn't seem to mind and proved more amenable to Ankhar's needs—especially after Ankhar appointed him the new overseer of the town. Then Ankhar collected more than a hundred ogre warriors, young bulls eager for mayhem and plunder.

Next he went to the town of Heart Eater, the other chief who had claimed Pond-Lily's affections.

Apparently, word of Vis Gorger's fate preceded Ankhar's arrival. In any event, Heart Eater organized two hundred ogre warriors, with twice that number of goblin spear carriers, and was ready and waiting to join the half-giant when Ankhar and his growing force arrived.

And so it went. The villages and towns of Lemish gave up their young warriors, willingly and with great expectations. They all joined the army of Ankhar the Truth. His force swelled by the day as he marched up and down and back and forth through the breadth of the land.

Until finally, he had amassed his horde of warriors and there was no place left in Lemish for him to go.

CHAPTER EIGHT

AMBUSH BY FIRE

Blayne Kerrigan didn't stay to witness the outcome of the battle in the orchard. Instead, he took two hundred skilled archers and the wizard Red Wallace, and speedily rode east to Vingaard Keep. They crossed the Stonebridge near the bank of the Vingaard—the bridge Jaymes had ordered Dayr not to guard in order to draw more of the Vingaard defenders into battle outside the keep walls.

The riders crossed the span just upstream of the confluence of Apple Creek and the much larger river. South of the creek, they raced westward along the road toward the advancing forces of the emperor. Soon they came up behind the position established by Lord Kerrigan before he had gone to parley with the emperor.

A deep ditch had been excavated across the road, which was anchored by steep, rocky hills to either side. A number of men were waiting behind the dirt wall that had been thrown up behind the ditch, while many horses were pastured in the fields behind the hills. Blayne quickly located the officer in command.

"I have a thousand horsemen, and as many archers and soldiers on foot. We'll hold them up for a few hours," reported Captain Dobbs, a veteran of the keep garrison and the man in charge of this contingent. "But we won't be able to stop them."

"A few hours is all I'll need. Do you have the equipment I asked for?"

"Yes, sir, right over here." The captain led him to a small compound, where bulky saddlebags—two hundred pairs—had been prepared and laid out for Blayne's inspection. Each set included quivers of arrows, a stout bow, jars of pitch, some webbing to wrap around the arrows, and dry matches.

"Excellent," pronounced the young lord. "Any word on how far away the emperor is?"

"Only a couple of miles and coming fast. They didn't waste much time after the battle at the ford."

"No—he always was fast on the march," acknowledged Blayne, wincing. "But it might give us enough time."

"Good luck, sir," offered the captain.

"And to you, too," Kerrigan replied, heading for his horse. That mount, like the rest of the two hundred, had already been outfitted with the bulging panniers. The rest of his band mounted and they cantered away. No longer did they follow the road. They took to the fields, coursing around the southernmost of the twin hills where the Vingaard line was situated.

Blayne had hunted, prowled, fished, and camped on those lands since he was a small boy, and he needed no map or guide. He had a specific spot in mind, and the fast-moving column crossed several fields of grain—though the young lord made sure to steer his horseman along the lanes between the tender plantings—and quickly passed under the shade of overhanging trees.

The Southwood Forest was not a cultivated grove, like the

apple orchard, but a deep and ancient wood of dense trees, drooping, mossy branches, and heavy thickets. Few pathways crossed through the forest, but Blayne knew how to lead his column rapidly through the woodlands. When they approached the mouth of a wide gulley at the far side of the forest, he signaled for his men to dismount. The band gathered around him, alert and unafraid.

"Take the webbing from your saddlebags and wrap it around the foreshaft of each arrow, extending about a foot back from the head. Use the pitch to hold it in place. I want every man to have at least a dozen of these fiery missiles ready to shoot in the next ten minutes."

While his men went about making the preparations, Blayne and Red Wallace advanced on foot to the mouth of the gully. Taking cover behind a cluster of large trees, they looked down on the paved road where, already, the emperor's army could be sighted, no more than a mile away.

"If we have timed it right, the horsemen are in position beyond the road," Blayne said.

Almost immediately those words proved correct as the first of the Vingaard delaying tactics began to play out. They watched as hundreds of cavalrymen, lancers mounted on fleet, unarmored horses, burst over the ridge on the far side of the road and came pouring down on the flank of the emperor's column. The Crown Army cavalry rode to intercede, charging from the front and rear of the column. The two men watched as a frantic battle erupted, men and horses cut down by the score, hooves trampling the wounded, grit and resolve driving each side.

The Vingaard riders had the advantage of surprise, and in their first rush, they split the converging force of Crown horsemen. The road was lined with heavy wagons lumbering toward the keep, and the lead lancers actually reached some of the wagons. They were not the bombards—Blayne could see those wagons far to his left, at the rear of the column, but even so, the riders speared some drivers and caused great confusion in the dense column.

Spearmen had been marching along near the wagons, and they leveled their weapons into a phalanx and pressed forward. Confronted with a wall of steel spearheads, the lancers had no choice but to withdraw. Still, they did so with élan, splitting into small groups and striking at unprotected sections of the baggage train as they jumped over the ditches and darted into the fields beside the track. One heavy cart overturned, tangling four horses in their traces, dumping crates of supplies all across the road.

Finally the harassing lancers were driven off. Whole ranks of spearmen formed up and advanced up the hill toward the crest where the riders had disappeared. They arrayed themselves along the height. Soon companies of the Crown riders, spearheaded by heavily armored knights, also climbed those hills, pouring over the top. Blayne could imagine them riding against the light cavalry on the other side of the ridges, and he could only hope his horsemen would ride away from the uneven challenge. His lancers would have to be ready to perform the next step in the elaborate dance.

At about that time, horns brayed, off to the right. The wagon train came to a halt as more soldiers—both cavalry and infantry, hurried forward to either side of the road.

"They've come up against the ditch," Blayne guessed.

Red Wallace nodded. "It will give them pause, certainly. We will strike while they are distracted."

"Agreed."

Quickly the two men returned to the band of riders to find

that the men had successfully rigged plenty of arrows with straw and pitch. The young lord directed his men to advance stealthily on foot, each man leading his horse, as they moved parallel to the road, along the bed of the wide gully. They were yet a mile from the enemy, and the steep walls of the winding ravine effectively masked their approach.

Periodically, Blayne would scale those walls, checking their location against the wagons, until finally he slid back down and ordered his men to mount up.

"Those bombards are right in front of us now, just off in the distance. They're guarded by a dozen companies of spearmen and riders, but with a little luck, those fellows will be distracted pretty thoroughly."

At that point, the deep ravine petered into a shallow cut, and the mounted men in the lead of the column could get a look at the road and the ridge beyond. Blayne studied the large companies of soldiers protecting his prize and found himself holding his breath.

"There they are!" exclaimed Wallace at the first sign of movement on the opposite ridge.

Just as planned, hundreds of the Vingaard light cavalry reappeared, abruptly spilling over the crest. With lances leveled, they bore down in a charge toward the wagons containing the massive bombards, whooping and shouting like wild men. Also as planned, the men of the Crown Army reacted quickly to defend their precious weapons, forming a three-rank line and extending their wings to the right and left in a sweeping, encircling barrier that stood between the charging horsemen and the precious guns.

That was when the light horsemen pulled back their mounts and milled about defiantly, just out of arrow range from the column's defenders.

Blayne looked at Wallace. "I don't think we'll get a better chance than this," he declared.

The red-robed wizard nodded in agreement.

"Light those brands!" cried young Lord Kerrigan. "We ride against the bombards!"

In the next moment, all two hundred of his men had touched flames to their pitch-soaked arrows, nocking the weapons onto the strings of their bows. They spilled out of the ravine in no particular formation, each man riding as fast as he could, determined to get off as many shots as possible. The wind snatched at the flaming arrows but only served to fan the small blazes. Blayne raised his bow and guided his horse with his knees, directing his charge at the closest of the three great weapons.

Amazingly, the Crown soldiers didn't at first notice the surprise attack. So determined were they to hold back the lancers on the north side of the road that Blayne's party had galloped forward for ten or twelve breaths without drawing so much as a warning shout. Finally, a commander, looking over his shoulder, spotted the flank attack and bellowed a sharp alert.

By then, the attackers were closing fast. The Crown companies were out of position, the footmen scrambling between the wagons, trying to form a wall of spears. The confused infantry effectively blocked their own cavalry from crossing the road, and the defensive line had to form only a few feet from the wagons. Mounted archers would have no trouble getting close enough.

Red Wallace bounced along on a fleet mare, readying a spell that—Blayne trusted—ought to destroy at least one of the bombards. The wizard would maneuver toward the last of the massive weapons, while the riders would concentrate their fire against the first two. The horses flowed across the ground, closing to five hundred feet, then three hundred feet.

The spearmen presented a bristling line, standing barely twenty yards in front of the road and the wagons. Blayne shouted, "Halt!" and the riders pulled up, still at a fair remove from the enemy footmen. The Crown cavalry was streaming to the rear, looking for a way to countercharge, but the delay was fatal.

"Fire!" shouted Kerrigan, launching his first arrow at the towering bulk of the first bombard. The target loomed like a mountain, impossible to miss—but somehow the sputtering arrow, trailing a column of smoke, wiggled awkwardly through the air and fell harmlessly to the ground in front of the spearmen trying to protect the bombards. Cursing, Blayne reached for another missile and struggled to light the pitch while his horse pranced beneath him.

But there were at least two hundred flaming arrows launched in the first volley, and a few of them did find the range. A pair smacked into the side of one of the bombard haulers, the impact driving the burning pitch deep into its wooden planks. Several more landed in the beds of the wagons, while a few of the near misses landed close enough to the big oxen hauling the guns that they set the creatures to bellowing and pitching in their traces.

Close by the young lord, Red Wallace had his spell ready and launched a bolt of lightning from one fingertip. The explosive charge shot through the air with a hiss and crackle, searing through the line of spearmen and striking the side of the wagon with a blast. Immediately that heavy bed was shattered into timbers and traces, one sturdy wheel wobbling away as flames consumed the wreckage.

Smoke was rising from many of the wagons, including the two bearing the remaining bombards. Another wagon, struck by accident, exploded in flame, spewing a huge column of smoke.

"We hit their powder supply!" Blayne cried exultantly. He released one then another arrow, which vanished into the smoke and fire. In any event, flames rose from all the wagons, and by now the Crown cavalry had begun to spill around the mess, hundreds of foes, lances leveled, thundering toward the attacking Vingaard riders.

"Pull back!" cried Blayne Kerrigan.

His troops needed no further encouragement. They spun their horses away, back toward the ravine and the tangled pathways of the Southwood Forest. By the time they vanished into the gap, the weary riders of the Crown Army had fallen far behind.

⊰⊱⊰⊱⊰⊱⊰⊱⊰⊱⊰⊱

"What in the name of the Abyss is going on back there?" Jaymes snarled, spinning his horse and staring in amazement at the column of smoke rising from the rear of the column. In the next instant, he put spurs to the steed and went racing back against the line of march, his horse dancing along the side of the road.

"Templar, follow me!" he ordered, coming on the Clerist Knight and his small company of priest-warriors. He didn't wait to see that they obeyed, but continued racing headlong to the rear.

The damage was apparent while he was still a mile away. At least one wagon had exploded into bits, and many others were burning. He saw the tail end of the Vingaard column disappearing into the woods and forgot about them—at least for the time being.

There would be time enough, later, for the enemy to feel his wrath.

He had to save the bombards, if at all possible. But by the time he reached the scene, he could see that one of the great barrels was enveloped by flames, and that the fire covered the wooden body of the great carriage supporting the gun. Even as the emperor watched, the wagon collapsed, and the timbers forming the bore of the great barrel started to blacken. A second bombard lay on its side, cracked and broken—by some kind of magic, he suspected.

The third and last cannon was wreathed in smoke, but the wagon was not yet engulfed by flames, not yet lost. Templar, his own horse lathered, galloped up behind Jaymes, and the emperor pointed angrily at the lone bombard in its cradle of vulnerable wood, just starting to catch fire.

"Put that out!" he ordered.

The Clerist immediately began casting a spell. Jaymes watched soundlessly, his teeth clenched and his jaw aching, as a cloud quickly formed above the burning wagon. In no time a steady rain began to fall, and a few moments later the flames had been reduced to sizzling, blackened embers. The lone remaining bombard had survived, essentially undamaged.

"My lord!" cried General Dayr, coming up to the site on a frothing horse. "What happened?"

"Happened?" retorted the emperor coldly. He thought for a moment, his eyes glaring at the dark forest where the attackers had withdrawn.

"What happened is that the fate of Vingaard has been sealed," he declared before turning his back on the damage and riding back toward the head of his army.

CHAPTER NINE

CASTLE KEEP

Selinda stared at the door to her room, the door that was almost constantly closed, tightly locked, and always carefully guarded, on the orders of her husband, the emperor. He was gone from the city, but his presence, his authority, seemed to linger everywhere—in the walls surrounding her, amid the guards who were the only people she saw, in the very air she breathed. She found herself turning quickly around several times each day, checking against the strong sensation he was in the room, watching her.

She wore the ring of teleportation from Coryn the White on her finger, nervously touching it as she looked at the door again. Selinda had been wearing the ring, staring at it, thinking about it, for a number of days. But she had been so worried about the unseen presence of the emperor that she had done nothing yet to activate the magical circlet.

It was not the closed, locked door that worried her, but rather those not-infrequent times when it swung open. Her guards were respectful, even kindly, and they often checked in on her to see whether she needed anything, how she was feeling, or simply to offer a bit of news or a home-baked treat from one of their wives. At first, Selinda welcomed the brief interaction with them, the few moments of conversation; otherwise her routine was monotonous. It lessened her sense of isolation to learn that a troupe of players had arrived in the city and were performing farces every evening, or that a cargo of fresh oranges had just arrived at the port.

But what if one of those guards came in to visit and found she was gone, thanks to Coryn's magic ring? Whatever consequences she imagined were too frightening to contemplate. It was this fear, more than anything else, that had stayed her hand for a week, since Jaymes had marched through the pass and onto the plains. Instead, she had spent most of her time studying the city, the sky, the mountains, and the bay, from her lofty window. She watched and she remembered and she continued to seethe.

As the days passed slowly, she found herself snapping at the guards when they came by. She complained about the quality of her food, even though it was always prepared and served perfectly. She demanded things—fabrics and thread, links of jewelry chain and baubles, paints and canvas—that she had no intention of using. What was initially sadness became anger, and then the anger became barely repressed fury.

Until, at last, she knew that she could stay in that place no longer. Having just sent away her supper, barely touched, she had a reasonable hope she would be allowed privacy for the rest of the evening. If not . . . well, she was finally prepared to take the chance. The time was ripe for her to visit the person she wanted to see.

She donned a cloak with a soft hood that would conceal her face and her golden hair, and she removed her jewelry—except for the magical circlet given to her by the white wizard. With her destination clearly in mind, she followed Coryn's instructions, turning the ring on her finger and imagining the place, calling up every detail she could remember.

The world faded away and she felt a momentary lightness in her stomach, the same sensation she'd experienced when she was riding and her horse took a high jump over a fence or stream. Selinda reached out to both sides, seeking something, anything, to grab for balance, but there was nothing there. She fought the urge to scream, but didn't want to alarm her guards. The nothingness that surrounded her was everywhere, and her panic surged.

And just like that, the feeling passed. She found herself standing in the vestibule of the great temple of Kiri-Jolith, one of the loftiest sanctuaries in Palanthas, which was exactly the place she had imagined as her destination. The unsettled feeling lingered in her stomach, and she breathed hard, but other than that, everything seemed normal. Instinctively wary, she ducked behind the nearest row of the columns that lined both sides of the great house of worship and waited for a moment, listening for any sound of alarm, any indication her sudden arrival had been noticed.

But all seemed quiet. Soon her stuttered breathing settled down, and as she touched the cool marble of a nearby column, she was reassured by its solidity. Looking around, she took stock of her surroundings. Though she was the lone visitor in the vestibule, a hundred or more voices were raised in a steady chant.

They were the prayers of vesperspeak, she knew, the ritual celebration of the clerics, apprentices, and acolytes that marked the end of church business for the day. She leaned back against the marble column and was reassured by the sounds that had been a part of her life since earliest childhood. The chants were in an ancient tongue, and she did not understand the words, but there was comfort merely in the solemn repetition. For long minutes she stood in the shadows, listening to the quasimusical prayers, which finally swelled to a crescendo that signaled the conclusion of worship.

Finally the ritual ended with a whispered benediction and a few moments of symbolic silence. Eventually Selinda could hear the low buzz of conversation as the clerics rose and offered each other good wishes before dispersing—some to their houses or apartments nearby, while others would make their way to residences in either wing of the great temple. She heard the soft rustling of robes and sandals as people filed out, past the shadowy alcove where she lurked. When most of the clerics had exited, she finally emerged and advanced into the great, vaulted sanctuary.

Some apprentices were tending to the many candles around the great room, extinguishing their flames, trimming wax, replacing tapers that had burned down too far. The apprentices took no notice of her as she quietly walked past them, keeping her hood over her hair and her eyes cast down. The great vault of the temple loomed high over her head, but the ceiling was as shadowy as the alcoves behind the columns, where the lighting was muted in deference to the just and mighty god, Kiri-Jolith.

Kiri-Jolith was the eldest son of Paladine and Mishakal, and in the absence of his sire, he had gained prominence in the worship of the Solamnic peoples. He was a righteous god of glory, honor, and discipline, known to favor the efforts of those warriors who fought bravely in a just cause. Soldiers who elected to fight to the death instead of retreating were exalted in the god's eyes. Courage was valued among his orders of priests and priestesses, many of whose number had been martyred over the years because of their unwillingness to compromise their beliefs.

The temple was the setting, Selinda recalled with bitter irony, of her marriage to Jaymes. Her wedding day—indeed, all the time surrounding that event—remained a kind of fuzzy memory, as if it were something she had dreamed, rather than experienced. The place seemed so much more real as she walked its halls, stone and solid and permanent. In her heart, the young woman understood that the *place* hadn't changed since her marriage, but *she* had.

She made her way to the left side of the great room and passed into the corridor leading to the Hall of Priestesses. Passing several young women who were moving quietly, almost gliding, from room to room, Selinda nodded pleasantly in response to their recognition. The wing she was in was the living quarters of a dozen of the senior female clerics as well as some fifty apprentices and novices, and the princess had visited there before. She turned into a small hall and went to the door at the end of the corridor. There she stopped, drew a breath, and knocked softly.

"Come in," came the reply, the last word rising in inflection welcomingly.

She opened the door and saw Melissa du Juliette. The young high priestess was hanging her golden robe on an elaborate rack. She turned and smiled warmly.

"Selinda! It's so nice to see you!"

Almost immediately after her greeting, however, Melissa's brow furrowed in concern. Selinda hadn't said anything, didn't think that her practiced expression revealed her inner torment, but her friend and counselor had clearly perceived her anguish.

"Please! Come in; sit down. Take off that cloak—it's *so*

stuffy in here." The priestess bustled around, pouring cups of tea.

The two women sat together on a low couch, holding their steaming cups, communing in silence. Selinda looked at Melissa, marveling at the young woman's composure and maturity. Though barely thirty, the priestess had demonstrated such a keen intellect, and was so clearly blessed by the stern god of right and justice that she had quickly risen to a high position in the church. She was one of two high priestesses in the temple at Palanthas—two high priests served there as well—and Melissa du Juliette was younger by twenty years than any of her three colleagues.

Selinda had known her most of her life. Always, she had been a person the princess could talk to or simply enjoy her presence. As a teenage novice, Melissa had been one of the older girls who shared advice, gossip, and good humor with the young daughter of the city's lord regent.

As they sat there, however, the wife of the emperor found herself at a loss for words. She was grateful that the priestess made no effort to draw her out, but seemed content to simply share the hot, spicy tea and sit quietly. Eventually, of course, the silence began to wear thin, and Selinda knew that she had to explain herself.

"I . . . I'm pregnant," she began.

"Selinda!" Melissa's face brightened, and she took both of the princess's hands in her own. Then she frowned and looked at her friend more carefully. "Is it troublesome already? Are you in pain? Do you fear you'll lose the child?"

"I don't know. I'm not in pain, but I am afraid. Afraid that something will happen . . . or, sometimes, I confess, simply afraid I will *have* the child!" Selinda blurted.

The tears came then, and she let them flow unabated. The

priestess gathered the other woman into her arms and held her, let the sobs, the anguish, run their course. Finally, the pregnant woman was able to push herself upright, draw a few steady breaths, and dry her eyes.

"I—I'm sorry," she said. "That hasn't happened before. I've been alone most of the time, and . . ."

"You don't need to explain—about the tears," Melissa replied. "But why do you grieve so? I understand your husband has taken his army through the pass, to Vingaard. Is that what worries you?"

Selinda shook her head. Somehow, she was strengthened by the thought of Jaymes Markham, and her apprehension became determination. "I felt this way even before he left. Indeed, I came to you because . . . because I am not sure that it is right to have this child. Perhaps I will be a poor mother—or what if it's a boy, and he grows into a man like his father? What if I simply lost the baby? Perhaps that would be best!"

The priestess looked sad, moisture appearing in her own eyes. "Oh, child," she said to the woman only a few years younger than herself. "Why? What makes you talk so wickedly?"

The princess raised her chin. "Is it wicked? What if the consequences of having the child are worse than the alternative?"

"Why do you say that?"

"It's my husband. He's a very dangerous man. He'll do anything to hold, to secure, his grip on power. The thing that would aid him the most in this goal is the birth of a son, an heir. Melissa, I don't love him anymore; I don't think I ever did."

"But your marriage! I was there, performed the rites. You were head over heels!"

"I was bewitched, Melissa! I must have been! That's the

only explanation. You recall, I met Jaymes on the plains while he was still an outlaw; he had a strong presence even then. I caused him to be captured by General Markus's men, and even in chains he seemed dangerous. When he first wooed me, I was cautious . . .

"But we shared some wine . . . and everything became very confused. My feelings for him changed in those moments, but it wasn't anything he said. It must have been some potion in the wine!"

"This is a serious charge. If true, he has done you a great wrong. But surely you can see that the child is guiltless?"

"There *is* no child! Not yet. But I came to ask you if there is a way to stop that child from being born."

"Selinda!" The priestess spoke with an air of resignation and finality. "What you ask runs counter to everything I hold sacred. I cannot help you in this matter. It is wrong." Melissa sighed sorrowfully. "Still, I am glad you came to see me. I wish you had come sooner."

"I couldn't risk it. I have been locked in my chambers ever since he left. I only came now with the aid of this magic ring, from Coryn."

"He *locked you up?*" Melissa's eyes widened in shock. "He has no right to do that! You're right about his power—he goes too far!"

"That's what I'm telling you about him. He doesn't need a right—he makes his *own* rights and expects the rest of the world to fall into line. Please—can't you help me?"

"I will try to help you but not in the manner you request. I understand that your husband, the man who calls himself 'emperor,' has much to answer for. What I suggest is we go, together, to talk to him, to confront him with these truths."

"What good will that do?" protested the princess.

"We have to try. Will you come with me?"

Selinda nodded. "But Vingaard is across the mountains, a week's ride."

Melissa nodded at the golden ring on the other woman's finger. "You have the means to make the journey, right there on your hand. And teleportation magic is not unknown to those in our order. We could travel together, through the ether. I need some hours to prepare the spell, so let us plan to leave in the morning."

Selinda thought about the journey. She felt nothing but anguish; there didn't seem much hope of gaining anything from confronting her husband. But she had to try something.

"All right," she said. "Let's go see him together."

⊱⊶⊷⊶⊷⊶⊷●⊶⊷⊶⊷⊶⊷⊱

Blayne Kerrigan lashed his horse and led his triumphant column across the Stonebridge. The men whooped and cheered as they approached Vingaard Keep, stirring equally enthusiastic cries from the many citizens lining the walls of the lofty castle. The three tall spires all flew the banner of the Blue Sturgeon, the keep's ancient sigil, and trumpets brayed a fanfare as the young lord and his warriors galloped into the central courtyard and dismounted in the midst of the frenzied populace.

The walls loomed high all around, white and pure and ancient. The three great spires lofted overhead, serene, aloof, grandiose. In the flush of Blayne's victory, those towers seemed as permanent as the rugged mountains on the western horizon.

"The emperor's great weapons have been destroyed!" boasted the young captain. "Make ready to hold the Stonebridge!"

Confetti rained from the high ramparts, and ladies—

dressed in gowns and jewelry, as if for a ball—waltzed with each other and embraced each of the sooty, sweaty riders as they dismounted from their blown, lathered steeds.

Amid the commotion, Blayne found his sister, Marrinys. She was less exuberant than some of the women, and he understood why. Placing his hands on her shoulders, he looked into her worried eyes. "You heard about Father?"

"Is it true he was killed by the emperor's men, taken at the parley?"

"Yes." The young nobleman didn't try to hide his bitterness. "And he will be avenged. For now, you should know the castle is safe—the emperor's great weapons have been destroyed!"

"I'm proud of you, Blayne," she said, hugging him. He held her tightly, felt the tremors of her grief. Forcibly he broke away, reminding himself that the first blows of vengeance had already been struck.

"We won't let Father be forgotten. But know this, my sister: the emperor's bombards will not destroy our home! And we did it, we attacked brilliantly, without losing a man!"

"I'm happy about that, Blayne. Really, I am. But I fear for the future. Even if he can't destroy this place from across the river, how long can we hold out here against his army?"

"I don't know, Marrinys. Not for sure. But I think we can hold out for most of the summer, if need be. We can cover the Stonebridge from these walls, and our catapults and archers will pound any force he dares to send across. And the longer we hold our defense, word of our courage and success will spread across Solamnia. In a matter of weeks, I expect rebellions to arise in other parts of the nation. We have an ally in Thelgaard, where Captain Franz—the son of the ruling lord—despises the emperor, and works on his father's loyalty. There will be unrest in Caergoth and perhaps even Solanthus. When fires of rebellion burn on all sides of him, the emperor will be forced to withdraw and alter his plans."

"I hope you're right, my brother. But even so, I'm afraid."

Blayne had no time for her concern; he was too busy sharing the sparkling wine of victory, pouring bottles from both hands. "Let's at least relish a moment of victory today! We can have hope for the future, finally."

She let him go, but her eyes remained troubled. She watched as his riders were toasted, and hoisted onto the shoulders of the castle's men-at-arms, and in more than one instance hustled off into the stables by pretty girls for more personal rewards. The scene brought a reluctant smile to her face.

Meanwhile the young lord found himself borne into the keep's great hall on a swelling tide of victorious Vingaard. Only when he was seated at the great table, still sharing drinks, waiting for the triumphal banquet to be prepared, was he reminded of a grim reality. He felt a gentle touch on his shoulder and looked up to see the red-robed figure of his—and his father's—closest advisor.

"You'd better come with me, my lord," said Red Wallace, his tone and demeanor sobering the other man's excitement.

"What is it?" asked Blayne, rising and following the wizard out of the hall when Wallace made no move to reply. In silence they climbed the winding stairs within the keep's tallest tower. The young lord's stomach grew queasy. Even the spectacular leaded glass windows, whose beautiful panes were known throughout Solamnia, could not ease the growing heaviness in his heart.

When they were about halfway up the lofty tower, Wallace led Blayne out onto a small balcony, a walled perch on the side of the spire that offered an unimpeded view to the south. Already the emperor's army was marching into view, great columns breaking off the road, forming camps along the ridge to the south of Apple Creek.

"That's no surprise," he informed Wallace confidently. "We knew they would come this far, and we'll hold them at Stonebridge, if need be."

"That's not what I wanted you to see," the red wizard declared grimly. He pointed to the west, where the road wound out of sight along the shallow valley of the creek.

Blayne saw it immediately: the long, trunklike shape rising from the bed of the wagon, trundled along by its team of eight massive oxen. He couldn't believe his eyes.

"One of the bombards survived?" he asked finally, his voice hollow.

"It would appear so," Wallace replied.

"But . . . but we destroyed them all! All three! They were burning as we retreated!" Even as he blurted out those words, Blayne realized how foolish they were. He could see with his own eyes that one of the great weapons had survived. Wallace said nothing.

"What do we do now?" the younger man asked, after a long time.

"It seems we have little choice. He can attack and probably destroy the keep from the safety of the far side of the bridge. I think you must submit, throw yourself on his mercy. Send a courier!"

Word of the bombard's appearance had spread to the great hall by the time Blayne and the wizard returned. The mood was somber and quiet, the crowd having thinned from hundreds to a few dozen loyal supporters. They listened with grim faces while the son of Lord Kerrigan dictated a note, specifying the castle's surrender, and pleading for the emperor's mercy. Within a few moments, a courier raced out of the gates, across the Stonebridge, and up to the army's initial picket line.

Blayne made his way to the gatehouse, intending to wait there for the courier's return. He was startled to see the man come galloping back, even before the young nobleman had made his way to the top of the wall. Hurrying back down the stone stairs, he accosted the rider as soon as the man dismounted.

"Did you speak to the emperor? What did he say?"

"He wouldn't see me," the courier replied flatly. "Instead, his guards told me to come back here, and to stay here. He said that our decision had been made, earlier in the day, when we chose to offer battle instead of acknowledge his right of rule."

"*That* was his answer?" demanded Blayne, appalled.

In the next instant, a sound thrummed through the ground, a powerful crunch that could be felt in the ground even before Blayne heard it in the air. Immediately after, he heard another sound—something exploding overhead. Looking up, Blayne saw a gaping hole in the side of the keep's loftiest tower. The colored glass, which he had been busy admiring just a few hours before, rained down from the shattered windows.

"I suspect," Red Wallace said soberly, as they joined the rest of those in the courtyard in fleeing to the shelter of the nearby buildings. "That the emperor has just begun to make his reply."

⊱•◦❖◦•⊰

"Fire away. Keep blasting until dark, and then zero in on the fires, if there's enough light to give you a target."

"Aye, my lord," replied Captain Trevor, the grizzled commander of artillery. If anyone had been more enraged than Jaymes by the loss of the two bombards, it was the gunnery officer. The emperor knew he would carry out his orders diligently and professionally.

The bombard was set up about a half mile south of the Stonebridge. From that distance, Trevor had calculated that the round stone balls fired by the gun could reach every part of Vingaard Keep, except the very tops of the high towers. And, as the gunnery captain had observed wryly, he didn't need to strike the tops of the towers in order to bring them down.

Jaymes walked a short distance to his command post, which had been established in a travelers' inn alongside the Apple Creek road. He passed through the main room, which, though filled with officers, was strangely silent. Jaymes did not desire the company of his men, not at that moment, so he made his way up the stairs. Several guards stood duty on the second floor, posted outside a suite of rooms where Lord Kerrigan's two companions were imprisoned.

Jaymes continued up the stairs. A wide balcony ran the entire length of the third floor, and from there he could watch the bombardment. There were a few captains there, and they made way for him. None tried to initiate conversation as the emperor sat at a table and sent a serving maid down to the bar for a pitcher of ale. When she returned, Lord Templar trailed behind her, and when Jaymes gestured to a vacant chair, the young Clerist sat down.

"My lord," he began, awkwardly. "The Vingaard messenger—the man you refused to see—brought an offer of surrender. Is it necessary to destroy the castle now?"

"I don't intend to destroy the castle. I'll be content with the destruction of those three towers."

"But those towers *are* Vingaard Keep, lord! They have stood for centuries—even through the great battles during the War of the Lance! They're landmarks on the plains, known to every

Solamnic—knights and citizens alike. Are you sure you want to bring these great edifices down? The rebels must surely have learned their lesson! I implore you, Excellency, consider carefully the lesson your own people will take from this action."

Jaymes looked past the Clerist and caught a glimpse of General Dayr engaged in intense conversation with his son, Franz. The older man seemed to be pleading; the younger was rigid, pale, his hands clenched into fists. Finally the captain stalked off but not before casting a venomous glance at the emperor. Jaymes met the look coldly, and was mildly surprised when the young captain didn't immediately turn away.

Instead, Franz glared mutely for several long heartbeats, before finally stomping through the door leading inside.

Jaymes turned back to the Clerist Knight, the man whose magic rain had doused the fires and allowed at least one bombard to survive the surprise attack. The emperor shook his head firmly.

"Perhaps the rebels in Vingaard *have* learned their lesson, but that's beside the point."

"But why? How?" protested the priest.

"Because I intend to send a message to everyone, across all of Solamnia. Only when the towers are destroyed, and all have heard the news, will the people understand my will is law. I will brook no opposition, no dissent—and I will crush even a whisper of rebellion!"

He turned to look back at the castle and watched as another ball crashed into the middle tower. Already much of the stonework, and all of the glass, had been destroyed. The spire wobbled like a tall tree that had suffered an almost fatal blow from a woodsman's axe. He was vaguely aware that General Dayr was watching the tower too, that the army commander's face was contorted in grief.

Why couldn't they understand? Were they *blind?*

Jaymes watched impassively as, a few moments later, the great spire leaned, swayed, and ever so slowly smashed down across the walls of the keep, raising a great cloud of dust and provoking screams of fear and dismay audible even from that distance.

Before the dust had settled, Captain Trevor had shifted his wagon, and the bombard began to chisel away at the second tower.

CHAPTER TEN

TUMBLING DOWN

Smoke and dust churned through the courtyard of Vingaard Keep. The base of the ruined tower stood like a shattered tree trunk, rising barely higher than the castle walls, its jagged, irregular silhouette outlined against the sunset. Tons of stone had rained down. Walls and ceilings, furniture, doorways, and the great curving stairway, all were broken and scattered widely.

For a moment there was silence, an absence of sound rendered all the more eerie for the fact that it followed the loud pounding of the bombardment, and toppling of the spire.

Then a child started to cry, its plaintive sobs piercing the silence and magnifying the terror. A woman ran from the keep, across the courtyard to the storage barn. She knelt over a motionless form just inside the door and also began to wail.

"I've got to go across the bridge and talk to him myself!"

Blayne Kerrigan fought against hands that tried to restrain him, struggling against his sister. With a groan, he struck the stone wall.

"This is my doing, my fault!" he insisted. "I have to see the emperor—surrender myself so that the keep can be saved!"

"You can't!" Marrinys declared, grasping him desperately. She had dark circles beneath her eyes, and tears streaked her cheeks as her body trembled under the fear and strain. "He'll throw you in chains . . . or kill you—like he did with Father!"

"I can't let this continue!" Blayne said, gesturing at the rubble that stretched across the courtyard. Two guards were escorting the wailing woman away from the barn. Limping figures emerged from the swirling smoke along the base of the keep wall, coughing; one fell flat, and his companion lifted him with a bleeding right arm. Everywhere the dust rose in choking clouds.

"I doubt that anything you say or do could stop him now," Red Wallace declared, supporting Marrinys Kerrigan against her brother. The Red Robe wore an implacable expression. If Blayne was frantic and guilt ridden, he remained stern and aloof.

The trio stood under the shelter of an upper rampart with a clear view of the destruction. After less than two hours of bombardment—some fifteen shots from the massive cannon—the first tower had collapsed on a mostly empty courtyard, with part striking the outer wall, crumbling the stone parapet halfway to the ground.

The garrison had abandoned the wall in time, but there were still a few casualties from stones showering across the keep and breaking through the wooden or thatched roofs of living quarters.

Another shot boomed out, a ball sailing past the second of the great towers. It was a poorly aimed shot, but it wouldn't take long for the gunners to correct the distance and begin to pummel the second spire. It would start with the next shot, or the one after that. Both of the remaining spires had been evacuated.

Blayne drew a breath and forced himself to speak calmly even as he disengaged his sister's hands from his arms.

"What else *can* I do?" he asked bluntly. "He's doing this because I dared to attack him, I know it."

"You must escape from here, and attack him again—as soon as you can!" Marrinys urged, showing a steely determination that Blayne hadn't realized his sister possessed. "Meanwhile I, myself, will go out and talk to the emperor, offer our capitulation—again—and try to persuade him to stop this senseless destruction."

"You?" Blayne asked, his voice choked by a tangle of gratitude and shame. "I can't let you—"

"She's right, yes, it's the only thing to do," Wallace interjected, once again taking the young woman's side. "Let your sister appeal to his mercy. You need to get away from here; you know we're not the only ones who think to resist the emperor's rule. Find some of the others, join forces, and forge a resistance."

"And you should go with him," Marrinys said, speaking to the wizard. "Your part in all these actions will become known—the emperor will have you arrested, or worse, if you stay."

"She's right again," Blayne said.

But Red Wallace demurred, shaking his head. "I believe, my lord and lady, that I should stay here in the city. I may be able to help if there are matters of occupation or . . . reprisal."

"But he'll be looking for you! Certainly his agents know of your importance to Clan Kerrigan. They'll—"

"I have means of disguise that are not available to others," said Red Wallace quietly. He made a quick, furtive gesture and before their eyes seemed to shrink, to age. His red robe faded to an ugly shade of brown, the silver threadwork vanishing entirely. When he peered at them from under his ragged cowl, he was an old man, withered and stooped and certainly no danger to anybody.

"Very well," Blayne agreed, nodding with satisfaction. "I will ride alone, and I will contact you as soon as I can." He held his sister close. "But you? How can I leave you to . . ."

"I will take care of myself. And I will bury Father with every honor he deserves, while you carry on the fight from far beyond here. You can send word to me, secretly, after you get away. Let me know where you are, and we will prepare to act together."

Another explosion burst from the ridge across the creek. They could spy the ball flying lazily through the air, looking no more dangerous than a child's toy. Then it struck the second tower thirty feet above the ground, punching through the masonry to smash and rumble through the interior rooms. Pieces of rubble rained down from the outer wall, which was immediately scored by a jagged crack. Many of the windows had been shattered by the concussion of the first shots; those few that remained shattered, adding jagged shards to the lethal chunks of falling stone.

Marrinys sobbed, and Blayne pulled his sister against his chest. It felt as though the weapon were aimed against him, and the missiles were striking his flesh, so deeply did the brutal onslaught against his beloved city wound him. And yet, he knew, there was nothing, absolutely nothing, he could do to halt the destruction.

"I'm going," he said bitterly. "I hate it and it shames me,

but you're right; it would be futile for me to try to speak to the emperor, and stupid to remain here and fall into his hands."

"Please be careful," Marrinys said, hugging him one last time.

An hour later, Sir Blayne Kerrigan, dressed in a plain brown tunic and leading a horse unadorned with armor or precious metal, slipped out a narrow door on the north side of the keep. He waited to mount until he was on a country path used by hunters and herdsmen, which extended all the way to the foothills of the Vingaard Mountains. The steed was a loyal animal, one he had trained since it had been a colt, and it knew how to move stealthily.

The young lord rode into the night, hearing the steady boom of the big gun as the miles slipped behind. When the second tower fell, he couldn't see it in the darkness, but he felt the tremor ripple through the very heart of Krynn.

⊱⋆⊰⋆⊰⋆⊰❋⊱⋆⊰⋆⊰⋆⊰

Jaymes drifted off to sleep some time during the night but was awakened near dawn by a gentle but insistent nudging from Lord Templar, the Clerist. The emperor, who was resting in a chair on the headquarters' balcony, pushed himself to his feet, shook his head once or twice, and very quickly was wide awake.

"What is it?" he asked before looking to the north. Dawn was pale in the sky, and he could make out the altered silhouette of the citadel. Where the three graceful spires had dominated the view just a day before, only one tower soared above the ancient fortress. There was a pervasive silence over the scene, and the darkness on the ground was given an eerie cast by a crimson glow emanating from deep within the piles of rubble around the castle walls.

"Why is it quiet? Why has the bombardment ceased?"

"Captain Trevor needed to cool down the bombard, so he had to interrupt the firing after the second tower came down. That was only a few hours ago, my lord. Trevor is down in the great room below and reports the cannon is nearly ready to resume."

"Good. Then tell him—"

"Excuse me, my lord," Templar said boldly. Jaymes stared at him in silence. "But there comes another mission from Vingaard. This time it is led by Lord Kerrigan's daughter, Marrinys. She begs an audience with you. And, my lord, I sincerely hope—on my own, and by the grace of Kiri-Jolith—that you will meet with her."

The emperor thought for a moment. Always a swift riser, he had no fog of sleep to shake away but instead reflected on the violent events of the previous day and the long night of bombardment. "Very well. Have her come up."

A moment later a petite young woman, barely five feet tall, came through the door onto the balcony. In the growing daylight, Jaymes guessed her to be about sixteen years old; she had dark, curling hair and slightly swarthy skin, clearly inherited from her father. He noted, with passing interest, that she was extremely pretty.

He also noted that her jaw was set firmly. But she seemed determined to keep her composure; she curtsied politely before addressing him.

"I have come to offer our submission, my lord emperor," she said, "and to plead for your mercy. Surely you can see that you have mastered us. What need is there to inflict more damage?"

"Where is your ne'er-do-well brother?" asked Jaymes. "I should have thought that such an offer would come from him."

She lifted her chin proudly, looking him squarely in the eyes. "He has left the city, my lord. He has chosen to become an outlaw."

"You didn't try very hard to stop him, did you?"

"What could I do?" she asked innocently. "Besides, my desire—my sole desire—is to stop the destruction . . . and to bring my father's body back home so that we may bury him properly."

Jaymes winced at her comment. He didn't want to recall the ignominious death of her father. Shaking his head as if to banish the thought from his memory, he looked down at the young woman. For some reason he wanted her to know the truth.

"My orders were to arrest Lord Kerrigan. His death was an accident; he charged onto the sword held by one of the guards. I did not order him killed."

"But he is dead?"

"Yes. His body has been prepared for burial and is even now being carried respectfully in one of the wagons of my train."

"What do you plan to do now?"

"The bombard is ready to commence a barrage against the third tower. It was my intention to smash them all, as a lesson to all that could not be mistaken by anyone in Solamnia."

"Surely that lesson has already made its impression, great lord! I promise, we in Vingaard will remember this day forever!"

Jaymes looked away. He rubbed a hand across his eyes, feeling the beginnings of a headache. It was harder to deflect the arguments of the girl than it would have been to debate her foolish brother, or the fierce nobleman, her father.

"I will only cease the destruction when I am convinced that you understand something."

"And what is that, Excellency? Please, tell me!"

"You need to understand that I did this for your own good!" he snapped, turning suddenly and looming over her.

Marrinys flinched but did not step away. Instead, she continued to meet his glare and spoke in a strangely different voice, with the real courage that was part of her heritage. *"How* can we understand that? Explain it—please, my lord!"

He sat down, gesturing to another chair. After a moment's hesitation, she took the other chair, sitting straight, knees together, hands clasped in her lap. She continued to look at him, eyes shining.

For some reason, he found her youthfulness, the naïveté of her expression, strangely compelling. He really *did* want her to understand his good intentions.

"Solamnia is a nation again—a single, united entity. It has not been such for more than a thousand years, and it will not remain so for long unless we all sacrifice, unless we all put our shoulders to the wheel of the common good."

"I see," Marrinys replied seriously. "I understand—it was a mistake to defy you. I know that my people understand that too."

"It was not the defiance of *me;* it was the refusal to work toward the great future of our nation! This refusal cannot be allowed to stand!"

"I give you my promise. I understand, and I will work hard to make sure that the people of my city understand as well. But you must—*please,* you must!—stop the destruction while there is still some of the keep left standing!"

Jaymes closed his eyes and pressed his hands to his temples. The sun was cresting the eastern horizon, and he suddenly felt very tired. He couldn't stand the thought of another explosion from the bombard. He wanted to believe Marrinys.

And so he did believe her.

"Very well," he said. "The bombardment will halt. You can return to Vingaard, and bear your father's body with you. My officers and I will arrive to accept your capitulation in two hours."

⊰◦◎◦◦◎◦◦◎◦⊱

Ankhar had good reason to be pleased. He had recruited a splendid army, with every savage warrior pledged to serve and obey the half-giant and his interpretation of the Truth. The great column had marched back and forth throughout Lemish, growing in numbers as it accrued from every tribe, every town and village. Eagerly the savage citizens of the barbarian lands gave him tribute, feted him and his legion, contributed more and more volunteers to his ranks.

He noticed with some surprise that his belly, the lumpy gut that had bulged over his belt, had grown flat and lean again. His legs had been weary, his feet sore during the first week of marching, but finally they were muscular and strong, sturdy as tree trunks. Even his mind seemed quicker. Pond-Lily flattered him continually, gushing about his prowess—in all endeavors—and he began to feel like a godlike champion once more.

Moving north and east, Ankhar even recruited from some of the restless ogre bands on the borderlands of Throtl—he had never used them as troops before, but they knew of his reputation and were eager to believe his promises of pillage, of riches and slaves. The young bulls were drawn from far and wide. Thousands upon thousands swelled his following. And, with Pond-Lily standing to one side and Laka on the other, Ankhar sat upon a great chair and reviewed his recruits. And he was pleased.

They were heading back to the west, coming up against

the foothills of the Garnet Range. The half-giant relished the smell of the wind blowing down from the high country, for it bore the scents he had known all his life. The ogress Pond-Lily had followed him uncomplainingly for all of their long march, and Ankhar felt generous and expansive as they came into those familiar, sweet-smelling hills. He hugged the ogress to his side with his brawny left arm, threw back his head, and bellowed in exultation.

"Est Sudanus oth Nikkas!" he roared, waving his emerald-tipped spear over his head. He was heartened by the great swelling of cheers from the ogres and hobgoblins who marched in the long, undulating file behind Pond-Lily, Ankhar, and Laka.

"You are remembering your first home, now." Laka cackled. "But you are a mighty king and can make a home anywhere in the world you choose."

"There are few places better than these mountains," Ankhar reflected.

"Bah!" Laka scolded. "Many places better! You just need better army to take them."

"How? Where can I get better army?" bristled the big half-giant, dropping Pond-Lily—who recovered with surprising grace, bouncing only a couple of times—as he turned to the withered, fiercely grinning shaman.

Ankhar gestured to the column of warriors, dominated by teeming numbers of hulking, muscle-bound ogres, which spread out through the light forest in the shade at the mountain range's base, extending as far behind him as Ankhar could see. "More ogres than ever! See the big bulls! How many tribal chiefs have I? More than anyone!"

Laka merely smiled smugly and squinted at the sky. "Look," she said, pointing to a circling eagle.

Puzzled, the half-giant observed the bird. The huge raptor wheeled and banked, gliding easily on the mountain updrafts. Barely moving those graceful wings, the eagle serenely tilted back and forth, watching the valley floor with deceptively casual interest. It soared with a freedom and majesty Ankhar could only envy.

A dozen rabbits, flushed by the activity of the encamping army, bounced through the grass, racing for the protection of the woods on the slope. The eagle tucked its wings and plummeted like a stone, coming down on the back of a large hare, breaking its neck with the force of the strike. Proudly the bird sailed upward, tearing at the warm flesh with its sharp beak.

"See how that eagle strikes . . . from the air? Kills quickly . . . by surprise?"

"Yes, I see!" Ankhar retorted in exasperation. "Of course it flies! It has wings!"

"Your army would fight better if it could fly," Laka noted.

Ankhar snorted indignantly. "And I could kill you with my breath if I was a dragon! But I am not a dragon. And my army cannot fly!"

"But what if you were to find some warriors, some flying warriors, who would join you in your glorious battles?"

"That fly like dragons, you mean? Where are warriors such as this?"

"There are some. They are not far away."

"Did you dream about these flying warriors?" he asked suspiciously. He had been exposed to many great and terrible things in the past as a direct result of Laka's dreams, so he didn't want to discount her suggestion out of hand. But neither was he willing to embrace the inevitable risks, at least not until he learned more. He would ask some questions, require some persuasion!

"Yes, I did," she replied triumphantly. "And I know where you can find them."

"Flying warriors?" he mused. They would be useful, to be sure. Face an enemy cowering behind a wall? Bah! Let them form a line of pikes? Hah!

That was enough thinking for the half-giant. "All right, we go," he said. "Pond-Lily, you stay here."

"Yes, my lord," said the ogress, bowing meekly.

And so it was, three days later, that the hulking half-giant and his frail, withered hobgoblin stepmother made their way high into a remote valley of the Garnet range. Ankhar left his army behind because Laka had assured him the warriors they sought would flee into hiding at the sight of a barbarian horde approaching.

His prospective allies remained utterly mysterious in Ankhar's mind, and he grew tired and weary of the new quest prompted by his stepmother. While he loved the mountains, he had forgotten how hard it could be to walk up and up and up for days at a time. He even missed Pond-Lily, who—despite her mental shortcomings—had a way of making the long, cold nights a good deal warmer and shorter. Footsore and grumpy, he was working up his courage to challenge Laka when he was distracted by a shape that dived from a nearby cliff, swooped past his head, and landed on the trail before him.

Great pale wings spread from the scaly shoulders of the creature, which snarled at him and Laka, opening a pair of tooth-filled, crocodilian jaws. And then it stood on its hind legs and drew a short steel sword from a leather belt.

"Stop!" it hissed. "And be afraid!"

Ankhar, in truth, had been badly startled by the creature's

appearance. It was a draconian, he noted at once, but of a type that was larger than any draconian he had ever seen previously. Furthermore, the draconian had a broad set of wings that spread much wider than the atrophied leathery flaps that allowed the standard example of the species to glide short distances while preventing true flight.

The creature was silvery white in color and almost as tall as the gaping half-giant. The hissing growls that issued from the draconian's maw were indeed frightening, and its flapping wings made it look even larger than it really was.

But the thing was *not* as tall as Ankhar—nor, he felt certain, was it as strong or fierce. The half-giant's surprise changed to anger and insult, and he lowered his spearhead, brandishing the emerald stone at his challenger's chest.

"Who are *you* to tell me to be afraid?" he demanded.

"I am Gentar—chief of the sivaks!" snapped the draconian, hissing, growling, and spitting.

Only then did Ankhar realize that other draconians were settling to the ground all around them. Within moments he and Laka were surrounded by more than a dozen of the creatures, each of whom was some nine feet tall—taller than a bull ogre—and continuously flapping their great, powerful wings. Others remained in the air, wheeling and circling, like bats. They flew with grace and power, and wore bands of leather strapped across their chests and girding their loins. The growling, hissing sivak draconians presented an impressive array of fangs, talons, and silver-bladed weapons.

"I am not afraid!" Ankhar lied—loudly, which was his favorite way to lie. "You fear me, or die!" He waved his emerald-tipped spear for good measure.

A blast of fire erupted from the ground in front of him, sending the half-giant tumbling backward. The blaze shot upward as if exploding from a deep hole, crackling and burning, radiating heat that forced Ankhar to raise a hand just to shield his eyes. He only barely managed to hold on to his spear as his jaw dropped at the sight of a slender, wingless draconian standing in the place where the column of flame had shot upward.

"You are Ankhar!" declared this new draconian. He was smaller than the other winged monsters, but there was something that suggested command about him. His eyes, slit with vertical pupils, nevertheless gleamed with intelligence, and his voice had a sibilant quality. And he knew the half-giant's name.

"Who are you?" demanded the one who called himself the Truth.

"I am Guilder," the creature replied easily, stepping forward, extending a taloned paw in a gesture of greeting. "Aurak draconian, master of these sivaks, and lord of this valley. I greet you in friendship and respect."

Guilder held that paw extended. Ankhar, watching suspiciously, switched his spear to his left hand and took the paw in his own—and immediately felt a numbing, chilling paralysis take root in his palm and start to run up his arm. Magic! He pulled his hand away with a roar of alarm. Weakness seeped through his flesh, and a wave of dizziness surged up through his mind.

"Take them!" cried Guilder, pulling his paw free, dancing away from the suddenly staggering half-giant. The aurak crowed in triumph and chanted words to a magic spell, wildly gesticulating.

His mother laughed shrilly, a cackling sound that made the half-giant wonder if she were going insane. Whose side was she on anyway? The aurak was still casting a spell, making grotesque sounds that rose to a crescendo and—Ankhar feared—a coming convulsion of magic.

Abruptly the sound of the aurak's spell-casting ceased, though he continued to work his jaws, frantically. But there was a glimmer of fear in the creature's slit eyes as the shaman's spell of silence disrupted the casting of whatever sorcery he had been preparing.

As one of the silvery draconians charged him from in front, Ankhar raised his spear by instinct more than plan, still holding the weapon awkwardly in his left hand. The green stone at the head of the weapon pulsed brightly, a flash of light brighter than the sun. The weapon almost seemed to draw the suddenly frightened draconian onto the weapon. Ankhar took heart from that flaring brilliance and thrust the spear forward with a triumphant bellow.

The green stone wedge pierced the draconian's chest and exploded through its back, halfway between those two suddenly flailing wings. "Die, wyrmling!" roared Ankhar, pulling the spear free. The draconian tumbled back and fell to the ground. Wings flapping, it thrashed and kicked for a moment, but its struggles quickly faded and it died in a spreading pool of black blood.

The other sivaks growled and barked and squawked, obviously dismayed. Several feinted lunges at the half-giant but retreated before he could parry against them. He spun through a full circle, feeling the strength returning to his numbed right arm. He still held the heavy shaft of his spear in his left hand, shaking it over his head, roaring challenges and taunts at the reptilian band. With his chest thrust out and his muscles flexing, he felt his mastery over the craven creatures and, like his mother, laughed out loud at their hissing, clacking, and flapping.

"Look at Arcen!" The aurak, Guilder, gasped in surprise as Laka's spell of silence fell away. He was pointing at the dead sivak, now sprawled motionless on the ground at his feet.

Slowly, with a strange rippling through its flesh, that silver-white body began to change. The shape writhed, its talons drawing back into the fingers and toes, its wings shriveling and shrinking. Ankhar was familiar with the gruesome death throes of lesser draconians—the baaz, who became hard stone statues when slain; or the kapaks, whose flesh dissolved into searing acid. But the sivak was strange and different: the draconian was changing shape.

With a violent convulsion, the scaly flesh of the creature's skin ripped apart. Its chest thickened, and its dragonlike face smoothed, the jaws shrinking until it resembled a more humanoid creature. With a gasp of disbelief, Ankhar suddenly realized that he was looking at the very image of himself! The corpse was wearing strange, ornate garments—nothing like the half-giant's leather tunic and leggings—but he was too stunned to take note of the garb.

"What foul sorcery is this?" he demanded, taking a step backward.

But the other draconians were not listening. They all recognized the image of Ankhar the Truth—but it was an Ankhar wearing a golden crown and wrapped in the robes that signified he was a great king. The aurak, Guilder, threw himself to the ground, pressing his face forward to kiss the half-giant's muddy boots.

"My liege!" he cried. "Forgive me!"

"Hail Ankhar!" croaked another of the draconians, the sivak called Gentar who had first confronted him. The draconian placed the tip of his great long sword on the ground and leaned the hilt toward the great lord. "Allow us to serve you, O mighty one!" he croaked.

"My power is my Truth!" bellowed the half-giant. *"Est Sudanus oth Nikkas!"*

"And we," Guilder said, speaking with bowed head from bended knee. "We will follow your Truth to the far ends of Krynn!"

<hr>

Deciding that they did not want to risk magically transporting themselves into the middle of a battle, Selinda and Melissa teleported safely to the yard of a country inn that the princess knew that was several miles south of Vingaard Keep. They arrived unnoticed and, in the early morning light, simply walked up the lane without being seen by anyone in the barely stirring household.

The two women were dressed in simple shawls and easily passed as farmwives when encountering dairymen or laborers on the dirt road that curled gently down the valley of the Vingaard River. That great flowage, a mile wide, spread to their right, but the keep itself and the town around it was obscured from their view by the ridge of low hills just south of Apple Creek.

They walked along in silence and after about an hour came to the crest of those hills. They both stopped and stared. The silhouette of Vingaard Keep loomed before them, but it was a sad, twisted mockery of the once elegant fortress. Only one tower could be seen, standing aloof and proud, with many black gaps where the once-beautiful windows had been. The other two towers were gone, replaced by stumps of rubble.

There was a picket of Crown Army guards at the crest, a dozen men-at-arms who stood near the road, watching to the south. They had clearly been observing the women for the past hour, but just as obviously did not perceive them to be any threat. In fact, they ignored them as they moved past until Selinda stopped and turned. She spotted the sergeant of the detail, a grizzled knight who was a decade or two past his prime, and approached him.

Curtsying respectfully, she begged his pardon for interrupting him at his duties.

"No problem! No problem at all, little lady. What can I do for you on this fine morn?"

"Is it safe to approach the castle? Does the battle still rage?"

The sergeant chuckled genially. "Not so much of a battle, really. The poor beggars were ready to quit at the first sight of the emperor's bombard. But he wouldn't let 'em—turned the cowardly curs right back to their walls, he did, when they tried to yield. He had to teach them a lesson, you know."

"He turned them down? When they offered to yield?" Selinda tried to keep her voice level even as her stomach heaved with nausea. She felt Melissa take her hand, the priestess squeezing it hard, trying to give her strength.

"Well, he had to, you see. Had to teach them the lesson."

"And now? Where is the emperor?" asked Selinda.

"Why do you want to know so bad?" asked the guard, suddenly suspicious. "You are a pretty thing, I'll say. But you know he's married, don't you?"

"I had heard that, yes," said the emperor's wife. "I'm curious, that's all. Do you think he will knock the rest of the castle down?"

"I don't think so. The lord's daughter came out to see him, in the wee hours it was. She went up and begged him to stop. She was up there with him a long time, but when she rode away, he called for a ceasefire. You can see they're taking the gun down . . . right there."

She looked and did notice the mighty bombard, the barrel lowered almost to a horizontal position as oxen were secured in the wagon's traces. Beyond, she saw a building, probably an inn, and recognized the three-symbol pennant that was the emperor's banner.

"Is he down there, then?" she asked, pointing to the obvious headquarters.

"Well, he was. But a few moments ago, he and a party of men, all decked out they was, road across the Stonebridge and into Vingaard Keep. Maybe he had some more terms for the little lady, eh?" he added with a lewd chuckle and a wink.

"Yes, maybe," Selinda replied disconsolately. Then she walked away from the sergeant with Melissa at her side. Instead of turning toward the castle or the headquarters building, however, she turned her footsteps toward the Apple Creek road, leaving the Vingaard, the castle, and the army behind.

The priestess walked with her in silence for a long time. Finally, she spoke. "You're not going to try to talk to him, then?" she said.

Selinda shook her head. "No, I'm not. I mean, in the end, there's really nothing to say."

The cleric of Kiri-Jolith nodded somberly, and again took her friend's hand. The Lady Selinda was right.

There really wasn't anything to say.

CHAPTER ELEVEN

CROSSING OVER

Marrinys Kerrigan proved an able administrator. By the time Jaymes, Dayr, and the Freemen rode into the courtyard of Vingaard Keep, she had ordered the vaults opened and somehow collected enough treasure to fill a small chest with gems and larger chests with steel coins. Jaymes didn't need more than a glance to see that the recalcitrant town's taxes would be paid in full.

"You're as good as your word," he said approvingly.

"I wish I could say the same about you," she replied, startling him with her vehemence. "But your word has been sullied by your disregard of the parley, more than you even know. The world will long remember how you betrayed my father under a flag of truce."

"I told you—I didn't plan to kill him! I gave no order to injure him. It was simply an accident." Once again, he found himself wanting her to understand and was irritated that she refused to accept his explanation. "Do you think I'm lying to you?" he demanded.

She shrugged. "What I think doesn't matter. Your intent

doesn't matter. What matters is that a good man, a Solamnic patriot, was slain when he went to you under a flag of truce."

"Your father's death was beside the point. The world must learn the price of defying the nation of Solamnia. That's why this whole campaign occurred." He gestured to the piles of rubble where the towers had fallen. "It is why *that* needed to be done."

Her eyes suddenly filled with tears, and she turned away from him. He grimaced, annoyed, impatient. "Do you need any assistance making funeral arrangements?"

"I can take care of things myself," she replied coldly.

"Very well. I'm detaching my engineering companies, leaving them here under your command. They'll rebuild the walls, where they were damaged by the falling towers. The fortress will be restored, intact, and once again you will able to defend against external enemies."

"It is not external enemies who did this!" Marrinys cried. "It is my own liege—my emperor!"

He flushed, clenching his jaw. Something in his eyes caused her to blanch, and she backed up a half a step. But still she was unafraid.

"And the towers?" she asked. "Will your engineers help to rebuild them as well?"

"That will be up to you." There was no point in talking to her any longer. "Good day!"

He spun on his heel, and as he walked away, he glanced at the scene in the crowded courtyard. Burly troops were helping to move the chunks of rubble out of the way. One of his engineers had backed a wagon with a block and tackle mounted on the bed up to a swath of ruined stone. Officers were issuing orders.

Another wagon rolled in with the priest of Kiri-Jolith,

the cleric who had accompanied Lord Kerrigan to the parley, sitting in the front. The priest dismounted and beckoned to some men from the castle guard. They started to remove a litter from the back, which bore the body of the slain nobleman. Jaymes watched impassively as they bore the dead man into the keep, entering a side door, since the main entrance had been devastated by an artillery ball.

Looking around, the emperor saw General Dayr waiting at the gatehouse. The emperor walked over to his army commander.

"I want you to take a message to Dram Feldspar, at New Compound," Jaymes said.

"Of course, my lord."

"I want him to begin work on a dozen new bombards. He's authorized to negotiate payment with the mountain dwarves for as much steel as they can give him. Also, I want to increase the next commission of black powder to a hundred kegs, as well as a thousand balls of ammunition. Dram is authorized to contract to the hill dwarves for sulfur and saltpeter. The new order is effective immediately."

Eyeing Dayr, Jaymes continued, "I don't want there to be any misunderstanding about these orders. I will need the bombards as soon as he can finish constructing them—certainly at least two of them can be done before the end of summer. And I will take delivery of the powder and balls in small batches, as they become available."

"Certainly, my lord." Dayr said, looking away then turning back to Jaymes. "May I ask if there's a reason you're worried about a misunderstanding? Might the dwarf be reluctant to follow your orders?"

"No, of course not. But I trust you to see that Dram receives the order and carries it out."

"Of course. And your orders for the Crown Army? Shall I hold them in place here?"

"No. Take your army back to Thelgaard; you can expect to stand down for the rest of the year unless something untoward happens. But keep the garrisons sharp."

"Yes, sir. Naturally. Are you taking the legion back over the pass to Palanthas?"

"No. I'm putting them into permanent camp a few miles up the river from here. Vingaard will not be given a chance to forget about them. I intend to have General Weaver practice the legion in open field maneuvers on the plains since there's a lot more room here than there is beside the city and the bay."

"Of course, Excellency," Dayr said, saluting crisply.

Those dispositions made, Jaymes turned at last to his horse. He would ride with the full company of Freemen, a hundred strong; they would escort the wagon containing the tax payment. Palanthas was seven days away, a journey that would take him over the pass in the Vingaard Range, and past the High Clerist's Tower.

Those mountains were etched along the western horizon, jagged and imposing, with a crest marked by numerous glaciers and snowfields. Some of those peaks were dazzling and white, while others were gray and ominous, shaded by the thick clouds of a massive thunderstorm.

He suddenly missed his wife very much. Jaymes wished he were back home already. He had little spirit for the long ride over the mountainous terrain.

But it was time to get started.

⊰·ᴏᴇ·ᴏᴇ·ᴏᴇ·ᴏᴇ·⬙·ᴏᴇ·ᴏᴇ·ᴏᴇ·ᴏᴇ·⊱

Blayne Kerrigan pulled his oilskin cloak over his head, leaning forward against the neck of his horse in a desperate

140

attempt to block out the torrential rain. He couldn't see the trail—such as it was—before his nose, so he clung blindly to the saddle. His horse forged ahead, shrugging off the water, shivering against the cold. It was a brave and steady animal and showed its true heart, heading resolutely into the savage weather.

But the mount was as weary as the rider. They had traveled hard through the night, entering the mountains not long after dawn, following a hunting trail Blayne remembered from earlier trips. The trail ran along the bed of a ravine and climbed steeply upward for many miles.

After the all-night ride, the storm had broken on them about noon, and for the rest of that day, they pressed through a steady rain that occasionally, as at that moment, became a lashing downpour. Because of the steep walls rising to right and left, it was practically impossible to get lost, even with the almost complete lack of visibility, so they simply continued blindly, stolidly onward, past a stream spilling down a rock-filled channel in the middle of the ravine.

Blayne had nervously watched the water level increase during the course of the rainy afternoon. In places where the ravine walls closed in, there was no dry land between the intermittent streams and the rock wall, and at times the horse surged through water up to its knees, driving forward until the passage widened and it could again scramble up onto what passed for dry land.

They were hampered by visibility and fatigue and couldn't maintain their pace after dark. Blayne looked around for a place to stop for the night. But the ground was steeply sloping there and everywhere was exposed to harsh elements. He remembered the presence of a rocky overhang, which would provide minimal shelter, a mile or two farther on, and he resolved to keep going. How different it was from the last time he was on that path. Then he had been on a carefree hunting adventure; at that moment he was fleeing for his life.

It was his father who had first brought him to those mountains. There, Blayne had learned to shoot a bow and arrow. The deadfalls of the forests had burned in their campfires, and Lord Kerrigan had regaled his only son with tales of Vingaard Keep, of the heroes of the past, the War of the Lance, and the battles against minions of evil. Always that great keep had awaited their return, secure on the plains, master of the great, placid river.

His thoughts wandered until a surge of white water, swollen by the heavy rain, rushed around a corner of the ravine before him. The sudden deluge overflowed the banks, and a wave higher than his head came at him so fast that he had bare seconds to react. The horse reared in terror, hooves flailing, and Blayne slid from the saddle.

Landing on his feet, he sprang toward the ravine wall, scrambling desperately. His fingers clutched a gnarl of roots, his boots pounded and kicked, pushing up on rock edges. The water struck him with impossible force, and he was slammed sideways, hearing frantic whinnies as the flood swept his steadfast horse away.

But a thick root dangled just above him, and he seized it with one hand, then both. It was solidly anchored. He clung to the root as the water tugged at his legs, hungrily seeking to bear him away. Gradually he felt the strength of the torrent wane, the water receding until it dropped to his waist then slowly down the length of his legs. Only then did he try to move, desperately hauling himself up from the water onto the steep side of the ravine.

His horse was gone, surely dead. He had no food, no home,

very little hope. How long he stayed there, he had no idea, but when he awoke, he was surrounded by pitch darkness and frozen to the bone.

⊰◦⊙◦⊙◦⊙◦❈◦⊙◦⊙◦⊙◦⊱

Selinda materialized within her rooms, exhausted and disheartened and full of fear. Those emotions were exacerbated when she saw the outer door to her chambers was open, and several of the emperor's men-at-arms were searching through the place. One had a wardrobe open and was pawing through her dresses, ignoring the fabulous raiment in a desperate rummaging for . . . something. Another was on his knees, peering under her bed.

In a flash she realized they had discovered her absence.

"What in the name of the Oath and Measure do you think you're doing?" she demanded, forcing into her voice every ounce of authority she could muster.

"My lady!" cried the kneeling guard. "Thank Kiri-Jolith you're safe!"

"Why shouldn't I be safe?" she demanded. "Safe, that is, except from the presence of rude men who burst into my chambers without an invitation. I repeat, what are you doing?"

The guard in the wardrobe had withdrawn with as much dignity as he could demonstrate, closing the door behind himself and bowing to Selinda. "Begging your ladyship's pardon, but we came through the door when you didn't respond to our knocks—over the span of hours, of course! And when we came in, we didn't see you—"

He blinked and scratched his head. "That is, where *were* you, my lady?"

"I should think the wife of the emperor is entitled to a few moments of privacy," she said icily. "It is not necessary that you know everything about my room! Now, leave me, please. At once!"

The two men exchanged glances but wasted no time in retreating, whispering to their companions in the outer hall and bowing and scraping as they pulled the door shut behind themselves.

Only then did Selinda allow herself to breathe easier. Realizing she was trembling, that her knees seemed on the verge of buckling, she dropped into a chair and tried to collect herself.

Collect herself for what? The question rose up and challenged her almost as soon as her breathing returned to normal.

What in the world was she going to do?

❦

Jaymes drove the Freemen hard, riding past dark every night, rising before dawn and returning to the mountain road early each morning. His thoughts were focused on his wife: *she* would understand what had transpired; *she* would see the reason he had needed to show his mastery of the nation! He didn't stop to think about the matter rationally but just rode forward, thinking of Selinda and of the miracle of the child growing within her.

Anxious to keep moving, the column rode right past the High Clerist's Tower, without the emperor even thinking to stop and pay his respects to General Markus. That garrison commander watched from the High Lookout in some amazement as his lord and the escort of his loyal riders passed the crest of the pass and started on the long, downhill course to the great city by the sea.

So hard and fast did they ride that on the afternoon of the

fifth day, Palanthas was in their sights. Only as they drew close to the city gate did the emperor allow the column to slow. He was, after all, returning from a victorious campaign, and he would enter his capital with all the pomp and ceremony his station warranted.

So he slowed the procession to a proper march, and he and his men smartly returned the salutes offered by the guards at the gates. Still, it was all he could do to hold back his horse, to refrain from galloping to his palace on the great square, from bounding up the steps, racing up the stairway to the room where she was waiting for him. He felt a sudden flush of regret at locking his wife up in her rooms. He would apologize and explain; she would understand!

Riding through the city gate, he threw back his cloak and sat astride his saddle with his head held high. He glanced up at the tower of his palace, rising into view from barely a mile away.

He took scant notice of the citizens of his city, although the Freemen muttered among themselves that there seemed to be an unusually small and unenthusiastic turnout for the emperor's return. The great leader had eyes only for his palace, and when at last he rode through the gates, Jaymes dismounted quickly, strode through the front doors, and started across the hall.

It was there that he was met by his old sergeant Samuel, a garrison commander who had experienced all that the Age of Mortals had delivered unto Krynn. Something in the grizzled veteran's eyes gave the emperor pause, and he halted.

"What is it, Sam?" he asked, fighting to remain calm. "Is my wife unwell?"

"Er, no, Excellency. She seems fine. It's just that . . . well . . ."

The old soldier was uncharacteristically hesitant, and Jaymes had no patience for delay. "What is it? Spit it out, man!"

"Well, it happened about six days ago. We went to check on her, as we did nice and regular, just like you ordered."

"Was it the baby? Is something wrong?"

"No, well, I don't know. You see, she was gone when we looked in on her. And then she came back—just like magic, my lord."

⋘⊙∾⊙∾⊙∾⊙⋙⊙∾⊙∾⊙∾⊙⋙

Selinda watched Jaymes lead the Freemen back into the city. The emperor's column of a hundred knights came down the road from the High Clerist's Pass. They were trailed by a heavy wagon, and palace heralds shouted the news that the carriage bore the overdue taxes owned by Vingaard Keep to the national treasury.

Selinda noticed that the crowds of Palanthians—usually festive on such occasions—seemed to avoid the heralds. There were very few people lining the streets as Jaymes made his way to the palace, and those who were out seemed to be watching in sullen silence. The attack on Vingaard had certainly not been popular with the people of Palanthas.

Indifferent to his people, the emperor sat astride his horse, looking neither right nor left, Selinda noted. He accepted the effusive praise of the palace garrison with a casual salute as he rode through the gate. Stablemen vied to take his horse, but he ignored them as he entered the keep, vanishing from her sight.

Not long after, he was knocking forcefully at her door.

"Enter," she replied.

He came in, looking to her eyes like a stranger, though he was still the same man. Jaymes Markham . . . an outlaw when

146

first she met him . . . then general and ultimately lord marshal of a great army . . . and finally the emperor of Solamnia. A long, long time ago, it seemed, she had agreed to become his wife. The reasons for doing so seemed compelling at the time, since then they were vague and indistinct.

No, she did not love him. And yes, she feared him.

"Hello," he said. She was aware he was scrutinizing her. His narrowed eyes were dark above the neat beard. She noted more gray along his temples, and in that beard, than she remembered. Had he really changed that much in a fortnight? She watched him closely, saying nothing. She had nothing to say and felt at a loss for words.

"The guards tell me you gave them quite a start."

"How so?" she asked, feeling a jolt of terror.

"They thought you were in danger, had fallen or suffered some stroke in your sleep. But when they broke in here, after hours of trying to rouse you, you were nowhere to be seen, according to their report."

"I was . . ." She faltered. The lie that had diverted the guards would no longer suffice. "I was gone. I traveled to Vingaard. I wanted . . . I wanted to see firsthand the way you would rule your new, proud nation."

"Magic?" He frowned then glared. "You teleported! How?"

She didn't answer but unconsciously placed her left hand over her right, concealing the ring. The quick movement did not pass unnoticed.

"So you have a magic ring," he declared haughtily. "Don't you understand the dangers—to yourself? To our child?"

"I felt perfectly safe."

"I can't allow you to risk yourself and the baby like this." He took a step closer. He didn't appear so much angry as concerned. Holding out his hand, he spoke again, more gently but still firmly. "You can't do this again; I won't allow it. Give me the ring."

"No!" The word exploded from her lips, but Selinda didn't regret blurting it out. She felt a wave of relief, the first excitement of honesty. She took a step backward, watching him warily.

"Don't refuse me!" he snapped, his anger starting to flare. "I'll simply take it from you if I must."

"No, you won't do that, either," Selinda said. She stood at her full height, chin raised. Her fingers touched the little circlet of silver, ready to give it a twist, to activate the magic. "If you try, I promise by all the gods that I will use the ring to go away from here and never return."

"To where?" he asked, appearing—for the first time ever, in Selinda's experience—to be stunned.

"I won't tell you. But I will tell you this: I will not be locked up in this tower, not by you, nor by all the troops in your army."

He stood staring at her, mute, for what seemed like a long time. Finally he turned and stalked to the door. "This is not the end of this," he said before marching from the room.

❧⊷∞⊷∞⊷∞⊷❦⊷∞⊷∞⊷∞⊷❧

Jaymes was wrapped in a cold fury as he rode out of the Old City, lashing his horse into a gallop, scattering pedestrians out of his path. The steed galloped up Nobles Hill and clattered onto the paved road leading to his destination.

The great manor house was owned by Jenna, Mistress of the Red Robes. The powerful crimson-garbed wizard had been declared head of the Orders of Magic at the momentous Conclave that convened after the gods of magic returned to

Krynn. Coryn had helped Jenna attain that vaulted station against the ambitions of Dalamar the Dark, and in gratitude—and genuine friendship—Jenna had offered Coryn stewardship of her magnificent house.

It had been there, in her laboratory, that Coryn made the potion of enchantment Jaymes had used to bewitch Selinda—to woo her love, win her hand, and gain control of her fortune. That seemed like another lifetime, such a distant part of the past that the emperor could almost convince himself that it had never happened. But it had happened. Now, it seemed, his wife had magic on her side.

There, too, the White Witch and a younger Jaymes Markham had shared moments as lovers and friends. They had dreamed of a united Solamnia. That goal was key to their partnership.

Would that dream, too, end in ruin?

The emperor dismounted and stalked to the front door, which opened before he could knock. He halted momentarily at the sight of a young man dressed in the livery of an apprentice Knight of the Crown. A small fuzz of brown fur bristled atop his lip, an overly ambitious attempt at the singular mustache of a proud Solamnic Knight.

"Donny?" Jaymes said, taken aback. It had been more than a year since his last visit there. He was suddenly bemused as he confronted the fellow who was the son of the house's most venerable servant. "I didn't know you had taken the Oath."

"Yes, my lord," said the young man, beaming. "It's Sir Donald, now."

"Excellent. Your father must be very proud."

"Oh, he is, sir. Most definitely. I'm sure he would love to see you if you have a moment. I can get him right away."

"Actually, I'm here to see Lady Coryn on a matter of

urgency. Where is she?" His voice had suddenly hardened, and the change in his mood did not escape the young knight. Jaymes was surprised to notice a flicker of defiance in Donny's—Sir Donald's—face. The young man's first loyalty was to the mistress of the house, a fact that shouldn't have been surprising.

"Come in," the knight said after a moment. "I'll get her."

Jaymes waited in the anteroom, looking at those steps he had climbed so many times. The laboratory was up there . . . and her bedroom too. He had gone to each, in turn, and found strength and renewal with the woman so many knights called the White Witch.

The stairway seemed unusually bright in the afternoon sunlight spilling through the high windows. When Coryn came around the curve on the stairs, he realized that she, not the sun, was the source of the brightness. It was a magical effect, he knew, and resolved not to give her the satisfaction of shielding his eyes.

She halted several steps from the bottom, waiting for him to speak first, and he felt the rise of his anger. He was facing betrayal from women on all sides. Instinctively, he went on the attack.

"You gave a magical ring to my wife, didn't you?" he began, speaking harshly.

"You locked her up in her room when you left the city." Her tone was calm. "As if she were a criminal. That was something she clearly did not deserve."

"It was for her own good!"

"Who are you to judge what is good for the Lady Selinda?" Coryn challenged.

"I thought you were my ally!" Jaymes declared. "We are working together toward a strong Solamnia! Surely you understand the importance of keeping Selinda—and the child she carries—safe!"

"I'm not sure that we agree on what is good for your . . . wife." The reply was frank, her tone still cool and unapologetic.

"But everything is going according to plan," he protested. "We've come so far! Six duchies and regencies, united as a nation, facing a future in strength, as an empire! Just as we always hoped."

"What does that have to do with Selinda, with what you did at Vingaard Keep?" she said. *"This* is how you make a strong future?"

"It was necessary—"

"It was brutal and short-sighted," Coryn spat, her calmness shattered like a broken mirror. Her voice caught; tears swam in her eyes. "Much of what you are doing these days is brutal and short-sighted. You don't have any idea how the people of this nation feel. You want their respect, but all you gain is their fear!"

"You're the one who doesn't understand!" he replied. "I have carved a place for myself . . . and for this land. Turn your back on me, on this land, if you will. I can hold that place by myself."

"I wish you success in your attempt," the White Witch replied coldly.

"Do not dare to betray me again!" he warned.

"Go now," was her only reply.

The last word vanished behind the door the emperor slammed on his way out.

CHAPTER TWELVE

DAYS OF DECISION

General Dayr and his son accompanied their army on the southward march back to Thelgaard. It was a grim, businesslike procession, with none of the celebratory chatter and cheering that inevitably accompanied the return from a victorious campaign. Men and officers alike seemed subdued and introspective.

They had about the same distance to march as Jaymes and his Freemen, but they moved without the emperor's urgency. As a consequence—even though they marched across the plains instead of over a mountain pass—it took a few days longer for the Crown Army to reach Thelgaard than it did for the emperor to reach Palanthas.

Finally the long column of troops drew up to the ancestral home and castle. Despite being sacked by Ankhar less than five years earlier, Thelgaard had been restored as an impressive edifice. The outer wall and gates had been fully rebuilt, and several new towers added to the mighty keep.

"I'm going to spend one night at home and then go on to New Compound on a mission for the emperor," General Dayr said to his son as they approached the castle gate. "Would you care to come along with me?"

"Certainly, Father," replied Captain Franz.

"Good," said the older man, invigorated as they rode into the cool shade of the great courtyard.

On arriving home the general signed the orders dismissing his levied troops, allowing them to return to their farms and shops for the summer. He took some time to set up a training schedule and duty rotations for his permanent garrisons. He and his wife hosted a homecoming banquet that evening for his knights and their ladies.

The next morning he and his son ate a quick breakfast while their horses were saddled and their traveling kits were freshened by servants. Lady Dayr made no complaint—she had seen darker days—and merely kissed her husband and son good-bye.

They departed for the valley of New Compound, in the northern Garnet Mountains, only an hour after dawn. The two men had decided to travel alone, partly to make the trip almost a vacation, but partly knowing they had private matters to discuss.

The older man had been watching his son, noting the darkness that seemed to envelop him whenever the emperor's name was mentioned. After their first day traveling, with the responsibilities of army management and home behind them, General Dayr decided to broach the subject of what had transpired at Vingaard Keep.

"I picture the siege of Vingaard, even in my dreams," he said frankly. "As clear as if I'm standing there, the smoke of the gun still swirling around me."

The two men rode their horses at an easy walk, the flat expanse of the Vingaard Plains making for easy traveling. The ragged crest of the Garnet Range was visible on the horizon but still several days ahead.

"How can we ever forget?" Franz replied, the bitterness tightening his voice. "A year ago those knights were our friends, our allies. Blayne Kerrigan was a mate of mine when we were apprentices in the order of Crowns! How could it have come to this?" He turned in his saddle to regard the general with an almost pleading expression. "Father, we helped the emperor earn his place. At the time, it seemed like we were clearly doing what was best for the knighthood . . . and for our realm. Now I fear just the opposite."

"Don't rush to such a harsh conclusion. Keep in mind all that Solamnia has suffered over my—even your—lifetime: the Dragon Overlords, the Dark Knights, the sacrifice of our great god Paladine. One by one we fought through these challenges—and we survived!

"Then came the invasion of Ankhar's horde. Remember what it was like to see our home sacked, my son? To watch the death of the duke I had served all of my adult life?"

"The duke was venal and corrupt, Father—you know that! And he was weak. He wouldn't even fight, in the end."

"All true, but he was my lord, and I grieved when he died. And think of what you are saying because Jaymes Markham may be many things, but he is not venal, he is not corrupt, and he is not weak! And he is the lord of our united lands now! We have lived through dark and trying times, and perhaps such times call for a powerful, even ruthless, leader."

"But I thought the point of our striving was to lead us to a brighter future," Franz protested. "And yet it seems as though we have ushered in a new era of darkness. After all, the great towers of Vingaard survived all of the scourges you listed—only to be brought down by the one who set himself up as our protector."

"I don't have an easy answer," the general admitted. "But I plead with you: don't give up on Jaymes Markham yet. I remember how he led us, when the dukes of the noble knighthood were allowing the country to crumble around them. Without him, we—and our women and children—would be Ankhar's slaves, or dead."

"I acknowledge the important role he has played," Franz replied, "but I will not promise to follow him into the future."

From that position the young captain could not be swayed, and his father was wrapped in gloom and worry as they finally made their way onto rising ground, following the paved, well-graded road—of dwarven craftsmanship—that led them up a verdant valley to the thriving mountain town of New Compound. The two men had not been there since the early days of the settlement, and they couldn't help but be impressed by the many white stone buildings, the neat timber structures. A farmers' market bustled in the main square, which they could easily observe from afar since no wall surrounded the town.

"I've never seen so many well-fed dwarves," Franz remarked in some astonishment.

"Ahem, a tribute to their prosperity," his father replied.

They were warmly greeted by Dram and his wife, and the veteran general was moved to chuck little Mikey under the chin, a gesture that provoked an explosion of giggles. Ever hospitable, Sally Feldspar set about preparing a dinner while her husband and the two soldiers retired to the sitting room. There, the general presented a letter of instructions from the emperor, and the two men sat quietly while the dwarf slowly read the missive. When he finished—it took Dram several moments, though there was but a short page of writing—he sat quietly, his expression blank.

"Do you understand his . . . requests?" Dayr prodded gently after some time of silence.

"Of course I understand," Dram said impatiently. His irritation, Dayr sensed, was not with the messenger, but with the message. Abruptly, the dwarf looked directly at him. "So he has three bombards, but he wants a dozen more? And all this powder and shot?"

"Actually, two of the bombards were destroyed in the march on Vingaard Keep." Dayr went on to describe, briefly, that encounter, realizing that Dram had heard nothing of the developments on the great river. Throughout his report of the events, Franz sat mute, staring out the front window at the pastoral town, the green, encircling mountains.

"I remember Vingaard Keep," Dram said idly after the general had finished the explanation. "Quite a landmark it was. You don't see too many places like that, not built by humans anyway. It's a shame to think that it's gone."

"Well, not entirely gone," Dayr said awkwardly.

"Scarred beyond recognition!" Franz spat, drawing a sharp look from his father.

"Well, I understand what he wants me to do. It wouldn't be easy, mind you—my operations have slowed down quite a bit, and it would take some gearing up to build more of those bombards. I'm going to have to think it over. In the meantime, why don't we go into the dining room? If my nose is as good as I think it is, Sally has got something special coming out of the oven."

"Very well," said the general.

His son, staring at the dwarf intently, rose to his feet immediately, and the older man followed more slowly. Together, they trailed Dram into his dining room, knowing that the matter of the emperor's orders would not be settled the first night.

⊱⋆⊰⋆⊱⋆⊰⋆⊱⋆⊰⋆⊱

Blayne Kerrigan had no idea how he survived through that night, exhausted, numb, soaked to the skin, shivering uncontrollably, clinging to the root on the edge of the ravine wall as the raging flood cascaded and thundered below him.

When next he awoke, gray dawn permeated the ravine. The rain had ceased, and the flood had abated. There was enough ground for Blayne to slide down and brace himself on a couple of rocks, keeping out of the cold stream. He spared a few moments of regret for the loss of his horse, a loyal animal that the young noble had personally broken and trained some six years earlier.

But he had no more time for reflection. The road before him was steep and difficult, even more so since he would be traveling on foot and without supplies. But there could be no turning back: Vingaard was in the hands of the emperor, and Blayne was certain his patrols would be combing the countryside, looking for the enemy soldier who had become a fugitive outlaw.

Resolutely, he started upward, slogging along in his wet clothes. The exertion began to warm him, and by the time the first rays of the sun poked into the deep valley, he was dry, sweating, gasping, and dead tired. He followed the narrow path with stumbling footsteps, always ascending. He took note of familiar landmarks—a waterfall that had bemused him for a whole day, once, when his life was peaceful; a grove where he had stalked a mighty stag just a few years earlier; a steep side valley where he and his faithful hounds had once chased, trapped, and killed a cattle-eating bear. But he didn't linger at any of those places.

157

Most of his thoughts were of his father, and they were fond remembrances of the man who had taught him to hunt, camp, ride, and fight. Once, when he paused beside the becalmed stream to catch his breath, he looked into an eddy and imagined Lord Kerrigan's presence—not so much in the water, but inhabiting the whole place, in the stream and the mountains and the very wind.

"I will make you proud, my father," he whispered aloud.

Invigorated by the thought, he pushed himself to his feet and continued on, higher into the Vingaard Mountains.

There was a reason only the one road traversed the mountains—through the High Clerist's Pass—crossing by land from east to west side of the long, narrow range. Most of the valleys leading into the Vingaard Mountains eventually came up against sheer cliffs, dead-end canyons that presented the traveler with impassable rock faces, looming glaciers, and forbidding peaks. In a few—a very few—places, the grade was shallow enough for a narrow path to snake its way into the heights. But those trails were mainly fit for goats and mountain cats.

Blayne knew from his past experience that he had found such a path. By late afternoon, the grade had increased substantially, and he frequently had to use his hands to grab bushes, roots, or rocky knobs to propel himself up and forward. If his horse had survived, he would have had to abandon the animal because the ground was simply too steep, the trail too narrow. Before sunset he was treated to a respite when he stumbled upon a narrow valley. There a pair of waterfalls trilled down from the heights, and a crystalline pond showed proof of trout in its rippling surface.

Wearily he slumped onto a patch of grass beside the pond. His stomach growled, and for the first time he felt his hunger as an acute craving. Fortunately, his father had prepared him for that type of situation. Rolling up his sleeve, Blayne lay face down on the ground next to the place where the stream flowed out of the pond. Many fish were visible, swimming in both directions. He let his arm dangle in the water, motionless, until a fat rainbow trout swam by. With a quick gesture, he thrust his hand under the fish, hoisted it up, and flipped it, wriggling, onto the bank. With a single sharp move he cracked the fat fish on a rock and killed it.

He had no fire, nor any means to make one, but two slashes of his sharp knife cut tender fillets from the fish, and he simply ate them raw, carefully pulling out the tiny bits of bone. Before sunset, he had pulled four more fish from the water, eating two and wrapping the others in moist leaves. Stars sparkled in the sky as he finally stumbled away from the stream, seeking a place to sleep.

He found, instead, a man dressed in a gray robe, regarding him coldly with black, expressionless eyes. The stranger stood under a tree, and the young nobleman got the feeling that he might have been watching him for some time.

Blayne gasped aloud when he spied the man, immediately reaching for his knife. But that weapon fell from his suddenly cold fingers when the gray man waved a hand and muttered a soft word. The world began to spin, dizziness and disorientation drowning out the young noble's awareness.

"Sleep now," said the man in gray. "Rest tonight. Tomorrow, you will come with me."

※◇◎◇◎◇◎◎◇◎◇◎◇◎◇※

The Nightmaster again visited Ankhar when he and Laka had gathered his new horde into a great encampment, filling a broad stretch of fields and meadows near the northern edge of Lemish's vast woodland. The band had grown to number many thousands of warriors.

Perhaps it was not quite so numerous as the half-giant's first army, the one that had terrorized Solamnia for more than two years, but in several important respects the force was even more impressive: for one thing, about half the warriors in the new horde were ogre bulls, averaging nearly eight feet tall, each as heavy as two strong men. For another, he had the company of nearly fifty flying sivak draconians commanded by the spell-casting aurak called Guilder.

The rest of the troops were lackeys: many hobgoblins and goblins, together with a few ancient, battered draconians, that inevitably trailed in the wake of their mighty masters.

But they were the descendents of fierce warriors who had fought under the Dark Queen's banners in the War of the Lance, who had waged war against, and in the service of, the Dragon Overlords. A fraction had served under Ankhar in his previous campaign, and they were as thirsty for revenge as they were for plunder.

Some of his old captains, too, had returned to the ranks. The grizzled ogre chieftain Bloodgutter had come at the head of a company of nearly a thousand axe-wielding bulls and proclaimed he, himself, would batter down the walls of any fortress standing in the army's path. Impressed by his loyalty, and tusk-foaming ferocity, Ankhar had promoted him to General Bloodgutter on the spot.

The fierce warg rider Rib Chewer had also returned to serve the half-giant again. Rib Chewer brought with him hundreds of his clan, each mounted on a snarling, fanged wolf the size of a pony. Those warriors, riding fast across the plains and seemingly tireless, would be the fleet advance guard of his army, Ankhar decided. The flying sivaks would be his scouts and his eyes.

The ogres would be his fists.

"You have done well, son of the mountains," declared the Nightmaster, appearing—as ever—only after the last glow of the sunset had faded from the western sky. He materialized near the great fire where Ankhar sat with his captains, and his arrival provoked a great stirring and growling among the restive ogres. One, the captain called Heart Eater, leaped to his feet and took a step toward the small, masked human, only to halt in shock when the visitor raised a black-gloved hand.

"What witchery is this?" demanded Heart Eater, struggling and flailing as he tried to free his feet, which seemed to have become suddenly planted in the ground.

"Merely a precaution, to see you do not try and harm one of your master's greatest allies," replied the Nightmaster with a shrug. He gestured and Heart Eater twisted free. Off balance, the ogre smashed to the ground and bounced, growling, back to his feet. The others muttered warily but did not intervene.

"Or, perhaps, to see that your master's greatest ally is not forced to do harm to one of his loyal captains," continued the black priest, his tone casual. Still, there was power and menace in those words, and the bristling, growling Heart Eater saw the wisdom of returning sullenly to his seat by the fire. Pond-Lily, seated beside her lord and master, watched the exchange wide-eyed, while Laka—on Ankhar's other side—cackled in wry amusement.

"I have done as you . . . requested," Ankhar said, choosing his words carefully. His stepmother sat rigidly, her bright eyes shifting from him to the visitor. The emerald gems in the eye sockets of her skull talisman glowed, and she lifted the ghastly rattle above her head and shook it wildly. "I have an army, and my warriors are ready to march against the knights."

"Very good," said the Nightmaster. "Know that you do not march alone, that even as you move to attack, other armies—as well as smaller, more secretive factions—will move against the emperor and Solamnia. His fall is all but assured."

"Other armies? Will they claim his treasures before I reach them?" demanded the half-giant suspiciously.

The Nightmaster waved a hand, and Ankhar's worries seemed to evaporate. Even as the man was explaining that all the booty in the southern plains would be the property of the half-giant and his men, the horde's commander was no longer concerned with such questions.

Instead, he felt impatient. He wanted to go to war.

〰〰〰❦〰〰〰

Jaymes asked Sir Donald to take his horse back to the palace, announcing that he intended to walk. Before the knight rode off on the silver-saddled steed, the emperor lashed his cloak and helmet to the saddlebags. Instead he made do with a plain black cape. Pulling the hood up over his head, he walked down from Nobles' Hill with his head low, though his eyes and ears stayed alert. His mood was black; his anger felt like a burning coal in his chest. Two women had thwarted him, and he could strike at neither of them directly. Sooner or later they would regret their actions.

But that afternoon he would find an easier target.

Unrecognized, he passed through the gate into the Old City. No strong urge propelled him home—he had no stomach to deal with his wife right then—so he took a roundabout path, determined to see for himself what the mood in Palanthas was like. His footsteps soon carried him near the bustling waterfront, where a number of wide plazas served as day markets, with vendors offering everything from fish to sharp steel knives for sale. About the only commercial item prohibited from sale was slaves—that foul trade had been banned since the restoration of Solamnic rule under Lord Regent du Chagne—but Jaymes suspected that if he looked closely at some of the brothels or mercenary companies in the city even humans could be purchased.

However, he was not concerned with such matters of morality. Instead, his mind was on practical problems, and Coryn's words had warned him that there might exist dangers in the very city about which the emperor suspected little. Was the population rebellious? Was Vingaard Keep just the tip of a dangerous iceberg?

If so, Jaymes Markham would not remain in the dark for long.

The first place he stopped was a fish market right at the docks. He ignored the busy scenes of commerce, the nets full of glistening salmon being hoisted from holds, the icemen hauling their wagons of frozen water to the stalls, the merchants trying to sell their goods to the teeming throngs. Instead, Jaymes listened to the people who were not there to sell or buy, but merely to gab.

He heard one of the official heralds, proclaiming the relatively old news of Vingaard's capitulation. Jaymes had written the announcement himself, and—hearing it—regretted his choice of words.

"The recalcitrant Kerrigan clan has rejoined the lawabiding ranks of the Solamnic peoples!" cried the herald. "The daughter of the lord, Lady Kerrigan, has been appointed mistress of the keep. Her brother is declared an outlaw, and a reward of a thousand steel pieces is offered for his capture, alive. Alternately, if proof of his death can be produced, the reward is five hundred steel."

Jaymes heard people muttering about the announcement, some hearing the news for the first time, others reacting as though the herald's report was familiar. The emperor had intentionally left out any mention of the damage to the keep's legendary towers, as well as the fate of Lord Kerrigan. But the sad truth was spreading.

"Did you hear that Old Sandy—that's Lord Kerrigan the elder—was killed by the emperor when he came to his camp under a flag of truce?" whispered an old man, speaking to several young ruffians. He was a vendor of wine, who leaned on the counter of his tiny stall as he held the attention of a small group of onlookers. A hand-scratched sign hung crookedly on a post, announcing it as "Norgaard Eric's Prime Wine Shop." Though the fellow was speaking softly, his words carried to Jaymes's ears as the emperor, still cloaked, mingled with the crowd.

"Not only that, but his guns knocked the whole keep down!" a woman hissed, looking up to make sure the herald wasn't listening. She didn't show any concern about the strangers clustered around her and kept speaking. "Next thing you know, he'll be blasting down our own houses if he don't like the way we looks at 'im!"

"They say his own troops was on the point o' mutiny!" the old man interjected, trying to recapture his audience. "That he held a sword to his captain's own throat, ere the men would follow orders."

"How'd it come to this?" heatedly asked one of the young men. He was a furtive, swarthy type that Jaymes immediately pegged for a thief. There was the shape of a short blade under the hip of his tunic, though for the moment he seemed more interested in gossiping than in working his trade.

"We let 'im do it!" the woman replied tartly. "Just gave 'im the keys to the city, we did."

"Eh, it's the lord regent's fault. Givin' up his daughter like that to a hick warrior from the backcountry! Why, there's them say that he really did kill old Lord Lorimar, and 'e threatened to do the same to the regent, less he gave up his daughter."

"And the poor princess," said the woman, shaking her head and clucking her tongue. "Locked up in that castle like a prisoner, she is."

"Huh! Really? How d'you know that?" demanded the old man, obviously jealous of that fresh tidbit of information.

"Why, my son's a sergeant in the palace guard, 'e is," the woman insisted in a low voice. "Was him that looked in on her every day while the emperor was off makin' war."

Jaymes had been determined to listen in silence, but that remark upset him. Muffling his voice, he spoke from the edge of the group. "A sergeant, you say? Sure he ain't just a reg'lar ranker?"

"Sergeant Withers!" she shot back, offended. "Maxim Withers. You can see his name on the roster, you don't believe me!"

She suddenly squinted, trying to get a clean look at Jaymes, but he shifted slightly, using the shoulder of a burly dock worker so she couldn't see him. "Yes," she repeated firmly. "Our beloved princess wept and she wailed, I'm told! They were barely allowed to feed her—on the emperor's orders it was!"

"No!" gasped one of the listeners.

"That tain't the worst of it," the old woman said, her voice dropping low again.

"What? Tell us!" demanded the listeners.

"She's with child!" she proclaimed triumphantly. "The Princess of Palanthas is going to be giving the emperor an heir!"

"Ah, I ain't heard that!" said Norgaard Eric skeptically, trying to take charge of the gossiping again. He switched the subject, grousing about the city patrols that had apparently required him to close his wine-vending stall at sundown. The new rule had been one of Jaymes's innovations, and the emperor knew it had considerably reduced the drunkenness on the streets in the waterfront district.

Disgusted, the emperor moved on, though not without making a few mental notes.

He spent the rest of the day making his way through the city. In some neighborhoods the official heralds were actually jeered by people in the crowds, and everywhere the mood was touchy. The people were foolish cattle, he realized, who were distracted by any kind of gossip or provocation. By the time he approached the gates of his palace, throwing back his hood so he was immediately recognized, the emperor had made several decisions. Many of them would take a little more thought, but at least two of them he could act on at once.

"Find Sergeant Maxim Withers of the palace guard," he ordered the captain on duty. "Have him report to me at once. Oh, and send a detail to the waterfront district. There's a wine merchant there, calls himself Norgaard Eric."

"Yes, my lord," the captain replied, his eyebrows raised in mute question.

"I want his stock destroyed, and I think it would do him good to spend a few nights in the city gaol. See that it's done."

Knowing he would be obeyed—it was a good feeling, that

knowledge—Jaymes stalked through the door of his palace. He was hungry but would have a meal delivered to his office.

He had a lot of work to do.

⊰⊱⊰⊱⊰⊱⊰⊱⊰⊱

Dram couldn't sleep. He didn't want to disturb Sally with his tossing and turning, so he got out of bed, threw a fur robe over his stocky, muscular body, and went out to the front porch of the great house. The valley's crystalline lake shimmered before him, bright with the reflected light of a million stars and the setting of the silver crescent moon in the west.

He settled himself into his favorite chair and only then realized he wasn't alone. There was a man leaning against the railing at the end of the porch. He had been staring at the waters but turned silently to regard the dwarf. Dram's eyes were naturally keen in the dark, and he recognized the fellow immediately.

"Captain Franz," he greeted the son of General Dayr. "You're keeping late hours."

The young knight sighed and came over to take a seat next to the dwarf. "Well, I've had a lot of trouble sleeping lately. Ever since . . ."

"Since Vingaard Keep?" asked Dram shrewdly.

"Yes. I'm loyal to the knighthood, sir. I really am. But it felt like, what we were doing, marching on, firing on a keep of our own people, was a great injustice."

The dwarf fell silent for a moment. "Sounds like the Vingaard knights made a pretty good attack on Jaymes's army, if they burned up two of his bombards."

"What choice did they have?" shot back the young captain.

Dram merely shrugged. "I'm not saying they had choices,

167

not good ones, anyway. But I can't think of anything more likely to arouse the emperor's ire. He couldn't let an affront like that go unpunished."

"Is he willing to punish the whole of this nation?" demanded Franz.

The dwarf shook his head. "I don't know what he's willing to do. I never did. But I have to admit I don't like the sound of his plans, if his letter to me is any indication."

"Is that why you're down here in the middle of the night?" asked the knight. "Because you can't sleep either?"

"Something like that," Dram replied. "It helps me to think, out here with the stars and the lake and the mountains. I come down here more nights than I'd care to admit to Sally."

"So you admit that you, too, are troubled by the emperor."

Dram didn't answer, and after a while Franz rose to his feet. Stretching, he looked at the vista in the valley then turned back to the dwarf. "I appreciate your hospitality, putting us up in your own house. And I appreciate you listening to me. I try talking to my father, but he doesn't want to listen. I think he's *afraid* to listen, sometimes."

"Well, your father is a very wise man. And a courageous one, as well. I wouldn't expect to hear that he's afraid of anything. But he might have the wisdom to be cautious."

"Yes, I know. And I'm sure you're right. Good night," Franz said, going back into the house.

Dram sat out there until dawn started to color the sky. He went back in and snuggled next to his wife as the day grew brighter, and still he couldn't sleep. When Mikey, in the next room, started to stir, he got up to get the boy so his wife could have another hour of rest.

And when he met General Dayr and his son for breakfast,

as they had planned, he had finally decided what to say.

"Tell Jaymes I got his orders. I read his letter. I understand all his needs and wants," the dwarf said gruffly.

"And?" prodded the commander, sensing there was more.

"Tell him if he wants more bombards, he'll have to make them himself."

CHAPTER THIRTEEN

ARTICLES OF LAW

G arrison Sergeant Maxim Withers, much to his surprise, received a curt note from his captain: the emperor wanted to see him, personally. Withers carefully polished his boots, shined his armor, and made sure his flowing mustache was thoroughly combed before he reported for the audience. He marched in to the emperor's office, saluted smartly, and waited for Jaymes Markham to finish reviewing some of the important-looking papers that were scattered across his desk. Finally, the great man looked up.

"Sergeant Withers," the emperor said coldly, stirring the soldier's anxiety. "I have decided to reassign you. Sometimes duty in the palace, or in the city, softens a man, and I would hate to see that happen with an estimable fellow of your quality."

"Excellency, I'm afraid I don't understand."

"Oh, you will." The emperor was smiling, though his tone was most unpleasant. "I'm assigning you to the garrison command of the Northpoint Lighthouse, effective immediately. There is a supply ship departing the docks with the evening tide. I expect you to be aboard."

Withers swayed, feeling a little sick to his stomach. He knew the Northpoint Lighthouse was a huge tower on a rocky islet just beyond the northern terminus of the Bay of Branchala. A perennial flame burned at the summit of the tall spire. It was fueled by oil pumped by the garrison. The light of that fire was reflected and amplified by great mirrors that were visible for dozens of miles out to sea. The installation was beloved by mariners as a sign of safe harbor ahead.

Yet the place was not viewed so favorably by the men assigned to keep the fire burning. The lighthouse was staffed by a garrison of twelve men-at-arms and a single sergeant. Since it was miles from the mainland, and scores of miles from the city, the troops were stuck there for a term of three months, during which time they lived on the remote, otherwise uninhabited, islet. Stormy waters often surrounded them, so supply and replacements ships were unpredictable, often delayed for weeks or months. And the smell of the perpetually burning oil was notorious to passing ships and often sickened the guard contingent.

"I have decided that there is too much instability in the operation of the lighthouse," the emperor continued. "Staff, especially the command sergeant, replaced every three months leads to inefficiency. Therefore, your term will last for a full year!"

Withers, aghast, dared to ask Jaymes the reasoning behind the posting.

"Ask your mother," the emperor retorted. "It seems you converse with her about all manner of things that are within the purview of this palace and not the subjects for marketplace gossip."

Chagrined, the veteran guard slunk out of Jaymes's office, grateful he still had his life and some semblance of his rank.

A short time later, the captain of the gate guard came in and reported that the wine merchant known as Norgaard Eric had been put out of business, his stock dumped into the gutters of the marketplace. No doubt a few bottles of the higher-quality product had been salvaged by the city guards for their own enjoyment, but the emperor expected as much and didn't care to inquire.

"Let him languish in the gaol for a fortnight. And tell him to watch his words when he's released, or the next time it will cost him his tongue."

"Aye, my lord," said the captain, bowing quietly to his stern, forbidding lord and, with a wary eye on the emperor, withdrawing from the office.

Jaymes spent the whole night at his desk, drafting and redrafting orders, calling for scribes when one parchment was done, turning to the next even as those servants began making copies. He worked by the light of several bright lanterns, and threw away a quill every so often as they became overworked, cracked, and useless. "More ink!" he demanded several times through that long night. When his hand cramped up, he flexed his fingers and picked up another pen. When his back became sore, he rose from his chair, stretched for a moment, paced a few times around his office, and sat back down to continue writing orders.

By dawn, he was finished. In the space of eight hours, he had authored a dozen new laws and prepared a detailed statement to be read aloud by a dozen heralds. The announcement would be called out every hour by each of the heralds throughout the day, and every day for the next two weeks. Additional copies were prepared and dispatched by mounted couriers to city rulers in Vingaard, Thelgaard, Solanthus, Garnet, Caergoth, and the lesser towns of the realm.

The copies completed, the criers headed off to begin their day's work. By the time they were finished, the people of the city would know that it was a crime to criticize the emperor's motives as he led Solamnia into the future. It was sedition to discuss the emperor's actions in a way that would reflect poorly on Jaymes or his officers. Criticizing the government in small groups—any scurrilous gossip against the state—was also a criminal offense.

It was against the law to interfere with, heckle, or otherwise obstruct an official herald in the conduct of his duties. Removing or tampering with the official scrolls posted around the towns and cities of the realm was an act, not of vandalism, but of rebellion against the state. Those who would publish pamphlets, posters, or newspapers of their own needed to have those publications approved by the emperor—or his local representative, for areas beyond Palanthas—before public dissemination.

Those who violated the edicts would face a wide variety of sanctions, including imprisonment, public humiliation, loss of property, or worse. True sedition would result in exile or execution. Conversely, the new laws built in many rewards, mostly financial, that allowed loyal citizens who reported on the disloyalty of their neighbors to profit handsomely, often with a portion of the properties seized from the designated rebellious miscreants.

Satisfied with his long night's work, the emperor did not go forth to listen to the announcements and observe the reaction of his citizens. He knew what the heralds would say, and he knew the new laws would be obeyed.

Besides, he was exhausted. When the last crier had left the palace, he devoured a cold breakfast, eating by himself, and went to his private chamber. There, he stripped off his clothes and crawled under the covers.

But it was several hours before he could fall asleep.

Blayne knew he was a captive, utterly under the control of the man in the gray robe, even though no rope or chain had been used to bind him, no gag placed across his mouth to keep him from crying out. He plodded along behind the man without uttering a sound of protest and, despite his profound weariness, without collapsing to the ground. In a sense, it was a relief to turn his life over to another person, to be freed from the terror of flight, of trying to make his way alone through the mountains.

It was not until dawn broke around him that he began to question everything about the strange experience: his own thoughts and emotions, his remarkable endurance, the sense of cooperation and comfort he felt with the unique man. He was no longer cold, despite the fact that the fellow had made no fire. He was no longer wet, though the air remained damp and dew was heavy on the grass, rocks, and boughs of the surrounding trees. Somehow he felt strong enough to keep going, though he had managed only a few hours of frozen, cramped sleep during all of the previous forty-eight hours.

And through it all the young nobleman remained strangely content, numb but in a pleasant, almost dreamlike state, as he followed the gray stranger up a grueling and dangerous climb.

They followed a steep, half-hidden path that Blayne hadn't even known about, leading away from the placid lake where he had caught the trout. They wended their way up a steep-sided gorge, finally moving through a pass so narrow that they needed to move in single file. Sheer walls of rock rose to the right and left of them, culminating in summits hundreds of feet over their heads. The pass twisted around like a winding corridor, shadowy and cool even though sunlight and blue sky were visible far overhead. In places the cliffs loomed so close that they overhung the path, looking as if they were ready to collapse on them at the merest whisper of sound or swirl of wind.

But when they finally emerged from the narrow slit of the pass, they arrived in a sheltered valley hitherto unsuspected even by the young nobleman who had grown up hunting and climbing in those mountains. The land before him was flatter and more verdant than any place he knew about in the whole of the Vingaard Range. Not only did he spy farms and mills and clusters of buildings that indicated the existence of several towns, but there were encampments across every bit of level ground, tents as far as the eye could see. A thousand cook fires glowed in the early-morning mist, and a whole army seemed to be living there, going about its morning meals and ablutions in such an utterly secret place.

"Who *are* you?" Blayne croaked, finally finding his voice.

He suddenly found that he again possessed his free will—and that the fatigue of his long flight had caught up with him. He staggered and allowed the stranger to offer him an arm in support.

"Just a bit farther and all your questions will be answered," said the man in the gray robe. "For now, it is enough to know that I am a friend to you—and an enemy to the emperor."

That was enough to keep him going. An hour later Blayne found himself seated in the parlor of a large house. A beautiful young woman with striking albino features had brought him a cup of hot tea, and he was sipping the liquid gratefully, sitting beside a roaring fire, gradually getting his bearings. The gray man had led him to the house then disappeared somewhere in the back of it. When he returned, when Blayne was nearly done with his tea, he was accompanied by a man in a black shirt and leggings.

"Thank you for bringing me here," said the young noble-man sincerely. He knew enough about the stranger to believe him when he said they shared the same enemy. "I presume you will tell me more, when you're ready."

The gray man smiled, a kindly expression full of sympathy and understanding. "I appreciate your patience. My name is Hoarst, and this is Captain Blackgaard. It is he who has established the little outpost, and this is his house."

"I've hunted these mountains all my life and never even knew there was a valley like this up here. I can't understand how it has gone undiscovered so long."

"I can tell you that this is a very magical place," said the captain. "Through the centuries many dragons have flown over-head, some carrying human riders. And yet, when they look down, they spot only glaciers and barren rock. It is an illusion of nature, one which I gratefully used to my advantage."

Blayne looked bluntly from one man to the other. "You are enemies of the emperor? Do you know that he has killed my father, bombarded my home? I will devote the rest of my life to vengeance. If you can use my services, I will gladly join your force."

Blackgaard chuckled. "My force is quite large enough, don't you think?" he said dismissively.

The young nobleman's heart sank, but he could only nod. "I could tell as we approached that you must have thousands of men. Well-trained, well-equipped men. A not inconsider-able army. But why do you have them here, locked up in the mountains?"

"Picture where we are, in your head. What do you see?" prodded Hoarst.

"You're in the high Vingaard Mountains . . . maybe twenty miles north of the High Clerist's Pass. Is that right?"

"More like fifteen miles," Blackgaard corrected. "Hard mountain miles, but there is a certain route that will take us there. I have men excavating a concealed road even as we speak, to allow us to cross the steepest parts of the trail."

"I see, you could strike at the emperor there, cut him off from the plains! But . . . can't you use my help? I know how to wield a sword, even to command a company. I led the attack that destroyed two of his terrible cannons!"

"I had heard of that attack," the captain said. "It was well done. But no, I do not need you to join the ranks of my army."

"I understand your dismay," Hoarst said as Blayne slumped back in his chair. "But don't despair. You can help us greatly—in another capacity, not as a swordsman in the Black Army."

"What do you want? Tell me, whatever it is, I'll do it!" blurted the young man.

"Have you heard of the Legion of Steel?" asked Blackgaard gently.

Blayne nodded. "An ancient sect of the Solamnic Knighthood, as I recall. They used to be active in the cities, helped to ensure that no one leader became too powerful . . . too enamored of his own . . ." His voice trailed off, and he nodded. "They were dedicated to preventing someone like the emperor from seizing too much authority and control!" he realized.

"You are correct in almost every respect," Hoarst said. "You only err in assuming that they are gone, a part of the past."

"Do you mean they still exist?"

"They exist, and they strive to limit the emperor's power in every way they can. They operate a cell in Palanthas that is desperate for fresh blood. Especially noble members, young men who have been trained in the ways of the Solamnic Code."

"People like me! They could certainly use my contacts in

the city. Yes—by all means! Let me find the legion, offer them my help. Together we can bring down Jaymes Markham. Send me to them, and I will tell them of your army, your position here in the mountains.

"I admire your passion," said Captain Blackgaard. "Now we must talk of your circumspection."

"Please, explain what you mean," urged Blayne, eager to do whatever he could to win the approval of the men.

"It is better for us all if the legion doesn't learn of our existence until the time is right. Indeed, no one in Palanthas must know. The emperor has too many ways of learning what's going on in his city, and even a whisper of suspicion could be enough to thwart our plans."

"I understand. Your secret is safe with me," pledged the Vingaard nobleman.

"Yes," said Hoarst quite confidently. "I'm sure it is."

"Tell me what you want me to do."

"You will go to Palanthas and make contact with the Legion of Steel. There is a man in the Westgate garrison, an archer named Billings, who can assist you. Tell him the truth—that you have evaded the emperor's minions in Vingaard and crossed the mountains on foot. That you would like to work with the legion to stop the man who destroyed your home."

"Without mentioning you or your operations here in the valley?" Blayne asked, and the other two nodded. "Yes, I can do that."

"That is no more than I expected you to say," Hoarst noted, obviously pleased. "Now you must rest and restore your strength. In another day or two, we will see you on your way."

⊱⊰⊱⊰⊱⊰◉⊱⊰⊱⊰⊱⊰

General Dayr worked on a message to the emperor, trying unsuccessfully to couch Dram Feldspar's refusal in gentler terms than the dwarf had used. In the end, however, it was a hopeless task, and with a sigh he simply wrote to Jaymes and matter-of-factly described the meeting in New Compound. He finished the letter, dusted it with sand to dry the ink, and was sealing the scroll when his son came up to his study in Thelgaard Keep.

"There's a courier just arrived from Palanthas," Franz reported. "He says he brings an important message from the emperor."

"I'll see him at once," said the general.

A short time later, he was unrolling a hefty pack of scrolls, five sheets all rolled together and placed in one tube. The courier had been dismissed to get a meal and some well-deserved rest—he had made the ride in less than ten days—and only the general's son was present as Dayr read the first scroll. He put it aside without comment, but his heart was sinking as Franz picked it up and started to read. Before he was halfway through the second scroll, Dayr heard Franz's snort of outrage.

"That's enough!" snapped the older man. "These are direct orders from the leader of the nation!"

"Orders to gag the mouths of his own people!" Franz snapped back. "Whoever heard of passing laws that prohibit talking! Maybe next he will ban eating? Or having babies?"

"I told you—that's enough," declared Dayr, standing and confronting his glaring son. The general had not progressed even halfway through the several scrolls, but he had seen enough to realize that Jaymes was presenting him with a whole new set of laws, legislation that would create criminal activity out of a number of simple things the people of Solamnia, of all

Krynn, had long taken for granted. How the people would react to those laws, he couldn't predict, but he was determined to bring his own son to heel before Franz said, or did, something that could be construed as treasonous.

"Are you really going to post these laws, Father?" demanded the captain. "As if what happened to Vingaard Keep wasn't enough—now he tries to control the conversations that go on in the marketplaces, in the *taverns?*"

"I don't know what I'm going to do about it!" Dayr retorted, drawing a look of surprise from his son. "But I will not tolerate treason in my own household. You will watch your tongue, or you will leave. Now!"

"Maybe you don't know what to do about it," Franz said, his tone contemptuous, "but my own decision is easy." He stalked to the door, pulled it open, and pivoted to glare at his father.

"Goodbye," he said, walking away.

✦❀✦❀✦❀✦❀✦❀✦

The Nightmaster had provided Ankhar with a detailed map, and with a little help from Laka, the half-giant had studied the map until he was pretty sure he understood what all the pictures, symbols, colors, and lines depicted. He thought of employing some of the flying draconians to get a more first-hand report, but in the end he decided not to risk allowing them to be seen.

Besides, the enemy layout was actually rather basic. The knights had established a series of picket forts along the borderlands with Lemish. They were garrisoned by only a company or two apiece and were meant to serve as tripwires to alert their comrades if anything untoward happened from the wilderness to the south. The map, and the dark priest's counsel, showed Ankhar that a very large force of Solamnic Knights, including cavalry, archers, and infantry numbering in the thousands, was posted in a permanent camp some ten miles north of the border. That force was expected to mobilize and come to the rescue of any of the garrison posts in the event of a cross-border incursion.

Based on that knowledge, and his long experience fighting the knights, Ankhar had formed a plan to surprise and confound them. He gathered his captains together at the edge of the Lemish forest and explained the plan to them. The big ogres were there, and Rib Chewer the warg rider was there, as well as the chief of the draconians, Guilder. The latter's slender, reptilian body seemed to spark and pulse with its own kind of internal lights, and as a consequence, even the biggest ogres gave him a wide berth.

The headstrong ogres, knowing that the enemy lay in camps just over the horizon, were all in favor of bursting from the woods, charging north at full speed, and overrunning any outpost of Solamnics that they encountered on the way. Bullhorn and Heart Eater both advocated that tactic, but the half-giant was grateful that the veteran Bloodgutter—his new general—persuaded his fellow ogres to at least listen to Ankhar's strategy.

"You see fort out there?" the half-giant demanded, silencing the others with a glare, barely holding his exasperation in check.

They were clustered behind a curtain of foliage, vines and creepers and swamp flowers that blocked them from view as they gazed out over the open ground to the north. Less than a mile away, they could spy the knights' outpost—a small, square compound protected by a wall of logs. Several men rode horses in a lazy patrol outside the wall, and a lofty tower, also erected out of logs, allowed a handful of lookouts to get a commanding view.

"Yes," growled Heart Eater sullenly. "My axers could rush out and destroy it before humans have time to turn around!"

"My clubs could smash it to pieces!" Bullhorn added. "Kill everyone!"

"I know that!" Ankhar retorted. "But there are ten forts like that. All along here, by Lemish woods. Not strong forts, but strong enough."

"If not strong, why we not kill them right away?" pressed Bullhorn.

"Because men in those forts *want* us to attack them. That's why they are there! Sure, we wipe out fort, but not before men in fort light signal fire, put up big smoke cloud. Horses ride away, tell everyone we attack."

"Smoke cloud not scare me!" declared Heart Eater.

"Smoke not to scare you—smoke is to call knights from big camp. They see smoke, they ride out and attack us."

"Then we kill them!" Bullhorn concluded. "After we smash fort."

"Listen! Just listen!" Ankhar drew a deep breath. He looked at Laka, and she raised her talisman, rattling the skull with the glowing emerald eyes, and that produced a general silence. "Lots and lots of knights are in big camp. Many soldiers sleep; they live there. They not watch for us because these forts are here. But tonight, there is no moon. We go—all of us go—between two forts, very quiet. We march all night, and come to big camp. We attack there, when the sun comes up, and kill many, many knights."

He exhaled, finally sensing that he had their attention. "Then we come back and smash all the forts," he concluded.

"All right. We try your plan," Heart Eater said, nodding

and scratching his bulging chin.

"And what about my flyers?" Guilder, the aurak, wondered gutturally.

"I have a plan for them: they fly over knights' camp and land on other side, where horses are. Scare all the horses, and the knights cannot ride."

Guilder nodded, hissing his approval. Bullhorn, too, agreed with the plan, and at last the scheme was set. The great column gathered at the edge of the woods, still concealed by the dense foliage. With some difficulty, the captains persuaded their troops to wait for the signal to move out.

"You two will wait here," Ankhar told Laka and Pond-Lily seriously. "I send for you when fight is over."

Pond-Lily nodded vacantly, staring at him with the limpid puddles of her small, deep-set eyes. Even Laka, to the half-giant's mild surprise, accepted her role of waiting, perhaps understanding that she was no longer capable of keeping up with a night-long march.

Darkness was complete a few hours later, and Ankhar led the great column, thousands of ogres marching on foot, between two of the border outposts, the forts with the towers and horsemen that could be seen from the woods and were spaced about every five miles along the line. Moving quietly, with many whispered admonitions to avoid making any noise, the band somehow escaped notice as it swept toward the great garrison camp, the place where the real defensive force awaited, all unaware.

Dawn turned the eastern sky blue as the ogres came into sight of the vast wall around the fortified camp. Made from sharpened birch stakes driven into the ground to form a palisade, the barrier would have been a formidable obstacle to goblins, hobgoblins, even some ogres. But Ankhar had taken note of the weaponry preferred by Heart Eater's warriors, and his plan was shrewd.

"You lead the way," he said to the strapping bull. "Use your axes and break down wall—make many holes. The rest of us come after you, charge through holes, and kill the knights."

Naturally, Bullhorn raised some objections—"Why Heart Eater go first?"—but was mollified by the argument that the axe-wielders had a special job in the attack. Guilder, concealed by a spell of invisibility, quickly ventured out for a look and was pleased to report the vast horse corrals on the north side of the camp were very lightly guarded.

"We can stampede the herd," he reported with confidence.

The ground was still shrouded in shadow, though the sky grew steadily lighter as the ogres spread out into a line more than a mile long. There was as yet no sign that they had been noticed when, at Ankhar's command, the monstrous warriors raised a great shout and charged forward en masse.

Almost immediately a trumpet brayed within the Solamnic camp. Ankhar loped along in the front rank, and from within the palisade he heard orders shouted, cries of panic and alarm, and the frantic neighing of horses. All the while his ogres pounded closer, the ground trembling under their massive, lumbering weight. A few arrows arced from behind the palisade, many falling harmlessly to the ground, a few puncturing the flesh of the hulking attackers.

But it took more than one lucky arrow hit to stop a massive ogre. The brutish warriors who were struck typically plucked the annoying missiles out of their hides and cast them away—the glancing wounds merely enhanced their fury, their determination to wreak terrible havoc. Tusks slick with drool gleamed in the eerie darkness. Eyes wild, throats hoarse, the horde swept closer.

Soon the picket wall loomed before them, and Heart Eater's axemen attacked with a vengeance, whipping their heavy, bladed weapons through roundhouse swings, right into the bases of the stout timbers. Several of the posts snapped free with the first blows, while others could withstand only two or three smashes before splintering.

Looking up, Ankhar's heart filled with pride as he saw the company of sivak draconians, some fifty strong, flying overhead, winging toward the great corrals.

The attackers pressed forward, and the logs of the palisade toppled inward on the knights and infantrymen who were scrambling to the defense. Some men were crushed outright, while the rest were forced to back out of the way, beating a hasty retreat before the barrier collapsed on top of them. Bloodthirsty howls rang out along the whole mile of the front as ogres spilled into the breached camp and lay about with axes, clubs, swords, and spears.

Ankhar's army hit the fort like a wave, a tide surging against a picket fence, finding gaps in the barrier, crashing and seeping through. Like water, the warriors spilled through the gaps, widening them, dragging down more and more of the birch poles as the trickle became a flow and the flow became a flood.

The half-giant yodeled a great battle cry, feeling a joy he had not known since his defeat in the foothills. This was the life! He thrust with his emerald-tipped spear, piercing a footman like a piece of meat on a spit. With the limp body still hanging from his mighty weapon, he smashed to the right and left, stabbing another swordsman, smashing the weapon—and arm bones—of a frantic archer. Blood ran down the shaft, slicking his hands, and he relished the moment.

Finally he gave the spear a contemptuous flip, tossing the

slain man from the end of his weapon, while he looked for his next victim. The ogres were roaring everywhere, smashing through the Solamnic camp. Their quickness belied their huge size as they rumbled through tents, kicking through cook fires and mess halls and canvas-sheltered armories where the knights' weapons had been neatly stacked.

Human warriors were still scrambling from their tents, strapping on breastplates, sometimes fighting without boots or helmets. Officers screamed and shouted, directing their troops this way and that in the face of howling, growling foes. Often the tents were cut down even before the men emerged, and the trapped humans flailed around under the smothering tarps while ogres gleefully danced across the heaving fabric, bashing it down any place where it moved.

One knot of men fought in a little circle, shields raised and swords brandished as the attackers swirled around them. Bullhorn led a charge, crushing the captain of the company with a powerful downward smash of his club. The circle breached, every man fought for his own life as dozens of ogres pierced the formation. Any place a human looked, there was a deadly enemy, and in a few moments, the last of those brave men had been battered into a slain, bloody pulp.

A trumpet brayed from the rear, and a column of horsemen bearing lances charged the ogre line. They were not many in number, but several of the brutish attackers went down, stabbed by the long spears rendered especially lethal by the driving power of the charging horses. Their armor was incomplete, but the knights wore breastplates and helmets, and their horses were saddled securely. Ankhar wasted no time wondering how they could have equipped themselves and counterattacked so quickly; instead, the half-giant bellowed furiously for a response from his followers.

Ogres rushing behind him, he raised the glowing spear and charged at the leading horseman, a knight with a gray mustache and long, silvery hair. The man lowered his lance and urged his warhorse forward, and the half-giant halted. Bracing his feet and crouching, Ankhar bashed the long weapon out of the way. But the horse surprised him, lowering a shoulder and knocking him backward.

The half-giant barely maintained his footing but recovered quickly, and the two combatants circled as the battle raged around them. Each held his long weapon with the deadly tip aimed at his opponent's chest. Pacing sideways, Ankhar looked for an opening, while the knight rested in his saddle as if he were a part of the horse. His shield firmly held over his chest, the knight peered over the top of the metal barrier, keenly studying the half-giant's maneuvers.

Ankhar lunged, and the steed skipped sideways. Then it reared suddenly, flailing with its great hooves. When the half-giant charged, the horse veered again and the rider jabbed quickly with the lance. Once again, Ankhar parried with the Shaft of Hiddukel.

With a sharp kick in his horse's flanks, the knight suddenly attacked. The massive horse bared teeth like some kind of nightmare steed and rushed at Ankhar, intent on trampling him. The half-giant crouched, aiming his spear at the horse's breast, but the man again used his lance to knock the great weapon, the Shaft of Hiddukel, out of the way. Ankhar tumbled into the dirt, rolling away from the charge, barely holding onto his precious spear.

Springing to his feet with a growl, he sprinted after the horse as the steed pivoted and reared, those massive forehooves lashing at the half-giant's face. He felt a glancing blow on his cheek and staggered back. Surprise gave way to rage, and he bored in, driving between the flailing hooves, sticking the spear right through the horse's muscular chest. The mount reared back with an earsplitting shriek, toppling onto its side, fatally wounded.

The knight tried to leap from the saddle as his horse went down, but his foot stuck in the stirrup. With a strangled curse, the man sprawled on the ground, his leg trapped under the thrashing, dying horse. Ankhar yanked on his mighty spear, but the Shaft of Hiddukel was stuck fast. Releasing the weapon, the half-giant hurled himself on the knight, bashing the lance out of the way, smashing a huge fist into the shield so hard that the man gasped and lay momentarily stunned. With one massive hand, Ankhar seized the stunned warrior by the neck and squeezed until he heard the snap of bone.

Pushing himself to his feet, the half-giant took hold of his weapon with both hands. He put a massive, booted foot on the dying horse's chest and pulled with all his vast strength. At last the weapon, the emerald head glowing all the brighter for its soaking in blood, burst free. Raising it over his head, Ankhar shook the weapon at the sky, howling like a maniac to celebrate his personal victory.

Before him he saw a knot of fighting around the gate at the northern end of the great camp. Some of the sivaks had landed there, where they were fighting furiously, holding the passageway against knights who were trying to reach the horses. Quickly the half-giant rallied a hundred ogres and charged toward the draconians. Beyond the corrals, he saw a deluge of sparks and flames, sputtering lightning, and dramatic pyrotechnics. Guilder Aurak was there, casting spectacular—if relatively harmless—spells. The effect on the horses was the important thing, as more than a thousand of the normally steady mounts panicked and stampeded away from the battle, away from the camp, and away from the knights who depended on them for mobility and survival.

When next he looked around, Ankhar saw that the last pockets of defense were being mopped up. Some ogres plundered the extensive food supplies piled behind the kitchen tents while others were hoisting grotesque trophies, including the severed heads of their enemies, and dancing about in triumph and glee.

"Enough!" roared the half-giant in a voice that rumbled even over the celebratory chaos. "We feast later. Remember those forts! Now is the time to go back . . . and to kill them all!"

With howls of anticipation, the ogres responded to his command. Ankhar himself would remain in the conquered camp—he made sure that a message was conveyed to Pond-Lily and Laka, inviting them to join him in his luxurious surroundings—while thousands of ogres spread across the plains, intent on wiping out the border outposts to the last man.

The half-giant chuckled, a sound of genuine happiness that had not erupted from his chest in several years. It was good to have an army again, good to march, to fight.

And it was good to kill Knights of Solamnia.

CHAPTER FOURTEEN

PALANTHAS AND HER PASS

L ord Regent Bakkard du Chagne watched the city of Palanthas from the serene height of his Golden Spire, the tallest tower on his palace. It was an ornate building, which he had ordered erected on the slopes of the mountains rising above the city and well outside the wall. It was nightfall, and the lights were twinkling throughout the great metropolis. Ships in harbor were draped with navigation lanterns, which winked in the placid waters of the bay. It was not hard for the lord regent to imagine he was looking down on a field of fireflies, insignificant creatures bustling around in the illusionary comfort of their own short-lived brightness.

He liked the feeling of superiority provided by his lofty vantage. From his palace, his tower, he had the sense he was looking down on the lesser beings of the world like a farmer might look down on the ants in his garden.

But there was a very potent ant in that garden.

Unlike the lord regent's edifice, high outside the city walls, the palace built by the emperor was situated right in the middle of Palanthas, facing one corner of the great plaza. Du Chagne could see the emperor's residence clearly from there, and—if the truth be told—he spent far too much of his time staring at that garish, ostentatious structure. He had worked hard to rein in the powers of the upstart ruler, but thus far he had been thwarted at every turn.

Du Chagne's wealth, the magnificent cache that had brightened his world and shed its enchanted light across his city from the top of this very tower, was sadly depleted. The hoard had been claimed by the emperor and spent on public works such as the horrendously expensive widening of the road over the High Clerist's Pass. The city was a seaport, by all the gods! A narrow, twisting road had served Palanthas throughout the centuries, providing all the land connection with the rest of the world that the city needed . . . or desired. Why was it necessary to widen and smooth that thoroughfare? Of course, increased trade had been the result, but the city's greatest tariffs would always be collected at the docks. Didn't Jaymes Markham understand that?

Even Bakkard du Chagne's own daughter, who had been the regent's most significant pawn in the power game of governance, had been co-opted by the usurping emperor. She represented great power to whoever claimed her and, for reasons du Chagne had never fully understood, she had given herself to Jaymes Markham.

Even in his aloof aerie, Bakkard du Chagne heard rumors and kept his finger on the pulse of the city and the empire's government. He had heard the gossip that his daughter might be pregnant and that she was no longer entirely happy with the choice she had made. There were still ways, perhaps, that the lord regent could put his powerful pawn back into play. He had already sent out a valuable agent, preparing a contingency, hoping to retrieve the Princess of the Plains.

There were other biting ants in the city as well. During his term as ruler of that place, the lord regent had been awarded the loyalty of the Solamnic Knights, as was his due as their lawful lord. But there always had been knights, a secret legion of them, who had resisted his will, had worked to hinder him at every turn. Those knights still existed, and though they were not the emperor's tools, they stood in the way of the lord regent's resurgence.

He had a plan for them as well.

He did not hear the newcomer enter this room—he felt more of a chill, like a metal gate closed across the door to a stove—but neither was he surprised to welcome that particular visitor. Du Chagne turned to notice the Nightmaster was standing quietly, well away from the windows, waiting to be noticed.

"Well?" asked the lord regent. "How do matters proceed? Are you nearly ready?"

"Yes," came the muffled voice from the behind the black gauze. "Yes, my great master—our minions are now prepared to strike."

<hr />

Blayne Kerrigan felt almost at home in the camp of the force known as the Black Army. His host, the gray wizard Hoarst, was unfailingly pleasant, courteous, even solicitous. Blayne had been given the freedom of the valley, joining Hoarst and Captain Blackgaard for meals, even sharing the charms of a slender elf maid who, he learned, was one of several beautiful females who inhabited the gray wizard's domicile.

Hoarst seemed not the least bit jealous, even encouraging the lass to go off alone with the young nobleman. From her, Blayne learned that it was only the albino woman, Sirene, who seemed to arouse any sense of possessiveness in the delightful, cultured magic-user. While his nights were busy enough, during the days Blayne was allowed to sleep late, and he was tutored for a few hours in the routes through the mountains. He observed the road that Blackgaard's men were constructing, and realized it would provide a route for the High Clerist's Tower to be assaulted from the north—an unprecedented flanking of those ancient walls.

Finally, Hoarst told Blayne that it was time for him to go on his important errand, and the young lord was all too willing to comply. He was provided with an old nag of a mare to ride, the horse that would take him down to Palanthas. The steed was by no means the best that he could have drawn from the well-equipped herds of the Black Army, but—as Hoarst had counseled—it was best for the young nobleman to enter the city in a nondescript fashion. He needed to look like a humble country squire coming to the city looking for work or apprenticeship.

The Gray Robe warned Blayne that the emperor had posted a reward for his capture. With a little bit of shaving and some hair dye, the knight had completely altered his appearance, darkening his skin and shortening his long black hair. He felt quite confident he would not be recognized, even if he should encounter someone who knew him in passing—a distinct possibility since he had lived in Palanthas for five years as an apprentice Knight of the Crown.

When he could see the spires of Palanthas rising before him, he guided his horse off the main road onto one of the farm tracks that curled along the ridges to the west of the city. From there he could see the Bay of Branchala winding off to the north and the lofty palace of the lord regent dominating the city from its foundation on a slope. Closer, against the city's defense, he saw his objective: the gate in the west wall of the Old City.

Heart pounding, Blayne followed the road down from the ridge and toward the city gate on the west side of the Old City wall. That was where the man named Billings was posted, and where Blayne was eagerly headed. It was all he could do to let the nag shamble on at her leisurely pace when what he really wanted was to spur toward the gates and get on with his mission. But Hoarst had impressed on him the need for disguise and discretion, and he was determined not to let down the man who had saved him in the wilderness and who shared his desire to bring down the emperor of Solamnia.

How difficult would it be to meet up and recruit the Legion of Steel? Blayne had wondered about that for most of the long ride down from the mountain heights. The organization had been around for a long time, always existing on the shadowy fringes of the knighthood. They were traditionally loyal to the Oath and the Measure but sometimes had proved a nuisance to the men who attempted to rule. Working outside the rigid hierarchy of the orders of Rose, Sword, and Crown, the Knights of Steel could venture certain strategies and employ unconventional tactics that would have scandalized the more hidebound members of the Solamnics.

And what did he ultimately expect from the Black Army and its captain? The force was capable and well trained, certainly, but how could it hope to stand against the four huge armies under the emperor's command? It counted some three thousand men—less than the number Blayne had standing with him at Vingaard. And the emperor had brushed those troops aside with only two of his four armies! But for now, Blayne was willing to place his trust in the two leaders in their mountain valley. Truthfully, the young lord was glad simply to have been given a role in their rebellion.

Attracting little attention, he and his old horse ambled through the open gate, joining a small trickle of farmers, merchants, and laborers who were entering or leaving the city past the indifferent supervision of a small company of guards. The men-at-arms were swordsmen, Blayne noticed, whereas he was seeking an archer. He dismounted and led the nag toward the public watering trough just inside the gate and looked around for the garrison's bowmen.

He spotted a stone blockhouse inside the wall. The top was flat and high enough to provide a view—and field of fire—over the wall. Several men were up there, and they were carrying bows and wore quivers bristling with arrows. Lashing his horse to a post, he walked over and spoke to the lone guard sitting outside the door.

"I'm looking for Archer Billings," he said. "Is he here?"

The guard looked him up and down for a second before sniffling noisily and running the back of his hand under his nose. He tilted his head toward the open door.

"Look in the back room," he said. "He's off duty right now."

Blayne walked into what was obviously a barracks, passing through a room with a number of unoccupied bunks. Passing through another door, he found a room with many tables and chairs, most likely the mess hall. A dozen men sat around in there, listlessly pursuing games of cards or knucklebones, sharpening arrowheads, or carving away on small scraps of wood or, in one case, the ash haft of a new bow.

"Is Archer Billings here?" he repeated.

"I'm Billings," said one man, unusual in that his black hair and swarthy complexion was much darker than all the other men in the company—but a plausible match for the disguise Blayne wore. It would be easy for someone to believe they might be countrymen. Billings had been sitting alone in one corner of the room, whittling what looked like a curling pipe out of a small piece of wood.

The bowman put his work in his pocket and squinted at Blayne. "You bring me a letter from the homestead?" he asked.

Blayne hoped his relief didn't show, but that was exactly what Hoarst had told him Billings would say. He went through the reply he had been rehearsing on the long ride to the city. "No letter, but I have news from some old friends."

The archer rose to his feet and stretched easily. He was a tall man, lanky and thin, and moved with catlike grace. "I'm off duty until sunrise. Let's go have a beer, and you can tell me all about it."

The other bowmen didn't so much as glance up at them as the two men left. Blayne collected his horse and followed the tall archer as Billings led him a few blocks down a city street. They reached the door to a nondescript tavern—the noble-man couldn't even read the faded sign over the door—and after Blayne had tethered his horse, they went inside. The front room was mostly empty, with just a few dockworkers drinking cheap ale at the bar. The archer simply nodded to the innkeeper and led his guest through a door and into an even darker room in the back.

"Welcome to Palanthas," Billings said, gesturing to a chair beside the lone table. Blayne took a seat with his companion, and the innkeeper bustled in with a foaming pitcher and a couple of glasses.

"Thanks, Wally," Billings said, pressing a coin into the man's hand. "We'll be all right for the time being."

"You got it, Hawkeye," said the innkeeper, bowing and retreating.

Blayne looked at his companion curiously.

"A nickname," Billings explained. "I'm a pretty good shot with my longbow," he added, filling their glasses from the pitcher. When he was done, he set the beer down and looked at Blayne long and hard.

"Now," he said. "Tell me what's up."

⊱⊶⊷⊶⊷⊰⊰❀⊱⊶⊷⊶⊷⊰

Selinda looked out the window of her room, watching the city as nightfall drew its curtain across Palanthas. Candles sparkled from countless windows. Lamplighters were busy igniting the wicks in the oil-fueled beacons that brightened all of the major intersections. Vendors and merchants wheeled their carts back home as the markets closed, while other sellers of different goods moved into the alleys, whispering invitations for darker and more secret commerce. People mingled, talking and laughing. They thronged on the main avenues, but even on the side streets there were many small parties finding their fun through the night.

What was the point of it all? Of any of it?

Her hands moved almost unconsciously to her belly. She could begin to make out the subtle roundness there, though the pregnancy still did not show through the contours of her clothing. It was still hard to believe she was carrying a human life within her—and harder to believe that that life had been kindled by the emperor, Jaymes Markham.

"What kind of child will you be?" she whispered to herself.

And what kind of world would that child grow up in? That was a question she didn't give voice to at all.

Feeling the weight of approaching darkness, the princess sighed and turned away. But the shadowy confines of her room were no consolation. Even when she lit a lamp and a half dozen candles, she couldn't banish her uneasiness, her despair. Her door was closed and there was no longer a guard posted there to block her exit; her husband had abandoned that tactic, tacitly acknowledging the freedom she had been granted by the magical ring.

Yet she had not used the device since that terrible trip to Vingaard, when she had recognized the hard and violent truth of the emperor's reign. Since then she had remained in her room for most of each day, though she went to other parts of the palace when she knew her husband was not present. That night, he was working in his office several floors below her quarters, and since she would not take the chance of encountering him in the hallways, she would not leave her room.

But the restlessness was growing intolerable, and she was thinking about the ring of teleportation, of the freedom it gave her—should she only choose to exercise its magic. And in that instant, impulsively, she decided to go.

Her destination wasn't terribly important; it was simply that she wanted to be out of there, to go to a place of her own choosing. She took a few moments to don sturdy walking boots and a practical gown and cloak of quality that would mark her merely as someone of reasonable means, not suggest any tie to nobility or, more significantly, to the emperor's household. When she had made her preparations, she went to the window again, pictured the place she longed to be, and twisted the magic ring on her finger.

The sensation was familiar by now, no longer dizzying or disorienting. She materialized on the street before the great Temple of Kiri-Jolith, the same building where she had gone to see the high priestess Melissa du Juliette. She hesitated, listening to the familiar, comforting chants of the vesperspeak. But she did not go inside the temple.

Instead, she turned and walked along the wide avenue, enjoying her freedom. She ambled along the wide street, smiled at a pair of soldiers who offered her greetings, and smelled the salty breeze coming from the great waterfront.

The maritime air seemed to call to her, and she turned along a cross street, heading north. It was not a wide roadway, but there were people about, and the sounds of flutes and lyres emerged from an inn at the corner. It was called the Goose and Gander, she noted from a brightly painted sign. Raucous laughter erupted from the inn, followed by a spontaneous song, and she envied the carefree people enjoying the simple pleasures of night life.

But she wasn't tempted to enter the inn, because the lure of the docks drew her along. So she passed the noisy inn and moved along the narrowing street. It was a part of the city that was unfamiliar to her, and she felt a tingle at the thought she was exploring new territory. Not terribly far away was the haunted wasteland of the Shoikan Grove, which gave her a thrill even as she turned a corner to give a wide berth to the ancient place of dark magic.

She noticed that there were fewer people about there, but there were still lively outposts. She passed one called the Boar's Head and another very large establishment called the Fist and Glove. Each was the site of raucous revelry; in the latter she clearly heard the sounds of voice raised in drunken anger, followed by the crash of crockery then furniture. Quickly she hurried on, feeling just a little vulnerable as she noticed that the street before her grew dark and empty.

There were fewer inns and taverns there, and they tended to be darker, smaller, and seedier than those in the temple neighborhood. Even so, most had sounds of boisterous and good cheer as she passed. She heard laughter from one, loud and dissonant lyre music in another. From a third came the sound of a female's scream—not screams of fear so much as playful and flirtatious, she decided quickly. Yet the screams, too, caused her to hurry along.

Selinda was startled by a movement in the shadows as she neared the last street before the docks. Pulling back with a gasp, she saw a short man leaning out of a dark doorway, gesturing to her. A strange, sweet smell lingered in the air, and she heard bizarre music, softer and more lyrical than the jigs and ballads that were the usual fare.

"This way, mistress, to some of the finest delights Krynn has to offer. Please, not even a small fee for such a beautiful lady. Come in, and you will be amazed."

"What kind of delights?" she asked, intrigued in spite of her misgivings.

"Great wonders from the East, mistress. Spices, drinks . . . even herbs for smoking. This is the only place in Palanthas to find them."

She hesitated, undecided. A pair of young women came along, giggling, and they gave her amused glances before they turned and passed the short man into his dark entry. He winked at them, and they laughed easily.

Why not? Selinda asked herself, and there was no good answer. She had come out to experience the life that was banished from her royal palace, and why shouldn't she do just that?

"All right," she said with more confidence than she felt.

"Right this way," said the man, who walked with a pronounced limp. He turned back into the doorway, and she followed him into the shadows.

⋈⊷⊶⊷⊶⊷⊛⊶⊷⊶⊷⊶⋈

Jaymes put down the letter from General Dayr. His head hurt—that had been happening a lot lately—and he suddenly felt very tired. Leaving the parchment on his desk, he rose and went to the window, looking out over the city of Palanthas. It was night, but there was light everywhere, from the streetlamps, the windows of homes and inns, even silver moonlight reflecting on the bay.

But he didn't see any of it.

It seemed even Dram had betrayed him. The dwarf refused—he outright *refused*—to build the bombards that Jaymes required. "The emperor can build them himself" had been the phrase in General Dayr's letter, and Jaymes could almost hear the gruff old campaigner issuing the challenge in his gravelly voice.

But *why?* What could possibly have happened to cause the dwarf to turn against him like that, acting just like . . . like the foolish rulers of Vingaard! The person he trusted the most in the world, the one he knew he could count on in every extreme, the dwarf who had become very, very rich because of his service to Jaymes Markham—his old friend Dram had refused his duty to the emperor.

Had the treachery been perpetrated by anyone else, Jaymes would have been consumed by terrible rage, obsessed with the need for quick, severe retribution. Why, when it was Dram who betrayed him, did he feel only a consuming weariness, a darkness that even the sparkling illumination of his beautiful city could not dispel. He felt a tightening in his throat he didn't recognize, so long had it been since he had given way to any such effeminate emotions.

As he had been doing more and more, he admitted to himself that he missed—really *missed*—Selinda. Her appeal for him had been born in her beauty, and in the unattainability of her position as the daughter of the Lord Regent of Palanthas. Later he had been drawn to the power she represented, which he knew would augment his own power, and the nearly inexhaustible funds that would become his to share by right of empire and marriage.

Yet in the too few years of their marriage, he had come to appreciate her for her intelligence, her wit, and her wisdom even more than for those surface traits that had first drawn his attention and his interest. Her fierce independence, he remembered wryly, had also been attractive once: she had confronted him alone, in a ruined basement, all the while suspecting that he was a desperate assassin. And she had fooled him with her girlish enthusiasm, leading him into a trap so her father's knights could capture him with ease.

How ironic, then, that those knights served him now, but the woman who had lured him into chains was lost to him . . . lost at least as a partner, as a helper, as an ally. She would bear his child, true, and that meant something. But he was enough of a realist to know there would be no more children, that he would never again take her to bed. Even that, which he desired, was beside the point in his moment of darkness. He simply wanted to *talk* to her.

Making up his mind, he left the office and quickly climbed the two flights of stairs to the floor where she lived in her suite of rooms. Surprisingly, he found himself taking the steps two at a time and forcing himself to slow to a natural walking pace as he approached her chambers. Stopping outside her door, he breathed deeply a few times before knocking. There came no answer. He hesitated a moment then knocked again, listening carefully.

The silence beyond the door was complete, utterly undisturbed. He tried the knob and found it locked. His hand tightened on the latch, knuckles whitening, and for a moment he was possessed by an almost irresistible urge to smash the barrier down, to splinter it into a hundred pieces.

But immediately that urge passed. He released the door-knob almost gently, turned, and walked back to the stairs. He descended them slowly, deliberately, going back into his office, seeing the letter on his desk. Contemptuously he swept the parchment onto the floor and stepped onto it with the heel of his boot. Forcing thoughts of his wife into a corner of his mind, he thought back to Dram.

So the dwarf, too, would dare defy and betray him? Well, there was only one way to treat such a betrayal. He sat down at the desk again, thinking furiously. The Palanthian Legion was still in camp at Vingaard. The emperor could ride there with the Freemen and put that fast, mobile force on the march. He could cross the plains and reach New Compound with five thousand men within another week. If he needed to, he could draw reinforcements from the Crown Army for as he marched, he would pass Thelgaard Keep.

He knew Dram had not fortified his mountain town. Would he do so since he had thumbed his nose at Jaymes? It didn't matter: once the emperor and his troops got there . . .

Once he got there . . . what?

Jaymes leaned back in his chair, pressing a hand to his eyes. The missive from General Dayr, the letter that respectfully reported the dwarf's refusal to work on any more bombards, lay on the floor, a dark heel print smudged onto the back.

And the thought kept hissing like a snake in his ear: Where was Selinda? Where was his *wife?*

Too many questions and, for the moment, too few answers.

Jaymes rose and paced around the spacious room. It was his usual way of thinking and planning, but just then it seemed aimless, leading him nowhere, offering nothing in the way of insight or decision. He was almost relieved to be interrupted by a knock on the door.

"Come!" he snapped.

It was General Weaver, and one look at the ashen face of the veteran Knight of the Rose drove all other concerns from the emperor's mind. "What is it?" Jaymes demanded.

"My lord, grave news," replied Weaver, coming into the room. By all the gods, was the man trembling?

"What?" repeated Jaymes.

"Word from the Lemish frontier. The message was sent magically from our Kingfishers in Solanthus. It . . . it seems that Ankhar has attacked again. He's come from the forest with a new horde—thousands upon thousands of ogres. They wiped out our border defenses in a single attack. Now he's on the march into the plains."

⊱⊶⊷⊶⊷⊶❁⊶⊷⊶⊷⊰

"Come with me, my dear," Hoarst said to Sirene. With a sly glance at the other women, all of them seated around the breakfast table, the albino rose and followed her wizard out of the kitchen.

"Yes, my lord," she whispered at the door, allowing her long fingers to trail down the back of his smooth cloak.

"Alas, I need you for serious work," he said, giving her a playful squeeze as he opened the door to his small laboratory. Barely more than a poorly furnished closet—a very poor cousin to the vast installation Hoarst had created in the great hall of his own castle—the gray wizard used the place as his workshop while he remained there with the Black Army.

"I need to make a potion," he explained. Dutifully she held out one of those slender fingers as he picked up a sharp lancet.

204

His hands caressed hers, and he smiled kindly as he shifted a small glass vial on the table. He pricked her finger lightly, and she smiled at the gentleness of his ministrations even as several drops of crimson blood dripped from her finger into the vial.

"That is all," he said, releasing her. "You go rest, now. I'll have the other girls bring you some broth or tea."

He was already busy as she departed, crushing herbs with a mortar and pestle and magically igniting the burner on a small stove. Within half an hour, he had a small vial of potion, chilled from boiling to moderate temperature by the quick murmur of a cooling cantrip. With the vial in his hand, he went to find Captain Blackgaard.

With the potion tucked into a pocket of his robe, Hoarst mounted a spirited gelding beside the Black Army commander on his stallion. The two men cantered across the valley and up the road that was being chiseled through the jagged crest of the mountain ridge. At the top they halted, and Hoarst handed the vial to the captain.

With a mock toast, Blackgaard gulped down the contents. Immediately he released the reins of his horse, kicked his feet out of the stirrup, and rose from the saddle, gliding aloft.

"It works—I can fly!" he declared.

"Good," Hoarst replied. He spoke a spell that bestowed the same power on himself, and together the two men soared upward, passing the sheer cliffs, rising effortlessly to the very crest of the long, tall ridge. They crossed another valley—a gorge, really—where the Black Army engineers were building a slender bridge high above a raging torrent. Blackgaard pronounced himself pleased with the progress of the span, the last link in his road.

Finally Blackgaard and Hoarst the Gray stood on top of a

pinnacle of rock, high above the road and the pass, higher up even than the summit of the High Clerist's Tower. They looked down upon the narrow passage, the only connection between the city of Palanthas and the whole vast lands of Solamnia across the plains.

A column of knights was riding along that road, moving quickly through the pass without pausing at the great fortress. The garrison troops of the tower had turned out to watch the column pass, and even without benefit of magic, Hoarst was able to identify the tall rider at the head of the column. The white banner of his personal guard, the Freemen, trailed over the group as they picked up their pace, starting down the long, winding track to the plains.

"The emperor rides to deal with the threat that he knows," the Gray Robe said in satisfaction. "He attacks the army that he sees as a threat to his new nation."

"Do you think Ankhar will be able to withstand the knights if the emperor marshals his armies?"

Hoarst shrugged. "It is not important. The significant detail is that all of his military strength is on the east side of the Vingaard Mountains now. This pass, below us, controls all access to and from the city."

Blackgaard nodded. "And my army is only a day's march away from here. We can catch up with them down the road as soon as that bridge is finished."

"The fortress is still a challenging target," Hoarst noted. "But I believe my magic will be able to help you gain the top of the outer wall."

"Good—that's all I need. If I can obtain the wall, the fortress will fall. And when I take the fortress—"

"And when you control the fortress, you'll control the road to Palanthas," Hoarst concluded.

The captain nodded in agreement. He drew a deep breath, as though he couldn't quite grasp the enormity of their opportunity. But he had seen the maps, the dispositions, and he saw the future.

"Then inevitably the great city must fall."

CHAPTER FIFTEEN

A WHOLE NEW WAR

It was only natural that, after the great victory on the border, the ogres of Lemish would want to celebrate for a few days. After all, they had destroyed a great army camp and a dozen frontier outposts with very few losses among their own forces and almost total annihilation of the enemy troops. Indeed, if any of the knightly forces had escaped, they had done so without attracting the ogres' notice. The victorious army gathered at the site of their original triumph. In a nod to hygiene, Ankhar the Truth ordered the troops to haul the bodies of the slain knights more than a mile away onto the plains, downwind of their encampment.

After that task was completed, Ankhar turned them loose. He had learned quite a bit about managing an army during his first campaign against the knighthood. As a result, he let the ogres and their lesser allies gorge themselves on captured food rations and drink themselves silly on the many expropriated casks of rum, dwarf spirits, and ales. He participated in the guzzling, the wild dances, and the general feasting. He was grateful that he had brought Pond-Lily from Lemish so she could share his triumph, admire his prowess, and warm his bed at night.

But after two days of merrymaking he remembered he had more important matters to concern him. As the conquerors began to exhaust the captured stocks of liquor, the half-giant ordered his troops to assemble on the morning of the third day. Those captains who were slow to rise—which included all of them except Bloodgutter—were roused with heavy kicks of the half-giant's own hobnailed boots. Those captains, in turn, were hastily scattered to administer the same persuasion to their men. Sounds of groaning and thumping, retching and grousing, echoed through the messy camp.

Within a few short hours, the whole force had been roused and prodded into some semblance of an assembly—that is, they all stood in a great circle, while Ankhar mounted a flat-topped boulder in the center. Already the tallest warrior in his army, he strutted and puffed atop the rock, relishing his power and glory.

"You ogres! You gobs and hobs! You are part of a great army!" he bellowed, his voice roaring across the plains. Even so, the army was too large for those in the back to hear, so Ankhar paused to allow his captains to repeat his words, relaying the message to all.

"We killed many knights and footmen here on the border. But this is just the beginning!" His words were met with great shouts of approval, and he bared his tusks in a grin, letting the admiration of his army wash over him like a warm wind.

"Today we march! We take war to the knights wherever we find them! We kill, and we take booty. We will be rich, my warriors!"

Again his words provoked cheers. Ankhar raised the Shaft of Hiddukel over his head, and the green light emanating from the massive wedge of emerald seemed to cast all the plains in that same hue.

"I am Ankhar! I am the Truth! The Prince of Lies is my only master! And you, my warriors, are the Swords of Truth!"

The half-giant turned slowly through a complete circle, brandishing his mighty weapon, showing the glowing spearhead to all his troops. They cheered and shouted and bellowed as he grinned broadly.

"Now! Today! We march!" he shouted finally, gesturing to the west with the shaft. Immediately the ogres surged in that direction, hobs and gobs scattering to get out of the way of their massive comrades.

There was no strict formation to the march, though the veteran wargmaster Rib Chewer managed to gather his thousand wolves and their goblin riders together at the fore of the army. The fleet, savage mounts loped ahead of the mass, scouting for enemy resistance, making sure no devious ambush lurked hidden in a ravine, along a riverbank, or was masked by the tall grass.

Guilder the aurak probed into the future with his spells and peered into distances ahead of even the fast-riding warg riders. The sivaks flew overhead, returning to report there were no knights, no companies of human warriors, anywhere in their path.

"On all the plains," crowed Laka to her son, proudly. "There is none who dares to stand against you!"

The old shaman held her rattle high then, with startling abruptness, swept up into the air. She cackled gleefully, clutching the wooden handle, allowing the brightly glowing talisman to bear her back and forth in the skies over the army. She was flying!

"Come down here this instant!" Ankhar barked.

She only laughed, flying higher. "See the power of Hiddukel!" Laka shouted. "Behold the might of the Prince of Lies! He bears his humble servant in his mighty fist!"

She swept higher, so all the warriors could see her and be impressed. They all gaped in awe as she finally swooped down to land breathlessly before the astonished figure of her stepson, Ankhar the Truth.

"How did you do that?' he demanded.

"I watched the dracos. I prayed to my Prince. And he bade me fly!" she replied, gloating.

There was a new swagger about her as she strutted up to the company of sivak draconians and their captain, Guilder. They greeted her warmly, as one who had demonstrated a power they thought only they themselves possessed, and Ankhar was amazed.

But it was time to resume the march. Heart Eater, Bullhorn, and Bloodgutter pushed through the mass of ogres, coming to march close beside the army commander. They thundered along, each captain burly and powerful, master of a whole tribe of ogres. They stood only shoulder height beside Ankhar, though each of the trio seemed to bask in their master's glow, puffing up in his shadow. They competed with each other over who would stand closest to Ankhar, elbowing and jostling, snarling and snapping their jaws.

Even so, none of them barked so much as a protest when the withered old hob-wench pushed between them next to her stepson. The bull ogres meekly deferred to Laka. As always, she clutched her death's-head rattle, and she regarded the half-giant seriously as she fell into step beside him.

"This way is Solanthus," she declared, pointing in the general direction of the front. "You go to make war on that city again?" The tone of warning in her voice was unmistakable.

And the warning was well warranted, Ankhar knew. After the initial victories of his first war, the entire campaign had come down to a long, tedious siege of that city at the northern terminus of the Garnet Mountains. For more than a year, he and his troops had surrounded the place, camping within view of the walls. One attack had even breached the walls, and for a few glorious hours, the attackers had charged into the city, running amok, burning, looting, and killing.

But in the end, Ankhar's army had been repulsed and the lord of the knighthood had brought his own troops to the relief of the city. Ankhar had withdrawn to another battlefield, where, a few weeks later, his army had been broken, his dreams shattered. His mother was clearly worried he intended to repeat that pattern.

The half-giant chuckled, pleased at his own cleverness, before he replied. "No," he said. "We don't go there. But I want the knights to *think* we will attack Solanthus!"

"Ah, clever, my son. Where do we really go, then?"

"That," he said, his chuckle growing into a hearty guffaw, "is a surprise!"

><೦೦-೦೦-೦೦೦೦-೦೦-೦೦-೦೦><

Waiting frustrated men of action, and the gray wizard Hoarst and Captain Blackgaard, their preparations completed, chafed and stewed in the secret valley north of the High Clerist's Pass. The Black Army, some three thousand well-trained and well-disciplined troops, equipped with the best weapons and armor steel could buy—and magic could conjure—also detested the delay. They had been drilled to the point of exhaustion, and the captain wisely released them from training for a few days, and still they waited.

They would not risk everything by a premature attack,

and so they bided their time until they received the message they awaited.

That message inevitably came at night, borne by a black-cloaked, whispering figure who arrived with suddenness at headquarters. The Nightmaster was not unexpected, but even so, his teleported arrival caused a cook to drop a tureen of soup and sent a half dozen guards lunging for their weapons.

"Hold, men!" Blackgaard ordered as his own heart skipped a beat. He glared at the cleric, who had materialized without warning in the anteroom of the captain's manor, just as he and his staff were sitting down to a late dinner. A sharp reproach rose to his tongue, but a moment's thought—not to mention the cool, unreadable expanse of black gauze covering the high priest's face—caused him to draw a slow breath instead of complaining aloud.

"Greetings, priest," he said. "You're just in time to join us for dinner."

"I have no need of such sustenance," the Nightmaster replied with a dismissive wave of his hand. "I need to speak with you. I come with news."

"The wizard will be here shortly—ah, here he is now. Hoarst, come in," Blackgaard said as the Gray Robe entered through the front door. His white-skinned woman, the concubine he called Sirene, glided silently at his side.

A kitchen orderly mopped up the spilled soup, while the dozen or so officers at the table waited expectantly for whatever would happen next. "You men, go ahead and eat," Blackgaard said, glancing at them. He nodded at the Nightmaster and the Thorn Knight. "We can talk in my office."

"Wait for me here," said Hoarst, disengaging Sirene from his arm. She went over to the dining table, where the officers quickly shifted to give her plenty of space on one of the benches. Her eyes never left the tall, gray-haired figure of her wizard as the three men departed through another door.

"What news from the city?" asked Blackgaard as soon as the door closed behind them.

"Events progress as we planned. The Legion of Steel seethes against the emperor's new laws and stands ready to rise against him. All that is required is the provocation, the catalyst—and the archer tells me that he has already arrived in the city."

"Good," Hoarst said, nodding. "His rage burns within, unabated. It is a spark that shall serve as splendid kindling."

"We watched the emperor and his Freemen ride through the pass several days ago," Blackgaard said. "I have no word directly, but I think he must be out on the plains by now."

The Nightmaster nodded. "My auguries have shown him to me. He gathers his troops on the plains and moves toward Solanthus."

"And the half-giant?" asked Hoarst, raising an eyebrow.

The masked priest chuckled dryly. "He has erupted from Lemish with all the thunder and storm we could wish. The whole of Solamnia—at least, Solamnia east of the mountains—is in an uproar. All their attention, all their fear, is fixed upon our erstwhile ally."

"Good!" declared Hoarst. "It seems the great oaf still has value to us."

"But my men die of boredom here," Blackgaard noted. "They must have action soon, or they will lose their edge. Discipline is good for the time being, but idleness is the enemy of discipline. My soldiers will need every advantage when they attack. Even coming by surprise, and outnumbering the tower garrison by ten to one, it will not be easy to breach those ancient walls."

"Soon," counseled the Nightmaster. The masked face turned to Hoarst. "You have one more task to perform, do you not?"

Hoarst nodded as Blackgaard glanced at the Gray Robe. "What's that?" Blackgaard asked, startled.

"I must return to my fortress to work," said the wizard. "It will take me three or four days, but when I return, those ancient walls will no longer be much of an obstacle."

~~~~~~~~~~~~~~~~~~

Jaymes had reined in his horse, stopping to look up as he rode past the Stonebridge that crossed Apple Creek at the bank of the Vingaard River. He saw that the wall around Vingaard Keep was almost completely repaired. The scarred stubs of the fallen towers, on the other hand, were still there, proof of the violence that had transpired.

For a moment the emperor wondered about Marrinys Kerrigan, how she was faring with the rebuilding. For some odd reason, he wondered if she would ever forgive him for the devastation he had wrought. With a grimace of irritation, he dismissed the thought: such concerns were a weakness he could not afford. In another few moments, he had turned south along the Vingaard road, and the damaged fortress was relegated to memory.

Often during the long days of riding, he thought of his wife. It was only a week ago that he had received the sudden news of Ankhar's invasion and departed Palanthas before dawn. Yet he couldn't forget that before leaving, Jaymes had called on Selinda in her chambers and learned she had not yet returned from wherever it was she had gone on the previous night. Worry, fear, and anger vied within him whenever he thought of his wife. He wasn't accustomed to a problem that was out of his control. He couldn't stop thinking about her, about home and impending fatherhood.

At last, following the great river as it swept into the plains, Jaymes and his Freemen drew near to the camp of his most steadfast troops.

The Palanthian Legion had received orders by courier, and the men were mustering for the new campaign. Even before Jaymes and his Freemen rode down from the High Clerist's Pass, the five thousand troops had broken down their permanent camp, organized their weapons, horses, and equipment, and made ready to march.

"Secure those tarps!" Jaymes barked, passing a wagon where the waterproof cover had begun to slip. "Pick up the pace," he shouted to the captain of a company of lancers. "We need to move—I want thirty miles behind us by nightfall!"

With Sergeant Ian at his side, Jaymes rode at a canter at the front of the vast column of his legion. The troops, who had lived in their camp beside the Vingaard for more than a month, started southward. With many a marching song rising from their ranks, they trekked all day, starting an hour before dawn and not making camp until an hour after sunset. At that pace, it was only three days before they arrived at the great Middle Ford, where the wide river flowed across a smooth, hard bed. Given the dry weather of the past season, the water was no more than three feet deep in midstream, and the troops didn't hesitate to march right through.

General Dayr, with six thousand men of the Crown Army, awaited the emperor on the east bank of the river. Jaymes and Dayr rode their horses off to the side and watched as the huge, ox-drawn wagon supporting his single bombard rumbled up and out of the river. The stolid creatures pulled the wagon easily over the bank, and it trundled off toward Solanthus. A hundred other wagons, none of them quite as large, trailed after, while the file of the legion's column snaked into the distance to the front and the rear.

"What's the latest word from the border country?" Jaymes asked, removing his helmet to mop at the clammy sweat on his head.

"My son is scouting the invaders," Dayr reported. "After overrunning the frontier outposts, Ankhar spent a few days camped on the ruins. But now he's on the march and seems to be heading for Solanthus. He travels in strength and is moving quickly."

"He always was a fast marcher," Jaymes replied, nodding. "That as much as anything was how he was able to out-maneuver the dukes."

"Well, he won't steal a march on us," Dayr replied. "The Sword Army is fully mustered, gathered in and around Solanthus. Add them to your legion and my Crowns, and we should be able to field a force greater than the half-giant's by a few thousand men."

"Cavalry?"

"He's got those same warg riders. Franz tells me they're doing a pretty effective job of screening the main force. My son is on the trail, but the wolves keep him from getting close enough to get a real look at the horde."

Jaymes nodded. "The old brute has learned a thing or two about making war, it seems. Well, we'll have to assume he's moving on Solanthus. But be prepared for any tricks. I would be surprised if he laid siege to the city again—it didn't work out so well for him last time. But I can't figure out what else he could be doing."

"Yes. I've been wondering about his movements." Dayr removed his helm and scratched his head. "We defeated him pretty certainly last time. Why would he attack Solanthus again?"

"Arrogance? Vengeance? No, I've been asking myself the same questions," the emperor admitted. "He does not strike me as one who has a death wish."

"No, certainly not. He's a wily old brute and, above all, a survivor."

Jaymes nodded in agreement. "We'd better be ready for a surprise. Remember the old maxim: don't try to imagine what your enemy *will* do; instead, think about what he is *capable* of doing."

"He could come around north of the city," Dayr acknowledged. "General Rankin is deploying his cavalry up there. They wouldn't be strong enough to stop him, but at least we'd get a warning if he shifted that way. And the Garnet Range stands in his path if Ankhar tries to go south of the city. I don't think he would try to take his whole army through there."

The emperor stared in that direction. The Garnet Mountains were not visible from that distance, but he knew those heights were just over the horizon. "Maybe. Maybe not," he allowed. "Those mountains were once his home, after all. And he's used them as a hiding place before."

Suddenly he thought again of his old companion, the dwarf who had refused his direct orders to manufacture additional bombards—and who lived in a valley high up in those very mountains.

What was Dram doing?

⊱✦⊰

"Where is that damned steel?" Dram demanded of no one in particular. He stood at the top of the watchtower his dwarves had just completed, a sturdy stone structure dominating the

218

road that led into New Compound from the heart of the Garnet Range. The tower, of necessity, had been hastily constructed, but dwarven skill insured the stones were tightly meshed.

Dram had learned of Ankhar's resurgence barely a fortnight earlier, when three bedraggled survivors of one of the border outposts had staggered into New Compound. Exhausted, battered, and half-starved, the three men had made their way through the mountains, barely avoiding the patrols of wolf-riding goblins that seemed to be everywhere. After reporting their news and getting some solid food and a hot bath, their leader—a grizzled sergeant who had seen fifty years—had voiced the opinion that a major war was under way.

The mountain dwarf had reacted with decisiveness. He had immediately sent to Kayolin an order for all the spring steel that could be scrounged up. His legion of dwarf workers, more than a thousand strong, had been pulled off mundane duties and assigned to quickly create defensive obstacles around the town. The watchtower was one such installation. Others included a fortified wall at each of the two passes leading into the valley, as well as a walled compound in the center of the town. The splendid bridge with its three arches had been mined with casks of powder, so it could be destroyed with only a few moments' warning. Dram had supervised every aspect of the defenses—issuing orders, coordinating workers and tasks, and allocating personnel and materials.

Only one member of the community had proved resistant to the mountain dwarf's instructions.

"You've got to leave now!" he had barked to Sally, barely an hour after absorbing the news of the invasion. "Take Mikey and get back across the plains to the Vingaard range. I'll call you back here when the danger has passed."

"I will do no such thing!" she retorted predictably.

"But—the baby—"

"The baby belongs with his mum and pap," Sally shot back. Her voice softened and she touched Dram on the shoulder, a gesture that never failed to soothe his deepest agitation. But he shook her off.

"Look. You heard the man. That damned half-giant has thousands of ogres, and he's just fifty or sixty miles away from here."

"He's on the other side of the mountains," Sally replied calmly. "And I think Jaymes and his knights will have something to say about it if he tries to march around Solanthus."

Jaymes! Dram felt a twinge of guilt. No doubt his old friend had received word about the dwarf's refusal to build him additional bombards. Of course, that refusal had been overtaken by events—Dram would gladly build more cannons as fast as he could—but he found himself thinking he had betrayed his greatest friend.

Just as he couldn't do anything about getting Sally to leave, there was nothing to do about that at the moment. Like every other dwarf in New Compound, she had thrown herself into the defensive preparations, supervising teams of leatherworkers who were busily turning out stiff, arrow-resistant tunics for the defenders of the town. She, like Dram, hoped battles would be fought elsewhere, that their peaceful valley was in no danger. But they would be prepared.

Dram stiffened abruptly, spotting a small caravan of mule-hauled carts coming into view down the mountain road. Rogard Smashfinger had come through! Each of the carts was loaded with the steel bands he needed to make the new bombards. He counted a dozen of the little wagons and guessed that there would be enough of the strong metal to make an equal number of the big guns. He glanced back to the lakeshore, where the ironwood planks were already assembled and a score of massive wagons had been prepared.

Now he had the last of his necessary ingredients. But would he have enough time to do the work?

There was no way to know.

CHAPTER SIXTEEN

MOUNTAIN DARKNESS

B layne Kerrigan moved quietly down the darkened street, counting the doorways on his right. Archer Billings had given him very specific instructions, warning him there was no sign, no outward indication, of the secret meeting hall. Finally he came to the thirteenth door, the one he had been told to find. He hesitated and for a fleeting moment felt like turning and running away.

A glance over his shoulder failed to spot anyone on the street, though the young noblemen had the distinct feeling that he was being followed and observed. He remembered the tragedy of his father, thought about the emperor whose power smothered everything in the city, and found the courage to press on.

The building was seedy and rundown, with boards nailed over the windows. No sound came from within. He tried the latch and found the door unlocked, just as the archer had told him it would be. Pushing the door open slowly, he expected the loud creak of rusty hinges and was surprised when the door glided easily, effortlessly inward. With a quick step, he was inside. The door shut behind him, and for a moment he was enveloped by darkness and silence.

But it was just for a moment; almost immediately he felt strong hands grasp both of his arms. He struggled instinctively, but felt the iron grip of his captors and knew that he was firmly held. He lashed out with a kick, only to bang his shin painfully against something; the blow produced a metallic *clang*.

Light seared his eyes. It was only the flame of an oil lantern, but the sudden brightness was painful. Still struggling and half blind, Blayne was trundled along like a squirming child, through another doorway and into a larger room.

It might have been the hall of a moderately prosperous inn: a large stone fireplace on the far wall held a huge pile of glowing coals, while several long tables, each flanked by a pair of arches, took up most of the space. The ceiling was lost in shadows, though he saw beams and arches connecting to a central pillar. To his left was a long bar. There was no other exit or entrance visible.

More interesting than the room itself were the occupants. There were a dozen men in there, all regarding him suspiciously. To a man they wore the handlebar mustaches of the Solamnic Knights, yet the men were not dressed in armor, nor did they display the heraldry of their order on their tunics. Instead, they looked more like thieves, wearing dark cloaks and old, well-worn boots. A few had hoods pulled over their heads, while several wore ratty gloves with fingers missing. Not one was smiling; on more than a few faces, he noted stares of suspicion or outright hostility.

The two men holding his arms were the largest fellows in the room, and they also glowered down at him. Apparently they didn't like what they saw, for their iron fingers dug more deeply into the flesh of his arms as Blayne was roughly propelled toward a table in the center of the room.

A single man sat there, slightly older than the rest to judge by the creases around his eyes, the traces of gray in his mustache and his long hair. He stared at Blayne while deliberately pulling a long dagger from his belt. Never taking his eyes off the visitor, he started to trim his fingernails with what was obviously a very sharp blade.

Blayne ceased to struggle against the tight grip of the two men. Among the several warnings Archer Billings had given him was an indication that these men were perfectly willing to use violence against their enemies. With that in mind, the young lord didn't trust himself to speak, but he tried to remember the legacy of his birth as he held his head high and levelly met the gaze of the man.

"Who are you?" the fellow with the knife demanded after what seemed like a very long silence during which he kept trimming his fingernails.

"I am Sir Blayne Kerrigan of Vingaard Keep," he replied proudly.

"Ah, I have heard of you," the man replied with a snort that could have indicated derision or amusement.

"Perhaps I could say the same thing, if I knew who it was I addressed," Blayne retorted sharply. "Why do your men hold me so rudely? And who are you?"

The man did laugh then, loudly. "Perhaps my men hold you because you entered like a thief—silently, stealthily. Perhaps we should cut your throat, *Sir* Blayne, like we would any other thief?"

"But I am not a thief!"

"Why do you come here, then?"

"A man from the city guard sent me. I am looking to make contact with a group of brave people opposed to the tyrannical emperor, and he said I would find them here. They are—"

"Don't tell me what 'they' are!" the man snapped back. "Who is this man who sent you to our door?"

Blayne drew a breath. "He told me that I could identify him to . . . the men I met, but only if I was satisfied that I had come to the right place and found them."

"And, Sir Blayne, are you so satisfied that you can speak now, or do I need to exercise some further persuasion?"

The man continued to wield his knife, whittling away at his fingernails with as much ease as skill. The light from the oil lamp caught on the steely blade, reflecting brightly in Blayne's eyes. He took a chance.

"The man was Archer Billings of the city guard. I was sent to him by a mutual friend who is not of the city. I came here because the emperor slew my father, treacherously, and then destroyed the towers of Vingaard with his bombard. He must be stopped!"

"Now there, lad," said the man, clearly enjoying himself. "You surely have heard that it's a crime to express such sentiments? Most especially it is a crime here in Palanthas, the very heart of the emperor's realm? You could be subject to, oh, I don't know, imprisonment or loss of property. Exile, maybe. Hanging! Why, the emperor might even *scowl* at you!"

The last line provoked coarse laughter from the rest of the men. Blayne could hear the mockery in the fellow's words but sensed that it was not he who was being mocked, but rather the emperor himself.

Blayne felt his courage reborn. If he had somehow come to the wrong place, he would not be cowed into disclaiming his father, his quest. But he was certain that they were the right men and the room was the place that he sought.

"I care nothing for the emperor's laws!" he declared

passionately. "They are an abomination of the Oath and the Measure. He fears his own people, even as he claims to have their interests in his heart. He is a despot and must be brought down."

"Well, my young lord," said the man, "it may be that you *have* come to the right place and are speaking to the right fellow." He stood up; somehow the long-bladed dagger vanished into the folds of his cloak as he held out a strong hand. Blayne took that hand and shook it, impressed by the firmness of the dry grip.

"I am Sir Ballard," he said. "And your archer friend—I know of him as well—spoke the truth. We are the Legion of Steel in Palanthas. And the emperor is no friend of ours."

›‹⊰⊱⊰⊱⊰⊱❦⊰⊱⊰⊱⊰⊱‹

Magic wrapped the gray wizard Hoarst and Sirene in a whirlwind sensation, transporting them together from the camp in the Vingaard Mountains to his stronghold across the plains in the Dargaard Range. They arrived in the huge laboratory, the vast chamber that had once been the great hall of the castle.

Many of the wizard's other women, more than a dozen of them, had been living there in his absence, and he was pleased to note the fires were lit and the rooms had been kept warm and clean. The women gathered quickly when he shouted out his arrival, delighted to see their master.

"Bring me a cask of the dry white wine from Nordmaar," he snapped to a pair of strong blondes who hailed from that country. "Lara, you start a fire under my largest caldron. I want it blazing hot. Use the hard coal. Dani, Kammra, Tenille, go to the cabinets and bring me ten jars of down feathers, a dozen silk fans, and a cask of whale oil."

He stopped to consider: he had water in plenty but needed a few other ingredients that he would have to select himself. "The rest of you, prepare us some food. And see that Sirene gets a hot bath. I want all of you to gather in the lab at sunset tonight!"

"Yes, lord! As you command!" they chorused and scurried off to do his bidding, with two of the youngest girls taking charge of the albino. When all were busy, Hoarst left the hall and entered the connecting corridor leading to his chambers. But he did not climb the stairs.

Instead, he went to the plain door near the kitchen and touched it, sensing the power of his wizard lock. He was pleased but not surprised to note the door had not been disturbed in his absence.

With a murmured word, he released the locking spell and opened the door. A thin, steep stairway led down into the shadows, and he had to turn sideways to descend the narrow steps. A single word ignited a light spell on his belt buckle, illuminating his way as he plunged deep into the passages under his ancient keep.

At the bottom of the steps, a narrow corridor led to the right and left. He turned left—for the other direction was an illusion, and though it appeared to be a long, straight passageway, in actuality it led to a cleverly concealed trap over a large pool of acid. Anyone who went more than ten steps in that direction would fall through the floor and into the pool. They would not come out again.

Hoarst continued down the narrow passage, each footstep kicking up little swirls of dust that danced in the light of his spell. He passed a number of side passages to the right and left and took the third corridor on his right. That led him to another intersection of passages, and again he made the correct turn.

There was only one way to walk through those dark corridors, he knew: each false move led to a death certain, violent, and inescapable. One trap would crush an intruder with a slab of rock weighing many tons. Another opened into a chute that plummeted into a hundred-foot-deep pit; the bottom of the pit was layered with spears planted, sharp tips up, in the ground. A third, one of the most ingenious, would pour oil over any trespasser and then, a few seconds later, release a cascade of bits of phosphorus that would ignite a searing, completely lethal blaze.

After a hundred and fourteen steps, Hoarst turned to the left into a corridor that looked just as ordinary as any of the rest. He came to a mundane-looking door, confirmed with a gentle touch that his locking spell was still intact there, and with a single word released the door, pushing it open to enter the most secret, most cherished of his rooms.

The light spell still gleamed from his belt buckle, but that pale brightness was completely overwhelmed by the brilliant glow emanating from a dozen different places in his treasure chamber. Jewels and scepters, a crown, and a magnificent wand all shone with magical light. A chest, overflowing with coins, glowed crimson as though from the embers of a fire. Yellow and green light rose from statues and paintings, while a magical chandelier—perpetually illuminated—brightened the place more than a hundred candles.

Hoarst spent a few moments perusing his trinkets, fondling the limitless piles of coins, admiring his favorite painting—which displayed a partially disrobed woman beside a deep, clear pool—hoisting a prize scepter, and cradling the hilt of a splendid flying dagger.

But business, not pleasure, had drawn him there, and he had precious little time to waste. He moved to a jar that was full of powdered flakes of gold. He needed both hands to hoist the heavy vessel until he slipped it into a bag of holding. Then he was able to suspend it from his belt as if it were a small purse. He found another small chest, one containing pure, crystalline diamonds, and added that to the bag. After a moment's thought, he dropped the enchanted dagger into the bag as well.

Securing the wizard locks behind him, he went out through the dungeon tunnels and back up the long stairway, returning to his lab to find that the women had followed his instructions precisely. A great fire burned under his cauldron, and the wine and other ingredients had been brought over to the nearby table, where they were neatly arrayed.

He dined in the laboratory, mixing and working through the meal, then chanted spells and wrote arcane symbols deep into the night. The women tended the fire while he slept, and he continued to mix and cook for all the following day. Powdered gold, its weight equivalent to two thousand pieces of steel, was added. He put the diamonds—ten times the value of the steel—in his grinder, and reduced the precious stones to powder after an hour of hard labor.

For six more hours, the huge cauldron boiled, the magical potion taking effect until, finally, there was only one thing he needed to add.

"Sirene, come here," he ordered.

The albino woman came to him immediately, willingly. She was clean and perfumed following her bath, and he was pleased. She well knew that albino blood was rare and much treasured as a spell component, and once again she proudly held out a finger, ready for the prick of his lancet.

"Do you need another drop of my blood, my lord?" she asked, relishing the power of her special status, inwardly sneering at the jealously of the other women.

"You understand me too well," he said with a smile. "But this is a very special potion with very special requisites."

The magical knife was in his hand, but she was looking only at his eyes.

"I am sorry to tell you this, my dear," he explained. "But this time, I need all of it."

✦✦✦✦✦✦✦❋✦✦✦✦✦✦✦

Selinda returned to the little inn at the end of the dark alcove the next night. Though there was no sign outside the place, she learned from other patrons that it was called the Hale and Farewell, in honor of the parties sailors had before their ships left port for long voyages. She learned the proprietor was the man who had spoken to her outside the alley the first night she stopped, and that his name was Hale. People referred to him as Lame Hale, and he seemed to take that reference to his gimpy leg with fine good humor.

The third night she teleported from her room directly to the alley, very much surprising Lame Hale as he leaned against the dirty wall and scouted the street for prospective customers. But he seemed glad to see her again, and she enjoyed his compliments. She was soon inside and being welcomed by a host of familiar customers. She didn't lack for an invitation to sit at a table with a group of travelers or share some gossip with some of the lady merchants who held court in the corner room.

The sailors told stories of exotic ports and terrifying storms, and she relished their tales of adventure. There were old soldiers too, and—for a drink or two—they could be coaxed into recounting campaigns against the Dark Knights, surreptitious missions under the realm of Khellendros, or battles against Ankhar the Truth on the central plains. Selinda stayed late each time she visited the place—usually the sun was coming up by the time she went home—and she always departed on foot, waiting until she was out of sight of the Hale and Farewell's front door before teleporting home.

She told no one her name, and no one asked. She was treated well, as befitted her beauty and the generous tips that she left following each visit. The exotic music, oily and smooth and a trifle atonal, appealed to her in ways that the flutes, lyres, and drums of other local musicians did not. On her second visit, she had learned the unusual musicians and their instruments came from so far away that they were unknown on most of the continent of Ansalon.

It also pleased her to go to a place where no one knew her as the wife of the emperor, where her legacy as the Princess of the Plains, the woman who would help unite Solamnia, was mere myth. She had grown up in the city, a daughter of privilege, and—when she was honest with herself—she admitted that she was spoiled by her rich father. If he hadn't exactly been doting, Bakkard du Chagne had never allowed her to want for any material things, and she came to adulthood expecting that as her due. Her marriage to the most powerful man in her world had done nothing to lessen her sense of entitlement, but it had walled her off from life.

There in the dark inn, those walls were broken. She laughed at the sensation of complete freedom and relaxed among the jovial strangers. She even joined in the gossip about the emperor, which was surprisingly common. Everyone had an opinion of her husband, and most opinions were unfavorable—though a few of the veteran soldiers spoke up for the new discipline and pride of the Solamnic nation. Others mocked Jaymes as being afraid of his own shadow and paranoid to the point of lunacy with his edicts and restrictions. If the new edicts had put any fear of reprisal into her new friends, they certainly hid the fact very well!

On her fourth or fifth visit, Lame Hale came over to sit at her table. She nodded a greeting to him.

"I am delighted to see that the mistress finds my humble establishment to her liking," he said with an easy smile.

"It's a lovely place," Selinda declared. "Everyone is so nice, and you have such a splendid mix of people from all over."

"Ah, yes. And don't forget the music!" He gestured to a slender, pale-skinned musician who was working with some kind of flute that was as tall as a long spear. The man was producing notes that seemed to transcend scale, just then playing in a mournful minor key that made Selinda feel achingly sad.

Hale cleared his throat. "Perhaps I could introduce the lady to something new?"

"Perhaps," she said. "What did you have in mind?"

Hale whistled loudly, and one of his serving maids hustled over to the table. Like all of the inn's maids, the young woman wore a gown that dipped very low in the front and was braced with a knee-length skirt. She curtsied to her master.

"Bring the gracious lady a Red Lotus," Hale said in his soft but curiously seductive voice. He turned back to Selinda. "It is another concoction that comes out of the east. I believe you will find it very pleasing."

And indeed, Selinda did. The drink was tart, with a hint of some kind of berry that covered up stronger, unusual tastes. It felt soft yet prickly on her tongue, and when she sipped it, she found the sensation strikingly pleasurable. Before she knew it, her glass was empty, and Hale was motioning for another . . .

And another after that. It seemed the drink was focusing her thoughts, heightening her awareness, and she found herself laughing very loud at something—she couldn't say what it was. The lights were suddenly very bright then seemed to fade almost to black. They flared up again with a sudden, wavering brilliance that she found absolutely hilarious. She wondered at the fact that no one else seemed to take notice of the distortion, but she didn't wonder very much as the music started up again.

A fiddle player had joined the man with the exotic flute, and they picked up the tempo into a lively jig. Suddenly Selinda was up and dancing, and everyone was clapping in time to the music, cheering her on, and it was simply the most wonderful, exhilarating experience in all of her life. Laughing, she encouraged the musicians to play an extra song, and was terribly disappointed when, a long time later, they pleaded the need for rest.

She felt a little unsteady on her feet as she made her way back to the table, where the proprietor still sat, beaming happily at her. He was such a *nice* man!

"Perhaps the mistress would come with me now?" said Hale.

A glimmer of alarm tried to find its way through her fuzzy brain. But all she could think of were Hale's eyes, so dark and mysterious and utterly, completely compelling. "Very well," she said, realizing that she had to speak very slowly to make herself understood. "But where are we going?"

"This way," he whispered, pointing to a dark hallway at the back of the inn.

"Why?" she tried to ask. It seemed like a very long way away, but she was terribly curious. Slowly, she pushed herself to her feet, surprised at how strong his hand was as he helped her up.

"Don't worry, and don't wonder," he said softly. "I promise you that it will be a magnificent surprise."

"The knights have an army in front of the city of Cleft Spires, and another army marches this way, across the plains," reported Rib Chewer. "Many horses in the north. With knights. And long spears."

Ankhar nodded. He was not surprised by any of the reports, and he knew better than to ask the rather stupid goblin for precise calculations. The City of Cleft Spires, he knew, was Solanthus, thusly called because of the twin blocks of stone that loomed high above the center of the place. He knew the city was cherished by the knights and that they would move to protect it from any threat.

But he had already made a different plan, and the scout's reports only reinforced the course of action he had chosen. Solanthus lay over the horizon, only about twenty miles away, west and a little north of his position. The Garnet range loomed directly to the west, with the tops of the peaks concealed behind a mass of dark clouds that promised heavy rains, possibly even snows, in the high country. Ankhar smiled at the thought.

He gathered his captains, as well as his stepmother, for a conference. The ogres were restive and grumpy, having marched farther and faster in the past fortnight than at any previous time in their lives. Still, they looked at him respectfully, and Ankhar took heart from the fact that they were still prepared to follow him.

"Up there!" he said, pointing into the mountains. "Knights are all before us, on plain, in city, north of city. But they are not up there."

"We find treasure and booty in the mountains?" asked Bullhorn skeptically. "Or just cold and snow and hard rocks for beds?"

"We will not stay in the mountains," Ankhar said. "We just

go through them, and come out the other side. The knights look for us over here—and we are over there!"

He gestured in triumph to the lofty ridge, hoping that his plan was sinking in.

"Over there!" cried Laka, cackling shrilly. "Across the mountains—there we find treasures, and slaves, and war."

For a moment the ogres looked skeptical. Finally, General Bloodgutter roared out a challenge. "We march! Who is afraid of the mountains?"

Bullhorn raised his face toward the heights, and bellowed his own challenge. "Mountains will not stop me! Go over mountains! Make war!"

"Over mountains! Make war!" The chant was soon picked up by the rest of Ankhar's captains. A few moments later, the great horde turned from the flat plains into a valley that, Ankhar knew, would take them all the way to the summit of the range, and still remain north of the vexing mountain dwarf realm of Kayolin.

On the other side of the crest, he knew of a wide river valley that would lead them down to the plains. No one lived in that valley; he knew because he had marched through there only a few years before. No one was there to stop his plan.

CHAPTER SEVENTEEN

TAKING THE TOWER

Hoarst returned to the Black Army with a small keg in his bag of holding. It contained perhaps two gallons of precious liquid—very precious in so many ways, he thought a little wistfully. Would he ever find another concubine quite like Sirene? He doubted he would. But like a passing breeze—or a teleporting wizard—that regret vanished when he beheld the neat rows of tents, arrayed at the southern end of the hidden valley in the Vingaard range.

It was time to get to work.

The companies of Blackgaard's force, ten units of three hundred men each, had moved there. They would travel light, leaving their tents and baggage behind, because, after all, soon they would all be sleeping comfortably in the High Clerist's Tower.

Hoarst found Blackgaard sharpening his sword in the predawn mists. The Gray Robe was interested to note the commander did that mundane chore himself, but he made no mention of it.

"The bridge was finished just yesterday," the captain reported to his mage. "Your timing is impeccable."

"Good." Hoarst patted the bag of holding. "I have the means of attack right here. It all went as planned."

The bulk of the keg had vanished within the magical confines of the container, but Blackgaard understood his companion's gesture. "Excellent," he replied. "It's time to move out."

The columns of companies quickly fell into line and started up the steep road, switching back and forth to ascend the sheer wall that was the valley's southern barrier. Their goal was only fifteen miles away, and Blackgaard intended to have them in position by nightfall, so they could have some rest before making the attack after moonset, in the darkest hour just before dawn.

The Black Army marched with the ease of a veteran formation. The soldiers were mercenaries, true, instead of men who fought for colors, state, or oath, but they were the finest, toughest mercenaries in the world. They took pride in their reputation. No untoward click of metal against metal, no cursing or grumbling or even careless stumble would mar their advance.

Within an hour the leading company reached the crest of the ridge bordering the valley and led the column out of the sheltered vale and into the windswept wilderness of the high Vingaard range. As if crossing a line of demarcation, they left the fields, pastures, and groves of their own settlement behind and entered a realm of stark gray stone, white glaciers, deep chasms, and lofty peaks. There were no trees there and few stretches of level ground.

The captain's engineers had done a splendid job on the road. It would not suffice as a trade caravan route—it was too steep—but it was wide enough for five men to march abreast, even where it was scored along the side of a sheer cliff. After crossing the first ridge, the route cut along the precipitous side of a mountain, staying a hundred feet below the crest for the sake of concealment. Descending gradually, it curled around the shoulder of the solid massif then dropped sharply to pass between a pair of conical summits.

Beyond, the route was confronted with the obstacle of a half-mile-deep chasm—the barrier that had prevented any previous attack against the tower from the north. But the bridge that had been erected for the attack was a true work of art, slender and graceful, spanning the narrowest part of the chasm on a single arch. The stone surface thrummed to the march of the Black Army and carried the whole force safely across by midafternoon.

There was one last ridgeline to crest, and there the companies narrowed into double, and finally single, file. That part of the route, scaling the highest summit, was of necessity rough and ill-prepared. Since it was close to the fortress, the diggers had worked only very cautiously there so as not to risk discovery.

Night was falling as they approached the summit. Blackgaard had previously scouted out a shallow swale near the top, and there he put the small army into an overnight bivouac. There were a few stubby cedars growing in the little valley, but Blackgaard would allow no fires. Even though the rising ridge blocked their line of sight to the fortress, the smell of smoke had been known to thwart a surprise attack.

Lying on the hard and rocky ground, the men slept as much as they could, which was not much at all. Mostly they watched the red moon, then the white, slowly traverse the night skies. Lunitari set behind the western slopes at about midnight. Solinari, closer to full and trailing behind his red cousin, did not set until past three. Only the stars, far more of them than a man could count, brightened the vast arch of the cosmos.

Then it was time to move out.

Hoarst went first, leading a single company of three hundred handpicked men. As they crossed the summit of the ridge, their target came into view. Even in the moonless night, the alabaster walls of the High Clerist's Tower stood out against the black mountain range. Dominated by its tall, central spire, the fortress had stood in that spot since the Age of Might, a symbol of the Solamnics' mastery of that corner of Krynn. Lesser towers, immense walls and gates, and the secondary fortress known as the Knights' Spur, all stood as reminders that the place had held out against great armies many times in the past.

The lead company started down the bed of a narrow ravine, descending sharply. Occasionally the path twisted around to give them another glimpse of their destination, but mostly it was a deep, narrow trench and all they could see was a narrow sliver of sky overhead.

The Thorn Knight was the first to reach the base of the ravine. They were less than a mile from the north wall of the tower when Hoarst called a halt. His men gathered around as he reached into his bag of holding and pulled forth the cask that he had brought from the Dargaard range. The wizard produced a very tiny cup and opened the spigot. One by one, his three hundred men were given a sip of the potion that had been brewed at such cost.

When they were done, the wizard dropped the keg on the ground. It was no longer needed—like the drained corpse of Sirene, it was an empty shell that had to be unsentimentally discarded. Hoarst lifted his hands, outlining his gestures with the tiniest hint of light magic so that his men could observe him. With one smooth gesture, he commanded them to move out.

Swiftly, silently, and magically, his company of soldiers began to fly.

⊱⚭⚭⚭⚭⚭⚭⚭⚭⚭⚭⊰

General Markus was restless, unable to sleep. Always an early riser, on that morning it seemed as though he had not been able to close his eyes for more than a moment or two all night. Giving up sleep as a lost cause, he rose, dressed himself in his leather garrison tunic with the red rose emblazoned on the crest, and decided to walk the parapets of his mountain fortress.

He found the guards awake and alert, as he knew they would be. Most of the defensive positions of the High Clerist's Tower overlooked the road through the pass. That was the highway Jaymes had ordered widened, the route where the emperor's army had marched to and from Palanthas. Nothing stirred on the road that day.

Markus had been the commander of the tower garrison since shortly after the defeat of Ankhar's army. Jaymes Markham had given the trusted, veteran captain the choice of going back to Caergoth, to command the Rose Army, or of taking command of one of the remote outposts in the outer empire. Markus had leaped at the chance to come to the tower and never regretted the choice.

There he was his own master, and the master of a place that was hallowed throughout the long history of his order. He trusted his men, and they all but worshiped him. There were no politics, no distractions—thankfully, no women!—and there he could live the austere soldier's life that he loved. It was a life of duty and service, maintaining the security of a very important landmark.

He never forgot the fact that the High Clerist's Tower was a bastion of the ages, the site of some of history's greatest battles. It was the battlefield where Sturm Brightblade, the knight who restored honor to the Solamnic orders during the War of the Lance, had fallen. It was where the Heroes of the Lance had slain their first dragon. And it was the key trade route of the new Solamnic empire. Every night, no matter how ill he slept, Markus went to bed proud he did his job to the best of his abilities.

Why, then, did he feel such unease and disquiet?

Still restless, the veteran captain moved from the gatehouse through the lower courtyards, where all was quiet. He climbed the towers on the curtain wall, finding the sentries awake, bored but watchful. He considered going all the way up to the High Lookout—the loftiest spot in the whole tower, except for the tiny enclosure known as the Nest of the Kingfisher, atop a narrow spire—but he knew there were trustworthy guards up there, and it would take him until dawn just to climb the hundreds of steps.

Instead, he made his way to the northern walls of his great fortress. They looked down into vast canyons, utterly dark and silent, and up on frowning cliffs and jagged peaks. There were places in view that were higher than the fortress walls, but they were too far away for archers, or even catapults, to come to bear. The night was motionless, dark with shadows.

"Eh?" croaked one of the knight guards from the outer parapet. "What kind of bird—?"

The sound died out in a gurgle of air and blood. Markus had been a soldier all his life; he knew the sound of a throat being cut.

"Alarm!" he cried. "Raise the alarm. Light torches, by Kiri!"

Immediately fires flared into being, a dozen brands igniting across the many ramparts. For a horrified instant, the captain could only gape in disbelief. His lofty parapet, nearly a thousand feet above the canyon bed, was swarming with attackers clad in black leather armor. They came not just over the walls, but also from the base of the interior wall and tower—and many were dropping right out of the sky!

The defenders never had a chance. Markus's knights, the men who so adored and trusted him, fought bravely, but there were only twelve men posted on the remote platform, and they were swarmed by at least ten times their number. Each knight faced two, three, even four attackers at once. Steel slashed at them from every direction. And the enemy were skilled attackers.

Markus saw the last of his men die—within seconds after the battle had started—before managing to retreat into the tower's interior, pulling the heavy iron-banded door shut behind himself. He dropped the bar and braced it with his hands.

The alarm was ringing across the pass. Torches flared all over, as men sought targets and shouted questions and challenges.

A sergeant pounded by the steps below Markus, carrying a torch and holding his sword at the ready.

"General! What's going on?" he cried.

"Up here!" Markus cried. "Two hundred men, maybe more, have gained the north parapet—right outside this door! Get reinforcements up here on the double!"

"Yes, sir!" The veteran soldier sheathed his sword and sprang down the stairs, his torch flaring. Markus still had his hands on the locking bar, but he grew more and more unsettled when there came no attempt made to force the barrier.

A moment later the general heard dozens of boot steps pounding up the stairs. He went to an arrow slit and looked out, wondering why none of the attackers had started to pound on the door. Markus could only hope that fresh troops arrived in time to help him make a desperate stand.

But when he looked out the arrow slit, he saw why the attackers weren't pressing the attack there. The reason was clear and astonishing: they weren't trying to batter down the door because they were simply flying away, soaring through the air to attack another position.

⊰⊶⊙⊷⊙⊷⊙⊷❀⊷⊙⊶⊙⊷⊙⊷⊙⊷

Hoarst and his flying company struck three different parapets, all positions high up on the north wall. In each place they killed the posted guards and created such commotion that additional troops from the tower's limited garrison were dispatched to the critical juncture. And by the time the reinforcements reached each scene, the attackers were gone. Soon the whole tower was ablaze with torches and littered with dead bodies.

The High Lookout bristled with archers, and arrows were launched against bats, clouds, and imaginary targets in the sky. Hoarst would send his men against the lookout soon—they had about an hour of time before the potion of flying wore off—but first he had an even more important objective.

The Gray Robe's advance company swept downward, off of the high wall, toward the north gate. Only about a dozen of his men had been lost in those initial skirmishes, and Hoarst took the rest in a long, sweeping descent from the lookouts and into the courtyard that was just within the fortress's northern gate.

There they found several dozen guards, and there the flying soldiers of the Black Army attacked ruthlessly. Half the defenders fell even as the attackers were dropping to the

243

ground, swords extended and chopping. For a few moments, a melee swirled in the courtyard, blades clashing and men shouting, screaming, and dying.

Hoarst saw a knight rushing toward the massive rolled chain of the portcullis. He knew that if the man released the chain, the heavy barred gate would come crashing down, and it would take at least an hour for his men to hoist it up again.

The wizard pointed his finger and spat a word of magic. Arrows of light and energy, deceptively beautiful yet terribly lethal, shot from Hoarst's fingertip. Two, four, six of the magical arrows seared into the back of the running knight, dropping him to the ground, his body blistered and bleeding. The stricken man reached out a desperate hand toward the chain release, but another attacker was there. The Black Army man crushed the knight's hand with his heel of his boot then stabbed him through the neck with his sword.

The Thorn Knight was pleased. As the last of the defenders were dispatched, he looked up at the massive gates, studied the mechanisms, and spotted the great capstans that would pull the portals open.

"Go there, men!" he cried, highlighting the machinery with a ghostly spell of brightness. "Turn the winches!"

⊱⊰⊱⊰⊱⊰⊱⊰✹⊱⊰⊱⊰⊱⊰⊱⊰

"Charge! Double time, men—to the gates!"

Captain Blackgaard was leading the attack on foot—the steep and rocky slopes were not fit for horses—and the bulk of the Black Army surged after him in a long file. The nine companies on the ground swept around the base of the great fortress, which was protected by the cloaking shadows in spite of the torches flaring all along the high parapets.

As the alarms spread above them, they emerged from the

shadows and raced toward the great barrier of the north gate.

Finally they came around the last corner of the bastion to see the great gates looming before them. Blackgaard felt a momentary panic when he saw the impassable barrier still blocking them. There came a creak of sound followed by a first tentative movement—and then he thanked his gods and all those who would make him rich, as the mighty portals began to swing open.

Hoarst had done his work well.

⊱⊰⊱⊰⊱⊰☙⊱⊰⊱⊰⊱⊰⊱

Markus looked down to see thousands of men, all clad in black, pouring through the open gate. The advance guard of flying soldiers, meanwhile, had claimed the gateway into the central part of the tower, forced an opening, and slain the few defenders who blocked their path.

The general took a look across the courtyard toward the redoubt known as the Knights' Spur. It was a side tower separated from the bulk of the fortress by a deep channel, which was crossed by a single bridge. If the defenders could get across there . . .

The thought died as he saw fifty black-dressed soldiers already patrolling that rampart. The small bridge was being raised; the Knights' Spur was soon closed to the defenders.

Clashes raged throughout the great fortress. Outnumbered and surprised, most of them awakened from a sound sleep, the Knights of Solamnia nevertheless gave a good account of themselves. They fought in twos or threes, each man watching his comrade's back. The attackers were cut down by the score. More by instinct than anything else, however, the knights were gradually retreating toward the southern end of the fortress.

Already the attackers, with so many gates opened by the flying advance guard, were pouring around every wall, tower, and courtyard on the north side. They swarmed through the central courtyard. The great tower in the center of the fortress had fallen, and enemy archers had replaced the knights on the High Lookout, raining their deadly missiles down on the defenders.

Here and there a sergeant organized a counterattack, or a dozen men burst through an encircling line of black-clad attackers. The Solamnics fought bravely and died, falling back steadily. The fortress was too big, had been breached in too many places for them to try to hold more than a small corner of it against the overwhelming numbers.

"Rally to me, knights!" cried Markus to his surviving men. "We'll hold them at the south gatehouse!"

His men arrived in pairs and trios, a pathetically small number, all of them fighting their way to the general, many dying in the attempt. Dressed in silver mail shirts or even silken pajamas, they stood back to back when they could find companions, dueling—and dying.

Still, the Solamnics took a terrible toll on the attackers. They knew every nook and cranny of their great fortress and had the advantage of lethal traps that had been carefully laid over the years. More than two hundred of the attackers perished under a crushing rockslide, triggered when a sergeant released a trapdoor over a constricted corridor. Dozens of black-clad soldiers fell as they pressed through darkened hallways defended by unseen knights. A whole company of the Black Army—three hundred men—died horribly when they were trapped in a courtyard that was flooded with oil and subsequently ignited into a cauldron of screaming men and stinking, burned flesh.

But in the end, the overwhelming number of attackers simply had to prevail. When a hundred men were slain charging across an exposed courtyard, two hundred survived the charge to sweep the beleaguered defenders from their positions. When a corridor floor dropped away, spilling two hundred Black Army soldiers into a subterranean aqueduct and certain death by drowning, four hundred replacements took a new route and massacred the knights who had sprung the trap. Wherever the defenders met with a momentary success, the attackers changed tactics, came around from a new direction, and carried the fight.

Finally Markus had fewer than a hundred men left, huddled together on several sections of the outer parapet. They formed two lines, facing west and east, blocking the ramparts on top of the walls as the attackers swarmed into them. For a few moments, the Solamnics stood, steel clashing against the attackers, killing two or three of the black soldiers for every one of their own casualties.

Markus looked to the sky, which was paling with dawn. The flying soldiers had disappeared. Knowing they must have used magic to take to the air, he realized the foul enchantment had worn off, that the enemy was once again grounded, like his own men.

"Fall back to the south gatehouse!" he ordered. "We make our stand there."

The men retreated with the discipline one would expect of Solamnic Knights. There was no panic, not even when a new rush of the black attackers surged through a side door and took the skirmish line in the right flank. Two or three men fell, but the rest wheeled back toward the great metal door that led to the massive gatehouse.

But then the doors to that gatehouse burst open, disgorging

a fresh company of the enemy, three hundred strong or more emerging to form a phalanx. The defenders were trapped in a vise. Enemy archers began to open up on them from higher platforms, and it broke Markus's heart to see brave men fall without even being able to strike a blow at their distant attackers.

It was not far from this place, General Markus remembered grimly, that Sturm Brightblade had died. The Blue Lady, Kitiara, had killed him here, and in that courageous moment the Orders of the Solamnic Knights had sprung back to life. The Oath and the Measure had been redeemed, the honor of Vinas Solamnus restored.

"Hold, there!" he called as two more knights fell. A young apprentice, not yet bearded, rushed into the breach, hewing and hacking at the black-clad attackers, and the new line held—for a moment, until the lad was felled by an arrow plunging from high above.

Markus was down to only a dozen men, and they were beset by hundreds of attackers on all sides. His bloody sword was a heavy weight in his hand, but that was nothing compared to the burden dragging down his heart.

Another knight fell, so close to him that his blood spilled across Markus's boots. The general tried to step forward and avenge the man, but the killer backed away from him, and five or six of the attackers rushed in to take his place.

Markus never saw the one who killed him, the keen blade lancing in from the left, stabbing under his rib cage, driving up to pierce his great heart.

"Est Sularus oth Mithas," he groaned. My honor is my life.

And on that day, it was his death as well.

CHAPTER EIGHTEEN

ᐊᐁᐅᐃᐁᐅᐃᐁᐅ ᐊᐁᐅᐃᐁᐅᐃᐁᐅ ᐊᐁᐅᐃᐁᐅᐃᐁᐅ ᐊᐁᐅᐃᐁᐅᐃᐁᐅ

PERIL

ᐊᐁᐅᐃᐁᐅᐃᐁᐅ ᐊᐁᐅᐃᐁᐅᐃᐁᐅ ᐊᐁᐅᐃᐁᐅᐃᐁᐅ ᐊᐁᐅᐃᐁᐅᐃᐁᐅ

T he latest reports still have Ankhar closing in on
Solanthus," reported Captain Franz. The Crown
officer sat astride his lathered charger. The young man's face
was lined with sweat, caked with dust. But he had ridden up to
the emperor and his staff at a gallop, and his voice displayed
only calm assurance, no fear.

The leader of the White Riders had been out on patrol for
more than a week and had just located the marching column
of the Palanthian Legion and his father's Crown Army.
Dismounting, Franz saluted his father, General Dayr, and
turned to address Jaymes. "But I have to tell you, Excellency,
that those reports are four days old. My outriders have not
been able to penetrate the screen of warg cavalry, so we
don't have concrete information on the whereabouts of his
main body."

"Well, let's start with some facts," Jaymes said, thinking
aloud. He had maps in his saddlebags and a whole library of
them in one of the command wagons, but his memory had
etched every detail of those plains into his mind; he didn't

need to consult any documents to lay out the situation on the plains.

"He hasn't come within fifty miles of the city—that much we know."

"Correct, my lord," the knight captain reported. His gaze was steady on the emperor, and he spoke levelly, without emotion, though resentment simmered behind his eyes. "The screen of his riders extends that close to the city, but they haven't pressed my outposts."

Jaymes turned to another nobleman, a high lord of Solanthus who had joined his force the previous day. Lord Martin had been a stalwart commander in the city's defense, and he had led a brave company during the Battle of the Foothills. The emperor couldn't help but think Martin merely looked old and tired. His hair had thinned, and what remained of it had turned white. His pale blue eyes were watery and didn't seem to focus clearly.

But Lord Martin had always been a reliable man, and he was his best bet there and then. Jaymes spoke bluntly.

"Your garrison is at full strength. Would it help to send a few regiments of infantry to reinforce?"

"I don't think so, Excellency," Martin replied. His voice was as strong as ever, Jaymes was pleased to note. He recalled, too, Martin had lost a son in the battle that broke the siege. In the immediate aftermath, the nobleman had been fully engaged and his help was vital in winning the conclusive actions of the war. But afterward, surely the personal tragedy had taken its toll on him.

"We have enough to man the city walls with the complement of troops already in Solanthus," the lord reported. "And those walls are as high and as strong as ever. The breach at the Westgate has been fully repaired—in fact, the gate is taller and thicker than it was before Ankhar's monster smashed it down. There's plenty of food in the granaries. Even so, I don't think there's anything to be gained by bringing more hungry mouths behind the walls."

"I agree," Jaymes said. He glanced at Franz again and was startled to see the naked hostility there. The emperor's eyes narrowed. "Captain?" he said curtly.

"Yes, Excellency?" A mask fell across the young officer's face. But Jaymes made a note to remember his hidden feelings.

"Is there any chance Ankhar has moved farther east, into Throtl, or the Gap?"

"No, Excellency. I've sent three platoons of lancers all the way to the northern edge of the Darkwoods, and there has been no sign of anything that way."

"So he's back there somewhere, behind Solanthus?" General Dayr speculated. "I suggest we find him and attack, Excellency. We have the Crown Army here, with your legion, and the Sword Army gathered at Solanthus. United we'd have more than enough strength to collapse his pickets, and destroy him once and for all."

"We could do that, if indeed he's over there," the emperor replied. "But I'm not ready to take the chance."

"What chance?" Captain Franz blurted out, his face flushing. He blinked in the face of Jaymes's glare but didn't back down. "We know where he isn't, just like you said! So he has to be down there, east of the city."

"No, there's one more possibility," the emperor replied. "What if he took his army into the mountains?"

"But why?" Franz objected. "He'd be trapped in some box canyon or dead-end valley. There's no place an army could cross over the crest of the range!"

"Not an army of knights, perhaps," Jaymes replied. The young man's outburst forgotten, he spoke thoughtfully. "But Ankhar doesn't march with wagons and war machines. He doesn't even have horses. And he knows those mountains well—they're his home, after all."

"Do you think he'd go there now?" General Dayr asked. "Because if he did . . ."

"He could outflank us all and make for any part of the southern plains. He'd be far ahead of us and we couldn't do a damned thing about it," Jaymes concluded. "And the more I think about it, the more I'm certain he's not anywhere on these plains at all."

"If that's true, what can we do about it?"

"I'll leave the Sword Army near Solanthus for the time being; General Rankin can keep an eye on things around here. General Dayr, you will march eastward with the Crowns for thirty miles and set up a temporary camp. I want you to be ready to move in either direction at a moment's notice."

"Yes, Excellency. Of course. And the Palanthian Legion?"

"I'll lead them myself. We'll march toward the mountains. The legion isn't big enough to stop Ankhar by itself, but if he does try to come through the high country, we'll be waiting to give him a nasty surprise. I expect we'll be able to hold up his progress until you arrive to help finish the job—hopefully once and for all."

"May all the gods hear you," Dayr replied sincerely.

⊱✦⊰

Blayne woke up suddenly, sensing that someone was in the room with him. It was night, and the cramped little boarding house cubby that had been his home in Palanthas was utterly dark. It should have been utterly silent, as well. But Blayne had heard something, a soft sound that had interrupted his sleep. And when he listened, he plainly discerned the sound of breathing.

"Who's there?" he demanded, sitting up, reaching for his matches. With a scratch against the striking board, he smelled sulfur and heard the wooden chip burst into flame. He even felt the heat of the little fire on the fingertips holding the match.

But his room was as dark as ever.

Magic!

The skin on the back of his neck prickled, and he thought about his short sword—suspended from a hook on the back of the door, way across the room. "Who's there?" he asked again before cursing and shaking out the unseen match as the flame seared his fingertips. "Why can't I see?"

"It is important that my identity remain secret."

The cool voice startled him, brought him bolt upright on his grimy mattress. Blayne discerned no threat in the voice, rather more a tone of almost paternal affection, as though his visitor were a revered counselor—even though he had never heard the voice before.

"What do you want?" he asked.

"I bring you news—good news, from your friend in the gray robe."

"Finally!" Blayne cried involuntarily. He blushed over his outburst—and because he had just inadvertently confirmed to the unseen visitor his connection with Hoarst the Gray. "I mean . . . I have done what he asked when he sent me here. But I feared he had forgotten me."

"Not at all," said the other man with an avuncular chuckle. "And he will be pleased to hear of your success—as I am pleased."

"So . . . you also know about my mission in Palanthas?"

"Yes. The Legion of Steel is an important component in our plans, as the nation moves beyond the reign of the emperor. I take it that you have made the necessary contact with them, then?"

Blayne considered for a few moments, wondering how much of his secret mission he should be divulging to the mysterious stranger. It seemed the man was a confidant of Hoarst's and that he already knew a great deal about Blayne. After all, the young lord had taken his room in a shabby inn with the clear intention of remaining incognito. Yet somehow, the stranger found and knew him.

"Why this peculiar darkness?" Blayne asked bluntly. "I sense that you've cast a spell to block any light in my room."

"It is very important no one know who I am," replied the man, his easy tone indicating he took no offense at Blayne's question. "That is all. You can trust me; I am a friend."

And, in truth, Blayne felt he did trust the man. Of course, he didn't know about the charm spell his visitor had cast, the subtle magic that made pleasing the powerful cleric's every word. Nor could he see the black mask the Nightmaster wore across his face.

So Blayne told him all he had learned during several meetings with the secret order of knights known as the Legion of Steel.

"There are about a hundred of them in the city, organized into six cells," he reported eagerly. "I've only been to visit one of the cells, of course—that's deliberate on my part. But they have been preparing for their day ever since the emperor passed his new edicts."

"Excellent. One hundred knights is a few more than I had expect—that is, *hoped*—to find here," the other man said.

"But you said you brought news for me! From Hoarst," Blayne remembered suddenly. "What is the news?"

"Ah yes, that. Good news, indeed. The Black Army has taken over the High Clerist's Tower, and even now our mutual friend sits in control of the pass," the stranger explained.

"They took the tower?" Somehow, the truth of that seemed rather daunting to Blayne. It was good news certainly, but still . . . suddenly, rebellion did not seem like an ideal thing to support. Actual conflict was being waged. The thought—the reality—was unsettling.

"Did the garrison fight? Were there many killed?" he asked anxiously. "On either side?" he added quickly.

"There was no bloodshed, none whatsoever," said the kindly visitor. "It seems that disgust with the emperor is growing like a well-watered crop, all across the land."

That was a surprise; Blayne would not have expected the duty-conscious General Markus, one of the emperor's most loyal adherents, to surrender so easily. But it made the good news better.

"That crop has been watered with my father's blood," Blayne remembered bitterly, wondering if he was trying to remind his visitor or himself. "It is time the emperor reaps his violent harvest."

❧◦❀◦◦❀◦◦❀◦❀◦◦❀◦◦❀◦❧

Selinda tried to scream, but her throat was so dry that no sound emerged. She struggled to move, to break free from some kind of cloaking net that inhibited her movement, but felt as though her whole body were encased in heavy mud. The tiniest effort, such as wiggling a finger, was a great challenge. Actually running away, she discovered, was quite out of the question.

Where was she? How did she get there? Her eyes were open, but she saw only a vague, almost black grayness. Had she been blinded?

She had the vague sense that a lot of time had passed since she had last been aware of her surroundings. Some memories returned, slowly . . . the smoke-filled inn, the exotic music . . . people were laughing—*Selinda* was laughing—overcome by hysteria. She recalled her dance of wild enjoyment, the boisterous cheers of the other patrons. That drink! A lotus . . . something . . .

And Lame Hale.

"Hale!" she called angrily—or rather, tried to call. But still her mouth seemed to be filled with cotton; her tongue, her lips were unresponsive to mental commands. She tried to move again and failed—and for the first time realized that she was physically restrained. Her vision was clearing slightly. She made out a growing illumination, a spot that might have been a window, and the shapes of worn planking on the ceiling over her head.

She was lying on her back, on some sort of mattress. Her hands were over her head, each bound by the wrist to some sort of thick restraint. With a shudder of relief, she realized that at least she was still dressed; indeed, she was wearing her own clothes—she could feel the familiar, rare silk nestled against her skin. But what was happening to her? How had she come to such a pretty pass?

"Ah, my dear. How nice to see that you are awake."

The voice came from very close beside her head, and she started in panic.

"Hale?" she asked, recognizing the voice. "What did you do to me?"

"Nothing . . . yet." The smirk was evident in his voice. "You are worth far more to me intact than damaged."

"My worth? What in the world are you talking about? Are you planning to *sell* me?"

"Very astute!" said the man. She could make out more details finally, and when she twisted her head slightly, she saw him out of the corner of her eye, sitting smugly against the wall of the room. Selinda tried to think, to clear the fog from her mind and hatch some sort of plan. But all she felt was a headache. "A splendid-looking creature such as yourself will fetch a fine price in the east."

"But—how dare you!" she spat. "Why, they'll be looking for me!"

"I haven't failed to note that you invariably visit us alone, my dear. I am guessing, with a fair degree of certainty, that you haven't told anybody where you are. So let them look for you—within a few days, you could be hundreds of miles away from here. I have only to give the order, to make the deal."

Selinda fought against the tears that threatened to blind her. She would not give him the satisfaction! Instead, she cast about for some idea, anything, that might give her cause for hope.

"Of course, it may be that there are buyers closer to home who would be interested in possessing one such as yourself . . . a woman as beautiful as a princess, if truth be told."

Cold terror shot through her. Did he know who she was? Could he use that information to hurt her or the emperor?

Or the city of her birth?

And then, with a glimmer of optimism, she remembered her ring. She couldn't see her finger, but surely the ring was still there—it *must* be there. If she could just touch one hand with the other, twist the ring on her finger three times, she would be able to teleport out of there, back to her palace room, that former prison that suddenly seemed so inviting and secure, a safe refuge against the many dangers of the world. She wasted no time in regretting her actions but tried to imagine a way to get the man to ease his guard.

She let go a deep, unhappy breath and slumped back on the bed, motionless. Her despair was not an act, but her loss of strength was. Stretching her legs, she realized her feet were bound too. The room was shabby and plain, and she guessed it was probably somewhere in the back of the inn she had visited so many times.

But nobody at the inn knew who she was, and nobody at the palace knew where she was!

"That's better. It will go easier for you if you don't struggle so much. Those ropes can chafe terribly, I have learned."

"I understand," she said meekly. "But I am terribly thirsty, and my shoulder is sore. Could you loosen those ropes, just a little? My feet are bound; you know I'm not going anywhere."

"I suppose a little slack wouldn't hurt, so long as you promise to behave," Lame Hale said with a sneer that made her skin crawl.

"I promise," she replied as sweetly as she could through gritted teeth.

He leaned forward and pulled on the rope. Her right hand came free, and in the same instant she pulled it around to her left, groped with her fingers, felt for the metal band, her magical tool of escape. But she couldn't feel the ring, couldn't feel anything but her cold, clammy skin!

"Oh?" said Hale calmly, reaching out to grasp her hand again, bringing it back to the post where he secured it tightly again. He showed her the glimmering circlet of silver, shining in his hand, and looked at her with mock innocence. "Were you looking for this little bauble?" he asked.

Ankhar's route took him and his column of ogres and hob-goblins right past a broken-down cabin near the upper reach of the mountain valley.

"Do you remember this place?" he asked his stepmother, pausing to look at the wreckage, feeling an unfamiliar lump of emotion in his throat.

"Yes," she said in a muted voice. "Here I save you from Bonechisel. You were just baby."

He chuckled, touched. "Yes. Then I grew up. Nobody saved Bonechisel from me."

Proudly he showed the place to Pond-Lily. "I was born here! My first home!"

The ogress was delighted and wanted to stop and ooh and ahh over the place, but Ankhar couldn't spare the time for such trivialities. "We march now," he said. "Come back later, after war."

They moved on up the valley toward the crest of the snow-covered mountain range. The ogres, draconians, gobs, and hobs of his army all followed behind, unquestioning of their lord's intentions, strategies, and plans.

"Even then, I saw greatness in you," Laka said proudly. She put a withered claw of a hand in Ankhar's, her bony grip barely wrapping around his smallest finger. "Now, you carry greatness for the Prince of Lies."

Ankhar proudly carried that greatness right up to the crest of the Garnet Range. The valley terminated in a couloir that was surrounded by looming mountain faces that were very steep but not quite precipitous. The half-giant himself led the way on a remembered goat path, kicking through a steep, melting snowfield for the last thousand feet of the climb. He came through a narrow pass between two great peaks and immediately started downward.

The column of ogres and hobs trailed out behind him, moving single file over the lofty ground, snaking into a line more than two miles long. Ankhar was already out of the snow, picking his way around a clear, blue pond, while the tail end of his army was still waiting to begin its ascent.

But the half-giant was in no great hurry. He paused at the pond's outlet and, with a few deft stabs of his emerald-tipped spear, pulled a half dozen plump trout out of the water. Pond-Lily set about making a fire, while more ogres, as they arrived, spread out along both sides of the stream and tried to duplicate their chieftain's success.

By the time some two hundred drooling, snapping monsters loomed over the water, every one of the fish had been spooked, and the ogres of the advance entourage had to settle for watching Ankhar, his ogress, and his stepmother share the tasty morsels from the stream. That they did with remarkable patience, as the rest of the army continued to slowly make its way over the high saddle.

The procession continued far into the night, and several hobgoblins fell to their deaths as cooling temperatures turned the slushy snow to ice. But the rest of the troops made it before dawn, and Ankhar woke well rested and ready to lead his army to lower elevations.

"Move out!" he ordered cheerfully after a repast of leftover trout. He ignored the grumbles and complaints of those warriors who had just finished the previous day's march an hour or two before.

"Easy walk today," he encouraged. "This is a wild place—deer and trout for all, if you keep eyes open. We go through woods all the way down to the plains, and there we can make war. No people until we come to the cities on the plains—and then we kill, and we feast, and we drink!"

Heartened by that prospect, the army marched along easily, emerging into a larger valley, where the half-giant was startled to discover a smooth, paved road—a feature that had not been there in his childhood, nor when he had campaigned through there some four years earlier.

Still, the road made for good walking, and the army fell into a semblance of a military formation, advancing three or four ogres abreast, lumbering freely down toward the plains. The half-giant did not waste any brain power wondering why anyone would build a paved highway through the wild valley . . .

Until they came to a curve in the road and Ankhar stopped, utterly astounded by what he saw lying before him.

"Huh?" he said to Laka. "Someone put a town here."

CHAPTER NINETEEN

꒰⊹꒱ ꒰⊹꒱ ꒰⊹꒱ ꒰⊹꒱ ꒰⊹꒱ ꒰⊹꒱ ꒰⊹꒱ ꒰⊹꒱

EMBATTLED COMPOUND

꒰⊹꒱ ꒰⊹꒱ ꒰⊹꒱ ꒰⊹꒱ ꒰⊹꒱ ꒰⊹꒱ ꒰⊹꒱ ꒰⊹꒱

The town of New Compound occupied the flat shore of a long lake resting in a steep-sided valley. Geography had defined how the town was designed. The precipitous mountain ridge to the west, which plummeted directly into the deep, clear lake, was too steep for building. The stream flowing out of the lake was deep and rapid, and curled back and forth through the valley leading from the town down to the plains. The stream cut across the entire valley, surging up against the cliffs on the east side of the valley. Consequently, the dwarves had built a sturdy bridge across the stream right at the edge of town. That bridge allowed easy travel from the town down to the plains, along a smooth, paved road.

The bridge also provided easy access to the town for any invader coming from the plains, so it had to be defended. Dram's dwarves had built two towers within the town that overlooked the bridge, while preparing trenches and a palisade on the far side of the span. As a last resort, the mountain dwarf had mined the bridge with many kegs of black power, rigged to fuses that could be ignited from either tower. If dwarves had to retreat across the bridge, then the stone structure would be exploded—they hoped while a hundred ogres were trying to cross!

It was a good plan, except it didn't take into account one variable.

"You mean they're coming *down* the valley? From the high mountains?" Dram asked Rogard Smashfinger in disbelief. The dwarf from Kayolin had just arrived with several hundred doughty warriors and bore that sobering piece of news.

"'Fraid so," grunted the forger-turned-steel-merchant. "We had to move out on the double just to get here before them."

Dram looked up the valley in dismay. They had erected no defensive positions in that direction. The stream flowing into the lake meandered there, but it was shallow and broad, with a gravel bottom. A four-foot-tall dwarf could ford it in any one of a hundred places; it certainly wouldn't deter a charging band of ogres.

Dram turned to his father-in-law as Swig Frostmead came up to the pair of mountain dwarves.

"How many fighters do you have on the other side of the bridge?" he asked Swig.

Dram was trying hard to remain calm, summoning the steadiness that had preserved him through dozens of battles in his life. But in those days, there wasn't any threat to Sally or little Mikey—and worrying about them was making all the difference in the world. Dram Feldspar was shocked to realize his knees were shaking.

"Steady there, son," said the hill dwarf. "We need you now."

"Yes. Yes, of course," Dram snapped, drawing a deep breath. "Now—answer my question!" he demanded with his customary bravado.

"That's more like it," Swig declared, clapping him on the shoulder. "And we got about four hundred, to answer your question. What do we know about them brutes up the valley?"

"One of our scouts spotted them yesterday, watched them come over the crest of the range," Rogard explained. "He couldn't get a count, but there's thousands of 'em. Mainly ogres, it looked like."

"Great Reorx's nose!" cursed Swig. "That's a fair lot of muscle against our little town."

"And they're coming down the valley," Dram muttered grimly. He looked at the towers, the hastily erected wall, and the mined bridge ready to be demolished. Ankhar had stolen more than a march on him; he had rendered Dram's entire defensive strategy obsolete.

"Curse that stubborn daughter of mine!" Swig muttered grimly. "And what kind of husband are you—that you didn't *make* her leave?"

Dram snorted. "I was in the next room when *you* told her she had to go, remember? It was me that brought the ice pack for your eye."

"Aye," Swig said, more than a little proud. "You've got yerself a prize in that girl, you do."

"I know," Dram said, trying hard not to think about Sally, not right then.

He, Rogard, and Swig stood on the town's broad central plaza, a partially paved field overlooking the lake. The dwarves of New Compound were gathering around them, streaming from their houses and shops, coming down from the mines and forests where they had been working. Soon virtually every resident of the town, male and female, had answered the emergency summons.

"All right, then," the mountain dwarf said gruffly. "Let's get to work."

He stepped up onto an empty barrel that had been rolled into the middle of the square, turning slowly through a full circle, meeting the eyes of as many townsfolk as he could. Their voices stilled. With a full-throated shout, he broke the news.

"Here's how we stand: eight hundred hill dwarves, two hundred and fifty mountain dwarves, and a hundred humans who've decided to stick around and fight on our side. We don't know how big a force is coming against us, but a good reckon is that it will be twice our number in ogres alone. And they've got hobs along with 'em too. They're just around the bend, up the valley, and will reach the town limits in an hour or two.

"So the question is this: Do we pack up and skedaddle, getting out of here fast with whatever we can carry, and hope that these brutes don't chase us down the valley faster than we can run? Or do we stay here and fight for this place, our town and our factories? Our bridge and our houses?"

"Fight!"

Dram didn't see the female dwarf who shouted first, though she sounded an awful lot like Sally. That first cry was echoed almost immediately from a score—a hundred—throats, until the whole town was shouting its determination to give battle, to hold the ground they had claimed for themselves only a few short years before.

And so the issue was decided.

"Swig Frostmead, take three hundred hill dwarves down to the shore. You'll stop 'em if they try to come along the edge of the lake. Rogard Smashfinger will take the mountain dwarves and hold the logging sheds and powder factory at the south edge of town. I'll watch from here with the rest of us, as a reserve force, and we'll counterattack where we can do the most good. Any questions?"

"How do we make sure they save some ogres for us in the reserves?" quipped one burly lumberjack, a man who had taken well to life in a dwarf town.

That provoked a laugh, and the meeting broke up, each fighter grabbing his favorite weapon and heading to his assigned position. Sally stayed behind with Dram; Mikey went with the other children, who were being taken by some of the elders up a narrow side valley, the only other easy route away from New Compound. It was a dead end, leading to a box canyon where a number of mines had been excavated, but they should be safe there.

The children would take shelter in one of the deepest mines. If the dwarves were driven from the field, the survivors would seal off the entrances and hide in the mines along with the young ones. Enough food had been stored there for a month or more of siege.

By the time they had spent a month in the mines, Dram firmly believed, the emperor's armies would have arrived to free New Compound, and Mikey—and all the other kids of the town—could come out to play under the sun and breathe the air of freedom.

Either that or by that time, they would all be dead.

⋇⊙⊛⊙⋗⊙⊛⊙⋗⊙⊛⊙⋗

The Nightmaster moved invisibly through the streets of Palanthas. He departed from his temple, a secret shrine beneath the ground near the center of the city, and rose up through a grate in the street. As stealthy as the wind, he flowed above the ground, unseen, unheard, not even sensed. The gate in the city wall was nothing to him; he simply drifted up and over the wall as a cloud of gas and continued toward his destination beyond the old city.

Approaching the palace of the lord regent, the high priest of Hiddukel disdained the gates and stairways and courtyards. He rose through the air like a bird—or a bat—coming to rest on a lofty balcony. Though the night was warm, the doors leading into the palace were closed and barred. No matter: the Nightmaster dissolved into a pool of vapor on the paving stones of the balcony.

Still soundless and unseen, he flowed through the narrow gap underneath the door. Within the chamber, he took a moment to coalesce, watching the man who was poring over a scroll, working sums and subtractions with a *scritch scritch scritch* of pen on parchment.

Lord Regent Bakkard du Chagne had not weathered his change in status very well, reflected the Nightmaster. The lord, who had been the unchallenged master of Palanthas until the emperor had come to power, had grown overweight and round-shouldered. His hair, always thin, was nearly gone, the few remaining strands were pale and pathetically stringy. Though three bright lanterns were arrayed on his table, he still leaned low, his face near his writing, squinting as he studied his figures.

Abruptly he looked up at the place where the Nightmaster was hovering invisibly. "I thought I felt you!" he snapped. "What do you want?"

The high priest of Hiddukel sighed and materialized to stand on the floor, his features—as ever—concealed by his black mask.

"Trying to squeeze the last drop of blood out of each coin?" he asked drolly, enjoying du Chagne's flash of anger as the regent stiffened and turned his face toward his visitor.

"How dare you speak to me like that!" he spat.

"A mere joke between old friends," replied the cleric. "I meant no disrespect."

"You forget yourself, my old ally," said the lord regent. "I know the truth about you, and for that knowledge I will demand respect and obedience!"

"Very well, my lord. I apologize." Even as he spoke, the priest felt a tingle, his pleasure kindled by his companion's anger. Ever it was with the minions of darkness: they thrived on conflict, violence, and fury.

Du Chagne sat, glowering, and the priest pulled out a chair and sat across the table from him. "As a matter of fact," the black-masked man went on, "my visit should please you as well."

The lord's eyes narrowed, and he looked at his visitor shrewdly. "Oh?" he inquired noncommittally.

"You should know that all the pieces of our plan have been put into place. The time has come to act, and if we are decisive, the emperor's reign may come to an end within the next few days."

"What do you mean, exactly?" asked du Chagne.

"I mean the emperor is gone from the city. The High Clerist's Pass is closed to him, so he will not return in any timely fashion. I have troops coming to the city and will see that they enter."

"Troops? You mean Dark Knights?" asked the lord.

"Yes, in fact. But they will encounter no real resistance. The city garrison is not only toothless, but riddled with spies."

"Do you forget the foe that vexed us through our previous reign? The Legion of Steel! They have agents everywhere, and as much as they hate the emperor, they will surely rise up against a coup of Dark Knights. Don't underestimate the Legion of Steel!"

"Good news there, too, my lord. Of course I know the legion to be a formidable enemy. But now I have, after years of trying, figured out a way to neutralize them. An unwitting pawn has been placed in their midst. As soon as the Black Brigade reaches the city gates, you must be prepared to reclaim your seat as lord regent of Palanthas. And the new Solamnic nation will be no more."

❦

"Can you hold this place with only five hundred men?" Blackgaard asked Hoarst skeptically. The Thorn Knight and the captain stood in the Nest of the Kingfisher, the little parapet that jutted above the High Lookout at the pinnacle of the High Clerist's Tower.

The troops of the Black Army were assembled in the many courtyards that surrounded the broad base of the great spire. But there were not as many soldiers as either man would have liked to see: the fanatical defense of the Solamnics had claimed the lives of more than a third of the army's three thousand men.

The Thorn Knight shook his head. "I don't think so. Do you?"

"No," the mercenary captain replied. "We would be subject to the same kind of attack that we ourselves employed against the garrison. I should say we need more than a thousand swords to do an adequate job."

"Which leaves less than eight hundred for the march on Palanthas," Hoarst replied. "Rather too few, I think."

"Damn those traps!" snapped Blackgaard. "Three hundred good men, burned alive! And how many more drowned, crushed, or mangled?"

Hoarst shrugged; the past was past. "Well, there is one

way I could bring more troops here," Hoarst said thoughtfully. "It would require an unusually powerful spell, but I believe I could make it happen."

"You could?" the captain asked hopefully. "How? From where?"

"I could borrow them from our former master," Hoarst said in a tone dripping with irony, "and his army on the plains."

"But they're hundreds of miles away!"

"That, of course," the Thorn Knight replied mysteriously, "is where the magic must come into play."

"Surely you can't teleport an entire army?" Blackgaard probed, very intrigued.

Hoarst shook his head. "No, the teleport spell works only for one person at a time. Perhaps I could cast it over and over, but that would be inefficient."

"Then how will you do it? And how confident are you that you can pull it off?"

"Confident enough to suggest you take all but two hundred of your men with you to Palanthas. I will depart for my own castle and make the preparations there. Within a few days—certainly before the Solamnics can react—I will have a full garrison here.

"I rather look forward to facing the emperor here," Hoarst added. "Ogres throwing rocks from these walls will cost him half his men. And the other half will die trying to scale the ramparts."

"What about his cannon?"

Hoarst shrugged. "He only had one left when he marched across the plains. Even if it survives his campaign against Ankhar, it won't be enough to bring down this great fortress. This tower is ten times larger than those spires of Vingaard, after all. And if you recall, I destroyed half of his battery at the foothills battle with but a single fireball."

"I do remember," Blackgaard said, nodding. "It was the high point of the battle, from my point of view. Things turned sour on us not too long after that."

"This time," the Thorn Knight said confidently, "the outcome will be sweet, not sour."

"Very well," said the captain. "Then I will take the rest of the brigade and march on Palanthas."

"Where the gates will open before you and the Solamnic Knights will fall."

Hoarst looked to the east and wondered how many days it would be—weeks, more likely—before Jaymes Markham brought his army up that road. It did not matter.

Whenever he came, Hoarst would be ready.

※※※※※※※※

True to Dram's estimate, the ogre army came around the bend in the road just over an hour later. The dwarf recognized Ankhar, swaggering along at the front of his horde, and felt a familiar rush of adrenalin as the enemy force spread out. The old campaigner had learned a thing or two, the dwarf was forced to acknowledge: instead of attacking in haste, his army was ordered to halt.

Together with a few huge ogres and that shriveled witch of a hobgoblin, the half-giant climbed a low knoll on the edge of the valley and peered at Dram and New Compound from across the distance, appraising the lake, the precipitous walls, and the bridge that was the only route leading north out of the town. Dram was disturbed to see a couple of unusually big draconians with the half-giant, and he wondered what other surprises Ankhar had in store.

A half hour later, the little party trooped down the hill,

dispersing into different sections of the barbarian horde. It looked as though the half-giant were intending to attack head-on but also dispatch a secondary force along the lake. Smart moves, Dram thought grimly. He or Jaymes would have done the same thing.

Dram looked ruefully at Sally, who was holding a black-smith's hammer with a haft almost as long as she was tall, and forced a smile of encouragement. She looked back at him and grinned cheerfully.

Then the ogres roared into the attack. They came in a rush, and Dram knew that Rogard Smashfinger's mountain dwarves at the edge of town would quickly be overrun.

"Charge!" he cried, dashing forward as fast as his stubby legs could carry him. He waved his own weapon of choice, a keen, double-edged axe, and felt a primeval thrill as hundreds of dwarves echoed his battle cries and joined the attack. Then he remembered that one of those dwarves was Sally, and the momentary joy vanished into a cold, doomed feeling. He spared a glance over his shoulder and saw that she was running right behind him; she winked, hoisting her heavy hammer without any apparent exertion.

Heartsick, he realized that she was sensing that primitive battle lust, which had animated so much of his life, for the first time.

The bulk of the ogres smashed against the two sturdy build-ings where the mountain dwarves had elected to make their stand. Timbers shook and groaned, and the drumbeat of blows rang out like the thunder of a great storm. Many ogres spilled between the factory and the logging shed, crowding onto the main road into the village. It was there that Dram led his counterattack.

Within moments the ogres were upon them. Dram dodged the first blow from a heavy club, swinging upward to disembowel a huge, lumbering bull. The brute uttered a fearsome wail and toppled, flailing. With a nimble dodge, the dwarf ducked out of the way then scrambled up on the still-twitching corpse to swing his axe through a slashing circle, holding the middle of the ogre line at bay.

"Look out!" Dram heard Sally cry, and he threw himself down behind the dead ogre's shoulder as a great spear stabbed past where he'd been standing. The head of the weapon was stone, a glowing green emerald, and recognizing the talisman, the dwarf shouted his defiance and spat a curse of instinctive hatred.

"You!" he roared, popping up and swinging for the haft of the spear with his axe. It was Ankhar himself, the half-giant looming over him, who barely managed to sweep his emerald-tipped weapon up and out of the path of the dwarf's wild blow.

Dram pressed his attack, scrambling over the corpse, swinging his axe in a frenzy. Ankhar snarled and snapped with his great, tusked jaws, but the dwarf was too quick. Skidding down to the ground again, he swung his axe at the half-giant's tree-trunk-sized leg.

But the hulking attacker displayed quick reflexes, backing away only far enough to evade the blow then pivoting and stabbing forward with that great spear. Dram parried the blow, planting his feet.

"I'll distract him!" he heard Sally hiss into his ear. "Go for the kill!"

"No!" he cried, appalled as she darted past him and brought her massive hammer down—hard—on Ankhar's foot. With a roar, the half-giant kicked his heavy boot, the blow catching Sally in the head, flipping her backward like a rag doll. She flew over Dram's head, and he feared she was dead until he heard her spitting curses—the most musical sound he had ever heard in his life.

He renewed his attack with a frenzied, slashing series of swings. Each blow forced the hulking foe to step backward, and the dwarf's momentum carried him in so close that Ankhar could not strike with his long-hafted spear. He tried to kick at Dram, but the dwarf's axe bit home, slicing through part of the half-giant's boot and provoking a howl of real pain.

Ankhar hastily backed away, yielding his place in the fight to a pair of ogres who lunged in from either side. Dram cut one of them down by slashing his hamstrings, and the second one fell with his belly sliced open. By then, alas, the swirl of battle had carried the enemy commander out of sight in the melee.

He went to look for Sally, finding her where she had landed, with a thud, on the road with her back against the factory wall. Her right eye was swollen nearly shut, and she seemed a little dazed as she beamed up at him proudly.

"I saw you chop him in the foot!" she cried, getting up to rejoin the battle. "The same foot he kicked me with!"

"Sally! By Reorx, I thought—you had me—I was so—"

"Oh, be quiet and kiss me. I'll be fine," she said. Right after Dram obliged, she added. "And it looks like we're kicking them out of town."

Sure enough, he noted, the ogres were pulling back from the main street. The drumming on the walls of the logging shed had ceased, and there, too, the attackers were retreating—at least for the moment. The brutes seemed content to taunt and roar at them from several hundred paces away, staying out of arrow range.

But the respite was brief; he saw Swig Frostmead come running up from the plaza. His presence that far from the lake could only mean bad news, and his words confirmed Dram's fears.

"They're coming along the shore!" Swig reported breathlessly. "It was a slaughter over there; I lost a hundred dwarves, and the rest of us fell back. The town will be lost."

≍⊙⊚⊷⊙⊚⊷⊙⊚⊷❦⊷⊙⊚⊷⊙⊚⊷⊙⊚≍

Ankhar limped up to Laka and Guilder, ignoring—for the moment—the pain in the foot that had been so cruelly slashed in his clash with the dwarf. He would probably lose a toe, but for the time being he had more pressing concerns. He had seen Bloodgutter's charge carry the fight along the lakeshore, routing the dwarves who had tried to stop them. The enemy's defenses were breaking there, and it was time for the half-giant to play his surprise trump card.

"Go now," he said to the hob-wench and the aurak. "Fly, and take the sivaks! Go to that bridge we saw and land on it. With all your warriors, hold it, and do not let the dwarves get away."

"Yes, lord," Guilder replied. "We will take the bridge and hold it, as you command."

"Aye, yes—we'll hold it with steel and claw, and with the power of the Prince of Lies!" Laka pledged gloatingly.

"How will the Prince help hold the bridge?" asked Ankhar warily.

"With a wall—a wall of the dark god's magic," his stepmother explained mysteriously. "It will fill the dwarves with terror."

"Good," the half-giant muttered. "Build this wall on the bridge; terrify the dwarves so we can kill them all!"

He watched in awe as his stepmother hoisted her death's-head talisman and rose into the air, taking flight. The aurak cast a magic spell to follow her, while the sivaks flapped their great wings. All together, more than forty of them zoomed into the air, soaring high above the stunned, disorganized dwarves.

Their destination was the bridge—the only route of retreat out of the town.

✦◦❂◦❂◦❂◦✦◦❂◦❂◦❂◦✦

"It looks bad," Dram said, agreeing with Swig's assessment. "Let's hurry to the bridge, then. Sound the retreat!"

He grabbed his wife by the arm and turned to go. He glanced over at the stone bridge, pretty on its three neat arches, that was the only way out of town except for the narrow side valley leading up to the first mines excavated at New Compound.

"Up there—look!" Sally cried suddenly, looking elsewhere.

"By Reorx, what's that?" demanded Dram, at first thinking that a dense flock of massive vultures had soared down from the mountains. Very quickly he saw that those vultures had legs and arms, tails and crocodilian faces, and that they carried very deadly looking weapons in their hands. "Flying draconians?" he cried in alarm. "Swords up—make ready for attack from above!"

But it was immediately clear that those draconians were not going to swoop down on the thousand alert, aggressive dwarves milling in the center of the town. The formation flew past the dwarves, high up and out of arrow range, and the creatures started to dive down. Dram and Sally exchanged frightened looks.

Their objective was the bridge. The flying draconians came to rest along the length of the span, turning the neat stone structure into an organic arch of flapping wings and hissing, clacking jaws.

At the same time a new, dangerous commotion arose from the south. The ogres and their allies were attacking along the entire front, bursting up from the lakeshore, scrambling through the lumber yards, pushing up the main road, and pouring down every side street. Dram immediately saw the peril—retreat was cut off, and the waves of attackers had them trapped on all sides.

"We've got to clear the bridge!" Dram cried.

"I'll go," Swig shouted back. He was closer by a hundred yards, and with a loud, "You louts, come with me!" he rallied two hundred dwarves to his side. They sprinted for the bridge.

Squinting past them, Dram realized someone was waiting for them on that bridge. A grotesque creature, a withered old hobgoblin dressed in feathers and beads, was waving a club that seemed to be made out of a human skull, dancing and chittering at them. She was perched on the highest arch of the bridge.

"It's that old hob-witch," the dwarf said to no one in particular as he was running hard, breathing hard, and surrounded by other dwarves. "She was with Ankhar every step of the way. But she's not going to stop us, not with a hundred draconians. We'll cross that bridge and set off the charges and buy ourselves a little time."

Just then the hob-wench shrieked triumphantly. When she waved her wand, it crackled with flame, green fire sizzling all around her. She howled in exultant glee as sparks flowed onto the paving stones of the bridge, spilled over the sides, and hissed into the water. A wall of fire erupted, completely sweeping across the width of the span, soaring high, searing hot. Gouts of sparks cascaded down, tumbling along the paving stones, making the bridge so hot that even the draconians leaped and scampered to get away.

One of those sparks made swift contact with the fuse of the largest demolition charge, which led to a huge cask full of black powder. The powder exploded in a searing flash, blowing the entire middle arch of the bridge—not to mention the cackling hobgoblin and several dozen draconians—into tiny bits and pieces.

A column of fire spewed straight into the air, shrouded by smoke. A moment later the huge sound of the blast, a single, startling *boom,* swept over New Compound. The noise echoed off the cliff walls over and over.

And even before the noise faded and the dust settled, Dram knew that their only retreat from New Compound had been cut off. They must stay there and die.

Or they could desperately seek hiding places in the mines with their children.

CHAPTER TWENTY

OUTMANEUVERED

Selinda didn't yield to her despair until Lame Hale left her alone, after once more tying her securely. She had never felt so alone, so overpowered and completely helpless. Hale could do whatever he wanted with her, and no one would know. The dam of her emotions burst, and she sobbed until her heart was drained.

At some point she drifted off to sleep, though it was an uncomfortable rest, and she felt constrained by the bonds on her wrists and ankles, tormented by dreams of an unimaginable fate. Sometimes her tormentor was Lame Hale; sometimes it was her husband or father. She was by turns drugged, bound, or imprisoned, but always compelled to move in some direction she didn't want to go.

When she awakened, she had no idea how much time had passed. She felt better somehow, and her mind was clearer. She found she could think more clearly, though that was little comfort as her only thoughts were questions. Why was Hale doing this? What was to be her fate?

She was frightened but had regained some equilibrium

when the door to the room opened and Lame Hale entered. Perhaps she would learn something, though what she learned might be better not to know.

Her captor brought a waterskin and, limping over to the bed, held it up so she could sip some liquid. She lifted her head then fell back and glared at him. She spoke through the fuzz in her mouth.

"Is this water? Or is it another dose of your Red Lotus?"

Hale chuckled, a cold and unpleasant sound. "This is just water. The lotus is far too precious to waste on one who is already a captive." He looked oddly thoughtful. "I have already been paid very well, but I have to maintain my profit margin."

Reluctant and distrustful but overwhelmed by thirst, she took a few sips of the water. Insofar as she could make it out, the taste was pure, and though she distrusted Lame Hale, the water felt good.

For the moment it seemed as though Lame Hale were concerned primarily with business. In fact, he suddenly sounded a lot like her father—more concerned with making steel than with her emotional needs.

"We have a schedule to maintain, and I must deliver you on time. Your ship is sailing on the evening tide," he informed her, speaking as if he were reading from a bill of lading. "You will be taken aboard at the last moment, under careful guard. And you should know that if you raise any sort of alarm, the captain would much rather throw you overboard than have to explain your presence to the authorities."

"Where is the ship going?" she asked, heart sinking.

"Oh, you'll find out soon enough. Don't worry yourself about things you can't do anything about. My mother always told me that," he said cheerfully. "Some of the best advice I've ever received."

"I'm surprised to hear you even had a mother," Selinda retorted. "Which plane of the Abyss did she come from?"

The man blinked as though he were offended and she felt a momentary glimmer of satisfaction.

"That's enough talking," he snapped, getting to his feet. "It's time for you to go to sleep!"

"No!" she protested. Sleep was the farthest thing from her mind.

Yet even as she spoke, the word came out slurred, thickened by her clumsy tongue. What was happening? Her eyes flashed to the waterskin then saw the gloating on Lame Hale's face.

"You . . . you drugged . . . drugged . . . !" She couldn't even finish the accusing sentence before darkness claimed her again.

⤟⊰⊱⊰⊱⊰⊱✹⊰⊱⊰⊱⊰⊱⤞

Even as the debris from the blown bridge continued to rain down from the sky, splashing into the water, Dram realized the near-hopelessness of their situation. The only path of retreat for the dwarves was gone; if they tried to run through the woods and cross the stream lower down, the ogres could chase them down and slaughter them with ease.

The ogres who had been charging around the lake once again started forward, while the closer wave of attackers—which included the half-giant Ankhar—crowded the road into town. With the enemy closing in on New Compound from two directions, the defenders had only one choice, one place where at least they could hold out for a while—the same place where the elders and children had gone to seek shelter before the battle.

Glancing up the valley at the heights looming over the town, Dram saw the three mine entrances gaping darkly from

281

the mountainside. Each was a large, square hole with a steep approach; a few stout dwarves might be able to hold the gap indefinitely.

"To the mines!" Dram bellowed, waving his arms. He was gratified when dozens of dwarves, hearing him, echoed the call.

"Flee up the ridge and into the shafts! We'll make our stand at each entrance!"

The cry spread. The dwarves moved as one away from the town, racing up the many steep paths leading to the nearest belt of mine tunnels, carved into the ridge looming directly over New Compound. The healthy helped the wounded, while some of the steadiest warriors—including Dram and, to his chagrin, Sally—fought a desperate rearguard battle against pursuing ogres.

Dram and Sally stood side by side on one narrow trail. They pounded their axe and hammer down into the faces of the few ogres who tried to climb up. One of the brutes tumbled back down the mountain, his face split by Dram's blade; another dropped like a felled ox when Sally's hammer connected with his skull. Their ogre companions held back for a moment, but when Dram charged toward them in a frenzy, swinging his axe through vicious circles, their pursuers decided that it would be better to go back down and loot the town rather than chase the crazy dwarves into their holes.

Fortunately, the plunder spread and the pursuit waned—no ogre wanted to leave the best booty to his companions—and the fleeing dwarves quickly scrambled higher and higher. Soon the first of them were filing into the mines, the rest queuing up outside each of the three tunnels.

Gradually the entire surviving population of the town disappeared into the mines nearest to New Compound. The first to enter continued to move deep into the mountains, while the last of them gathered at the tunnel mouths, ready to make a stand. Weapons at the ready, Dram and Sally took their places with a few other sentinels at the mouth of the central mine; other warriors were posted at the mouths of the mines to their right and left.

Their positions were strong; even if attacked, only one ogre could enter a mine at a time, and with two or three dwarves in his path, the defenders should be able to hold for a long time.

And the mine shafts, Dram well knew, were more than a mile deep. They were stocked with many casks of fresh water and a smaller amount of nonperishable food. If the ogres quickly sacked the town and moved on, they might just manage to survive.

⋅≈∘≺∘≈∘≺∘≈∘❁∘≈∘≺∘≈∘≺∘≈⋅

"Oh, come in, Melissa," said Coryn, answering her front door herself because Rupert was running errands in the market. "It's been too long!"

"Thanks for seeing me," said the young high priestess.

"Sure. Come up to the laboratory. I am making a potion and need to keep an eye on the temperature."

The high priestess of Kiri-Jolith followed the white-robed wizard up the wide marble staircase leading to the second floor. Sunlight spilled through a row of windows on the south wall of the long laboratory. The workroom of magic was neat and tidy in a cramped kind of way. Volumes of books lined the shelves, with similar bindings catalogued on the same row. Components were stored in matching white bottles with labels and black stoppers; the different sizes of bottles were all lined up with matching sets.

The place had been designed by Jenna the Red Lady, but

283

the priestess was not surprised to see that Coryn the White was adding her own touches while the house's owner, the reigning head of the Orders of Magic, lived in the Tower of High Sorcery in Wayreth Forest.

Melissa and Coryn, while not fast friends, had both been instrumental in disrupting the power of the Dark Knights in Palanthas. When the Knights of Solamnia launched their coup, the priestess had used spells of darkness and silence to help the rebels achieve surprise. At the same time, the white wizard had caused whole Dark Knight guard garrisons to fall asleep. Her lightning bolt, cast only reluctantly because she disdained killing, had broken the Dark Knights' defense in their last redoubt. After the battle, the priestess's powers had allowed many badly injured men to survive and recover from their wounds.

As Melissa du Juliette took her seat and Coryn adjusted the bellows and flue of her fire, the wizard sensed that the other woman had come to her manor on a matter of some grave concern.

"What's wrong?" she asked.

"Have you heard from Selinda lately?" the priestess responded. "She vanished from her palace chambers three days ago, and no one's seen her or heard of her whereabouts."

"No, I haven't heard from her or talked to her in some time," Coryn replied in a measured tone.

She was surprised at the jealousy she still felt toward the woman who had married Jaymes Markham. Her anger toward the emperor had faded during the weeks since she had seen him, but hearing the very name of the woman who was to bear his child caused her a strange disquiet.

Then, remembering the magic ring she had given to the princess, she also felt a stab of guilt. "She hated being locked up," the wizard said cautiously. "But she . . . she had the means to get out of there."

"I know. She came to visit me," Melissa said. "While Jaymes was gone to Vingaard, she used the ring you gave her."

"Oh?" Coryn didn't know what to say.

"Yes. Did she tell you how she felt about her pregnancy?" asked the priestess. Melissa was only a few years older than Coryn, but her eyes showed the wisdom of an elder.

The wizard decided not to dissemble. "She told me she wasn't sure she wanted the child. I—I gave her the ring because Jaymes was keeping her a prisoner in her room. I couldn't tolerate the thought."

"I think it was good you gave her the key to at least some degree of freedom," Melissa said. "She told me the same thing about the baby. She was terribly frightened—of so many things—but eventually we teleported to Vingaard to confront Jaymes. When she saw the damage he had done to the keep there, she lost heart and decided not face him. So we came back home."

"I didn't know that," admitted the enchantress.

"There is more. A guard—he didn't know who we were—told us that the daughter of Lord Kerrigan had come to see the emperor the night before, to plead with him to cease the bombardment. Apparently she came in the middle of the night and stayed until dawn. And that is when he ordered the gun to cease firing. When Selinda heard that news, she was deeply upset."

"I can understand why," Coryn declared, nodding and feeling a pang of heartache for her rival. "Have you seen her since then?"

The priestess shook her head. "I went to call on her yesterday, just to say hello, and the guards told me she hadn't been seen for days. They were terribly worried, of course, and wondering if they should send word to the emperor. But he's on the other side of the mountains, looking for Ankhar. What could he do from there? And besides, she could be anywhere in the world."

"Yes." Coryn said, grimacing. She shook her head. "This is my fault. If I hadn't given her that ring—"

"Don't talk like that!" Melissa retorted. "We both know he had no right to imprison her. You gave her the means to get out of her cell! That wasn't wrong."

The white wizard sighed. "Do you have any ideas where she might have gone?"

"I . . . I hope she isn't trying to do something—to hurt the baby," the priestess admitted. "I fear for the state of her mind."

"So do I," Coryn replied earnestly.

"I was hoping we could look for her together," said the cleric.

"Combining our skills, yes. I will seek her with magic."

"Very well," said Melissa du Juliette. "And I will try to gain an answer from the gods."

⋉◑◓⋊◐◓⋊◑◓⦿◐◓⋊◑◓⋊◐◓⋊

Ankhar watched with numb disbelief as the massive tubes of the uncompleted bombards burned. In a mad frenzy, the ogres had tossed the unfinished barrels into a great heap, doused them liberally with oil, and ignited the conflagration. Normally the half-giant would have relished such a fiery spectacle, proof of his army's triumph. But the emperor's guns had been decisive against Ankhar in the Battle of the Foothills. Those great weapons, the next generation of savage new armaments, were destroyed without firing a shot. He wished that he could have had a chance to use them.

Worse, the great, searing explosion of the bridge had cost him the life of the person dearest to him in all the world.

"Laka!" he wailed, slumping to the ground, beating the stones of the plaza with his fist.

Pond-Lily watched him warily from nearby. She was still bleeding from the cuff he had given her when she had first offered her sympathies. Her eyes grew moist as the half-giant pressed his face to the paving stones, groaning and wailing.

When he finally caught his breath and raised his head, he saw that his ogres were watching him in amazement. Some of them had stepped away from him as he thumped and wailed, while others—including Bullhorn and Heart Eater—had actually sidled in closer. These two would bear watching, the half-giant suddenly realized.

Ankhar got on his feet with a snort. He reminded himself he could not afford to show weakness, especially not after his warriors had won another great victory—destroying and sacking a town belonging to the ogres' traditional enemy, the dwarves.

Thrusting his chest out, he swaggered around the central plaza, sneering at the great fire rising from the cannon factory, then turning to scowl at the still-smoldering remains of the stone bridge. Some of the buildings in the town were burning heartily, while others were still busy being trampled, plundered, and looted.

Naturally, a dwarf town had plenty of inns, and already a dozen massive kegs of dwarf spirits had been trundled into the street. The taps had been opened, and ogres were lining up in order of physical prowess, tilting forward to fill their gullets with the fiery, intoxicating brew. Whoops and hollers rose from the conquering brutes, and as more and more spirits were consumed, the scene degenerated. A tailor shop was ransacked, and a dozen grotesque brutes began to strut about with undersized dresses and fancy coats draped all over them. A sword smith's shop yielded up its contents after an ogre smashed down the door, and in just a moment, five clumsy sword-wielding ogres—unused to the keenness of dwarven steel—were bleeding from deep, accidental cuts.

Meanwhile, Ankhar seethed. The dwarves had for the most part escaped. He glared up the hill at the three dark holes where they had vanished. And again he remembered his mother, violently slain by the trap so cleverly laid by those fiendish dwarves.

A familiar figure clumped up to the half-giant, and Ankhar recognized Bloodgutter. The ogre general, veteran of so many campaigns and conquests, remained aloof from the chaotic celebrations of novice raiders. He looked with contempt at the drinking and looting.

"We go down the valley now? Attack humans on the plains?" Bloodgutter asked, pointing toward the low country. Though the bridge was gone, the stream was not terribly deep, and it was clear the ogres would be able to wade the flowage and complete their crossing of the Garnet range. Once on those plains, as Ankhar had promised, they would be able to go anywhere they wanted.

The half-giant blinked. Yes, that had been his plan. And that plan had worked very well, except for the unexpected obstacle in their path of the newly sprouted town. Even the dwarf town had barely slowed up their advance—the whole attack had taken only a couple of hours—though the celebration threatened to take all night.

In the morning, as planned, they ought to just march away and leave those dwarves hiding in their holes.

"No," Ankhar decided grimly. "Not right away."

"Stay here what for?" replied the ogre bull.

The half-giant pointed at the mine entrances. "We go up there where dwarves hide. We kill them."

"What if stay in holes?" inquired the ogre, thinking it over.

"Then we bury them. Let the mines be their graves," Ankhar replied, satisfied that, one way or another, his mother would be avenged.

⊱⊷⊶⊷⊶⊷⊶❂⊷⊶⊷⊶⊷⊶⊰

Leaving the more heavily equipped Crown Army in its wake, the Palanthian Legion made a forced march of seventy-five miles in a little more than two days. That was a splendid accomplishment by any measure. Even so, they were two dozen miles away from the feet of the Garnet range when they came upon a lone dwarf, battered and bloody, staggering toward them across the plain.

"New Compound is lost, Excellency!" the dwarf declared, falling on the ground even as Jaymes, leading the legion, rode forward.

"How?" he demanded. "Was it Ankhar?"

"Yes—and a horde of ogres. They came down from the heights, surrounded the town, and sacked it."

"The dwarves? Did they flee?" asked the emperor, appalled by the news.

"No, lord. The bridge was destroyed, and they were trapped. Many were killed, but the survivors and women and children took shelter in the mines."

"And what then?"

"I confess, I fled the place, my lord. I was responsible for carrying away the news. But before I left, I saw the ogres head up there, to the mines. They climbed over the mouths, and started to fill them with rubble. They threw in great boulders, hundreds of them. It looked like each of the tunnels was being completely sealed."

Buried alive. Jaymes felt a shiver of claustrophobic dread. "How long ago was this?"

"Two days ago they attacked. I slipped out of there the dawn before this day."

"Then Ankhar may still be up there? In the mountains?"

"I believe so, Excellency."

The emperor looked to the south. From where he sat his horse, the crests of the Garnet Range stood out in clear relief. The mouth to the valley of New Compound remained out of sight, but he knew it was somewhere out there, not far, in the misty lowlands.

"General Weaver," he called out.

"Yes, my lord," replied the commander of the Palanthian Legion, urging his horse out ahead of the rest of the column, which had halted.

"The half-giant and his ogres are still up in the valley of New Compound, distracted by a clash with dwarves. Their options of escape are limited. We might be able to trap them there."

"I understand, Excellency. What are your orders?"

"Send riders to General Dayr of the Crowns, and General Rankin of the Swords. Have them bring up their armies as quickly as possible."

"Certainly, sir. You realize, it will be several days before either of them arrive on the scene."

"Yes, I do. That's why my legion will take the lead. We're going to march into that valley, pin the ogres in the mountains, and destroy that monster and his followers once and for all."

CHAPTER TWENTY-ONE

TRAPS AND PRISONERS

Blayne moved quietly down the dark street. It was his fourth visit to the legion's headquarters, and he felt every bit as nervous and furtive as the first time. But he had no trouble identifying the door, opening it, and slipping inside. And after entering, at least, he wasn't manhandled by the guards. Instead, they waved him through, and he found Sir Ballard in the usual meeting hall, waiting with a full complement of fifty or sixty men of his secret legion.

Clearly they were beginning to trust the nobleman from Vingaard; never before had Blayne seen more than a dozen legionnaires there. They made room for him at the head table, one man even bringing him a mug of cold ale. He nodded at a few he recognized.

The friendliness was not universal. Across the table sat a dark-skinned knight he had never seen before, and Blayne was surprised at the suspicion and hostility he noted in the man's black eyes.

"Wet your whistle," Ballard said encouragingly. "We've got a lot of planning to do." Noticing that Blayne was staring at the dark-skinned knight, Ballard chuckled. "Sir Jorde," he said, gesturing to the dark-skinned man. "I'd like you to meet Lord Blayne Kerrigan, now the rightful master of Vingaard Keep."

"Hello," Blayne said as pleasantly as he could. Jorde replied with a slow, deliberate nod.

Gratefully, Blayne took a drink as Ballard, who seemed to be in command of that unit of the Legion of Steel, explained.

"There are two more companies in the city, each awaiting word from me that it is time to move," the knight said. "The legion is ready to retake our city and restore rule based on the Oath and the Measure. But we need time to implement our plan—more time before the emperor arrives here with his own army."

"I understand," replied Blayne. "And I have good news on that score. I have just received confirmation: the High Clerist's Tower has been liberated by rebel forces. It surrendered without resistance to a band of fighters. They have manned the battlements and are prepared to block the pass against the emperor's passage."

"That's good news, if true," Ballard said. "A good garrison—say, a thousand men—manning the walls in that bottleneck will be enough to impede a whole army."

"But where'd they come from?" Sir Jorde asked curtly. "I'd wager it would take a lot more than a thousand men to pry that fortress away from Markus and his Rose Knights."

"It was an army of rebels—a small one, but several thousand trained men," Blayne explained. "They were gathered in a secret valley not far from the tower. They're friends of mine; they took me in when I fled Vingaard Keep in front of the emperor's men."

"These rebels—are they men of Vingaard too?" asked Ballard.

"Well, no," young Kerrigan admitted. "At least, I don't know them as such. I think they have come from all across Solamnia, everywhere people have become fed up with the emperor's edicts."

Sir Ballard fixed the lord with a piercing, suspicious look. "Well, it's a curious development. I thought General Markus was the emperor's man all the way, so I'm surprised to hear he would surrender without a fight. How good is your source of information?"

Blayne stiffened. Should he take offense? How good *was* his source?

When he considered the circumstances, the unseen man cloaking himself in magic and visiting Blayne in his small room in the thick of the night, he, too, wondered if he were being deceived.

But no, that was impossible. The man must be trustworthy. Blayne's concealed visitor had known too much about Hoarst and the Black Army. It was Hoarst who had guided him to Archer Billings, and Billings who had put him in touch with the legion. The only explanation was that his nocturnal visitor was in league with Hoarst.

"I believe it's reliable," Blayne said. "I got it from a source connected to the man who sent me here."

He had expected that explanation to be sufficient, but Ballard seemed surprisingly unmoved. "We'll have to watch and wait, to be sure," the legionnaire said. "But at the same time we'll get ready to move at a moment's notice." He turned to Sir Jorde. "Can you send a man up there to check it out—as fast as possible?"

The dark-skinned knight nodded. "I'll send my fastest rider

at once." He rose and, without a second look at Blayne, headed out through a door at the back of the room.

Ballard took a drink from his mug and changed the subject. "With the emperor's legion out in the plains, there are only a few places in Palanthas that we need to infiltrate and control in order to effectively seize the city," he said. "The palace on the central plaza, of course. The headquarters of the city guard, in the mayor's office—the guard will not offer resistance if their commanders order them to stand down—and of course, the three gates leading through the Old City wall. We'll be stretched pretty thin."

"I have good news there too. The rebels in the High Clerist's Tower have sent a number of men, something like a thousand, down the road to the city. They should be here in a matter of days, and they'll augment our numbers and help us."

Ballard nodded. He didn't seem to take the news of reinforcements with as much enthusiasm as Blayne would have expected. Instead, he cleared his throat, looking at the lord from the corner of his eye.

"Then there's the lord regent's palace, outside of the walls," he said. "Have you considered whether or not du Chagne will ally himself with us or stand against us?"

"I had intended to ask him to be our spokesman," Blayne said. "That is, if you agree. His differences with the emperor are well known. He's the only one with the authority to inspire the people to support our . . ." He hesitated, groping for the right word. "Coup," he concluded, realizing he had to accept the fact.

"I agree," Ballard said. "He was our leader until the emperor took control a few years back. He's not really a military man, but he's always had the sense to leave that department to others."

"For better or worse," one knight muttered. "Remember his dukes?"

Ballard shrugged. "Aye, but the people will respect him. Still, the emperor married du Chagne's daughter. Will that complicate matters?"

"No," Blayne replied with certainty. "If anything, it's a point in our favor. I have it on good authority that the two men hate each other, and that the daughter is much the sticking point."

"Well good, then. I'd heard rumors of that myself but couldn't be certain whether or not they were true. A fellow of noble blood such as yourself no doubt has better contacts for courtly gossip," Ballard added dryly.

"I suppose so," Blayne said, embarrassed in spite of the fact it was probably true. "In any event, I suggest we go to see the lord regent at once and bring him in on our conspiracy."

"Once again, I agree," Ballard said. He nodded at the younger man's half-full mug. "Now, drink up. We've got work to do."

⸎

As a mountain dwarf, Dram should have been right at home in the dark, crowded tunnel of the mine shaft. After all, he hadn't even seen the sun for the first decade of his life and had spent most of his youth in the great, subterranean, halls of Kayolin. Many mountain dwarves lived their entire lives underground as the natural course of things.

But he was surprised to realize he actually missed the daylight. For the past three days, as some thousand of his townsfolk had huddled with him in the narrow, sunless tunnels, he had come to realize how much he had fully embraced life on the surface. He didn't feel claustrophobia or fear, but he had really come to cherish the world of fresh air, sunlight, stars, wind, and sky.

How long would it be before he sampled any of those joys again, if ever? The ogres had sealed the three tunnel mouths very thoroughly. They hadn't even attempted to attack the entrenched dwarves, no doubt perceiving their disadvantages: because of their size, one ogre at a time would have had to fight against two or three dwarves at each narrow passage. So Ankhar had shrewdly ordered his ogres to toss large boulders into the mine entrances. The bombardment had seemed like a game to the brutes, as they competed to see who could throw the largest rocks with the most force.

A few dwarves had tried throwing the rocks out as fast as they were coming in, but they had been pummeled. When the third dwarf had fallen with a crushed skull, Dram had ordered the rest to withdraw deeper into the mines. The ogres had wasted little time in sealing off each hole, and even after all evidence of the sun had been blocked off, the dwarves could hear more and more rocks *thunking* and *crashing* into the pile. The result was a plug that was probably more than a hundred feet thick—and many, many tons of weight—blocking the mouth of each of the three mine entrances.

"Pop?" asked Mikey, climbing into his lap. Sally and about a hundred others were sitting or lying nearby; the place near the mouth of the center tunnel was one of the widest spaces in the network of tunnels. They had been eating and sleeping there since the siege began.

"Yeah, Mike?" Dram said, forcing a jovial tone into his voice.

"Go outta here?" The little tyke pointed a chubby finger toward the massive pile of rocks blocking the mine tunnel.

"Well, you see Red and Beebus over there? And Damaris?

It's their turn to dig now, and when they're done, it'll be my turn again. And sooner or later, we'll have all those rocks gone and go outta here."

In truth, the excavation was far more involved. Three diggers worked shoulder to shoulder, sometimes standing, other times kneeling, or even lying down to pull a stubborn piece of debris out of the way. Other dwarves loaded those rocks into mining carts, while still more trucked those carts deeper into the mine, where the excess rock was unceremoniously dumped into plunging, unused shafts. The same work was going on in the other two tunnels, Dram knew; there were side passages connecting all three mines, so in effect the whole town was sheltering in a network of tunnels that formed an underground fortress.

But it was a fortress with very limited food supplies. Originally they had provisioned the mines with enough victuals for the approximately three hundred children and their caretakers to survive for a month. There were four times as many dwarves in there as originally anticipated, with most of them needing significantly more food than a child. Dram had ordered the food to be strictly rationed almost immediately after entering the mines.

At least they had fresh water from several natural streams descending through the interior of the mountain ridge and enough air for them to breathe comfortably, thanks to some long ventilation shafts extending to the top of the ridge. Considering the fact they had no way to get out of there, their fortress was more of a prison—which was all right temporarily, as long as it didn't prove a tomb.

Easing Mikey down to the floor, Dram got up and went to check on the progress of the work. "How much farther?" he asked Red, who had been one of the miners who originally excavated the tunnel.

"I'd say eighty feet," the hill dwarf, nicknamed for his long, fire-colored hair and beard, replied. He wiped his brow, studying the chisel marks on the wall that served as calculations. "They really sealed us in."

"Need more help?" Dram offered.

"Not for now. Sit down, take your rest. There'll be plenty of work for you later."

Dram went back to his place and sat down, grateful when Sally slipped her hand into his. Mikey sat between them, slowly drifting off to sleep. Swig Frostmead came over, his face locked in a frown. He was on the verge of some loud complaint when he noticed the sleeping lad.

Glumly, Sally's father sat beside Dram, watching the workers. Finally, he leaned over and whispered into his son-in-law's ear.

"Why didn't you think to store a few kegs of spirits in here?" he wanted to know.

⊱⊶⊙⊶⊙⊶⊙⊱⊙⊷⊙⊷⊙⊷⊱

Selinda was aware of voices. She tried to move, to speak, but no noise came from her lips. For a panicky moment, she feared that the hateful Lame Hale had poisoned her with another lotus drink. The sounds around her were vague and indistinct and did nothing to refresh her memory, to enlighten her.

But after a while, straining her ears, the voices started to make sense.

"Ten prime diamonds, and a large bottle of the potion. That's a fair price for this merchandise, I agree."

Selinda recognized Lame Hale's voice, and her throat constricted at the thought that *she* was the "merchandise" at the heart of the negotiation.

"I agree as well." The second speaker's voice was muffed,

298

as though he spoke through gauze or something.

The princess tried to open her eyes, but the lids refused to move—almost as if they were glued shut by some gummy substance. Frantically, she strained, trying to move, to speak, to see.

"Now get her out of here!" Hale said. "It makes me nervous, and she's been here too long already!"

"I intend to."

Selinda heard someone come close, felt a presence—like a cold, black shadow—loom over her. Abruptly a cold, clawlike object brushed her hand, and a painful shock pulsed through her body, forcing an involuntary scream.

Immediately her eyesight cleared, and she found herself looking up at a faceless man, an image of darkness that utterly terrified her. After a moment she realized that it was a person concealed by a black mask, but that only added to her fear.

"Get up, my dear," he commanded in a clipped tone. "You will find that your limbs are quite capable of functioning again."

Wiggling her fingers, lifting an arm, Selinda was surprised to see he spoke the truth. She forced herself to a sitting position, swaying dizzily. The man was standing very close to her, and she nearly gagged on the stench of foulness and decay that seemed to permeate his black robe.

"You aren't going to take her out the front door, are you?" asked Hale, alarmed.

"Of course not." The masked man stared down at her. She felt like a mouse under the keen stare of a circling hawk. "Stand up," he said.

She did so, still dizzy, bracing herself against the bed. A momentary thought of flight entered her mind, but she banished it just as quickly. Even if she were steady enough on her feet to try to make a getaway, she sensed power in the man's voice and knew that she couldn't resist if he simply ordered her to stop. He must be some kind of wicked priest, she deduced, but she couldn't guess which god he served.

"I know you have powerful friends," he said to her, mildly amused. "So you must forgive a little spell that will mask you from magical detection."

The priest pulled a dirty black powder from his pocket and sprinkled it over Selinda. She wanted to shake her head, to lift her hands and brush it away, but her body would not obey her mind.

"That will suffice," he said. "Now we go."

He swirled his hands around himself and circled Selinda's head while muttering a deep, glottal chant. Almost immediately the room filled with gray haze, so thick Selinda couldn't see the walls or floor; then she realized that the room itself had disappeared. She felt the sensation of standing in an immense space, but she could see nothing beyond the tip of her nose.

She experienced that clawlike touch again and gasped as the priest took her hand. Every fiber of her being compelled her to pull away, but once again she felt powerless. "You do not want to escape me . . . not here," said the black-masked man. "You would wander for very many lifetimes and never find your way back home."

Terrified, she felt herself pulled along, dragged and stumbling across some kind of smooth, hard surface. She looked down but couldn't see anything except the gray haze. For a little while she tried to count her steps, but her mind was clouded, and the numbers swirled randomly in her head. Had they gone twenty paces, or was it two hundred? She had no way of telling.

"Now . . . here we are," the priest said finally. The grayness vanished and she found herself in a wood-paneled room lined with books. There was a fireplace—cold at the moment—along one wall. There were great windows, and she could see that it was fully dark outside.

The place was vaguely familiar—no, more than vaguely, she had been there many times! Why was her mind so thick?

"I have her, my lord," said the priest, addressing someone behind Selinda.

She turned and gasped out a single word. "Father!"

Then the contents of her stomach rebelled, doubling her over, forcing her to retch all over the expensive imported carpet.

❦⊶⊷⊶⊷⊶⊷❦⊶⊷⊶⊷⊶⊷❦

"Excellency! The men are tiring badly. Are you sure you don't want to stop for a few hours to let them rest?"

General Weaver's question was legitimate since the army had been marching hard for three days. But the emperor had no patience for questions or delays. Jaymes had traveled that valley many times. He knew that New Compound was a two-hour march away—two hours if they could at least maintain their crawling pace!

"No rest!" he snapped. "There'll be plenty of time for that after Ankhar is dead."

He knew the risks he was taking. Bringing a fatigued army directly into battle from a forced march tempted disaster. But it was a calculated risk too, for he reckoned the ogres would be celebrating chaotically after driving the dwarves out of New Compound. Most likely the great majority would be drunk or groggy with powerful hangovers. If he delayed, his men would have time to rest, but the enemy would have time to recover as well.

And there were other risks. What if Ankhar was planning to withdraw back up and over the Garnet Mountains? They might lose his trail entirely! And how many dwarves had he killed? Was Dram alive . . . and Sally? What about their little son? With a twinge, Jaymes realized he hadn't been there to see the lad in more than a year.

Curse Dram for a fool anyway! If he had built those bombards—ah, a foolish complaint at the moment. The big guns could reduce a fortress, but they would have been useless against ogres swarming down from the mountains. By the time the gunners were readying their second or third shot, the battery would have been overrun.

"Move!" demanded the emperor, picking up the pace of his own marching. He had dismounted hours earlier, striding on foot so as to set a better example for the men. He was grateful for the good dwarven road, smooth and gently graded, carrying them steadily and quickly up the valley toward New Compound.

He recognized a ridge before them, a moraine running perpendicular to the valley floor. It was the last obstacle before the town, and he halted his army. Ordering them to deploy on both sides of the road, he advanced carefully to a crest with General Weaver and Sergeant Ian.

They spotted the smoke even before the town came into view. Crouching, moving through some underbrush to the side of the road, they made their way to a decent vantage, where they could look over New Compound without being observed.

The great fire in the plaza was the central feature of the view, still casting a plume of smoke more than a mile into the sky. At the base of the blaze, smoldering rather than flaming, lay the charred ruins of nearly a dozen bombard tubes. So Dram had started manufacturing them after all!

And Ankhar had destroyed them and so much more. Jaymes took in the blackened warehouses, the splintered tangle that had been a neat lumberyard. The doors of every house he could see had been smashed in, with personal belongings, fabrics, and furniture scattered around in the streets and yards. The emperor's jaw clenched in fury, and his eyes narrowed to mere slits, glaring with hatred at the damage that had come to the place—to *his* place!

For if Dram Feldspar had been the caretaker of New Compound, Jaymes Markham had been its creator. His orders had caused it to be built there, and his steel had funded its operations. It would be his soldiers who avenged its destruction.

His narrowed eyes took in the military features of the valley. The once-splendid stone bridge—Dram had been inordinately proud of the structure, Jaymes thought—was a blasted ruin. Beside the wrecked span, the ogres had placed log bridges across the stream at several places, obviously readying for a march down the valley. But bridges could work in both directions, Jaymes knew.

At the moment the ogre army looked more like a disorganized mob. A few of the troops were up on the mountainside, apparently inspecting the rock piles where the dwarves of New Compound had been buried alive. The others were carousing through the ruined town. From where Jaymes was, it appeared as though nearly all were drunk. Certainly they were not expecting battle.

"We're going to strike at once," the emperor declared curtly.

"Certainly, Excellency," General Weaver declared. He gestured to the base of the cliff wall to the left, where a dense pine forest concealed the ground. "I suggest we send a flanking force through there, and take them from two sides at once."

"No time," Jaymes retorted after a brief pause. "The ground is too rough for troops; it would take them hours to get into position."

"Perhaps a reconnaissance up there, my lord?" Weaver suggested.

"No, I cannot accept any delay!" snapped the emperor. "They are ripe for attack now—surely you can see that. We strike at once!"

"Of course, Excellency."

The two men quickly made their way back to the legion. The skirmishers had deployed in front, with the ranks of the light infantry arrayed behind. Jaymes was pleased to see the three companies of New City men who had been mauled so badly at Apple Ford claimed positions in the center of the line. They would redeem themselves, he knew. The heavy infantry and cavalry formed a third line, with the archers ready close behind.

"I want a general advance!" Jaymes ordered, once again climbing into his saddle. "All infantry units, close in on the double! I want the cavalry ready to charge as soon as I give the words. Go in quietly at first, but as soon as they see you coming, I want you to shout your loudest—break their morale from the very start!"

With a flick of the signalman's flag, the great lines began to move up and over the moraine, breaking into a trot as they hurried down the smooth, grassy slope on the far side. In a moment they reached the river, the well-drilled units smoothly forming columns to rush across the three log bridges Ankhar had so thoughtfully put in place for them.

Hundreds of men were across the river by the time one of the ogres in the town raised a howling alarm. His cry was answered by the challenge of five thousand human soldiers as the first ranks of Palanthian Legion hurtled into the attack.

The ogres were clearly shocked by the sudden appearance of the army of humans. Many turned to fight, while others simply fled through the streets of New Compound, toward the great plaza along the lake.

"Go!" cried Jaymes, spurring his roan in the lead of the attack. "Cut them down!"

Giantsmiter was in his hand, and he slashed through the face of a foolish ogre who had turned to gape at the unexpected attackers. Arrows flew over the front rank, plunging among the disorganized barbarians. Men split into companies and platoons, charging into buildings where they saw ogres taking refuge. A dozen bulls, some staggeringly drunk, were trapped in a pigsty, and men with spears stood around the fences and stabbed until all of them were dead or dying.

There were no dwarves in view, so Jaymes could only hope they were still behind the stone barricades in the mines. He slew ogres wherever he could find them and cut down a few hobgoblins for good measure. The fierce exultation of battle filled his heart once again, and he was startled by the savage delight he felt. It had been a very long time since he had wielded his blade against a foe.

And where was Ankhar? Reining in just for a moment, allowing the tide of his men to sweep past, the emperor sat his saddle and looked across the melee raging through the town. He would find the enemy commander and make sure he never made war again.

It was a personal matter.

CHAPTER TWENTY-TWO

THE SECOND BATTLE OF NEW COMPOUND

"Why not send Bloodgutter's ogres into fight now? Look! We lose battle!" demanded Bullhorn, frightened enough that he dared to challenge Ankhar's plan with his question.

The human soldiers were storming through New Compound, and Bullhorn's ogres—who, as novices to conquest, had been more stupefyingly drunk than most—were being butchered by the score. Half the town already seemed in the attackers' hands, and yet a whole bunch of Ankhar's army wasn't even fighting!

"Where is Bloodgutter?" Bullhorn wailed, trying to ignore the throbbing in his head. "Make him fight too!"

"No!" roared the half-giant. "I stick to my plan!" He raised his fist but was satisfied when the ogre chief backed away without further protest.

The bull was simply too stupid to see the plan was, in fact, working to perfection. Events had begun when Rib Chewer's scouts had reported, a day earlier, that a fast-marching column of humans was approaching the valley of New Compound. Ankhar had been careful to post those scouts, while cautioning the goblin warg riders to avoid discovery. The speedy gobs on their wolves had observed the approach of the enemy column without being detected.

Never very smart with numbers, the goblin chief nevertheless had managed to convey the fact that the new force was not as large as the great armies they had faced a few years before. He was also astute enough to deduce that the human war leader himself—he called himself emperor!—was leading the army.

So Ankhar had made a few stealthy preparations. General Bloodgutter proved himself worthy of his rank as he kicked and cajoled his two thousand veteran warriors away from the booty of the dwarf town. Marching them around the fringe of the valley, he had concealed them in a band of rough forest at the very base of the eastern precipice. Ankhar was pleased and impressed by the fact that, even as the enemy attack unfolded, Bloodgutter's ogres had remained quietly hidden—just as the half-giant had ordered.

Rib Chewer and his riders, on their fierce, lupine mounts, he had positioned behind the stocks of wood along the lakeshore, where they could not be observed by anyone coming up the valley. The goblins had not fed their mounts for more than a day, and the huge, shaggy warg wolves were ravenous and ill tempered—just waiting to be unleashed on the unsuspecting foe.

As a final touch, Ankhar had ordered two of his few remaining sivak draconians—most had perished when the bridge exploded—to wait by his side. They would fly to Bloodgutter when the time was ripe, and Ankhar would spring his trap.

He snorted in amusement, even as a dozen of Bullhorn's ogres, bloodshot eyes wide with terror, were cut down by swordsmen not so very far from where he stood. The humans were advancing into the plaza, coming around both sides of the massive, smoldering pile of ashes left over from the great victory fire.

The enemy general was the one who had led the armies that defeated Ankhar in his earlier war, the half-giant knew. That disgrace was about to be avenged.

"Silverclaw! Crookfang!" barked the one called the Truth.

"Aye, great lord!" replied the two sivaks, bowing to the ground, flapping their great wings in readiness.

"Fly to the woods," Ankhar ordered. "Tell General Bloodgutter that it is time for him to burst forth!"

⊱⊰⊱⊰⊱⊰❀⊱⊰⊱⊰⊱⊰

"Now!" Jaymes ordered. "Lancers, charge!"

The ogres had done exactly as he had expected, falling back across the wide central plaza but forming only an irregular defense on the open ground instead of seeking shelter between the buildings and sheds across the square. Lacking pikes, holding a front that boasted several ragged gaps, they formed a perfect target for a lethal cavalry charge. It was a marvelous situation!

And in the perfection of the situation, the emperor felt a sudden misgiving.

Angrily he tried to shake away the nagging feeling. After all, his enemies were drunk, obviously, even staggeringly so. Jaymes himself had slain an ogre who had been too busy puking in the gutter that he could barely raise his head as death rode him down. How could a foe like that be capable of battlefield deviousness?

But, Jaymes reminded himself, Ankhar had proved during the course of his earlier campaign that he was capable of learning lessons from his failures. After all, he had adopted a reserve; he had learned to array spearmen against cavalry; he had practiced feints and diversions and even, after the siege of Solanthus had been broken, mastered that most difficult of military tactics, the fighting withdrawal.

Why, then, should he expect the half-giant to behave stupidly when things mattered the most?

Narrowing his eyes, Jaymes watched the lancers charge across the square. They tore into the ragged line of ogre warriors, slashing and stabbing. Horses reared and kicked, smashing hooves into roaring, tusk-filled mouths. Steadily the invaders were being beaten and pushed back; the disciplined Solamnic riders held their line, refraining from impetuous pursuit—as they had been trained to do.

The emperor had spotted Ankhar himself. The enemy commander stood upon the stone roof of a low, dwarven house. There were several ogres and a couple of draconians up there with him, and he was watching the fight—which should have been a disaster, from his point of view—with no outward evidence of dismay or consternation.

This realization sounded the final alarm inside of Jaymes.

"Trumpeter! Sound the recall!" the emperor shouted.

Immediately, the brassy notes of the horn rang out. The lancers reined back, reluctantly allowing the stumbling ogres to escape as they looked back in some frustration at their army commander. But they were well-trained Solamnic Knights, so they backed away, keeping their horses—and their keen, bloody lances—trained on the shattered, fleeing enemy before them.

That was when Jaymes saw the two draconians with Ankhar take flight. He noted with some surprise they were sivaks. Those aloof and fearsome dragon-men had not served the half-giant in his previous campaign, and the emperor wondered at the meaning of their presence. Were they fleeing a lost cause?

The sivaks flapped their wings and veered away from the legion positions. A few bowmen launched arrows at them, but the draconians were smart enough to stay out of range. Banking and leveling off, they skirted around the edge of the valley. Jaymes continued to watch as they abruptly dived and came to ground just before the fringe of pine forest at the base of the eastern cliff.

Those were the same woods, he realized, where General Weaver had proposed his flanking maneuver. Jaymes had discounted such a move as impractical, deciding the terrain was too rough for troops and that such a movement would only waste valuable time. Had he been too hasty? Peering at the woods, he saw meadows within the groves, and though much of the ground was rocky, there seemed to be space between the outcrops—most of it concealed by foliage—where troops could hide themselves very effectively indeed.

"General!" cried the emperor, attracting the attention of Weaver, who was directing the heavy infantry as it cleared the buildings on the eastern side of the town. A company of halberdiers were chopping at the barricaded door of a stout house, while spearmen swarmed around the place, stabbing through the windows and the few cracks that had been chiseled in the doors.

The commander rode over at a gallop.

Jaymes, meanwhile, ordered his lancers to redeploy on the near side of the square. "Regroup! Fall back to me! Form a line here!"

"Excellency?" Weaver asked, raising his eyebrows in mute concern.

Jaymes pointed at the woods. "Keep an eye on the flank—there might be something happening over there."

But the warning came too late. More than a thousand ogres suddenly spilled from the tangled, rocky wood at the slope of the cliff, emerging just where the draconians had landed. They came out like a tidal wave, heading straight for the legion's unprotected rear. They were fresh veterans, not the drunkards and hangers-on they had thus far battled in the town, and they came roaring and howling.

At the same time, a surging formation of snarling wolves, each mounted by a shrieking, painted goblin, burst from behind the lumberyards along the lakeshore. The warg riders raced across the plaza, straight toward the lancers, as the horsemen struggled to reform.

Both enemy reinforcements howled maniacally, closing in on the exhausted legion from the flank and the rear. Jaymes spared one glance back at the enemy commander, standing proudly on that stone roof. He couldn't be certain, but it looked as if Ankhar the Truth were grinning in cruel triumph.

✕◦◎◦◎◦◎◦◎ 🜨 ◎◦◎◦◎◦◎◦✕

"I see a spot of light," reported Rogard Smashfinger, falling back from the pile of rubble where he had been excavating for the past two hours. His shift was over, but he insisted on going back for a better look, so Dram joined him in crawling forward, over the jagged boulders that had been pulled out of the plug closing off the mine.

"By Reorx, you're right," Dram said. He wriggled around and called over his shoulder, "Send me up a pike!"

Someone passed him the steel shaft with a sharpened head; the quarters were too tight to swing a pickaxe. The dwarf jabbed and stabbed away at the slowly widening entrance. After almost half an hour of vigorous activity, he had one more rock to clear and used the pike to lever it out of the way. It tumbled down the mountainside and cleared a gap wide enough for Dram to stick his head out.

Conscious of his safety, the first thing he did was check for ogres in the immediate area. But there seemed to be none around; apparently they had all gone back down to the town. Looking below, where he heard the unmistakable sounds of battle, Dram could see why: a legion of knights were there and had already taken back half the town. But as he stared, a horde of ogres surged out of the woods behind the relief force. At the same time, a furious cavalry battle between human horsemen and goblins mounted on warg wolves began on New Compound's central square.

Dram went scrambling back to the huddled dwarves waiting deeper in the mine tunnel.

"The ogres are under attack!" he shouted, his words echoing loudly, almost painfully, throughout the tunnel. "Get out there! Follow me! Pull more rocks out of the way when you come!"

He pushed loose rocks before him as he squirmed out the narrow hole, knocked rubble out of the way, and shouldered aside a good-sized boulder that was blocking one side of the narrow tunnel mouth. That rock tumbled free, almost doubling the size of the opening.

Rogard and Swig Frostmead were close behind him, clearing more of the entrance and emerging in a shower of tumbling stones.

Two by two, then three by three, then four or five at a time, the formerly trapped dwarves pushed their way out of the mine, each one widening the gap just a little bit more, making it easier for those behind to scramble outside. In a few moments, a hundred dwarves had emerged, and the mine shaft was cleared to its normal width.

The rest of the residents of New Compound and the mountain dwarves of Kayolin, came spilling out in a rush and, forming in ad hoc ranks, they moved quickly down the slope toward the town. Each dwarf carried a weapon, and each dwarf heart was filled with the race's traditional hatred of ogres—and the burning desire to avenge the damage done to their once-peaceful town.

"Hurry up!" cried Dram Feldspar. He pointed at the ogres attacking the rear of the legion, identifying them as the most urgent threat. "Take them in the flank! Let's roll the bastards right up!"

"Who's the slowpoke?" cried Sally Feldspar, sprinting past her husband, hammer raised over her head, short legs pumping like pistons as she rushed down the hill.

Dram didn't even try to talk her out of joining the attack. Instead, he just did his damnedest to catch up.

❧◦❀◦❁◦❀◦❁◦❀◦❁◦❀◦❁◦❀◦❁◦❧

Jaymes watched as General Weaver rallied his rearguard in the face of the ogre menace pouring down from the woods. The legionnaires reacted quickly, and the New City light infantry took the first onslaught of the attack on their shields, battling with short swords and giving ground only reluctantly so that the troops behind them would have a longer time to form a more solid line.

The men who had routed away from Apple Creek fought with tenacity, courage, and a high cost in blood and lives. Slowly they inched backward, falling by the score during the brutal fighting, but buying precious time for the rest of Weaver's men to wheel around and better meet the surprise attack.

313

Inevitably, the sheer weight and numbers of the ogres drove the lightly armed men out of the way, leaving more than half of them dead or dying on the ground. The ambush was almost perfectly executed, Jaymes realized with a grimace. He had only himself to blame, having been fooled by that damned half-giant he had too easily dismissed as a barbarian. Weaver had his spearmen and halberdiers formed up; only to Jaymes's eyes they seemed a thin, tenuous line facing a torrent of howling ogres.

If they had any chance at all, it was a very slim chance. Then Jaymes saw movement on the slopes coming from the direction of the mines. It was a fresh brigade of troops, doughty dwarves racing downhill on stumpy legs, beards flying, axes raised.

"For Kayolin!" came one battle cry; "In the name of Reorx!" was another, and Jaymes knew that the dwarves of New Compound somehow had freed themselves from their prison in time to join the battle.

The dwarves spilled from the rocks and tailings of the slope, surprising the attacking ogres on the flank. Immediately the ogre force wavered, the enemy tumbling all over each other as they tried to turn and face the fresh danger. Quickly the dwarf charge shattered the attack and forced the enemy into desperate defensive maneuvers.

That left the emperor to rally his own troops in the center of town. He ordered his archers to concentrate their fire against the goblin warg riders, firing in volleys to maximize the impact of each wave of arrows. Dozens, scores, finally hundreds of the savage cavalry were raked from their saddles. The wolves, maddened by pain and hunger, were as likely to tear at their own dismounted riders as they were to continue the attack, and that allowed the legion lancers, once more formed into battle line, to charge across the square and scatter their foes before them.

Through the waning afternoon and into the evening the fight raged—in long clashes between the dwarves and ogres and in pockets of furious skirmish in the streets, yards, and avenues of the town. Gradually Ankhar's force was pushed back until it was compressed into a semicircle in front of the lake, with humans and dwarves pressing them from all sides.

The sun dipped toward the horizon, purpling the placid waters in a way that ought to have been beautiful—except that it was a valley of violence, suffering, and death.

The pace of the fighting slowed as warriors on both sides succumbed to fatigue mightier than any mortal opponent. Men collapsed from exhaustion; ogres stumbled to the lakeshore to immerse their heads in the cool water, uncaring of their unprotected backs. Horses swayed and drooped, unwilling to run any farther; saddle-sore riders dismounted to let their weary steeds drink and graze.

Still there were pockets of fighting. Dram led a band of dwarves into his own house and, room by room, cleared the enemy out. His heart was hardened by the battle, and that was a good thing; later it would break, he knew, to realize all the death and destruction.

Jaymes, too, was one of those keeping up the attack, rallying small groups of men, closing in on the shrinking enemy perimeter.

And so it was that, finally, Emperor Jaymes Markham found himself facing Ankhar the Truth. The two commanders came around the massive pile of coals on the plaza—all that was left of the burning bombards—and stood, weapons raised, while the troops of their respective armies seemed to step back and draw a collective breath.

The sword Giantsmiter blazed brightly even in the daylight,

but the spearhead on the Shaft of Hiddukel shined with equal intensity. Jaymes and Ankhar cautiously approached each other, surrounded by the shattered and burned ruin of a town that had been a pleasant sanctuary just a few days earlier. The fighting between the ogres and goblins, legionnaires and dwarves faded almost to a halt as warriors on both sides watched the two champions.

For a few moments, the pair simply circled warily, each looking for an opening. Jaymes held the hilt of his weapon in both hands, the blade—with its fringe of flaring blue flame—extended before him, the tip a little bit higher than the grip. Ankhar, in turn, held the thick shaft of his spear in just one hand, with the weapon nearly horizontal, held just above his right shoulder. Twisting to present his left side to his foe, the half-giant wheeled and danced.

His left hand was protected by a heavy gauntlet, and he waved this hand with deceptive carelessness toward the man. Jaymes feinted and his hulking foe thrust down hard with his gleaming spear tip. The emperor bashed the rod of the spear to the side, the keen sword trying to bite deeply into the wood. But the protection of the Prince of Lies obviously extended even to the haft of his mighty weapon, for the fiery sword struck the wood and merely bounced off without chipping or even charring the material.

The ogres formed a semicircle on the side of the plaza with the lake behind them; the dwarves and humans gathered opposite, with their backs toward the ruins of their domiciles and businesses.

When Jaymes circled warily with his back to the enemy, one of the ogres sidled forward, raising a club. Rogard Smashfinger fired a bolt from his crossbow, striking the brute in the chest with enough force to drive him backward and down. When a dwarf raised a hand to aim a throwing axe at the back of the half-giant's head, an ogre threw a skull-sized boulder that crushed the dwarf's shoulder before he could launch his throw. In that way, it was decided that the two sides would settle down and watch, letting the matter rest on the outcome of the one-on-one combat.

❦

Dram fidgeted and muttered, his hands clutching his axe with white knuckles, but he knew better than to interfere. Instead, he also watched, trying unsuccessfully to stand in front of Sally, to block her from any surprise volleys from the ogre troops. Naturally, she pushed through into the front rank, brandishing her hammer as firmly as Dram held his axe.

Jaymes made a sudden rush, swinging to the right then ducking left as Ankhar stabbed with the Shaft of Hiddukel and missed, sticking it instead into the ground. The human drove inward, scoring a hit on the half-giant's knee, but the massive fighter moved with startling agility, swinging his foot in a roundhouse kick and sweeping Jaymes's feet out from under him. He landed flat on his back and escaped a crushing stomp only by rolling desperately to the side.

In a flash the man was back on his feet, but the half-giant had the advantage. Ankhar was able to stab once, again, a third time, and with each attack Jaymes retreated. Blue fire met green, and sparks cascaded, swirling around the two combatants, searing the air with an acrid stench. With each blow, the blazing weapons grew brighter until even those at the fringe of the fight could feel the heat and had to blink past the brightness. Sweat lined the emperor's brow, and the half-giant's sinewy limbs were likewise slick with perspiration. For a long time, there was no sound from the crowd, only the grunting of desperate breathing and the scuffing of boots on the paving stones from the fighters.

Abruptly the human closed in again, raising his sword and whipping it downward with a sweeping blow. Ankhar stumbled over his own feet, spinning his spear sideways and gripping the haft with both hands. Once more Giantsmiter met the Shaft of Hiddukel, but the wooden haft resisted even that heavy blow. Fire surged from both weapons with explosive force, and the two warriors stumbled backward, Jaymes falling on his back and Ankhar going down on one knee.

Rolling to the side, the human rose into a crouch. His shoulders heaved with the effort of each breath, and the tip of his sword rested on the ground—as if he no longer had the strength to lift the heavy blade. Ankhar saw his chance and lurched forward, his movements awkward because of his own weariness. But the spear tip drove directly at the human's pounding heart.

Except Jaymes was no longer there. From some unsuspected reserve, he found the strength to dodge nimbly out of the way, and the emerald head of Ankhar's weapon sliced only the air next to his arm. Overbalanced, the half-giant fell sprawling.

Jaymes stood over him, sword upraised, keen blade aimed downward. Ankhar looked up and saw his own death writ in blue fire.

CHAPTER TWENTY-THREE

THE AGENTS OF CHANGE

Sir Blayne felt better than he had since the day, two months earlier, when he had destroyed two-thirds of the emperor's artillery by surprise attack. That elation had been short lived, of course; he expected a greater triumph the next time around, one that would last a long time.

He and Sir Ballard approached the palace of Lord Regent Bakkard du Chagne. Both men wore knightly regalia, emblazoned with the Crown in Blayne's case, the Rose for Ballard. Their boots and helmets were shined, their swords sharpened but sheathed. If all went well, their mission would not entail drawing those weapons. The two men drew up before the closed gates, where a pair of men-at-arms had been watching their approach curiously.

"I am Sir Ballard of the Legion of Steel, and this is Sir Blayne of Vingaard. We seek an audience with the lord mayor," Ballard declared, standing rigidly at attention. Like Blayne, he held his helmet under his left arm; neither knight saluted the common guards.

Blayne was amazed at how martial Ballard had made

himself look. After the scruffy clothes and irregular appearance of him and his men in their headquarters, the noble had
half wondered if they would be scaling the palace walls by rope
or sneaking in through the kitchen door after dark. Instead, they
marched straight to the front door and presented themselves
formally with a request for an audience. The audacity of it
nearly took the young lord's breath away.

The two guards hastily conferred, one quickly slipping
through the door. "Make yourselves comfortable, sir knights,"
said the other, gesturing to a nearby bench, which the stalwart
knights disdained.

In a few moments, the first guard came back, and he held
open the door. "It so happens the regent has a few moments;
he will see you now."

Without further word, Ballard and Blayne marched into the
palace, their feet moving in perfect cadence as they followed
the guard through a high-ceilinged, marble-floored hall. He
led them into a small reception room, where, despite the warm
summer weather, the windows were shut and a fire burned on
a large hearth.

The lord regent was a small, squat man who reminded
Blayne surprisingly of a frog. He appeared to be bald, though
a close inspection revealed a few thin strands of white hair. He
was beardless, with a receding chin, and his eyes were watery
and seemed oddly out of focus. There was nothing physically
appealing or powerful about him. Kerrigan suppressed a
sense of disappointment, reminding himself of the emperor's
many crimes. Surely *any* man would make a better ruler than
Jaymes Markham!

"My Lord Regent!" said Ballard, saluting with a clap of
his hand to his chest. Blayne did the same as his companion
introduced them.

"What did you men wish to see me about?" wondered du Chagne, who was obviously not one for small talk.

They had already agreed that Ballard, the older and more experienced fellow, would do the talking. Blayne stood at attention.

"My lord," Ballard began. "The state of affairs in the city and the nation have become intolerable. The knights of my legion, and many other orders, have determined the emperor is in violation of many laws, as well as traditions, customs, and in fact, the Oath and the Measure itself. He will be removed from command of Solamnia, and we most respectfully ask if you will return, in the interim, to the authority and role you adopted when the Dark Knights were driven out."

"You mean . . . you want me to assume the mantle of ruler of this city?" Du Chagne blinked his rheumy eyes, seeming surprised—but only mildly so—by the suggestion.

"That is exactly so, my lord. Rebels have already taken control of the High Clerist's Tower. They will prevent the emperor from returning to the city until the new order has been established. We have representatives in the temples of Shinare and Kiri-Jolith who are also prepared to accept a change in ruler. But we need a leader, someone the people can rally around. You, Excellency, are the only person in Palanthas who could fill that role."

"And you, young . . . Blayne Kerrigan, is it not? What is your place in all this?"

"Perhaps my lord has heard that the emperor murdered my father—under a flag of truce. It was that incident that propelled me onto this course. I vowed that Lord Kerrigan's death would be avenged, and this is a way to do it righteously."

"But two of you only? Surely there is a greater power at work here?"

"Indeed, my lord. The Legion of Steel has posted cadres to the two temples I have mentioned, as well as to the city garrison headquarters and to the gates. They will call upon the historic respect for the knighthood as a force for justice."

Du Chagne rose from his desk and came around to pat each of the men on the shoulder. "Thank you for this meeting. I applaud your courage, both of you. And what you are doing is only right and proper. I accept your commission."

"Very good, my lord," Ballard replied. "We have prepared an announcement. With your approval, we will have it read by the city heralds immediately."

"Ah, yes, good thinking," said the lord regent, who had seemed to grow a few inches during the course of the meeting. "Perhaps you could let me see it, for approval. Then we will waste no time in spreading the word through the city."

❀

Hoarst completed his meditations in the laboratory of the gray castle in the gray mountains of Dargaard. His women fearfully avoided him—his coldness and aloof manner did little to entice them—and he, in turn, ignored them utterly. For this task, he would work alone.

Blowing the dust off of an ancient tome, he opened the spellbook on his table and spent more than twenty-four straight hours studying the complicated workings of a dangerous and powerful incantation. He didn't sleep and only took small sips of water for sustenance. His entire intellect was devoted to the effort of absorbing the arcane symbols, mystical gestures, and almost unpronounceable sounds. Finally, certain that he could cast the spell flawlessly, he closed the book and made ready to leave.

Looking around at the huge castle, he shrugged off the

feeling that the place was even darker and grayer than it had been since he had lost Sirene. His kind did not permit regrets, certainly not when he had such important work to do.

Still, he reflected, perhaps later, when the matter was resolved, he would undertake a search, questing across Ansalon, across all of Krynn, for another white-skinned beauty . . .

It was time to go. His plan required several stages of precise magical accomplishment. To begin with, he had to locate Ankhar. He could cast a spell that would lead him to a specific object. The more unique and powerful the object, the easier it would be to find. The Nightmaster had given him the perfect suggestion: a potent artifact of the Prince of Lies, the emerald spearhead that tipped the mighty weapon carried by Ankhar the Truth.

When Hoarst cast the spell, it gave him a clear indication of where the artifact could be found. The Thorn Knight determined immediately that his target was in a valley of the Garnet Range. Next was teleportation. He would not be coming back to his keep, perhaps for a very long time, so he made his final preparations for travel carefully. He would carry his sharp dagger, a few spellbooks, a wide array of components, and small bottles of potion.

Using the Shaft of Hiddukel as a guide, he teleported himself through the ether, landing right by the side of the half-giant.

The gray wizard materialized on a wide plaza with a pristine lake nearby and mountain ridges flanking the horizons. Ankhar the Truth was there, and shockingly, he was engaged in a fight for his life.

A fight, by all appearances, the half-giant was about to lose.

A man Hoarst recognized as Jaymes Markham was standing over Ankhar, sword upraised, ready to strike the killing blow. The half-giant was sprawled on the ground, clawing for purchase, trying without success to evade the inevitable blow.

Hoarst wasted no time. He spat one word, pointing at the emperor, and released a stream of magic missiles from his fingertips. The first of the blazing bolts struck the man in his shoulder, knocking him back, breaking the line of the downward stab so the big sword not only missed the half-giant, but even missed the ground. Jaymes stumbled again, gasping with pain as the second bolt seared into his chest.

The emperor recovered quickly and used the blazing sword to knock away the next of the magic missiles . . . and the next. Parrying each, he kept the blasts from striking his body but was forced steadily backward, away from the half-giant who was gaping in amazement at his unbidden benefactor. Slowly, groggily, Ankhar pushed himself to his feet. By that time Jaymes had fallen back to the rank of dwarves ringing the plaza. The half-giant raised his spear and started toward the human.

"No!" Hoarst barked.

"Who are you to give me commands?" growled the half-giant.

"The one who would save your life—and your army!" snapped the Thorn Knight. "Now come with me!"

He tugged at the brutish commander's wrist, and perhaps because he was still stunned and shocked, Ankhar let himself be pulled along. Hoarst and the half-giant retreated through the line of ogres standing on the lakeside edge of the plaza. It was not hard to see the ogres were in dire straits: surrounded on three sides by superior numbers with the deep, impassable body of water at the rear.

"I can get you out of here right now! We'll carry the fight to a fortress in the emperor's heartland! Will you come with me?" demanded the Thorn Knight.

Ankhar cast an anguished glance at the line of knights and dwarves, rallying around their wounded leader. The half-giant growled, an ominous rumble of sound that came from somewhere deep within him. The massive body trembled, and Hoarst momentarily feared the brute would be guided by his savage temper.

But somehow the mighty leader shook off the temptation, merely smacking his fist into his palm with a great *thwack.* "All right," he said, glaring down at Hoarst. "How will you do this?"

"Form a line; have your troops hold out as long as possible while the enemy attacks. I am going to cast a spell that will create a door to safety. When you step through this door, it will take you to the fortress I spoke about. And you can bring as many of your ogres as are able to get away."

"Let me see this door!" demanded the half-giant skeptically.

"Very well. But once the spell is cast, I cannot change it. The door will last for some length of time, maybe half an hour. You should go through first, but tell your ogres to keep following you."

Ankhar glowered at Hoarst. "Why are you helping me?"

"You will help me if you come to this fortress," the Thorn Knight said honestly. "I need warriors, and you need a place where you can make a stand. I believe we are helping each other."

Once more the half-giant had to struggle against his own instincts to charge the enemy Solamnics and dwarves. Companies of humans were taking up positions on the flanks, other men and dwarves were bringing forward water, replacement weapons, and fresh horses. Clearly the respite in the battle would not last much longer.

"Cast your spell!" Ankhar ordered.

Hoarst nodded, ignoring the half-giant's brusque tone; there would be time for that later. He went to the wall of one of the great charcoal factories, behind a shed where they were for the most part out of sight of the enemy troops. He took several small diamonds from his pouch and pressed the hard chips of stone into the wooden panels of the wall, outlining a rough rectangle some five feet wide and almost nine high. Closing his eyes, he began to chant.

Ankhar knew enough about spellcasting that he simply stood there and watched while Hoarst worked his magic. It was a complicated chant, full of barely-human sounds, augmented with many intricate gestures of the spellcaster's hands. For sixty heartbeats, the Thorn Knight spoke, then for sixty more, barely drawing a breath. When he finished, the Thorn Knight staggered weakly, and only the half-giant's reflexive catch prevented him from falling.

"Look!" grunted one of the ogres.

Hoarst shook off the fatigue and did, indeed, look. The area outlined by the diamonds was a shimmering surface of blue light, with arcs of power crackling across it and sparks trailing to the ground. It hummed with an otherworldly force, a thrumming they could not only hear but also feel in the pits of their stomachs.

"What is that?" demanded Ankhar.

"It is the door—the door between dimensions!" Hoarst snapped. "Now let's go!"

"You go first," the half-giant prodded.

"All right," said the wizard. "I will. But you must come

quickly with as many ogres as you can; I don't know how long it will last."

Ankhar nodded and quickly indicated some of his warriors—and one terrified, plump ogress—bringing them into a queue next to the wall. At the same time, the humans and dwarves shouted their war cries and commenced another rush across the plaza.

Hoarst took one last look, then stepped into the blue aura, allowing the magic to sweep him away.

⋆◦◦◦◦◦◦◦◦◦◦◦⋆

At sunset scouts brought word that a brigade of troops was marching down the road from the High Clerist's Pass, coming to cement the coup that replaced the emperor with the lord regent in Palanthas. Blayne went to the city gate to await the arrival of the brigade. The men of the city watch had already been informed by decree of the new order and the lord regent's restored role. They willingly accepted Blayne's presence at the watch command station.

If events were progressing according to plan, the men coming down the road ought to be troops of the Black Army, perhaps even Captain Blackgaard and the gray wizard Hoarst. As darkness fell, Blayne ordered the watchmen to light lanterns around the gate in the light posts set out along the road.

The men of the Legion of Steel had taken control of the palace and several key locations in the city. The city guards had caused no problem once the authority of the lord regent was invoked to support the coup. Sir Jorde, with two dozen of his men, waited in the courtyard below the gate tower where Blayne was watching for the troops. Sir Ballard was also due to arrive.

The waiting seemed interminable, but Blayne's mood was lifted when the young nobleman felt a friendly clap on his shoulder and turned to see the first man he had met on his mission to Palanthas.

"Archer Billings!" Blayne cried, delighted to see the grinning guardsman. "It's a great day today, is it not?"

"It is indeed, sir. It is indeed!" agreed the bowman, who wore his usual battered short sword in the scabbard at his waist. "I take it you had a hand in this, my lord?" he asked respectfully.

"I couldn't have done it without you," Blayne said. "The legion was ready to move, but they just needed a contact with the rebels outside of the city. You facilitated that."

"The least I could do, m'lord," Billings said modestly.

He stepped to the parapet of the watchtower, peering into the courtyard below. "My, they do look like they've waited a long time for this," the archer said.

Jorde and his small company were dressed immaculately in gleaming armor in a mix of Sword, Rose, and Crown emblems. They were well armed and positioned in the shadows of the high walls. There were two gates, both leading into the gatehouse itself or the training yard around the barracks of the city guards.

"There they are!" shouted a watchman suddenly, and Blayne and Billings turned to look up the road. The column marched into view, the men in the black tunics and armor, and at their head rode Captain Blackgaard, the commander of the Black Army and the liberator of the High Clerist's Tower.

The advance columns of the Black Brigade were mounted and rode at an easy trot. The sentries on the city walls pointed and watched expectantly as the riders drew closer.

Blayne didn't hear who it was who shouted the warning,

but the words rose suddenly from one of the footmen outside the wall. "Beware! These are Dark Knights!"

"No!" cried young Lord Kerrigan. "That can't be!" But he realized even as he raised the protest that it was possible. Could he have been so stupid?

"I recognize that captain—he was the Butcher of the Dark Tower here, when Mina ruled!" cried another man.

"Close the gate!" Sir Jorde shouted to his men. They rushed toward the passage out of the courtyard only to have the gate slam shut in their faces.

And Blayne saw why: There was another man in the courtyard. He was dressed utterly in black, even to the point of wearing a mask over his face. His hands waved before him as he chanted arcane words—speaking in a strangely familiar voice. Almost immediately, a greenish-yellow mist swirled around him, a heavy vapor that seeped along the ground, filled the small courtyard, and rose to clutch at the legionnaires with sinister tendrils.

Blayne stared in horror as one of the legionnaires clutched his throat and doubled over, kicking violently then falling utterly still, his body grotesquely contorted. Another, then more of the trapped men toppled over, thrashing and gasping, though none of them struggled for more than a few moments.

"A killing cloud!" grunted Jorde, lunging toward the man in black. "We've been betrayed!"

The knight's sword was in his hand, but the other person—he was a priest of darkness, Blayne realized—held up a hand in a gesture that brought Jorde to a sudden stop. His face twisted in anguish. Staggering, the legionnaire dropped to one knee, swaying clumsily before falling on his face. Like the other victims, all probably dead by then, he vanished beneath the miasma of mist that oozed and billowed across the courtyard floor.

"No!" cried Blayne, starting for the stairs. "We've got to close the city gate!" He spun toward Billings, and that movement saved his life.

The archer had his short sword out and was driving the tip toward Blayne's back. The lord whirled away, pulling out his own weapon and smashing it sideways to block the blow aimed at him.

"You were more help than you'll ever know," Billings said tauntingly. "Bringing the secret knights out into the open, where the Nightmaster could find them!"

"You lie!" gasped Blayne, even though he realized it was the pathetic truth. In a frenzy he came at the other man, driving him back with savage overhand blows. The archer's face betrayed fear as he retreated until the solid parapet was behind him, fighting desperately to hold Blayne's furious attacks at bay.

But young Lord Kerrigan stabbed him in the right arm and, with a scream of pain, Billings dropped his sword. He squirmed back, between two of the battlements on the parapet.

Blayne charged forward, dropping his sword, pushing with both hands. Billings toppled over the wall, screaming for just a moment before he landed on his back, disappearing beneath the layer of gas that ebbed and flowed in the courtyard. Blayne watched for a moment, making sure that the traitor didn't get up from the ground.

By then the first of the Dark Knights were through the gates. Blayne frantically released the winch, and the portcullis came crashing down, splitting the formation in two. He looked down to see that only a score of black-clad horsemen were inside the city. They dismounted with smooth efficiency.

"Up there!" cried the masked priest, indicating the tower where Blayne stood alone. "Kill him and open the gates again!"

In a rush, the Dark Knights headed for the stairway leading up to the gatehouse platform. Blayne raised his sword, already slick with Billings's blood, and took a position at the top of the stairs.

He wondered what it would be like to die.

✕◈✕◈✕◈✕◈✕◈✕◈✕◈✕◈✕◈✕

Coryn teleported directly to the temple of Kiri-Jolith, where she startled Melissa du Juliette in the midst of her midday prayers.

"I'm sorry for intruding, but I think I've located Selinda!" the white wizard exclaimed.

"You found her? Where is she?"

"Actually, I've located the ring I gave her. It's in the city, near the waterfront. I can find the place, I'm certain."

"Let's go!" the high priestess said, dropping her prayer beads and throwing a ceremonial cloak over her shoulders. She snatched up a stout cudgel of ironwood with a steel cap at the head. Impressed, Coryn noted the formidable weapon and hoped they wouldn't need it.

The two women hurried from the temple, one in her robe of immaculate whiteness, the other in the flowing green garment of her high station. After a moment's consideration, they wrapped themselves in cloaking magic, muting the distinctive colors of their garments so it looked as though they were both wearing simple woolen cloaks. Coryn led them toward the waterfront, and they quickly made their way down a dark street, so narrow it was almost an alley. It was well after nightfall, and the darkness was thick around them.

331

"Hello, pretty ladies," came a voice from the shadows. "What brings such illustrious lovelies to our little corner of the city? May I welcome you to the Hale and Farewell? I am Hale, himself!"

He lifted a hand, indicating the dark door behind him. Coryn saw a flash of silver on his finger and felt a jolt of recognition. He wore the ring!

The man continued speaking as he limped toward the door to his establishment. "I guarantee you will find the finest—"

Hale never got to finish his remark as a blast of magic struck him from behind, propelling him into the door, which cracked and broke open under the impact of the man's body. He sprawled on the floor just within the entry.

But Hale was tougher than he looked. He jumped up from the floor, drawing his dagger as the two women pushed after him. An unseen force knocked him against the wall of the room, so hard that he slumped to the floor. Struggling against the unseen power, he dropped his knife and raised his hands in front of his face.

The two females came closer, and close up they looked very different than when he had accosted them on the street. One was dressed in a pure white robe, and the other wore a cloak of bright green, emblazoned with the fist of Kiri-Jolith. Hale uttered a strangled sound, holding up his hands as he struggled to his feet.

Melissa du Juliette, high priestess of Kiri-Jolith, raised a hand and the invisible hammer of her god—the force that had blasted Hale against the door—slammed into the man again.

Stunned, Hale collapsed to the floor, writhing in pain.

Coryn stood over him, the sheer brightness of her white robe causing him—and every other patron in the place—to throw up a hand against the blinding glare. "Where is she?

The woman who wore that ring in here?"

"I—I don't know what you're talking about!" Hale murmured, reaching to cover the ring with his right hand.

Coryn gestured, and a sparking missile smashed against his free hand, drawing a howl of pain. Hale lifted his burned, blistered fingers to his mouth, groaning.

"Tell us!" demanded the priestess. "Or her next missile will be a death blow!"

"She—I turned her over—she's in the palace! The lord regent's palace—he sent his agent to collect her!"

Coryn blinked in surprise at the news, but that didn't stop her from stepping on the man's ankle and pressing down with her weight. "Did you hurt her? Or her baby?"

"She's pregnant?" Hale gasped, clearly horrified. "But—but, she drank the Red Lotus!"

"If you gave her something that will hurt that baby . . ." Melissa warned.

"No, it's not that. By the gods, this is horrible! I never thought—ah, no! We *all* have to beware!" Hale wriggled pathetically, looking around in abject terror. "The Red Lotus—"

Nobody saw the man in black, sitting in a shadowy alcove near the rear of the room. He raised his hand and made a simple gesture. Hale grasped his throat, choking and retching horribly.

"Speak! What is it?" demanded Melissa, kneeling beside him, trying to pry his hands away from his throat. By the time they did come free, Hale was dead.

⤕⊙⊸⊙⊸⊙⊸❀⊸⊙⊸⊙⊸⊙⤔

"Ankhar escaped—with most of his ogres," reported Sergeant Ian.

"Where in the Abyss did they go?" demanded Jaymes, holding a poultice over his chest where the wizard's magic missiles had scorched him.

Ian shrugged apologetically. "I can't say, Excellency. But the prisoners swear there was a blue circle on the side of the building and that Ankhar and many of his ogres passed through it. Wherever they went, it wasn't inside of the shed. The wall is as solid as ever."

"Are you all right?" Dram asked gruffly, coming up to Jaymes as the man rose, head down, to stand amid the corpses of the ogres who had defended the route of retreat.

"I think so," Jaymes said, nodding feebly. He swayed weakly until Dram's strong hands took his arm, supporting him. The emperor cracked a small smile and nodded up the slope toward the three mine tunnels that loomed blackly overhead. "Nice timing on your attack, old friend."

"I could same the same for you. I think Ankhar would have waited us out forever—at least, until long after our food was gone. We were locked in a deathtrap of our own making."

"Who'd have thought the old bastard would come down the mountains at you?" Jaymes said, shaking his head.

"I guess *we* should of thought about it," Dram said, shuddering at the memory of how close to disaster they had come. "After all, he was in these hills before we were."

"Yes, those were the days," Jaymes said, again allowing that small smile. "Riding after goblins, collecting bounties, watching each other's backs—"

"And looking out for the knights at every turn," Dram interrupted. "Ducking and hiding like the outlaws we were. I never imagined you'd end up *commanding* the whole bunch of them Salamis!"

"Life has taken some funny turns I guess you could say."

Jaymes turned through a slow circle, scrutinizing the devastation that was everywhere in New Compound. He stared at the smoldering remnants of the great bonfire in which Ankhar had burned the dozen uncompleted bombards. The timbers hadn't burned away completely, and the massive rings of spring steel stood out like great hoops, but it was clear nothing would be salvaged from those ashes.

"I . . . I started to make them bombards," Dram said awkwardly. "But only after I heard Ankhar was on the march. I guess you got my letter?"

"Yes. You didn't like what I had done to Vingaard Keep, and you assumed I'd use the bombards against more cities, didn't you?"

"Would you?" the dwarf asked bluntly.

"I shouldn't have used them at Vingaard," Jaymes admitted, surprising even himself. "And no, I don't think I'd have used them anymore against my own cities, no matter what. I lost my temper when the young lord made a surprise attack and burned two of my guns."

Jaymes rubbed a hand across his eyes, wiping away sweat and grime. "He was a courageous fellow, gnat though he was. And he had good reason to hate me, I have to admit; his father died in my custody."

"Well, any way you look at it, it'll be a year or two before I can get operations up and running again," Dram said. "That is, if you decide you want another battery of guns."

Sally came up and Dram put his arm around her; they both looked expectantly at the emperor.

"You don't have to do that. Not now, at least. Go ahead with your mining—looks like you've got a good place for it. We'll see what the future holds, but if I use any more bombards, it will be against enemies from beyond Solamnia. Now I just want to get back to Palanthas and to my wife."

He winced as he said the last word, and Sally reached out and touched his hand. "Is . . . is everything all right there?" she asked.

"It's worse than you know," said a woman's voice. They turned in unison, stunned to see Coryn the White standing behind them. She had obviously teleported, and her face was grim, even dour. Her black hair was tousled in disarray, and there were scuffs on her face and hands. Her white robe with its silver embroidery was, as always, immaculate.

"What's happened?" Jaymes asked. He thought of Selinda, feeling a stab of fear in his belly.

"Selinda has been kidnapped. By all accounts, it looks like her father was to blame."

"Is she all right?" demanded the emperor, his face ashen.

"As far as I know. But there's more bad news: the Dark Knights have struck," she reported grimly. "They've captured the High Clerist's Tower, and they're trying to take over Palanthas and prop the lord regent back onto his throne," she concluded. "You won't be able to bring your army back to the city with them holding the pass."

Jaymes groaned, but his thoughts were already churning. "Can you take me back to Palanthas right away?" he asked Coryn.

"Yes. I was hoping you'd want to do that."

He nodded absently, turning to Dram. "Can you accompany the legion up the pass to the High Clerist's Tower? And bring all the casks of powder that you have?"

Dram nodded. "I'll be there—with enough to fill three or four wagons."

The emperor nodded gratefully, touching Sally on the shoulder. "I'm sorry to take him away from you, again," he said. "But I'll do my best to see that he's back here before you even know he's gone."

"Go," she said, sniffling. "Be quick about it! But . . . may Reorx watch over you."

"Thank you," he said before turning back to Coryn. She spoke another word, the magic swirled, and they were gone.

CHAPTER TWENTY-FOUR

COUNTERCOUP

"Y ou might have killed her!"

Selinda heard those words, spoken by an angry voice . . . a familiar voice . . . She tried to shake off the cobwebs fogging her mind and felt her unsettled stomach churning.

Father!

She was lying on a couch in the anteroom of his study. The loud, stern words were coming from behind the closed door. Her father was speaking to the one who had brought her there, she realized at once, the black-masked priest of an evil god.

Selinda tried to call out to her father, but again her body failed to cooperate. Instead, she tried to listen carefully, to hear the outside sounds over the frantic pounding of her heart and the labored effort of her breathing.

"She was in very little danger." That was the priest's voice, insistent but hardly apologetic. "And I brought her here at once, just as you ordered. Perhaps she is weakened by the pregnancy—I did nothing to harm her! Or else your other agent, the one who lured her into his place of business, might have given her something to make her ill. How far do you trust him?"

"Hale has always been a faithful agent," the lord regent said coldly. "He knows better than to displease me."

No! Selinda was repulsed by her father's words, almost gagging in horror. But the truth was plain: du Chagne had contracted Lame Hale to accost his own daughter! Hale had drugged her, tied her up, threatened her—and all at the command of her own father!

She pushed herself up into a sitting position, looking around, wanting only to escape. There was another door besides the one leading to her father's office. Standing unsteadily, she stumbled to that exit, tried the handle, and found it locked. Despairing, she returned to the couch and sat down, trying to collect her thoughts. Gradually she noticed there was only silence coming from the office. She wondered if the priest had left by some other route.

Abruptly, the door opened and du Chagne strolled in. "Ah, you're awake," he said with forced heartiness. "Do you think you can sit up? Would you like something to eat?"

She shook her head, looking over his shoulder. "Father! That man? Where is he?"

"The . . . the Nightmaster is gone."

"He's a terrible man, a wicked man!" she accused. "And so is Lame Hale!"

Du Chagne sighed, slumping wearily. "I had hoped things would turn out different," he started to explain. "I mean . . . this was meant to be for your own good! I hoped you'd understand—"

The outer door opened, and the Nightmaster came in, pushing Melissa du Juliette before him. Her hands were bound, and there was a gag wrapped tightly around her mouth. The priestess's eyes widened in dismay at the sight of Selinda and her father.

"Melissa!" Selinda cried, trying to rise as the priestess of Kiri-Jolith was roughly pushed onto the couch. The princess glared at the Nightmaster. "What do you think you—"

"She was spying on you," the priest said, speaking directly to the lord regent. "I caught her outside your window—levitating, of course. I'd slit her throat right now and be done with it."

Selinda's eyes widened in horror. She turned to look at her father and was horrified to see he was clearly thinking over the dark priest's advice.

"No!" shouted the princess, furiously leaping to her feet to confront the masked priest. He reached out a hand, touched her cheek, and she slumped back onto the couch. Desperately, she struggled to rise, tried to lift her arms, but she couldn't move.

She could see and hear everything in the room, but her muscles were utterly paralyzed.

✶⊙⊙⊙⊙⊙⊙⊙⊙⊙⊙✶

"I thought we would find Melissa here," Coryn said to Jaymes in some surprise. They had teleported directly from New Compound into the priestess's quarters within the temple of Kiri-Jolith. But the chambers were clearly empty. "She must have felt too much urgency to wait and gone directly to the regent's palace herself. Or perhaps she's merely scouting the scene. I really don't think she would go in until we arrived to help."

"Let's get going, then," Jaymes urged.

Again, Coryn cast her magic spell, and shortly the two found themselves transported to a small room. A glance out the nearby window showed that they were high above Palanthas, looking down on the city and the harbor from a lofty tower. Jaymes quickly deduced that they were in the Golden Spire of the lord regent's palace.

"We can go down the stairs and surprise du Chagne," Coryn explained softly. "He doesn't expect to see *anybody* coming from this direction."

They descended the spiraling stairs quickly but as silently as possible. Within a few moments, Coryn and Jaymes were crouching on the lowest balcony of the long stairway descending from the top of the Golden Spire. They could hear voices raised in anger emanating from behind the closed door of the lord regent's office. Two men-at-arms stood before that door, looking nervously at each other.

Jaymes pointed to himself, then at the guards, indicating first one, then the other. His hand clenched over the hilt of his sword, and the white wizard took his arm, looked at him, and shook her head. With an impatient expression, he held his place.

Coryn pulled a pinch of something from a tiny pocket in her robe. Gesturing to the emperor to stay where he was, she stood and started down the stairs toward the two guards.

They both looked up in surprise at her unexpected appearance. She smiled and murmured something, waving her hand before her face and opening her fingers. The pinch of sand she let go sifted down toward the floor, and the two guards slumped backward against the wall then slowly slid down to sleep on the floor.

Jaymes was already gliding down the stairs and drawing Giantsmiter for action. Coryn leaned her head against the door, listening. As Jaymes approached, she nodded, and he lowered his shoulder and hit the door with a violent crash.

Selinda lay on the couch, magically immobilized. Melissa du Juliette, still bound and gagged, was seated on the couch beside the princess. They heard the smash of wood and even without turning her head, Selinda could see that her husband, his great sword drawn, had come bursting into the room. Coryn was right behind him.

"Halt!" demanded the Nightmaster through his black mask, raising his hand. Magic pulsed through the room, and Jaymes stopped in his tracks, his body lurching forward while his feet remained fixed to the floor. He twisted, almost dropping his sword.

Coryn raised her hand, crying out a word that sounded like a terrible growl. A flash of light seared through the room, and Jaymes tumbled free, rolling once before bouncing, catlike, to his feet. At the same time, Selinda, who had been straining to see what was happening, felt her paralysis weaken. The magic holding her, as well as the spell restricting Jaymes, had been weakened by Coryn's counter-spell.

The princess wrenched her head around. Relief flooded through her—not at the prospect of rescue but because she was starting to regain control of her body. She twitched her fingers and felt a rewarding flicker of mobility. Still, she knew she was too weak to stand and couldn't quite gain control of her vocal cords.

Smoke swirled around them, and she saw the Nightmaster casting a spell, hurling a cloud of noxious gas toward the white wizard. With a sharp bark—like a guttural challenge—Coryn raised her wrist to parry the attack, and the cloud exploded, erupting upward to shatter a good portion of the ceiling. Dust and debris showered down. A beam broke free and tumbled downward, knocking the white wizard on the shoulder and sending her sprawling.

The Nightmaster was still there, standing in front of the cowering lord regent. "Kill them!" shrieked du Chagne. He was pointing at the emperor and the white wizard, but to Selinda's mind, he might just as well have been talking about his daughter.

The priest cast a spell, and a force of mistlike energy materialized in the air. It smashed into Jaymes, knocking him flat on his back. The magical hammer swirled upward and smashed down again, driving her husband's head hard against the marble floor.

Selinda's voice came back to her as she croaked out a scream.

Jaymes lay on his back, his sword arm stretched to the side. Once more the hammer of the masked priest gathered for a mighty blow, but the emperor reacted first. Pulling his weapon over his body, he took hold of Giantsmiter's hilt with both hands. When the magical hammer came down, the sword flamed and sliced cleanly through the enchantment. Springing to his feet, Jaymes closed on the Nightmaster, his face locked into a feral snarl. Coryn, groggy and bleeding, pushed herself to her feet, stumbling toward the lord regent.

Then the high priest spoke again, and the entire room was swallowed by darkness.

✦◦✦◦✦◦◦✦◦✦◦✦◦✦

Bakkard du Chagne felt himself seized by the scruff of the neck. The surrounding darkness was total, so the lord regent couldn't see who or what had accosted him, hoisting him off the ground like a child's toy, but he felt pretty certain that whatever lifted him had force much greater than any mortal's grip.

A chaotic tangle of noise surrounded him, and he tried to clasp his hands to his ears, blocking out the cacophony. But the power seemed to have a paralyzing effect because he couldn't move his limbs, couldn't feel his skin. He was consumed with terror, and the worst of it was he couldn't even scream.

Then as quickly as the raging storm had started, it broke. Du Chagne found himself standing on a solid surface, perched high up on a tower—a tower much, much higher than the Golden Spire of his own palace.

"Where in the Abyss are we?" demanded the lord regent, staggering weakly, nauseated at the prospect of the dangerous depths just below his feet. He barely noticed the vista of lofty mountains pressing in from all sides, nor did he take note of the famous, sprawling outline of the fortress around him.

"This is the High Clerist's Tower," the Nightmaster said.

"Why did you bring me here?" the lord regent demanded.

"It was either that or let the emperor kill you," replied the priest. "For reasons unknown to me at the moment, I elected to save your life."

<hr />

Blayne stood at the top of the steps leading up to the gate tower. The column of Dark Knights still milled around outside the gate, blocked by the portcullis he had just dropped, but there were a score or more of the attackers—including Captain Blackgaard—already in the city. The knights were charging him, coming up the stairway with swords drawn and murderous intent on their faces.

The young lord met the first of those foes with a savage downward chop, delivered with such force he shattered the knight's upraised blade and cut deeply into the man's face. Immediately twisting the blade free, he knocked a second knight to the side, sending the fellow tumbling back down the stairs with his throat cut.

But the stairs were wide enough for the Dark Knights to come at him two at a time and so they did. The next pair, no doubt gaining some respect for their opponent after seeing the fate of the initial attackers, approached more cautiously. Striking from below, they aimed at Blayne's legs, both stabbing simultaneously. The young lord couldn't parry two blows at once; he had no choice but to back away, even though that meant giving up his position at the top of the stairs.

He backed across the tower platform, moving into the corner and raising his sword as the attackers swept onto the platform. "Kill that one!" barked Captain Blackgaard, pointing at the young lord of Vingaard.

A trio of Dark Knights rushed at him. Blayne slashed to the right and left, cutting down two but leaving an opening for the middle attacker. That knight grinned coldly as he raised his blade. Then he croaked and stumbled sideways, an arrow jutting from the side of his neck.

Blayne wasted no time wondering who was shooting. He charged in a fury, cutting down another black-clad soldier and fighting his way toward the stairs. The other Dark Knights on the platform shouted in consternation as swords clashed against shields and other blades cut into flesh. A wild melee erupted, swordsmen ducking and dodging, parrying and attacking on all sides.

Captain Blackgaard stepped into Blayne's path, and the nobleman feinted a thrust at the mercenary Dark Knight's face. The veteran officer sneered and stepped back then charged again. Once more the lord struck high; once more Blackgaard parried the blow. Then too late, he saw his mistake. The lord stabbed straight ahead, driving his blade through the captain's belly, pushing him back and down with the force of the killing blow.

Then the new men, led by Sir Ballard, were all around. They spilled from the stairs to rush across the platform. Archers shot arrows at the Dark Knights who had been blocked outside the city gate by the closed portcullis. Unable to fight against those lethal missiles, the horsemen put spurs to their mounts and galloped into the night.

Only vaguely did Blayne understand that he had been saved, but when he finally realized who his savior was, he clasped hands with Sir Ballard and allowed himself a groan of relief.

The Legion of Steel was there.

⊱⚬⊰⚬⊰⚬⊰⚬⊰✿⊱⚬⊰⚬⊰⚬⊰⚬⊰

"Are you all right?" Jaymes said, kneeling beside Selinda while Coryn freed the bonds on Melissa du Juliette. They were in Selinda's rooms in the palace, having teleported there after the Nightmaster and the lord regent left the Golden Spire.

"Yes—I'll be fine. But the city—the coup?"

"I think the coup is falling apart. But I have to go out there and be seen. The people need to know that their emperor is back."

"Yes, they do," the emperor's wife agreed. She winced in sudden memory. "But Father! He—"

"I know," Jaymes said. "He's even more of a scoundrel than I thought he was."

"Where did he go?" Selinda asked.

"The Nightmaster's magic bore them both away from here," Melissa explained. "They could be anywhere."

"I have a feeling I know where they are," Jaymes said grimly. "And as soon as the city is secured, I will be going there. Now . . . I'm sorry . . . but I have to go."

346

"Yes—and good luck to you," said the princess. She made no move to embrace or to kiss him, and after a moment's hesitation, he turned and quickly departed, running down the palace stairs.

The princess collapsed back against the couch, trying to catch her breath and fathom all that was happening.

Coryn and Melissa du Juliette explained how they had tracked her to the Hale and Farewell, confronted Lame Hale, and brought Jaymes back to Palanthas.

"Thank you—thank you both," Selinda said gratefully. "What about that place—Lame Hale! He's a slaver, right here in Palanthas!"

"He's a dead slaver now," the priestess noted grimly. "Someone killed him with a spell while we were trying to question him. Everyone associated with that place will be dealt with. As we learned what was happening, the knights of Kiri-Jolith were moving into that place, rounding up everyone they could catch there. Their justice will be stern, and it is safe to assume the building has been destroyed, the proprietors slain or captured." She shook her head. "I do not envy the prisoners of the knights, if those prisoners are known to have abused a woman."

"Why did he pick me?" Selinda wondered. "Nobody in there knew who I was; that's one thing I liked about the place."

"Perhaps it was nothing more than a random accosting," the priestess suggested.

"I'm not so sure," Coryn said, surprising both of the women.

"What do you mean?" Selinda asked.

"I spoke to some of the customers in that place and the barkeep after we took Hale and found your ring. I'm convinced he did know who you are."

"But—how? I never revealed my identity!" protested the princess.

"That is a very good question. But the barkeep's story has led me to believe that Hale must have been trying to lure you, personally, into the place. I suspect he used charm magic himself. He was a sorcerer, though not a follower of godly magic."

"I still don't understand."

"Why did you go in there in the first place?" the wizard probed gently.

"I . . . I was just out walking. It felt so good to be free of my room, my guards . . . my husband. And I followed the inviting scent of the waterfront because it had been so long since I'd been there. At least, I thought that was the reason. And then this man, Hale, called to me as I passed on the street. I was frightened at first . . . but then, it just seemed like it would be interesting and fun."

Selinda felt sick and humiliated as she made her confession.

"And once you were inside? I understand you went there several times. Why?"

"Hale . . . well, he seemed so friendly. A good listener . . ." Selinda's voice trailed away. How could she have been so foolish? Or so lucky, she realized, considering the narrowness of her escape. "How did you find me?" she asked.

"The ring I gave you," Coryn explained. "Because I made it, its magic has a very strong connection to me. We noticed you had been missing over a period of days, so I cast a spell to locate the ring, and the ring led us to Hale."

Selinda slumped back in her chair, sinking into the cushions, weary and still frightened.

"There's more," Melissa said, looking at Coryn with a

raised eyebrow. The enchantress nodded, and the priestess continued. "Did you drink something called a Red Lotus?"

"Yes," Selinda replied. "That's how he knocked me out."

"There is some danger in that drink. Hale was terrified when he learned you were pregnant."

"You mean—the drink would hurt the baby?" gasped Selinda. She dropped her head into her hands. "Oh, by Kiri! I didn't want that! Not like this!"

"I don't think that's the issue. I don't think it would harm the baby. Hale did not strike me as the type to fear someone else's troubles, and yet he was unquestionably afraid when he learned that you were carrying a child. No, I am worried that it is something even more mysterious. The child might be a danger to others—maybe everyone—or maybe those like Hale, who do wrong. There's no way to know exactly what the danger is."

"He wouldn't say why? Did you ask him?"

"He died before he could tell us," Coryn said. "I feel certain he was assassinated to keep him from telling any more."

"I—I don't care," Selinda said bravely. "I am going to bring this child into the world and see that he—or she—is raised to know righteousness."

"What about Jaymes?" asked Coryn. "Do you intend to keep all this a secret from him?"

Selinda lifted her head. She felt her strength flowing back, though whether it was just from the tea or from something else, she didn't know. Pushing herself to her feet, she found she could stand on her own. It gave her great pleasure to walk to her windows, to throw them open, and to admit the pleasant summer air. Finally, she turned around.

"I will tell him everything . . . when this crisis is over. I will not burden him with my problems while he wages war to save the nation that we all want to survive." Her expression hardened. "I know now that he must have deceived me to make me his wife."

Coryn looked away, almost as if she were ashamed, a reaction that surprised Selinda. But the princess continued to explain.

"And he used me to legitimize his ascension to emperor. I was the Princess of Palanthas after all, and the gods only knew how many prophecies there were proclaiming that the man who married the princess would be the one to unite the cities of Solamnia into a nation again. He used that—and me—to elevate himself, to make himself the leader of a new empire.

"At first, it was a dizzy game to me, and by the time I started to wonder how or why it was happening, it was too late. And even now, I can see that Jaymes has been good for Solamnia, even if he was not good for me."

Selinda turned and regarded both of her friends, gratitude shining in the emotion of her eyes. "I thank you both sincerely for saving my life. I was a fool—an utter fool—driven by despair. But no longer."

Coryn was still looking away, so it was Melissa who spoke.

"No longer a fool, or no longer in despair?" asked the priestess pointedly.

"No longer either, I trust," the emperor's wife said. "I thought I was reclaiming my life when I broke free from my prison, but just being free isn't enough."

Her hand moved to her belly, which she stroked gently. "Jaymes has another campaign to wage—and he is the best hope we have of holding this country together and moving into the future. I don't love him—you both know that—but I have a duty to this realm. Whether it is because of who I am by birth or who I married, I do have a role to play. I am more than a woman, a daughter, a wife. I am a symbol of Solamnia. However, I will not be his wife anymore—not even in the privacy of our lives. He must know this truth."

She drew a breath.

"But neither will I betray him," she said.

⊷⊶⊷⊶⊷⊶✹⊶⊷⊶⊷⊶⊷

Jaymes made his way to the main gate of the city, where the Dark Knights had tried to force their way in. He found the place garrisoned by a mixed force of city guards and Solamnic Knights. They were commanded by an impressive-looking Knight of the Rose named Sir Ballard.

"They attacked here, from the mountain road?" Jaymes asked.

"Yes, my lord. A brigade came down, reportedly from the High Clerist's Tower. It is said to be in rebel hands, sir."

"Yes, I've heard that too. I'll be checking on it very shortly. What happened to the brigade?"

"Their leader was killed on this very platform. The rest of the Dark Knights retreated back up the road when they couldn't gain entrance to the city," Ballard reported, eyeing the emperor warily. "They almost forced the gate here. One man stopped them—the same man who killed their captain."

"Who's that?" asked Jaymes.

"It was me, Excellency," said Blayne Kerrigan, coming forward into the light. Jaymes immediately recognized the young lord. "I closed the portcullis when I realized the men were Dark Knights. But not before a number of good men, loyal knights, were killed by black magic and treachery."

"You saved the city of Palanthas from the Dark Knights?"

The emperor surprised everyone by throwing back his head and laughing heartily. "But you're an outlaw!" he declared. "There's a price on your head!"

"So I have heard. If that be the case, then I submit myself to your justice," Blayne said stiffly. "To do with as you see fit."

"As well you may! But I see fit to pardon you, young outlaw. As a matter of fact, I myself have spent more than a few years with a price on my head. It's good to have it lifted, is it not?"

Blayne allowed himself to smile for the first time, it seemed, in many weeks. "Yes, Excellency," he agreed. "Yes it is."

CHAPTER TWENTY-FIVE

PATHS TO VENGEANCE

Jaymes went to see Selinda in her rooms. There were several large trunks standing open, partially filled with clothes, while a pair of maids were busy gathering dresses from the wardrobes and carefully packing them away. When the emperor entered, the maids scurried out, leaving him alone with his wife.

"I'm leaving for the High Clerist's Tower," he said. "Coryn just returned with confirmation: not only did the Nightmaster and your father go there, but so did Ankhar—and a large number of his ogres. I'm going to end this once and for all."

"They can't be allowed to stay there, I know," Selinda replied. "I only pray this battle brings the war—all the wars—to an end."

He nodded with real sincerity. "I do too. It's been too long, too much fighting. I want to rule an empire at peace." Jaymes cleared his throat, looking at his wife awkwardly. "I will try to protect your father, if I can."

"Do what you must," she said curtly. "I now understand what I was to him, and that knowledge has hardened my heart." She looked more puzzled than angry. "He served the Prince of Lies! All of it, his whole life, was a lie! I'm glad to be free of him."

The emperor looked around, as if noticing the trunks, the empty wardrobes, for the first time. "I'll be back when this is over. It may take some time, a month or two, but I will come home before winter to this place . . . I hope I can come home to you, as well."

Selinda sighed, going over to the window and looking out over the city's central plaza. People were walking back and forth on the great square. A pair of musicians played a lute and pipe, trying to collect tips. The temples were busy, worshipers coming and going. The little stalls of the farmers' market were doing brisk business. It was a hot summer day, and children splashed in several of the great fountains around the square, while a few men-at-arms of the city guard ambled around, amiably watching the activities of the citizenry. She took it all in for a moment then turned back to her husband.

"This city is a good place to live in again. And so much of that is due to you. You have made mistakes—some of which are hard to forgive—but you have learned from those mistakes and grown stronger, greater."

"Won't you let me come back to you? Let me prove to you how I have changed?"

She shook her head. "No. I cannot."

He gestured to the trunks. "But where will you go?" he asked.

"I'm going to the Temple of Kiri-Jolith. There is plenty of room for me there, and I will be with Melissa. I have to do a lot of thinking, and talking to her helps me clear my mind."

The emperor winced almost as though he were in pain. When he spoke, his tone, his words, were uncharacteristically hesitant. "If . . . after that . . . after I come back . . . perhaps we could try again. I would like to have you at my side."

Selinda raised her head. The sunlight coming through the windows outlined her golden hair, rendering a shimmering corona around her scalp. "I will have our baby," she said, touching the subtle mound of her belly. "And you will have this child, as well."

Her voice hardened. "But you will never again have me. I know my destiny, and it is not to be merely a woman of the city. My fate is tied into the fate of the nation, and yours is to forge this nation, and the others of Solamnia, into an empire. I accept that destiny and will do what I can to help you hold this empire together.

"But I will not live in your house . . . or share your bed."

He nodded slowly, hiding his emotions well—except for a slight narrowing of his eyes. But he made no argument. For a few moments, he stood still then slowly turned toward the door.

"Good-bye," he said quietly. "May all the gods watch over you."

"And good luck to you," she answered. "I know you will have Coryn's help, and Dram's, and of course all your armies. But be careful."

"I will." Still he hesitated.

"I think she loves you. Did you know that?" Selinda almost whispered the words.

He looked at her, puzzled, not knowing how to respond.

"Coryn. I think she's been in love with you for years. Just . . . watch over her, too, will you?"

He nodded, finally opening the door. "I will do that," he said and slowly walked away.

The High Lookout on the High Clerist's Tower was host to a meeting of a number of eminent figures, a weighty enough gathering to justify the name of the platform not just in altitude, but in soaring rank. Ankhar the Truth was there, as was the Thorn Knight Hoarst. The former lord regent of Palanthas, Bakkard du Chagne, and the black-masked Nightmaster of Hiddukel, who had brought du Chagne there from the city, were also present.

The ogress Pond-Lily was also up on the parapet—she never strayed far from Ankhar, fearing she would get lost in the labyrinthine corridors of the great fortress—but she hung back near the door to the tower and looked fearfully at the four stern males, who paced and cursed as they argued among themselves.

The lookout was a ring-shaped space. Rising from the center of the platform was the narrow spire that supported the highest perch, called the Nest of the Kingfisher. There was one door leading from the lookout to the interior of the tower, which was merely a landing for the narrow flight of stairs spiraling up to the Kingfisher's platform, and a much wider set of steps curling downward to the many rooms, apartments, and other rooms of the interior.

The fortress sprawling hundreds of feet below the lookout was well-patrolled. Dark Knights were visible from above, posted on the parapets of the curtain wall and the gatehouses. Ogres lolled in the courtyards. To the northeast, on the tenuous road that Blackgaard's men had carved, a procession of soldiers bore heavy packs laden with grain and fruit from the farms in the secret valley.

"Why we hide here?" demanded Ankhar, his ham-sized hands on his hips as he glared accusingly at the others. "Inside walls? This is not how ogres fight! This is not how *I* fight."

"These walls are all that is going to keep you alive," Hoarst replied pointedly. "And the spell that brought you here saved your life, you might recall. The town of dwarves didn't give you any walls, and your ogres were dying by the score!"

"Bah!" The half-giant didn't want to hear it. But neither could he come up with a witty riposte, probably because the wizard spoke the truth. The defeat at New Compound still confounded, dismayed, and enraged the half-giant. How could it have gone so wrong when everything had started out so *right?* His brilliant battle plan—wasted! He growled deep in his chest, smashing his fist down onto the rampart, which knocked a piece of stone loose and bruised his flesh. He watched sullenly as the chip of stone tumbled down for a long time, finally shattering in the courtyard next to a very startled ogre.

"Look," the Thorn Knight said, striving for a reasonable tone. "We have a very strong position here. A thousand Dark Knights and a thousand ogres can hold this place for a very long time—perhaps forever. Nothing can move across the pass, and so we have cut Solamnia in two. Here, too, we control access to the secret valley to the north; the farms and herds there will give us all the food we need to stay holed up here for years if need be."

"For years! But what will happen when the emperor brings his army up from the plains!" du Chagne declared harshly.

"I am not afraid of the emperor!" Ankhar roared, the force of his voice sending du Chagne retreating behind the Nightmaster.

"We are not here because we fear the emperor," the priest stated coldly, "but because we can give him a battle to our advantage here. I myself will take command of the south gatehouse—that's the most likely place for him to come against us."

"I will see to the Knights' Spur," Hoarst said. "It's a good position for guarding the approach on the road up from the plains."

"And I will stay here, on the High Lookout," Ankhar declared haughtily, "where I can keep an eye on everything."

"What makes you think that will be enough?" demanded du Chagne, his voice quavering. "We all know he has one of his cannons left. He can set that up on the Wings of Habbakuk and blow this tower to pieces—even if it takes him all winter."

"True, that bombard is a threat," Hoarst allowed.

"Then why are you so sanguine about our chances here?" demanded the former lord regent.

"Because I intend to see that his vaunted bombard never reaches the pass," the gray wizard replied confidently.

><@><@><@><@><@><@><@><@><

Coryn and Jaymes teleported from Palanthas to the far side of the great pass. There they would wait for the Crown Army, the Palanthian Legion, and the dwarves of New Compound, all of whom were marching as fast as they could across the plains. Even so, they knew it would be several days before the troops arrived.

"We should find a place we can use for shelter and to keep an eye on the road," the emperor suggested. Coryn agreed and they started to ascend the wide roadway, remaining out of sight of the tower.

Nearby they found a small herdsman's cottage adjacent to the road, about a mile below the pass. The shepherd and his flock were apparently spending the summer in the high pastures, so the place was abandoned, and they decided it would be a cozy place to wait.

Jaymes took a walk up the road, going about a half mile before he reached the last bend below the fortress. He went far enough to look at the tower rising so high about the surrounding walls, gatehouses, and fortifications. He thought ruefully of General Markus, always the boldest of his commanders. He knew that Markus and his Rose Knights would have given a good account of themselves. He was sorry the old veteran was dead.

"We will avenge you, good knight," he said softly before turning and making his way down the road and back to the cottage.

When he got there, he found Coryn had made herself right at home. The white wizard had produced a wide array of objects from within her bags of holding, setting up a crystal ball on the little kitchen table, taking over a pantry to store her potions and little boxes of components. Her spell books went on a shelf beside the door.

As Jaymes entered, she was seated at the table, using the scrying ball to see what she could learn about their enemies.

"They're all in the tower," Coryn confirmed after quick scrutiny. "The Thorn Knight and the Nightmaster have both placed many spells of detection around the place, so I couldn't probe too deeply. But the ogres that fled New Compound are manning the walls, and Ankhar himself seems to be the one in command."

Jaymes gazed at her. Her black hair spilled across the back of her robe, lustrous and long, a sharp contrast to the whiteness of her garb. Those traces of silvery gray—premature in a sense, for she was still a young woman—only added allure to her appearance. Lost in concentration, she held her slender fingers to her chin, absently chewing on a nail as she studied the murky globe. Abruptly she looked up, surprising him as he stared at her.

"What is it?" she asked.

"I don't know. I've been thinking . . . how much we have been through together . . . and how grateful I am to have your help. Nothing I have accomplished would have been possible if I hadn't had your help, your support."

She smiled radiantly. "Why . . . thank you. You've never said anything like that to me before."

"You're right," he replied in some surprise. "I guess I never have. I should have before now. Long ago, I should have."

Coryn rose and came to him, taking his hands in hers, her black eyes looking up into his own dark gray orbs. However, her expression was cloudy and troubled. "I have done things for you that I would never have done for anyone else. I'm not proud of everything. It was all toward a good end I trust, but sometimes I do regret the means we employed toward those ends."

He nodded with understanding. She had brewed the potion he had used to win Selinda du Chagne's heart, to cause her to fall—at least temporarily—in love with him. It was not something they had spoken of since that time—nor was it mentioned at that moment. But Jaymes remembered how surprised he had been at Coryn's bitterness when he had explained he needed that potion. She had complied but had done the work in a cold fury.

Suddenly he remembered Selinda's words about Coryn. Were they true?

The white wizard turned and sat back down at the table, that time chewing on a strand of her hair as she peered into the globe again. Once, she turned to the side and saw that he was still watching her. She smiled warmly again and went back to her inspection.

Jaymes decided that almost certainly Selinda had been right.

≈⊶⊙⊶⊙⊶⊙⊷⊙⊶⊙⊶⊙⊶⊙⊶⊙⊷≈

The Palanthian Legion and the Crown Army marched up the road, climbing the pass from the plains of Vingaard toward the High Clerist's Tower. Dram and the dwarves came behind the human troops. The mountain dwarves rode on the driver's seat of one of the freight wagons. He had, for once, persuaded Sally to do the sensible thing and stay back in New Compound with her father and son to supervise the rebuilding that had to get under way. He missed her terribly but was glad she was not riding to war.

Five hundred dwarves accompanied Dram and his precious cargo. A mixture of hill and mountain dwarves, they had all volunteered to take part in the final battle of what the dwarves had taken to calling the Ankhar Wars. The dozens of wagons in the train were hauling hundreds of casks of black powder, each vehicle separated by some distance from the others to prevent an accident. One mistake with one wagon could turn into a disaster for the entire army.

From his seat on the first wagon, Dram was enjoying the sight of the mountains looming around him. The Garnet range was nice, with its snowy glaciers and vast pine forest, but the stark and rocky cut in the Vingaard Mountains had always appealed to him.

"Reorx knew what he was doing when he carved these grand peaks," he had remarked to the other dwarves as the saw-toothed ridge came into view. The walls rose up on both sides of the dwarf contingent.

The lone bombard was in front of him, hauled on its great wagon in the midst of the marching legion. Because the steep, uphill road was long and curved, the dwarf had a good view of the massive gun ahead as it lumbered along, hauled by oxen.

Suddenly, even as Dram stared at the bombard, the cliff ahead uttered a groan and gave way, a crack spreading across the near face of the mountain. The section of the road where the bombard had been traveling simply dropped into the chasm, carrying the gun, the wagon, the team of oxen, and more than a hundred marching men of the Palanthian Legion into the depths.

The landslide was so sudden, so pinpoint, that it could have been provoked only by magic, Dram realized at once. The dwarf caught a glimpse of two figures, men high up on the crest of the ridge on the far side of the valley. The hair at the back of his neck prickled, but he could only fume as their sole remaining artillery plummeted into the chasm and shattered into splinters far below.

His eyes shot back to the ridge top, but he was not surprised to see that the two strangers had disappeared.

⊱━⊰⊱━⊰⊱━⊰⊱●⊰⊱━⊰⊱━⊰⊱━⊰

"It was an earthquake spell, no doubt, and it took us a day to carve out a new road in the gap," Dram reported to the emperor three days later, when the column of dwarves at last reached the herdsman's cottage. "But we're here now. We lost probably a hundred good men. And unfortunately, we don't have the gun."

"Hmm, but you still have the powder, right?" Jaymes asked. He seemed surprisingly undismayed by the act of sabotage.

Looking around, Dram had to wonder if the emperor's stay in the little cottage—he and Coryn had almost set up housekeeping in the place, the dwarf had decided with a single glance through the door—was making Jaymes soft or even apathetic.

"Yep. Plenty of powder—'bout three hundred casks, give or take."

"Excellent," said the emperor. "Come with me."

They went to meet Dayr and Weaver, who were riding at the heads of their respective armies. Jaymes instructed them to put the men into large, comfortable camps on the Wings of Habbakuk, the flat plateaus spreading out a mile or so below the High Clerist's Tower.

"Tell them to pitch their tents securely. I expect we'll be here for at least a month or so."

Then the emperor led Dram, together with Generals Dayr and Weaver, and Captain Franz of the White Riders, up the road. A few hundred paces carried them around the last bend before the pass, where the High Clerist's Tower rose before them in all its majesty.

"We won't want to get too close to the walls; the ogres on the battlements keep launching boulders at anyone who comes within range. But I can show you everything you need to see from here."

He pointed out the great, self-contained fortress that was the south gatehouse, and indicated a wall of mountainside that was below the gatehouse, several hundred yards away and, thus, out of range of the ogre-thrown boulders.

"What about it?" Dram wondered aloud.

"Your dwarves brought picks and shovels, I presume?" the emperor asked.

"Of course. We never go far without them."

"Then I'd like you to get them started digging—right there. And don't stop until you have a tunnel extending all the way under the south wall, beneath the courtyard behind that gatehouse."

"You're going to try and mount an attack out of a tunnel?" Franz asked when no one else seemed inclined to question the mad plan. "They'll just drop rocks on us when we try to climb out! The first man out of the hole will have to face a dozen ogres!"

The emperor smiled, taking his objection in stride. "No, the tunnel will be a dead end," he explained. "There's no need even to break the surface into the gatehouse. But I want the tunnel big enough and deep enough to hold all three hundred casks of the black powder."

CHAPTER TWENTY-SIX

✥◐◓◒◐◓◒◐◓●◐◓◒◐◓◒◐◓●◐◓◒◐◓◒◐◓●◐◓◒◐◓◒◐✥

MINING FIRE

✥◐◓◒◐◓◒◐◓●◐◓◒◐◓◒◐◓●◐◓◒◐◓◒◐◓●◐◓◒◐◓◒◐✥

The dwarves set to digging with a vengeance, working around the clock, each team of miners putting in a twelve-hour shift. The tunnel began as a simple shaft bored straight into the mountainside. Only a dozen or so dwarves could work at a time, but as the hole grew deeper, more and more picks and shovels could be brought to bear. They made steady progress and after a week had progressed more than three hundred yards straight into the rock.

There the diggers began excavating a path breaking away to the right at a perpendicular angle. That tunnel would bore toward a large section of the curtain wall beside the south gatehouse. At the same time, the dwarves continued the original straight shaft, with even more workers chopping away at a time. When the original shaft had grown to six hundred yards long, a second tunnel to the right began to creep toward the tower. Both shafts were extended and widened, the second one pushing through the rock directly underneath the great gates.

In the lightless tunnels, the distinction between day and

night was meaningless, but that was no obstacle to the doughty dwarves. Dram was omnipresent, supervising the excavation with a keen eye and curt instructions to "shore up that archway" or "smooth off that knob." Under his direction the tunnels grew deeper and wider and stronger, with many hidden passages expanded.

The ogres and humans in the High Clerist's Tower watched the surface work from the walls but made no effort to interfere. All they could see were the periodic shift changes, as two hundred dwarves trooped out of the mountainside while another two hundred trooped in. They took note of the ever-mounting pile of tailings spilling from the mouth of the shaft and wondered at the excavation.

As a deterrent to interference from the garrison in the tower, Jaymes maintained several companies of infantry and cavalry units within a quarter mile of the southern gatehouse. If the enemy made a sortie out to attack the miners, the troops would counterattack immediately. But Ankhar obviously scoffed at dwarves digging holes and decided not to risk his precious troops in a fight outside the lofty walls.

If, in fact, Ankhar were really in charge. Despite the magical obfuscation created by the Thorn Knight and the Nightmaster, Coryn had continued her scrying of the enemy. Sometimes her searching could penetrate through the veils of secrecy, and several times she had reported arguments between du Chagne and Hoarst, or Ankhar and the black-masked cleric. The siege was taking its toll on the enemy, even before the first clash of arms.

Outside, the troops staged competitions and games in plain view of the walls. They marched back and forth in maneuvers, singing martial songs, and generally acting as though they were happy to be there. And the dwarves were truly happy;

the diggers were all experienced miners, and the work was very much to their liking. The thought that they would strike a devastating blow against the hated ogres—the same ogres who had destroyed their town—only added to their pleasure and fervor.

As a result, some nearly four weeks after the mine was started, the shaft was completed to Dram's, and the emperor's, satisfaction.

It was time, Jaymes declared, to bring in the black powder and to set a very long fuse.

⊱⊰⊱⊰⊱⊰⊱❋⊰⊱⊰⊱⊰⊱⊰

Ankhar paced the small circle of the High Lookout. That was as high up as he dared to go in the great fortress. The Nest of the Kingfisher, perched on its spire some fifty feet over his head, he judged to be too small to accommodate his size and weight. Anyway, from where he was he could see everything he needed to see. With Pond-Lily at his side, he watched the fortress and the enemy army and left the planning of the defenses to the others.

Despite his bluster about hiding behind walls, he had quickly concluded that was a very good place to live. There was plenty of food, and the officers of the Solamnic Knights had maintained a splendid wine cellar that had been requisitioned by the dark forces. When he and Pond-Lily went inside, they spent their time in a couple of very nice rooms high up in the tower. He had hobgoblins bring up his food and drink, so he never had to bother himself going up and down the long flights of stairs.

Occasionally he grew a little wistful, remembering Laka or the heady days of his great invasions out in the open air. He truly missed his stepmother, but when he cradled the Shaft

367

of Hiddukel in his arms, he felt the presence of the Prince of Lies and that brought Laka very much into his thoughts and feelings. She had been, and would remain, the central Truth of his life.

Wandering through the wilds, living outside in the wind and rain, trying to maintain order in a large, chaotic band of barbarians—those old Truths entailed a great deal of work, a significant amount of discomfort, and massive aggravation. He had realized during the weeks in the tower that he was really very tired being a great leader. Being there with Pond-Lily in the comfort of his fine rooms, was a much more comfortable existence.

On that gloomy late-summer afternoon, clouds glowered low across the Vingaard Range, and the threat of an impending storm crackled in the air. But the half-giant's rooms in the tower were rainproof, and Ankhar suspected that, come winter, they would prove quite snug as well. So he wasn't worried about the weather, or much of anything else, as he propped his foot on the parapet. The rampart was waist high to a human, but it came up only to Ankhar's knees and made for a comfortable brace as he looked out over the fortress.

There was the great gatehouse in front of him, manned with a hundred ogres and an equal number of Dark Knights, commanding the approaches from the south. The ogres had stacked great piles of boulders on the upper platforms and were prepared to rain those down on any attackers who came within fifty or sixty paces. Every once in a while, an ogre tossed one of those rocks in the direction of the dwarf miners laboring some three or four hundred paces away. The dwarves were well out of range of the impulsive attacks, but throwing the stones gave the ogres a bit of useful target practice as well as the grist for wagers and other amusements.

Protecting that garrison were two massive outer gates, a pair of portcullises that could be dropped at a moment's warning, and an interior set of gates that were just as massive as those in the outer wall. If an attacker somehow managed to penetrate inside, he would find himself in a deep courtyard, with commanding positions on all four sides where the defenders could pour a murderous fire of arrows, rocks, and burning oil down upon him.

The half-giant had learned that at the time Hoarst and the Black Army attacked the place, the emperor and his Solamnics had garrisoned the tower with only three hundred knights, far too few to defend the place. The Knights of Solamnia had paid the price when the Dark Knights flew up and landed atop the walls then opened the gates for their comrades outside. With that history in mind, Ankhar was glad for the more than two thousand ogres and Dark Knights who now patrolled the walls.

The half-giant spotted the Nightmaster, clad all in black, walking among the troops down there on the gatehouse ramparts. The priest had diligently overseen the preparation of the defenses, and Ankhar was pleased to have him down there. He was further pleased by a corollary benefit: having the cleric down there meant that the man was not up here with the half-giant. The sight of that veiled, featureless face never failed to send a shiver up and down his spine.

The Dark Knights, too, seemed inclined to avoid the half-giant in his lofty aerie, and Ankhar was not displeased by their wariness. After all, he had his woman and a cadre of loyal ogres and hobgoblins waiting on him. All was right in his world.

"How long we stay here, Ankhy?" asked Pond-Lily, sidling close.

He shrugged. "You like it here?"

"Yes, I do." She snuggled against him, sighing blissfully.

"Me too. Maybe we stay for a long time. Live here in winter, with fires on hearths to keep us warm." With a squeeze of his massive arm, he held her tight.

"I like that. But bad men—what if they come and fight us? What those dwarves doing anyway?"

Ankhar chuckled genially. "Dwarves, hah! We squash them if they come too close. And see little fort down there, pet? Bad men have to fight through that first!"

And right then, before his very eyes, that massive gatehouse simply disintegrated. He saw the explosion before he heard it: the platform where a hundred ogres and a hundred Dark Knights stood blasted straight up into the air, propelled by a gout of flame and smoke that seemed to erupt like a volcano from somewhere deep in the bowels of Krynn. Pieces of stone shot high into the sky, intermingled with lazily tumbling bloody figures of ogres and men.

Next he felt the pressure of the blast, a sickening lurch in the floor beneath his feet. The massive High Clerist's Tower swayed like a tree in the wind, and for an instant, the half-giant was certain he would be pitched over the low side and fall to certain death. Pond-Lily screamed, and for a moment, that piercing noise, coming from right below his ear, was the only sound he heard.

Finally the sound of the explosion reached him, a *boom* of noise louder than any blast of thunder he had ever heard. It felt like a punch to the heart and gut and deep inside his brain, knocking all the air out of him, smashing and staggering him. He tumbled back against the interior column, where the tower climbed to its lofty Kingfisher's nest, then slumped to a sitting position, stunned and staring. The first echo came then, almost as loud as the initial blast, and all he could do was numbly clap his hands over his ears.

Jaymes, Coryn, Dram, and the generals watched the explosion from a mile away. The dwarf let out a whoop as the column of debris—intermixed with smoke and searing balls of fire—spewed high into the air. The blast was tremendous, carrying away the entirety of the south gatehouse and a great section of the adjacent wall. Even the huge spire of the central tower felt the shock, swaying visibly back and forth. Churning upward, the mass of smoke and destruction billowed into the sky. Bursts of fire showed in the darkness of the cloud, and for a splendid few heartbeats, the great scatter of debris poised, almost weightless, in the air.

The smoke kept climbing, but almost immediately stones, rocks, and bodies rained back down across the pass, killing men and ogres of the garrison who had survived the blast but weren't quick enough to duck under shelter. One slab of wall, a hundred feet wide, smashed every Dark Knight on a nearby rampart above the curtain wall. A huge portcullis, bars twisted but still banded together, crushed three ogres who stupidly had raced outside the base of the main tower to gape in astonishment at the devastation.

Smoke spewed into the sky like a column of ash from an erupting volcano. Bits of wooden debris, much of it flaming, tumbled away from the murk, scattering like small meteors across the road, the mountains, and the interior of the fortress.

"Go now! Give them your steel!" Jaymes roared to the men and dwarves of his assembled, waiting forces.

As soon as the rocks and other shrapnel ceased to rain down, the dwarves of New Compound together with the infantry of the Palanthian Legion and the Crown Army rushed forward into the gap. Shouting and cheering, chanting hoarse battle cries, they erupted into the open. Dwarves banged their axes against their shields, and humans clattered their swords together, adding to the din.

The attackers swept forward in irregular formation—pushing through the choking smoke and dust, scrambling over the piles of rubble left by the shattering of the walls, stumbling and scrambling up the steep slopes. They charged into the gaping courtyards of the fortress. So much of the wall had come down that the attackers had dozens of possible routes leading right into the interior of the fortress. Quickly they rushed up stairs, claiming the tops of the walls to either side of the massive breach, and passed through the vacant courtyards, pressing into the fortress's interior buildings.

The dwarves, with Dram in the lead, charged to the left, sweeping up onto a standing curtain wall, rushing along the rim, one by one taking the towers that obstructed passage at intervals around the ring-shaped barrier. Axes and hammers smashed against closed doors, splintering the boards. The dwarves crushed ogre skulls and broke ogre limbs with abandon, as many defenders were still stunned by the tunnel blast. Whether the ogres were lying down, fighting, or running away, the dwarves of New Compound gave no quarter.

Following General Weaver, the men of the Palanthian Legion spread out in the middle of the fortress, capturing one courtyard after another. Several companies burst into the base of the great tower before the defenders could recover enough to close their gates, and soon the attackers found themselves in the deep passages where long ago the Heroes of the Lance had lured dragons to their doom with the Orb of Dragonkind.

From there, the attackers worked their way higher, charging up stairways, slaying any Dark Knights or ogres who stumbled into their path. The farther they got from the scene of the blast, the more organized were the defenders, yet the swiftness of the advance continued to carry the day. The knights and foot soldiers swept through a level of temples and shrines, another of garrisons and mess halls. Six ogres tried to hold at the top of a stairway. Weaver's crossbowmen shot them down with a single well-aimed volley, and again the emperor's men rushed up and past.

General Dayr led the footmen of the Crown Army to the right, with a large detachment under Captain Franz attacking the separate redoubt known as the Knights' Spur. They clashed with a line of Dark Knights on the drawbridge to that isolated complex, and again the charge swept right into the spur before the outer gates could be closed. Skirmishes raged in a dozen chambers, but the Crowns threw more and more men into the figh. The Dark Knights could only fall back or die.

Then Jaymes ordered the second rank—mostly heavy infantry—to advance in as close a formation as they could maintain through the rubble and debris. The field commanders would use the second wave as a reserve, concentrating them wherever the enemy seemed determined to make a stand. Some men cleared paths through the rubble, so the follow-up troops could fight more readily.

Then, finally, the emperor and the white wizard advanced, side by side, seeking an end to the matter once and for all.

⊱⋅⊰⋅⊱⋅⊰⋅❦⋅⊱⋅⊰⋅⊱⋅⊰

Pond-Lily was sobbing, and Ankhar cradled her under his big right arm. They leaned against the solid tower wall inside the High Lookout, watching as the attackers ran rampant through the fortress. The southern gatehouse, where the Nightmaster had pledged an epic defense, was simply gone, blasted into pieces by the unimaginable explosion. Those

373

pieces, the half-giant assumed, included the little bits that remained of the black-masked cleric. The gatehouse was merely a gaping hole, a smoky crater crawling with the figures of dwarves and the emperor's men.

Bakkard du Chagne burst out of the door from the tower's interior to find Ankhar and his ogress on the parapet.

"The emperor's men are in the base of the tower!" he cried shrilly. "They're coming up the steps! Our men can't hold them back."

"Coming up the steps of this tower?" asked Pond-Lily, gaping.

"Yes, you stupid bitch!" screamed du Chagne. "They'll be here any moment!"

Pond-Lily uttered a choking sob and buried her head in the half-giant's side.

Ankhar shook off his lethargy and shock to glare at the chubby, balding man. The former lord regent, used to obedience and command, nervous of disposition and irascible of temper, had been an annoying presence during their weeks in that confined space. The half-giant had tolerated him only because he had been brought there by and was under the protection of the Nightmaster.

But . . . he looked at the crater again. No one could have survived that. It seemed safe to conclude the Nightmaster was dead.

Ankhar released the weeping Pond-Lily, who merely watched in amazement as the half-giant grabbed du Chagne around the neck and easily hoisted him off the ground. The human's eyes and tongue bulged out, but the grip was too constricting for him to make any sound. He could only stare pathetically into the half-giant's eyes as Ankhar lifted him over the parapet and dangled him in the air, hundreds of feet above the violence-racked courtyard below.

Then the half-giant let the former lord regent go, and that was when du Chagne found his voice, uttering a piercing shriek that lasted a very long time—as long as it took for him to hit the ground.

CHAPTER TWENTY-SEVEN

GODS, MORTALS, AND MAGIC

Coryn and Jaymes strode side by side through the wreckage caused by the blast. Nothing about the smoking crater suggested it had once been a mighty gatehouse or part of any kind of structure. The broken rock was strewn haphazardly, with a shallow groove running through the middle to vaguely suggest where the explosive-packed tunnel had been mined underneath the ground.

The bodies of many men and ogres of the garrison had been blown to pieces by the explosion. Here and there lay a grotesque corpse—or a part of a corpse—but those, like everything else, were so coated with the ubiquitous gray dust that they resembled stone more than flesh. Coryn turned away from the sight of one apparently unmarked corpse, a dead Dark Knight pasted with so much fine powder that he looked like a skillfully rendered statue of a dead man.

"Over here," Jaymes said, finding a channel in the debris. They passed between shattered walls rising like jagged cliffs to either side of them, and the emperor had to clasp a hand over his face just to keep the dust from choking him. He felt it coating his beard and skin, saw it on his leggings and tunic and boots.

Yet when he looked at the enchantress, her robe was as immaculately white as ever. He could only shake his head in amazement.

"We need to climb up into the tower, see who's still alive up there, right?" he asked.

"Ankhar has been on the High Lookout many times every day," Coryn reported. "I'm guessing he has quarters somewhere high up in the tower."

"Yes," Jaymes agreed. "Let's go pay him a visit."

He came to a section of broken stairway leading toward the top of one of the walls. The outer portions of the steps had been blasted away, but some remained. Clasping the railing with his left hand, he stepped carefully upward, kicking loose rubble out of the way. Coryn took his other hand and climbed behind him.

From the top of the wall, they could see the dwarves surging around the top of the curtain wall. Already they were halfway around the main tower, closing toward the north gatehouse. Dayr's men were making good progress on the other half of the wall, and Jaymes had hopes that within another hour or so the entire perimeter of the great fortress would be in the hands of his men.

Of course, that still left the main tower, the mountainous structure that rose to its imposing height in the middle of the massive fortress. Sounds of battle rang from throughout that edifice as the two moved closer as fast as caution would allow.

They passed through a doorway where there had been heavy fighting. The bodies of three men of Palanthas were pulled to the side and arrayed in respectful repose, while a dozen dead Dark Knights sprawled just within the entry, just where they had fallen.

The pair started up the great central stairway, but after climbing fifty steps, they came up against the backs of a hundred of Weaver's legionnaires, who were engaged in a furious clash with a company of ogres who had barricaded the way with benches, tables, and other furniture. The heart of the skirmish was about one floor above them, and they couldn't see much, though they heard plenty of steel clashing, voices shouting and crying out in pain.

"We'll flush 'em out with steel, Excellency," a sergeant promised over his shoulder. "But it might take us an hour or two."

"What about elsewhere in the tower? How goes the advance?"

"They're blocking all the stairs now. We can beat 'em back one floor at a stretch—for as soon as we carry one stairway, we can outflank all the others on the same floor—but it's a damn tall tower and it'll take time, sir," the man concluded awkwardly.

"Carry on," Jaymes said, clapping him on the shoulder.

"There's a way we can get around this," Coryn said. "Come outside."

She led Jaymes through a door onto one of the small parapets that dotted the outside of the massive tower. They stood side by side as she pulled a small bottle from within a pocket of her robe. "It's a potion of flying," she said. "I've been saving my magic, but I think we might as well head straight to the top now."

"That'll give us the advantage of surprise," he agreed. Jaymes took the tiny bottle from her and quickly tossed back the bitter, burning liquid. The magic tingled through his limbs, and he merely had to will himself upward to rise from the parapet.

At the same time, Coryn cast a spell of flying on herself. Thirty heartbeats later, the wall of the tower slipped easily behind them as, like ascending birds, the magic-user and the emperor soared toward the High Lookout.

⊰⊱⊰⊱⊰⊱⊰⊱❁⊰⊱⊰⊱⊰⊱⊰

Ankhar held his spear in his right hand while clutching the waist of his ogress in his left. He could see the emperor's army was going to take over the fortress. For all the talk of high walls and gatehouses, the defense had proved hopeless. Hundreds had been killed by the initial blast, and those left alive were dazed to the point where many could not even fight. As far away as he had been, Ankhar still felt the stunning effects of the explosion and had just begun to recover his senses. But the tower would fall.

Even so, the half-giant did not feel much disappointment. He was prepared to die there that day. He did experience a momentary tug of regret when he thought of the winter he might have spent there in a snug room with a fire and a large bed and Pond-Lily. But he shrugged away the thought. He was a warrior, and it was fitting he should die in battle.

Just then, Hoarst and the Nightmaster came through the door from the tower to join Ankhar and Pond-Lily on the lookout. The ogress and the half-giant, standing at the parapet while watching the battles rage below, turned at the approach of the two men.

"So, you're alive," the half-giant grunted at the sight of the black-masked priest. "I thought you probably blew up." He gestured at the smoking crater where the gatehouse had stood.

"The Prince of Lies whispered a warning in my ear, and I

teleported away an instant before the blast," the Nightmaster said dispassionately.

"Hmm. You are favored by the Prince, indeed," Ankhar said, impressed. He thought of du Chagne, and wondered if he should tell the priest what he had done. But he merely shrugged that thought away too. Dropping the man from those heights had been one of the most pleasurable things he had done in a very long time.

At the memory, Ankhar peered over the edge, hoping something blocked the sight of the man's shattered body below. But something else—movement he did not expect to see—caught his eye.

"Oh, oh! Here comes the emperor and the White Witch!" the half-giant cried. Hoisting his spear over his head, the shook the weapon eagerly. "They fly like birds to us! Come here, birdies! At last—the birdies are bringing a fight to me, a fight for the Truth!"

In the next instant, the two humans, magically soaring, swept up and over the wall. Coryn paused in the air, hovering, while Jaymes stepped onto the platform, landing in a crouch and drawing his mighty sword. Ankhar raised his spear to greet the swordsman.

The Nightmaster, Pond-Lily, and the two wizards were all forgotten as the huge half-giant readied himself to meet his hated foe.

Then the Nightmaster cast a spell, and everything went dark.

⊱∘⊶∘⊷∘∘⊛∘∘⊶∘⊷∘⊶∘⊰

Jaymes came to rest on the parapet and immediately charged toward Ankhar—until the darkness spell blinded him and he halted, spun, and dodged instinctively. He heard a clatter of stone against stone and realized the half-giant must have stabbed his huge spear into the ground, just missing him.

"Light!" roared the great brute. "I must see!"

"Use the darkness, fool!" the cleric's voice hissed. "Strike about you!"

Air whooshed past Jaymes's ear, and he knew Ankhar was taking the priest's advice. The foe had a longer weapon, and he was too close already. The swordsman edged away, trying to keep away from the edge of the tower. Where was Coryn? Damn, he had to see!

"Burn!" Jaymes demanded, crouching and twisting in the magical darkness.

Giantsmiter erupted with crackling energy, limned with the searing blue flames. That fire pushed back the darkness in the man's immediate vicinity. Ankhar stood right before him, and the half-giant reared back, retreating from the lunging attack, vanishing again into the murk of the priest's cloaking spell.

Jaymes noticed the Nightmaster then, and he rushed at the priest with his weapon raised. The dark cleric cast another spell, this time causing an image of blurry force to gather in the air between the two men. The power of the great sword knocked the magic away, breaking the shimmering force field into shards, and the murk of the darkness spell broke as well.

"Look out!" cried Coryn. Flying, she swept around the central pillar, pursuing the Thorn Knight who was retreating in front of her.

Then something hit Jaymes from the side, and he darted out of the way of a deadly blow. Looking down in shock, he saw blood spilling from his hip. The chubby ogress, who was obviously Ankhar's consort, stood there, a bloody knife in her hand, which she was drawing back for another blow. With a quick slash of his great sword, Giantsmiter, Jaymes cut her down, half slicing her head from her shoulders before he spun back to attack the priest.

From somewhere out of sight, he heard Ankhar's wail of anguish.

The Nightmaster turned to run, reaching the door to the interior of the tower as the emperor charged, driving his blade through the black cleric's back. As the priest gasped and stumbled sideways, Jaymes spun on his heel, swinging the sword so the impaled man slipped off the end of the blade. He struck the edge of the parapet and, with a wrenching drive, Jaymes pushed him over the lip. The high priest of Hiddukel, already dying, tumbled downward to sprawl near the body of Bakkard du Chagne.

But where was Ankhar?

Jaymes spun again and saw the half-giant crouching over the body of the bleeding ogress, still making his keening wail. Then the big creature stood and beat his chest. With a cry of rage more animal than articulate, Ankhar turned and charged toward Jaymes.

The emperor blocked the attack with a two-handed cross parry but was forced three steps backward by the weight of Ankhar's rush. The half-giant smashed and stabbed with his spear, the emerald tip glowing like green fire, the monster's roars and howls ringing nightmarishly. Jaymes retreated around the central spire, allowing his attacker to expend his energy.

He goaded Ankhar with a feint then stepped back, and back again. Each time the half-giant stabbed at the human, he skipped nimbly out of the way. The big chieftain began to swing his spear like a club, and Jaymes evaded his blows, steadily falling back, going around and around the ring of the High Lookout. Ankhar's eyes bulged; his tusks were slick with drool and foam; his roars became more enraged. Finally, he swung his spear again, missing, letting the blow carry wide, and the swordsman saw his chance.

Giantsmiter came up, driving like an arrow, piercing that immense chest from the left side, stabbing under the chieftain's rib cage and slicing through the creature's heart. The sword forged to slay those of the giant races found a worthy victim in that great son of a hill giant and an ogress.

Ankhar sighed, a sound almost gentle in its rush of sound. The half-giant swayed, and Jaymes stepped back, pulling his weapon free from the deep, gory wound. The blade was no longer burning, as if the fire had been slaked by the hulking warrior's blood.

And when Ankhar toppled to the floor, his spear tumbled from his lifeless fingers, and the glowing brilliance in the emerald head flickered, faded, and finally went out.

✦◦✦◦✦◦✦◦✦◦✦◦✦◦✦

Coryn groped through the ether, trying desperately to track the Thorn Knight called Hoarst. He had opened a door between dimensions and stepped through, escaping from the High Clerist's Tower, from Solamnia, even from Krynn. But the white wizard had hurled herself after him before he could vanish entirely.

He lurked and swirled through the mists, evading and stalking at the same time. Magic flew at Coryn in darts and bolts, and she parried each attack, launching lethal spells of her own. He blocked and fled. She pursued.

The white wizard cast a lightning bolt at the gray blur somewhere before her and watched as her crackling spear of magic broke in two, passing to either side of the target. The gray mage spat back with a blinding array of colorful balls that whirled like scythe blades, and Coryn shrank herself to an insubstantial cloud, letting the deadly slashes whip right through her suddenly intangible body.

Solid once again, she blasted him with missiles and bombarded him with a fireball that erupted like a small sun in that murky cosmos. His gray robe singed, the Thorn Knight nevertheless ducked away without suffering any real damage. A blast of frigid air frosted her face and numbed her skin, but neither did she suffer lethal or crippling wounds.

Hoarst came at her suddenly with a barrage of smoldering, speeding boulders that blasted toward her like meteors. Her hand shot out, wielding a shield of magic that knocked the first of them to the side and sent the next ricocheting through the nothingness. The third she reversed entirely, and it shot back toward the caster.

The Thorn Knight barely dodged that counterattack, and once again fled through the mists. The Mistress of the White Robes sped after him, casting spells, drawing on the greatest depths of her magical powers. For countless and timeless miles, they battled. They passed oceans and moons, and whole dimensions swirled around them for less than an instant. Gods watched and wagered on the contest; worlds swept by in the blink of an eye as they raced and chased through the planes of all existence.

For one heartbeat there was utter blackness; in the next, it was as though they were in the middle of the sun. Coryn cast up a globe of protection and watched in horror as the plasma of life seethed and burned just beyond the barrier, trying to consume her. She veered away from the searing inferno, spotting her foe, and the chase moved on.

They were under the ocean; they flew through the sky; they stood on opposite mountaintops and hurled thunderbolts at each other; they penetrated to the very interior of the world—and out the other side.

They hurtled through space. The moons loomed as terrifying obstacles. Coryn knew those moons, for they were central to all the orders of magic, but they were deadly close up. The red moon, Lunitari, burned, its searing radiance blistering their faces, singeing their eyebrows, charring their magical robes. Then Nuitari, the black moon, suddenly appeared, almost invisible but fiercely powerful, a void so compelling, so hungry, it almost drew both of them in. Only with the greatest exertion did the wizards shear away, coming around the black moon, breaking free from its murk.

And in that new brightness, a white moon suddenly loomed before them, so silvery pure it was almost blinding. Coryn sped toward that moon, drawn by the pure beauty and gravity of its embrace. Hoarst followed, but he was screaming in terror, compelled closer by the unforgiving pull of the planetary body.

And there was no turning away.

⊱⊰⊱⊰⊱⊰❀⊱⊰⊱⊰⊱⊰

Coryn returned as suddenly as she had left. Her hair, where it had been barely flecked with lightness, had turned gray, though her face was unlined by age. She staggered wearily, collapsing into Jaymes's arms.

They settled to the floor of the High Lookout, their backs braced by the parapet. In the tower, the sounds of fighting were dying out. The Dark Knights and the ogres who survived, sensing certain defeat and knowing their leaders had perished, were surrendering, and the emperor's men were at last accepting prisoners.

"What happened?" Jaymes asked Coryn softly, holding her on the parapet, feeling her trembling slowly subside.

"The Thorn Knight met my god, Solinari—the white moon," she said. "He will not be returning to Krynn."

EPILOGUE

Dram Feldspar returned to his valley in the early autumn to find his house repaired and his wife and son—even his gruff father-in-law—weeping tears of joy at his homecoming. He vowed loudly and long he would never leave that place again. By the end of that first night home, he and Swig had brawled their way through the new front window, down the street, and right into the lake. Everyone agreed things were back to normal in New Compound.

In Palanthas, the princess gave birth to her baby in the spring. Immediately the nurses and physicians agreed all the auguries were promising. He had a healthy cry, his eyes were bright and curious, and his little fingers—ten in number, equaling his toes—clutched his mother's hand with a sturdy grip.

The emperor had an heir! A son!

If the child's mother, the Princess Selinda du Chagne Markham, wondered at all about the lingering effects of the potion called the Red Lotus, she kept her concerns to herself.

Jaymes Markham, the emperor, took up permanent residence in his great palace, overseeing the rule of Palanthas and also the surrounding realms of the new empire. His wife lived nearby, in the temple of Kiri-Jolith. They appeared together with their son soon after his birth, and the plaza was filled to overflowing with people who cheered and applauded their leader and his family. Jaymes and Selinda accepted the accolades with grace and good wishes in return.

Then they went back to their respective homes.

In the darker streets and alleys of Palanthas, Sir Ballard and the other knights of the Legion of Steel doffed their regalia and, dressed again in dark cloaks and fingerless gloves, frequented their secret alehouses. But the people—and the emperor—knew they were vigilant and watched over the welfare of the city.

Trade thrived in Palanthas and across Solamnia. Many goods came over the mountains, through the wide road over the pass, while the great seaport remained as busy as ever before. Kalaman, formerly a part of the First Empire, sent emissaries to Palanthas to inquire about rejoining the great nation in the new age. Ergoth, Sancrist, and Sanction all became important trading partners and allies.

The lofty spires of Vingaard Keep were rebuilt with funds from the emperor's personal treasury. The Kerrigan clan, under the leadership of the pardoned young lord Blayne, lived and ruled there. So, too, was the High Clerist's Tower restored where the explosion had damaged it.

And the secret of the black powder remained with the dwarves in their pastoral valley. The charcoal ovens were cool, no more spring steel was ordered from Kayolin, for there were no bombards in the making.

Nor would there be, unless the songs of war were given voice again.

ELVEN EXILES TRILOGY
PAUL B. THOMPSON AND TONYA C. COOK

The elven people, driven from their age old enclaves in
the green woods, have crossed the Plains of Dust and harsh
mountains into the distant land of Khur. The elves coexist
uneasily with surrounding tribes under the walls of
Khuri-Khan.

Shadowy forces inside Khur and out plot to destroy the elves.
Some are ancient and familiar, others are new and unknown.

And so the battle lines are drawn, and the great game begins.
Survival or death, glory or oblivion — these are the stakes.
Gilthas and Kerianseray bet all on a forgotten map,
faithful friends, and their unshakable faith on the
greatness of the elven race.

SANCTUARY
Volume One

ALLIANCES
Volume Two

DESTINY
Volume Three
June 2007

For more information visit **www.wizards.com**

TALADAS TRILOGY
CHRIS PIERSON

The War of Souls is over. Takhisis is dead. On Ansalon,
heroes and gods have banded together to save the world from
destruction. A new peace, of sorts, has taken hold.

Half a world away, on the continent of Taladas, the troubles are
just beginning. Sorcery, long thought lost, has returned to the
world. Disasters wrack the land, nations clash, and dark forces
stir in the aftermath of the Godless Night.

An ambitious barbarian unites the tribes, a victorious general
returns, and an elven thief tracks a mysterious enemy. One
will live, one will die, and one will wish for death. For ancient
powers are waking in Taladas.

BLADES OF THE TIGER
Volume One

TRAIL OF THE BLACK WYRM
Volume Two

SHADOW OF THE FLAME
Volume Three
March 2007

For more information visit **www.wizards.com**

A NEW TRILOGY FROM MARGARET WEIS & TRACY HICKMAN

THE LOST CHRONICLES
Dragons of the Dwarven Depths
Volume One

Tanis, Tasslehoff, Riverwind, and Raistlin
are trapped as refugees in Thorbardin, as the
draconian army closes in on the dwarven
kingdom. To save his homeland, Flint begins a
search for the Hammer of Kharas.

Available July 2006

For more information visit **www.wizards.com**

IN THE WAKE OF
THE WAR OF SOULS...

The power of the Dark Knights in northern Ansalon is broken.

The Solamnic order is in disarray.

And in a shrouded mountain valley, an army of evil gathers.

Against them stand a mysterious outlawed warrior, a dwarf,
and a beautiful enchantress. With the aid of two fugitive
gnomes, they will hold the banner of Good against the forces of
darkness. And from the ashes of war, a new Solamnia will rise.

THE RISE OF SOLAMNIA TRILOGY
BY DOUGLAS NILES

Volume I
LORD OF THE ROSE

Volume II
THE CROWN AND THE SWORD
June 2006

Volume III
THE MEASURE AND THE TRUTH
January 2007

For more information visit **www.wizards.com**

FOLLOW MARGARET WEIS FROM THE WAR OF SOULS INTO THE CHAOS OF POST-WAR KRYNN

The War of Souls has come to an end at last. Magic is back, and so are the gods. But the gods are vying for supremacy, and the war has caused widespread misery, uprooting entire nations and changing the balance of power on Ansalon.

AMBER AND ASHES
The Dark Disciple, Volume I
MARGARET WEIS

The mysterious warrior-woman Mina, brooding on her failure and the loss of her goddess, makes a pact with evil in a seductive guise. As a strange vampiric cult spreads throughout the fragile world, unlikely heroes – a wayward monk and a kender who can communicate with the dead – join forces to try to uproot the cause of the growing evil.

AMBER AND IRON
The Dark Disciple, Volume II
MARGARET WEIS

The former monk Rhys, now sworn to the goddess Zeboim, leads a powerful alliance in an attempt to find some way to destroy the Beloved, the fearsome movement of undead caught in the terrifying grip of the Lord of Death. Mina seeks to escape her captivity in the Blood Sea Tower, but can she escape the prison of her dark past?

AMBER AND BLOOD
The Dark Disciple, Volume III
MARGARET WEIS

February 2007

For more information visit www.wizards.com

R.A. SALVATORE'S WAR
OF THE SPIDER QUEEN

THE NEW YORK TIMES BEST-SELLING SAGA OF THE DARK ELVES

DISSOLUTION Book I
RICHARD LEE BYERS
While their whole world is changing around them, four dark elves struggle against
different enemies. Yet their paths will lead them all to the most terrifying discovery
in the long history of the drow.

INSURRECTION Book II
THOMAS M. REID
A hand-picked team of drow adventurers begin a journey through the treacherous
Underdark, all the while surrounded by the chaos of war. Their path will take them
through the heart of darkness and shake the Underdark to its core.

CONDEMNATION Book III
RICHARD BAKER
The search for answers to Lloth's silence uncovers only more complex questions, allowing
doubt and frustration to test the boundaries of already tenuous relationships.

EXTINCTION Book IV
LISA SMEDMAN
For even a small group of drow, trust is the rarest commodity of all.
When the expedition prepares for a return to the Abyss, what little trust there is
crumbles under a rival goddess's hand.

ANNIHILATION Book V
PHILIP ATHANS
Old alliances have been broken and new bonds have been formed. While some finally
embark for the Abyss itself, others stay behind to serve a new mistress – a goddess with
plans of her own.

RESURRECTION Book VI
PAUL S. KEMP
The Spider Queen has been asleep for a long time, leaving the Underdark to suffer war
and ruin. But if she finally returns, will things get better... or worse?

For more information visit **www.wizards.com**